SUPERMANNERISM

C. RAY SMITH, architecture critic and historian, was brought up in New York City, received his B.A. in English from Kenyon College and his M.A. in English from Yale University. He has written extensively about architecture and interior design for the past fifteen years. He is a member of the American Institute of Architects. He has served as Editor of *Interiors,* as Senior Editor of *Progressive Architecture,* and as Editor of *Theatre Crafts* magazine and the "Theatre Crafts" book series. He has contributed to the *Britannica Encyclopaedia of American Art, Art in America, Interior Design, Industrial Design, The New York Times, New York* magazine, *The Architectural Record, The Village Voice, Domus, Architecture and Urbanism,* and edited *The Shapes of Our Theatre* for the late Broadway stage designer Jo Mielziner. He also has lectured widely in architecture and design schools on the subject of new attitudes in American architecture.

SUPERMANNERISM

New Attitudes in
Post-Modern Architecture

C. RAY SMITH

A Dutton Paperback

E. P. DUTTON NEW YORK

Published simultaneously in Canada by
Clarke, Irwin & Company Limited, Toronto and Vancouver.

ISBN 0-525-47424-2
Library of Congress Catalog Card Number: 76:44664

for my son Sinclair Scott Smith

In words or fashions the same rule will hold,
Alike fantastic if too new or old:
Be not the first by whom the new are tried,
Nor yet the last to lay the old aside.

                                    Alexander Pope, 1711

Most so-called tastemakers do what they do
because they wish to separate themselves from the
rest of unrefined, vulgar humanity. So they say
that the shiny, the golden, and the large are not
good taste. But if what they now say is good taste
were suddenly accepted by everybody, the next minute
the tastemakers would go to gold tinsel. The most
important thing for them is to be different.

                                    William Snaith, 1964

It is central to the role of an architectural historian
to construct rational bridges of understanding between
society and man-made objects that both reflect and
influence social needs. Hence, the architectural historian—
like any historian—must always begin with at least two
large conceptual questions. What were the environmental
conditions surrounding the object of his interest? How
did the object of his interest reflect and influence these
conditions?

                                    Albert Fein, 1973

Art is to dare—and have been right.

                                    Ned Rorem, 1967

Contents

Color plates follow page 194.

List of Illustrations

Acknowledgments

This book has been supported by a grant from The Graham Foundation for Advanced Studies in the Fine Arts, in 1971, made when John Entenza was its genial and sympathetic director.

The book has also been supported by a grant from the National Endowment for the Arts in Washington, D.C., under the Architecture and Environmental Arts Program directed by Bill N. Lacy, whose influence as an architect and a critic is evident in the following pages.

I am indebted to *Progressive Architecture* for permission to use portions of this book that appeared in another form in that magazine. (When architects are quoted without sources being given, their words are taken from *Progressive Architecture* [abbreviated as *P/A* throughout] or from direct interviews with the author. Other quotations in the text are more fully cited in the Bibliography.) I thank Yukio Futagawa for permission to use portions of my introduction to his series "Global Interior," volume 6, *Houses in U.S.A. #2.*

I am also indebted to countless others: To the architects and designers whose works and words are the building components of my structure: to Hugh Hardy, who first showed me what the new was all about; to Peter Andes, who helped me distinguish the old from the new; and to Albert Fuller, who showed me how to tell it like it is; to Tibor Kerekes, Jr., who leveled a firm grammarian's mind at both my logic and my syntax; to Robert Fenwick and Wendy Crabb, who typed the text with my sometimes chaotic inclusions; and to my editor at E. P. Dutton, Cyril Nelson, and his staff, and many others—all of whom gave information and encouragement and cheered me on along the way—I express my warmest thanks and deepest gratitude.

This book was written between Thanksgiving 1971 and Thanksgiving 1973. It is based on my investigations into the new and developing approach to architecture and design, which I witnessed at *Progressive Architecture* magazine from 1961 through 1970. It was researched again between 1971 and 1972. Meanwhile, the writing in the field since the book was written has continued to explore many of the points discussed herein and has largely reinforced my overview of the new attitudes discussed.

New York City

May 1976

Introduction

A new design movement in America is radically changing our vision—our way of seeing things as well as what we see. It is revolutionizing our expectations of architecture, of design vocabulary, and of the design professions themselves. It is altering our cultural consciousness and reshaping the country—in the houses of the adventurous, in the environments of our universities, in the commercial and business spaces of our cities. The work of a generation of architects and designers linked more by attitude and education than by age, the new design began to sprout in the gentle spring of a decade ago, sported riotous flowers in the late 1960s, and is now in prime summer.

I call it *Supermannerism*. Partly, the term expresses the movement's mannerist aspect—its systematic manipulation of established principles, its alteration of scale, its reordering of surface detail—which is similar to sixteenth- and seventeenth-century Mannerism, but augmented. Partly also, the term denotes the movement's broader design vocabulary: a vocabulary expanded to include the vernacular, the anonymous, and such elements of our ordinary life or popular culture as comic books, as is inherent in the hyphenation Superman-nerism.

The new design is also a revolutionary liberation to encompass and include more "social and environmental reform" by which our designed environments can be improved. It includes a longer concept of design validity, a broader concept of our environment—to include space and our ecological system—and alternative systems of planning, designing, and construction. These systems focus beyond buildings—the end products of architecture—onto the other activities that comprise the full process of architecture. The aim is to provide better, more vital, and more human environments for people.

A far cry from the elegant serenity of classical modern design, the formal character of Supermannerism is frenetic and distorted, jazzy and exciting, like contemporary life. Following the Modern idiom, it is a new post-Modern design with new attitudes, methods, and inspiration. It accepts a new scope or scale of vision, of materials, and of architectural process. This new design draws its inspiration eclectically from a wide range of sources: turn-of-the-century American vernacular, the Shingle Style and Art Nouveau, the Bauhaus, and 1920s Art Deco. It is a romantic approach that emphasizes the angular form, the curving line, and the asymmetrical arrangement. Its ultimate aim is to destroy the rigid categories set up by the Internationalists, to eliminate the boundary between the "high art" of the academy and the "low art" of the vernacular and popular culture. It endorses what is vital, alive, and ever changing as a design expression of today's society. Its influence is most strongly felt in architecture, interior and graphic design, with some manifestations in landscape architecture and urban planning. It is a serious force in shaping a greater humanism in the architecture of the future.

Architecture, design, and all the arts, when they are valid, express the motivating social forces of their time, as well as the enduring values of our culture. Supermannerism expresses our age of revolution—revolution in every sphere and aspect of life—in the political and social order, in science and education, in morals and ethics, and in the aesthetics of all the arts. The past decade has been one of chaos and unrest, of upheaval in every area of society and of acute challenge to the assumptions of institutional and academic structures. It has been an age of thunderous political upheaval and ultraviolence, of stunning assassinations and bombings, of riots at home as well as abroad. It has been a decade of investigation and research beyond reasonable boundaries—in science and technology, in outer space and under the oceans, in social liberties and mass communications. In medicine, the very heart of man has been opened and transplanted; in education, classrooms and curricula have become open, fluid, and ungraded. The arts have registered and depicted these anxieties and demands: painting and sculpture, theatre and literature, music and fashion, architecture and design have expressed equally violent changes.

Supermannerism began its revolutionary approach around 1962 when man first soared out into space; when the—then nuclear disarmament, now peace movement—symbol was designed; when activists among ethnic minorities and the poor began to move toward a social and intellectual revolution. Around that time a group of pioneering architects and designers began to produce their first works. Their numbers, output, and influence grew through the period of unrest and flamboyance that was the decade of the 1960s; and on through the turning around 1970 toward greater sobriety. Now, after more than ten years of experience, experimentation, and development of their crafts, the Supermannerists are becoming major figures in public architecture, known to laymen at large as well as within professional circles. A greater part of our population is beginning to recognize and benefit from their clear-sighted invention and creativity, and from the understanding of architecture that their work has brought about.

Among those who most influenced the development of this new design and are its most prominent exponents are: Robert Venturi and his partners in Venturi & Rauch; Charles Moore and his partners Donlyn Lyndon and William Turnbull; Hugh Hardy and his partners in Hardy Holzman Pfeiffer Associates; Romaldo Giurgola and his associates in Mitchell/Giurgola; and Thomas (Tim) Vreeland, Jr. Others working in the idiom who came into prominence early are: Peter Millard, James Stewart Polshek, Hugh Newell Jacobsen, T. Merrill Prentice, Jr., Sim Van der Ryn, Louis Sauer, Denise Scott-Brown Venturi, Richard Saul Wurman, Barbara Stauffacher Solomon, Daniel Solomon, Robert A. M. Stern, Der Scutt, Hobart Betts, and Barton Myers. Of great importance also are the influential precursors who by venturing beyond the ideological boundaries of the "Second Generation of Modern Architects," to which they belong, led the way to Supermannerism: Philip Johnson, Paul Rudolph, Edward Larrabee Barnes, John M. Johansen, Joseph Esherick, Ulrich Franzen, Harry Weese, Ralph Rapson, Charles Eames, George Nelson, Alexander Girard, and, above all, Louis I. Kahn. Others working with some of the attitudes of and sometimes within the Supermannerist idiom, although springing from different educational backgrounds, are: Cesar Pelli and his design team, Walter Netsch, Jr., and his design team, Ronald Beckman and his Research and Design Institute. And, inspired by different historical influences but also working with some of the same attitudes and achieving related formal constructions, as I hope to show, is the group loosely known as the "New York School," including Charles Gwathmey, Richard Meier, Peter Eisenman, Michael Graves, and John Hejduk. Others whose work and outlook can be grouped squarely within the purview of Supermannerism include: Craig Hodgetts, Lester Walker, David Sellers, Michael Hollander, William Grover, Barrie Briscoe, Kenneth Carbajal, Doug Michels, Chip Lord, and countless students of architecture in the 1960s.

The decade of their heyday comprised three fairly distinct periods. From 1960 to 1964, during the recovery from a slight recession, the rumblings of revolution and activism began to be heard. An urge could be felt, restless, emerging, tentative: protest against the war in Southeast Asia, the rise of "black consciousness"; the beginnings of student activism. More gently, these years also produced the musical challenge of rock—the rise of the Beatles, Dylan, and a host of celebrated others. It witnessed the emergence of Pop art—Rosenquist, Lichtenstein, Oldenburg, Warhol, and so on. Then too, the New Theatre's shock of cruelty and of chaotic Happenings expressed the less gentle tenor of the day. In architecture, similarly, a new attitude—or series of attitudes— emerged. The work of a group of architects practicing in Philadelphia captured the profession's uncomfortable interest: Robert Venturi, Thomas (Tim) Vreeland, Frank Schlesinger, Romaldo Giurgola, and others began to be known in 1961 and 1962. At the time, the Richards Medical Research Building of Louis Kahn was being completed, his Salk Institute laboratories designed, and his work first being published. A similar group was emerging in California, at Berkeley, in those years: Moore-Lyndon-Turnbull-Whitaker, Joseph Esherick, and the "third generation" of Bay Area architects.

From 1965 to 1968 there was a middle period of blazing euphoria, as people broke loose and headed toward a happy, youthful, freaky, affluent, bumptious zenith. They were free, wild, noisy. Those were the days of long hair and hippies, of Haight-Ashbury and Flower Power, of drug use and dropout. Discotheques flourished, temples of blaring sound and light and dance. The Peacock Revolution put men into clothes that attracted almost as much attention as the mini- and micro-miniskirts. Op art vibrated and tickled our eyes with its seemingly kinetic sensations. Everything led to a new active individualism that was heralded by the slogan "Do Your Own Thing." Ideas about what art was, what was acceptable, and what was beautiful were challenged. The new design reflected this desire for individualism and liberation; young designers were flying high on doing and on joyous ebullience, on a new sense of actuality—all combined with a rare degree of assertive personal commitment. Young architecture students created a flash fire of social and optical activity that came to the profession's attention even before their graduations. Not content to wait until they became registered architects, students were up and doing—designing, building, and developing—almost as fast as their teachers were. Experiments in spontaneous and transitory environments, in witty and flamboyant optical tricks, and personal involvement in social architecture were the signs of the liberated day.

After 1969, the bubbles seem to have burst, the fizz to have subsided. A more serious mood set in. It was a period of economic recession and political retrenchment, although the last sparks of excitement lingered in such excesses as hot pants and "coke" use, ubiquitous pornography, and transvestite rock musicians. The seemingly endless, unendable war in Southeast Asia produced a widespread mood of embittered weariness. The environment and its ecology became major public issues, with such subheadings as pollution control, recycling, organic foods, nature communes, and simple handcrafts. The new sobriety was reflected in a religious revival: People of all ages turned to fundamentalist sects; stage and filmgoers watched *Godspell* and *Jesus Christ Superstar*. Popular music mellowed from rock to gospel and soul; discotheques, the Beatles as an ensemble, and many other rock heroes vanished. The New Journalists, who had written so breathlessly and vitally from the inside during the previous half decade, began writing about it from the outside. There was even an official word on the subject. In 1972, immediately after his reelection, former President Richard Nixon declared "an end to our decade of permissiveness." Even before, he had proclaimed that "the whole era of permissiveness has left its mark." He deplored the fact that "we have passed through a very great spiritual crisis in this country." He therefore proclaimed his personal conservative position, which he felt reflected the majority center of the nation, against "the enormous movement toward permissiveness, which led to the escalation in crime, the escalation in drugs . . ." In design schools there was a revival of interest in drafting skills and conventional building processes; some students went back to the drawing boards, working hard to learn how to design Frank Lloyd Wright-like oak bandings around doors and windows.

This fairly sudden shift reconfirmed our awareness of the speed of change in our times, the acceleration of events brought on by instant communication and travel, which was described by Alvin Toffler in *Future Shock* (1970). In the early 1960s speed, space, superscale, revolutionary involvement, and "tell it like it is" had collided with the standards of the previous generation, brought us up short against new realities, and rocketed aloft the new design. Then, in the late 1960s came the new sobriety—another apparent collision of attitudes—and many professionals and critics felt that as the first flashes of activism dimmed, as the counterculture seemed to outgrow itself, the new design must therefore die out like a passé fad. They had experienced Design Future Shock.

If a shift in interest occurred, it was no more an indication that the new design had failed than it was an indication that the social revolution had come to naught. Although by 1970 the general public was only beginning to hear of the new design and architecture, its effects were internationally visible in graphics, advertising, interior design, and countless pages of the professional press. Even though the recession of 1969 seriously curtailed design commissions and construction programs for all architects, the leaders of the new design movement are stronger than ever in their work in the 1970s. They are reaching their stride in making serious and widespread social contributions, as well as stylistic contributions, to our mass culture and to our urban centers.

What the new attitudes, processes, and sources of inspiration are that infuse this new design, how they came about, and how they relate to the spirit of our day is the subject of this book.

SUPERMANNERISM

The Catapulting Catalyst
of the Age

The new design is a radically different way of seeing and designing spaces. Space, in fact, is what brings the new design about, as I hope to show—that deep, outer space, first experienced directly by man in the decade of the 1960s. The space age rocketed us into a revolutionary new scale. Our minds now recognize a new measure of distance, of speed, of size, of location. We see our fellowman, not only face to face—by the "human scale" that, mercifully, will be always with us—but also at an interplanetary distance, from other celestial bodies. We have been to the moon; we have looked back and seen the earthrise from the moon. We have been there and back instantaneously, there and here simultaneously in the twinkling of a tube. Distances, time slices, and dimensions have dwindled, and vision, imagination, and physical scale have expanded to cosmic proportions.

The Russians lofted the first orbiting satellite—unmanned—in 1957, but Americans stole the stars with the first manned orbit around Earth when John Glenn blasted off on February 20, 1962. For seven years—scientists worked and people anticipated. No other event more captivated the imagination of man than landing on the moon. Then on July 17, 1969, the world watched transfixed as the Saturn missile carrying Neil Armstrong and Edwin Aldrin dwindled to a sparkling needle and was gone. They became the first men to set foot on another celestial body. That "one small step" was an incalculably "great leap" for the vision of mankind. The picture of the earthrise was a visible symbol of Marshall McLuhan's "global village," cf an inclusive view of

I

our natural habitat. More than airplane travel and science-fiction films, that photograph crystallized the vision of man for the decade to follow. "Spaced out" was a phrase of the drug culture and it was not merely coincidental that "out of sight" was one of the superlatives of the decade.

It would be glib to attribute to space exploration the sole cause of man's new epiphanic vision. Yet its impact has been as powerful and pivotal for the new design as for the rest of society and culture. It has dizzied those who were accustomed to the old views and brought a new awareness to designers and a new generation of clients. Architects worked at an enormous new scale of design. The world's tallest buildings of the 1960s revived the 1920s skyscraper ideal at even greater proportions. Complete new towns and megastructures were the order of the day. And for the Supermannerists, optical tricks in architecture explored vast perspectives and superscale images, often juxtaposed in double scale, as will be described in detail later on. Also, the breadth of the process of architecture as well as the options and possibilities open to new architects seemed to expand to almost cosmic dimensions, as is discussed in "An Inclusive Process."

Architect Craig Hodgetts has written that the view of Earth from outer space "was the beginning of a cosmological consciousness" out of which came the ecology movement, which he sees as

> the one issue big enough to hold all the radicals, and leftists, and Birchers, and, yes, the Ku Klux Klan, because it's the only issue that deals in the common currency of all our paranoias, and that's survival. We had known all along that the earth was round and surrounded by a transparent blanket of air, but it took that portrait of a tiny, radiant earth, somehow nobly alone in the vastness of space to fully realize the awful corollary of Adlai Stevenson's remark to the U.N. that we stand together, passengers on a little space-ship, dependent on its vulnerable resources of air and soil, all committed for our safety to its security and peace, preserved from annihilation only by the care, the work, and, I will say, the love we bestow on our fragile craft.

The space age revelation wrought another crucially significant change in our perspective. It made us feel that the impossible could be realized. If we landed rockets on Venus, Jupiter, and Mars—clearly the next step could be the stars. More than mere romantic yearning gave the song "The Impossible Dream" its popularity. If man could actually walk on the moon, he could do anything else he wanted to. If man could create the technology that made it possible to explore the universe, he could rise above "failures in nerve," as Arthur C. Clarke called them, and create the tools to conquer any impossibility in our society. Being actually able to see the whole earth, we could comprehend and correct its manifold social, ecological, and other imbalances—we could *do it*. We could find alternative systems for shaping and preserving our environment, now that we had a new whole view of it. We could reexamine our design processes, our forms, our design vocabulary, and our visual systems; we could perceive time lags and stylistic cycles within the cultural continuum and in the societal unity that our formerly limited vision could not encompass. Inevitably, those who believed "We can do anything" began to say: "But they don't want us to," when confronted with the ponderous inertia of the status quo. Came the revolution.

REVOLUTION, RELEVANCE, AND INVOLVEMENT

Endlessly, ubiquitously repeated throughout the 1960s the words *revolution, relevance,* and *involvement* became overworked to the point of cliché. "The Revolution" opposed everything, promised everything. Everyone was "involved" with "relevant" causes. This was not mere verbiage. Real, radical activism pervaded society, and it challenged established standards, fixed principles, entrenched institutions, rigid hierarchies, and all authority. Assumptions and taboos were shattered by an emphasis on self-expression and on the rights of the individual. Provoked by deep unrest on the part of socially, politically, and economically disadvantaged minorities—"the other America," as Michael Harrington termed it—the civil rights movement was in every sense a revolution. It gave rise to rallies, antipoverty marches, demonstrations, and ugly urban riots—a parade of protest unknown since the labor movement of the 1930s and the 1940s. Equally revolutionary was the peace movement, brought about by zeal for global justice and political autonomy, as well as by personal sorrow and moral indignation. First there were draft card burnings, then student demonstrations and violent campus riots.

Yet all was not strident rhetoric and physical violence. There were also genial anarchy, simulated blasphemy, and taunting irreverence—rambunctiously comic means by which the nonconformists played the witty gadfly to society, and used their personal freedom to their revolu-

tionary ends. The sex revolution, to cite an obvious example, did violence only to certain people's consciences and/or cherished conventions.
Sexual activities were depicted in books, magazines, plays, and films
more freely than ever before. Massage parlors became the euphemism
for bedrooms. Homosexuals came out of the closet and joined the gay
liberation movement. The goal for everyone was, as elsewhere, freedom
and openness; so long as there was no harm to anyone, you could do
what you wanted. In the 1920s "free love" had been pretty much
restricted to the upper classes; in the 1960s there was "free sex" for
all—young and old, healthy and neurotic, homo-, hetero- and altogetherness.

The sex revolution, if something of a game and a dare at first, was
clearly real, and its momentum was inexorable. There was a swing
toward togetherness of the sexes everywhere, with co-ed dormitories
adorning many a campus, and women invading all kinds of male bas-
tions. Sailors' language spouted from the mouths of delicate-looking
females. Our robust heritage of four-letter Anglo-Saxon words flourished as if a new Chaucerian age had dawned—although his sense of
irony and poetry was not so much in evidence. The women's liberation
movement surged through parade after march, and symposium after
rally.

Sexual liberation was also mirrored in the glass of fashion as clothes
demonstrated society's "bust out" for freedom. Women's clothes were
more and more designed to reveal rather than to conceal; skirts became
shorter and shorter—shrinking above the knee and then to miniskirt
diminutions, and finally to bathing-suit dimensions as hot pants. Bras
were discarded with an abandon that brazenly dared to be free or was
free to be brazen. Topless and see-through clothes were the daredevil
extremes of these permissive fads. Men caught the infectious spirit too.
The Peacock Revolution started when French and American couturiers,
steeped in women's clothes, began designing for men also. Boutiques,
beauty salons, cosmetics, perfumes, and wigs, which had formerly been
the exclusive province of women, were used by men in almost all urban
areas. Men began to wear necklaces, bracelets, colorful scarves,
flowered shirts, wild multicolored and bepatched pants and jackets, fur
coats, and virtually every female adornment. Not since the French Revolution had men been free to wear such finery.

Younger males began in the early 1960s to wear their hair longer
than at any time in nearly a century. The older generation was appalled
at this permissive "slovenliness" and at the early blurring of the distinc-

tions between men and women. Countless parental battles and even legal skirmishes with school administrators ensued on account of long hair on males, and billboards showed a long-haired youth with the slogan: "Beautify America. Get a Haircut."

Later in the decade, fashions further erased the distinctions between the sexes with "unisex" clothes, which were designed to be look-alikes worn by either sex, or both sexes. Tieless turtlenecks for both men and women helped to merge the two genders of attire. Around 1970, shoulder-strap bags and high heels became OK for men as well as for women, and in 1972 all classes and persuasions of men were sporting a single earring in the gypsy-pirate tradition. In this permissive blurring of the sexual distinctions, sometimes only long sideburns, beards, moustaches, and exposed hairy chests confirmed the happy distinctions between sexes that some clothes made ambiguous.

The blurring of these formerly rigid distinctions in fields other than architecture was similar to what occurred during the 1960s within the design professions. There, coincidentally, the distinctions between design and other fields, such as fashion, became more and more flexible. Architects who had been affronted by suggestions that their timeless work had anything to do with style, fashion, or fad began to recognize that these also were elements of any changing life activity. Critics of the old school decried this permissive society throughout the decade. By 1969, the discussion was public entertainment—and, presumably, mass outrage.

Bluntness and even blatancy in regard to sex was only one aspect of a much broader impulse toward realistic acceptance of any and all actualities. "The times they are a-changin' " sang Bob Dylan, the poet of folk-rock, who protested earliest and most convincingly in the world of popular music that there was a new generation on the rise with a new viewpoint. He expressed the popular consensus, a gutsy unpretentious new urge to "tell it like it is." Paul McCartney declared that the Beatles wanted their songs to have "some—reality" to show things as they are. It was a new theme for a populace brought up on romances, persuasion, and sentimental pleading to acclaim a straightforward vision of everyday life. The realistic new view looks at the whole picture, the totality of an event, back as well as front, bad as well as good, impossible as well as expected, taboo as well as traditional, and accepts the fact that all these exist, individually, distinctively, and that they can coexist side by side and interact with each other. The new realists want to eliminate public confusion and pretense that one thing is another. Aiming for a total view, they say, for example, that it is unreal for jet travelers going 600 miles an hour at 35,000 feet above the earth to pretend they are simply enjoying a gracious French meal; that is blinding oneself to reality. Instead, passengers should be given binoculars, good clear flight maps, and announcements of landmarks.

Realism, in this sense, expressed a different view of the world from naturalism, which focuses on the literal, physical data of our existence. Realism attempts to get at all the facts. It accepts the entirety of a situation in which, for example, an artificial convention appears. A true realism accepts the artificiality of the convention and finds a way to expose its overlay on nature in some honest, straightforward, direct, and meaningful way. So the New Theatre stripped the let's pretend of painted makeup, costume, and sets and put the audience in environmental jungle gyms; it showed them such symbolic, telegraphic, and fragmental signs as "river," "forest," or "hill," rather than reconstructing the entire geography in paint and canvas. In this same view Robert Venturi told city planners and architects that they "need not fight the impossible," and advocated that we cast aside our prejudices about what is good and bad, valid and valuable, and adopt a tolerant and more realistic attitude toward accepting what is. "Learning from the existing landscape is a way of being revolutionary for an architect" is the opening premise of *Learning from Las Vegas* (1972), the book the Venturis wrote with Steven Izenour. "There have always been children in monumental fountains," he reminds the smooth-water reflecting-pool purists, encouraging them to see life in its reality and to design for its totality. The reality slogan is a corollary of revolutionary defiance; it is a society-versus-elitist-academy attitude that acclaims design and architecture as essential for all men. But it is also a plea for the expansion of our social and aesthetic vision to include actual living patterns. As Ada Louise Huxtable wrote of Venturi's show at the Whitney Museum of American Art in 1971: "The response of the architectural profession to the 'reality' of America has been the turned back and object lessons in art and taste."

INVOLVEMENT AND COMMITMENT

This new realism incited the generation to rebel *against* existing systems, and *for* renewed commitment and dedication, for an increased degree of participation signaled by that tag word *involvement*. Everywhere in the arts there was an urge to become more involved in creating a new society with alternative life-styles, as well as with environments for that new society. People, not designs, were to come first. The New Theatre— Environmental Theatre, Experimental Theatre, Happenings, and the like—utterly unlike the traditional theatre of illusion, aims at involving its audiences more actively, more directly, with physical activity as well as with psychological activity. The New Theatre asks total involvement from its audience—to laugh, weep, and fear or, to be hugged, felt, fondled, or shouted at; it encourages its audiences to move about, run, dodge, and dance; sing, stomp, and shout; heckle and cajole; throw, tear, and pour; discuss, undress, dress up, and play. The New Theatre is political, democratic, and everywhere and sometimes it is boring, inept, and crude. But it offers a new choice of total involvement rather than passive participation.

The new architects and designers, similarly, strive to involve themselves with the visually illiterate as well as with the sensitive critics and the trained aestheticians. They emphasize their concern for the communicative, expressive qualities of buildings. They are struggling to bring architecture back in touch with the heartbeat and the fleshy hand of man. They profess a greater involvement with the user, the actual inhabitant of the building or furniture system, the actual manipulator of the designed object. It is obvious that this approach is based as much on intuition and superimposition of ideologies as any previous one. Whose involvement and how much involvement have never been determined by any statistical or quantitative scientific method. Real research into the physical and psychological needs of users remains an unfulfilled requirement. But the awareness of and necessity for such research have gained a new urgency as people and their activities have become the real determinants of designs.

The imperative of involvement has led architects and young designers to concentrate on social and political issues, such as mass housing and civil rights, which have little or nothing to do with formal or nonformal design and aesthetics. Rebellious professionals and students devoted themselves to community self-determination or to *advocacy planning*—a term coined by planner-sociologist Paul Davidoff in 1965. Advocacy planners involved themselves with a new kind of client —the urban poor, blacks, underprivileged or "disadvantaged" citizen groups. Their goal was to protect and help those groups speak for themselves in the fight against such bureaucratic impositions as urban bulldozer renewal and the demolition of their homes for expressways.

Groups of architects, architecture students, planners, and draftsmen—such as The Architects' Resistance, founded in New Haven in 1968—believed that architecture, "like other professions, is not an end in itself, but part of a political process, a process that should grant all people the right to control their own lives and be governed by human values, not material ones." Some advocacy planning groups did more than protest. Among them were ARCH, which stood for Architects Renewal Committee in Harlem, directed by Max Bond; Troy West's Architecture 2001 in Pittsburgh; and Boston's Urban Planning Aid (UPA) activated by Harvard and MIT planners.

Involvement in social issues was also expressed in concern for the quality of architectural education. Students publicly involved themselves in protest and revolution for curriculum reform, campus building reform, university building practices, and relevant social programs. They threw themselves into these causes in demonstrations, in designing placards, and in open forum discussions. From 1964 onward, architecture students appealed by letter at Pratt Institute for curriculum reform; boycotted classes at Syracuse University; threatened a walkout by the entire University of Houston; and otherwise protested at Ohio University, Yale, Colorado, Kansas, Virginia, Columbia, Harvard, Cornell, Michigan, Princeton, and elsewhere. They called themselves "young radical architects," "guerrilla architects," "dropout architects,' "environmental nomads," and "mind huns." Like other students, they wanted an education without hierarchy, without authority, without architectural crafts. And they made some progress in changing the old in favor of this new goal. Many educators believed that this concern with "environmental issues," "social attitudes," "behavioral patterns," "greater social consciousness," and "the human condition" is the strongest movement in architecture today.

"Energized by the chaos and urgency of the urban scene, mass needs, and low incomes," as Olindo Grossi, then dean of Pratt Institute, said, "architects have resolved to be involved." They prefer this to showing merely what Yale's Ralph Drury called "a growing sense of helplessness in the face of it"—implying the way of the past. "They believe the typical urban environment is inhuman and they want to do something about it," said Michigan's Robert C. Metcalf. They wanted to build housing; they have lived and worked in black ghettos and other blighted areas—both urban and rural. They have gotten actively involved in civil rights and actually did help to design for and build in depressed areas. Students involved themselves in such community design groups as Columbia's Urban Deadlock, Yale's Black Architects Workshop, Pratt's Center for Community Improvement. Numerous class projects were social causes, such as Houston's Black Building (see p. 203), Oklahoma State University's NAACP Freedom Center, and other social work in Philadelphia, Oakland, Detroit, and elsewhere.

YOUTH MOVEMENT

Almost entirely new in American behavior was this activism of students and the young—people in their teens and twenties during the 1960s. Whereas, for generations, students in other countries had rioted for their causes, primarily political, North American students had usually remained sequestered and passive in their intellectual enclaves. But in the 1960s young Americans changed, with defiant, eruptive violence, into moral and political activists. One student manifesto to create a "new world" proclaimed:

> We are challenged to break with the obsolete social and economic systems which divide our world between the overprivileged and the underprivileged. All of us, whether governmental leader or protester, businessman or worker, professor or student share a common guilt. We have failed to discover how the necessary changes in our social structures can be made. Each of us, therefore, through our ineffectiveness and our lack of responsible awareness, causes the suffering around the world.

Although the counterculture—activist, subversive, revolutionary—was conventionalized as a privilege of the under-twenties, not all the idols were of the students' age like Mario Savio, Rapp Brown, and Abbie Hoffman. More mature and more experienced practitioners and philosophers also had hero status—Buckminster Fuller and John Cage, for example. In the new design, a similar cyclic, generational interaction obtained: several generations were united by an unfettered approach of youthful idealism and exploration.

The Supermannerists recognized the design contributions of the young, interacted with them, and accepted their invention into their own more established practices. They employed their students and incorporated many of their design ideas—especially decorative and lighting schemes—into houses, offices, and other architectural projects. Moore and Venturi formed partnerships with architects who had been their students and who were as much as a decade younger. A number of young architects went into independent practice immediately after school, forgoing the customary apprenticeship, and became entrepreneurs and do-it-yourself architects.

If students in the 1960s interested themselves in revolutionary causes outside the classroom, inside the classroom their work evidenced more concern with style of presentation than with building design. Instead of the traditional methods of drawing and model making, they used new graphics (see pp. 130–137), new colors and materials, electronic sound reinforcement, photography, and projection techniques to present their proposed designs. It was symptomatic of the revolution in architectural education and involvement beyond the traditional boundaries of architecture. It was a way of saying: "Yes, we are architects, but we are also men and women; we have interests and concerns and causes beyond the world of architecture that we want to bring to the world of architecture."

Of the revolutions associated with youth in the 1960s the most controversial is the drug culture—an ethic that accepts the affects of grass and hash, mescaline and peyote, LSD and cocaine, and harder drugs as valuable, desirable experiences. Unlike the elitist society dilettantism of drug play in the 1890s and the 1920s, and unlike the opium craze of Thomas De Quincey and his peers in the 1820s, the drug culture of the 1960s seemed synonymous with the subculture, the counterculture, and all underground revolution. During the decade, drugs were linked to almost every social phenomenon in the centers of Western civilization. Without drugs, popular music and films would not have been the same; artists and architects would not have portrayed the same multicolored and ambiguous images of their new visions of space; a playful and voluble segment of our population would not have had much in common with a deadly serious segment—a seamy, ugly, vicious segment that was involved in addiction, smuggling, robbery, assault, and murder. Unknown numbers of architecture students, like their contemporaries in other walks of life, experimented with drugs as a life-style. Grass, peyote, and LSD experiences were adapted to "psychedelic" interior and graphic designs, resulting in nebulous wavy lines, ambiguous forms and textures, and flashing, pulsing light schemes. University of Houston students called it "LSDesign" and Chip Lord said "the first generation of hippie architects has come of age." Even older, established architects tried LSD and other hallucinogenic drugs in an attempt to find ways to free up their designs and design processes. California architect and teacher Sim Van der Ryn, who got into the new life-style of freedom, liberation, busting out to nature, and do-it-yourself crafts, said in an interview, "Drugs are important to a lot of people in making changes; they accentuate the thought process and the feeling process and help people find out what they are really feeling. Dope, loosening up, being interested in being out of doors is mostly just tuning into another consciousness."

What all these drug experimenters and regular users looked for in drugs was a means of forging beyond the plateau of the status quo, beyond what came to be personified as the Establishment—the political, social, intellectual, and emotional tenets of the previous decade of conformism. For the drug culture, this Establishment was a pervasive unreality, an obsolete structure that, for them, seemed so obviously to have failed. Drugs were seen as a means of defying these conventions and breaking down the barriers they seemed to form. The ultimate aim, however, beyond rebellion and rejection of established patterns, was "consciousness modification" or "expanded consciousness"—the ability to see and to feel new methods and alternative life-styles—whether social, moral, and ethical, or in design vision.

If multiform revolution and impassioned commitment are the major social forces of our day, what could the arts be in order to be valid expressions of their time? Can we expect them to express pastoral peace and refinement, or elegance and calm?

"What is happening today in architecture is a revolution," Kenneth Carbajal proclaimed. "Most of the profession is not even aware that anything is happening. Those who are aware credit it as a passing fad; they are unable to understand it. This is more than a generation gap; it is a cultural gap. And the gap is growing wider rapidly."

Other critics concurred: "It is a reaction against the prevailing orderly planning"; against "oversimplification of three-dimensional form"; against "sterility of contemporary rationalistic attitudes" toward architecture, as a "concern for a new philosophy based upon other mores than the hypocrisy of the establishment."

It was called "counterrevolution in design" by architecture editor Jan C. Rowan, "Not because young designers want to re-establish the old order, but because much of what they are fighting for is the undoing of several sacred cows of the revolution in architecture that took place in the first half of this century." And *The New York Times* architecture critic Ada Louise Huxtable wrote in the 1970s, "Call it breakdown or call it metamorphosis. But these are the terms, and the record, of a society in radical transition as that wrenching revolution is taking place."

An Inclusive Process

One of the goals of the new architects' rebellion was involvement in a fuller, more inclusive range of architectural activity than that engaged in, they felt, by previous decades of architects. Just as they expanded their vocabulary of architectural aesthetics, they exploded their vision of architectural activity. They wanted to involve themselves with more than the end products of architecture—buildings. They wanted to involve themselves in detailed planning and preprogramming methods; in aiding and increasing user self-determination; in entrepreneurship, development, and financing; in new design methods and presentation techniques; in such administrative procedures and systems as "critical path method" and "fast track"; in new construction methods and building systems; in design and construction by client-users as well as by architects themselves. Interestingly enough, much of this very broad concept was also enthusiastically endorsed by the Design Establishment.

The inclusive approach to the process of architecture had its roots in the Bauhaus, where it was held that a good designer could design, in a single continuum, the entire range of man's environment—from a teaspoon to an urban or a regional plan. All that was needed was care, and attention to changing scale. Later, Louis Kahn maintained that an architect could design special types of buildings, even if he were unfamiliar with them, simply because he was trained to solve problems, to determine what a building "wants to be"—in the way that "a spoon wants to be a bowl with a handle."

In the 1960s architects took the design continuum for granted and added to it implementation, financing, and the full range of the architectural process. They saw themselves as capable of giving "comprehensive architectural services"—a slogan of the American Institute of Architects during the decade of the conglomerate corporation—as leaders of interdisciplinary teams. A typical claim was: "On our staff are architects, sociologists, specialists in counseling psychology, statistics, computer simulation modeling, and programming, as well as assistants in social work, urban planning, and law." Yet what the AIA called comprehensive architectural services really meant only comprehensive—traditional —design and planning services. The new architects aimed to involve themselves in areas far beyond these traditional boundaries of their profession. And even within those boundaries, they rebelliously reordered priorities, insisting that process comes first, then product.

As Cesar Pelli explained in a design statement from his firm,

> When architects are asked to say something about their design philosophy, they usually talk about the object, the result. Today it is more important to talk about the process that leads to architecture than about the object. Each project is different from the next, so there are a number of processes going on at the same time. I believe each solution should grow out of the proper understanding of the problem. The key function in the design process is decision-making. Inspiration and source of ideas, although important are secondary.

As Joseph Esherick recounts, "In the early 60s I began to be more conscious of the process that I used." Sim Van der Ryn also said, "Around 1960 I began to deal mostly with process. The problem in architecture was that you were not getting the right information to make any good design decisions. I was interested in the programming of a building type, how could you come up with human information."

PREPROGRAMMING AND PLANNING

As architectural projects became bigger, correspondingly more detailed administrative processes had to be developed to aid in planning and in "preprogramming." Borrowed from the aerospace industry, this new preliminary process is called "systems analysis," "operations research," or "systems engineering." It attempts a scientific methodology of determining building requirements. Architects do not often do preprogramming and systems analysis on their own. Instead, they can avail themselves of services offered by a new breed of non-architect design professionals: aerospace engineers, management consultants, industrial designers, construction management firms, and city managers. Real estate researchers, financial analysts, market researchers, accountants, realty lawyers, and others who help prepare economic feasibility studies and programs also influence building programs directly. Bankers, insurance companies, traffic-parking consultants, land economists, power utility companies, computer software service firms, and many others get involved in setting "general guidelines" and even specific requirements for buildings.

"These non-architects do the analytic work that often determines the size and shape of buildings," wrote Paul B. Farrell, Jr., author of numerous articles on this involvement of professionals. "They determine whether or not buildings are needed, what type they should be, when and where they should be constructed, what the budget will be, who the occupants will be, and, often, what the manufacturing processes will be."

The Philadelphia city government commissioned Becker & Becker to prepare a program for its Municipal Services Building, which was subsequently designed by Vincent Kling & Associates. Paul Rudolph worked on his Southern Massachusetts Technical Institute campus plan with a program written by Arthur D. Little, and on Boston's Government Center with one established by Becker & Becker. What may not be so commonly recognized is that some of these firms have been engaged by architects themselves to establish programs.

The AIA's book, *Comprehensive Architectural Services* (1962– 1965), indicates that practice, as it becomes more complex, may have to be divided in several different ways. One of these ways may require architects to specialize in one phase of practice, such as design or supervision, and leave other phases, such as programming, to other specialists. They may even subcontract some of these services, the book notes, to non-architectural firms. There is the official word.

The new systems engineers and programmers say that they can apply scientific principles to program writing and thereby increase operational efficiency with resultant economies. One programmer scores on a more sensitive point: "An architect's fee is related to the structure that's built; our fees are not based on this. We have nothing to gain if a facility gets built or doesn't get built." And that valid reason for engaging non-architect programmers will obtain until architects have a similar basis for their fees.

For city planning, the systems approach attempts to bring cybernetic technology to civil systems and to architecture. Systems analysis conceives mathematical models to simulate urban design decision-making situations. Computers and sophisticated information retrieval devices are used by large architecture firms to achieve "scientific planning."

"Systems technology is primarily the application of managerial skills in integrating creative effort in the fields of science, engineering, manufacturing, logistics, and operations to accomplish some objective or goal," as one spokesman defined it. "These same capabilities can and must be brought to bear to solve the present and future problems of our environment," he added.

Christopher Alexander, one of the prominent computer specialists who captured the attention of the architecture profession in the 1960s, was interested in "inventing a language to prescribe the kinds of forms that a city should be constructed with, to specify the invariant characteristics of a city at all levels of its essential physical structure at all scales." With such newspeak, pundit Alexander's pronouncements about computers rivaled Buckminster Fuller's on physics and cosmology.

Systems analysts are especially concerned with the problem of adaptability to change. "The missile system is a determinant system," one of those specialists said, by way of example,

> and once that bird is off the ground it can only do certain things. The ability to change and do other things were designed out of it. In a city we do not have a determinant system but an open system, so a city is more complex and changing. Through a process of starting on two systems and working them in conjunction with one another then going to three to four to six systems, you can come to something pretty close to a living system.

And living systems were the new goals of architects and designers in the 1960s.

At a time of increasing specialization and technology, the systems analysts showed a way of planning based on minute, or allegedly minute analysis of environmental conditions, environmental subsystems, and their interdependence and interaction with human factors or systems. The justification was that "no one should be allowed to exercise whims and fancy in the design or such megasystems as regions, cities, transportation networks, health facilities, and the like," as one architectural educator said. But what was not proved was the accuracy of the analysis in determining the interfaces between mechanical or environmental systems and human systems.

"Systems analysis, although it relies on quantification," Sim Van der Ryn said, "relies even more heavily on qualitative statements, on human judgment, intuition, and values." Those committed to this subprocess as a science did not easily agree. But Van der Ryn insisted: "Systems analysis in architecture begins where social and human problems interact with the institutions and building forms that have been devised to meet these problems." Systems analysis of client needs showed, said Van der Ryn, that "the building system—a determination of *how* best to build—comes much after the program system—establishing *what* to build."

But is systems analysis actually being used for overall urban planning today? Joseph Passonneau, whose *Urban Atlas: Twenty American Cities, a Communication Study Notating Selected Urban Data* (1966), developed with Richard Saul Wurman, has quantifiable indications of density, income, and other urban statistics surprinted on a computerized grid, says of industry's involvement, "Systems analysis for city planning is mostly a dream right now, and you can only identify uses for it." Charles Diehl of Stanford Research Institute concurred, "Systems analysis is not generally in practice so far as city planning is concerned. Without much fear of contradiction, you could truthfully say that no one has really done a total systems study." And another systems analyst admitted, "The subsystems are rather well packaged, but the blend has been done only at the universities."

Where is the inhibitor? Basically, it is in the matter of changing scale: from the single building to the total city, from the transportation and sewage system to the total city system. These are the awkward and slow transitions of our day. It is a grand leap from the analysis of a transportation system, which is only one of many single systems, to preprogramming the overall suprasystem of a city. However, the technology is there and it has been employed to analyze and plan urban subsystems.

Not many young architects in the 1960s, including the Supermannerists, could become deeply involved with systems analysis or computers. They did not have large enough firms, resources, or projects to support or to require them. The technological process was too elaborate for their early commissions, and only a few had explored the techniques to any great extent by the 1970s. Those who did work with this scientific planning worked either in large architecture or design firms or with organizations of specialists in preprogramming, planning, and management consulting that did not go on to design buildings. Most significant was a new awareness of the need to join forces with non-architect specialists and of the need for concentration on each phase in the long and complex process of architecture. Systems analysis exemplifies the expansion of the process of architecture as well as of the increasing emergence of new specialists—as the split-off of the engineering field some sixty years before had created a separate profession.

A NEW KIND OF ARCHITECT

No longer content to wait for opportunities to design and build someone else's dream house, no longer content to let clients be the sole benefactors of their skills and organizations, a growing number of architects—including the young Supermannerists—expanded their services to include a do-it-yourself reliance on themselves as architects, entrepreneurs, developers, financiers, planners, contractors, builders, and decorators—as well as politicians and other paraprofessionals.

A new AIA code of ethics permitted American architects—like architects in other countries—to engage in building and contracting, acknowledging the need for an expanded concept of the process of architecture. If architects assumed the relatively new roles of contractor and entrepreneur, artists detached themselves from their artisan-craftsman roles and delegated the execution of their works to other industrial craftsmen. Eduardo Paolozzi could do this with collages, Tony Smith with his models as well as with his superscale wood and metal sculptures. It was analogous to the process of industrialized buildings.

The most prominent, successful entrepreneur/architect is John Portman, successful both aesthetically and financially, who from 1959 onward initiated, financed, developed, designed, and operated large hotel, merchandise mart, and office tower complexes in Atlanta, Dallas, San Francisco, New York, and elsewhere. Numerous other firms also became involved in land development projects or announced plans to do so in the future. Charles Luckman merged his architecture firm with the Ogden Development Corporation; Jules Gregory merged with two other

John Portman: Hyatt Regency Hotel, Atlanta, Georgia. 1967.

architects and designers; The Louis Bergen Companies, architects-engineers, became the architecture wing of Leasco Data Processing Equipment Corporation; Lord Y Den Hartog, architects and planners, became affiliated with an engineering firm and a power company; and so on. It made a glaring contrast with the unbuilt, idealized, urban-design easel drawings of Paolo Soleri and the form-givers of the previous decade, until Soleri's workshops actually began to build his utopian city, Arcosanti, and put him surprisingly in the category of entrepreneur also. "Only by assuming an active role in construction and real estate will the architect be capable of assuming the position of leadership he has talked about much of this past decade," Paul Farrell said in numerous lectures.

As Alvin Toffler wrote in *Future Shock,*

> It is conventional wisdom to assert that the age of the entrepreneur is dead, and that in his place there now stand only organization men or bureaucrats. Yet what is happening today is a resurgence of entrepreneurism within the heart of large organizations. The secret behind this reversal is the new transience and the death of economic insecurity for large masses of educated men. With the rise of affluence has come a new willingness to take risks. Men are willing to risk failure because they cannot believe they will ever starve.

Charles Hosford: Hosford house,
Kingfield, Maine. 1966–1968. *Photograph by David Hirsch.*

Young architecture students in the 1960s similarly began to view the traditional architect-client relationship as "a rather dreary conclusion to some turned-on ideas they had in school," said Chip Lord. Charles Hosford, for example, after graduation from Yale in 1964, involved himself in the construction and design of his own house in Maine as "the result of an insatiable restlessness to explore my own growth process in a situation where, unlike architecture school, effort yielded tangible results." He and others—like Peter Gluck, who also built in Maine in 1965—felt that six years of professional training was a lengthy and expensive preparation for spending an equal period as glorified drafts-men. So an underground, anti-Establishment student movement pro-duced "a fringe of self-determined people who are actively pursuing their own directions," as Richard Oliver observed. They became more and more their own clients, their own entrepreneurs and developers, their own financiers, their own builder-contractors, and began to realize their own ideas in building forms without waiting to finish school to achieve architectural registration through the lengthy established process of apprenticeship and licensing. They are do-it-yourself, personally in-volved architects.

Architecture Swings Like a Pendulum Do

In 1965 a group of lumbering mountaineers then at the Yale Architec-ture School started a project called Prickly Mountain—a sun-and-ski area near Sugarbush and Mad River, Vermont. They were putting down the Establishment by acting as entrepreneurs and land speculators, contractors and craftsmen, as well as architects, and doing the whole thing themselves before they were graduated or licensed. At the time it seemed like architectural blast-off.

Then twenty-six and still somewhat Beatle-browed, Bill Ringo Rienecke and David Sellers with Tom Luckey, Charles Hosford, Louis Mackall, and others were Samsons up there in that spectacular valley on their own six-hundred-acre mountain tract with their checkbooks and their folk songs. They were dressed in plaid lumberjack shirts over surfers' pullovers, with pants hung on wide elastic clip-on suspenders, and construction boots. Surrounded by the smells of damp, fresh-sawn lumber and the acrid propane-gas warmer, with the polyethylene sheets on the windows flapping in the breeze, they talked up their ideas, like, "beautiful"—particularly Sellers, who comes on with works like a Mack Truck.

David Sellers and William Rienecke: Tack House, Prickly Mountain, Warren, Vermont. 1966. *Photograph by David Sellers.*

"The architect is irresponsible today," Sellers said,

if he thinks he has to sit in his office and wait for some client to come up and say, all right, build me that. But I think the architect has gotta change his whole scope if he's going to survive as an integral part of our future society; he's gotta play the role of the entrepreneur as well. He's gotta combine Zeckendorf, the Rand Corporation, and a great architect all in one. And maybe that's more than one guy; maybe that's five guys working together.

Ringo Rienecke carried on: "It's hard to believe that an entrepreneur could come up with a better idea than some professional people who are spending their lives thinking about these things. A lot of architects have a lotta ideas about things that should be done, or possibilities, and they, you know, stow them away and do nice drawings about them. But they don't act."

What this new generation of architects was proclaiming is that architects ought to take the lead and go out and find an entrepreneur— or become one—saying that the country needs a new town over there or a community here, or that this is the right place for a new high-rise office building. And that's what they've done at Prickly Mountain. They got financial backing by persuading friends through their bumptious energy and dynamic talk, and they bought the land themselves and built houses to sell, themselves. They sold parcels to other young architects, who want a share of the speculation game and flock up there to build for-sale houses.

When asked why he was so unusually interested in economics, Sellers burst out,

I'm not "interested"; I *have* to know it. Architects who don't know how things are paid for, and who don't know why things have got to make money, I think, are irresponsible to their field. Architecture has got to be a profit-making thing; there's no question about it. It's a commodity; it's a salable item; and it's gotta be made to work for somebody, or else he's not going to spend dough on it. The least responsibility you have, if you want to put up a building for some guy who is going to put out a lot of money, is to be economical and efficient. But most architects can't make anything that his client can afford. Any half-wit speculator seems to be able to make something that doesn't leak, stays warm, and you can see out of, and he usually does it so people can afford it—and he gets rich. That seems out of the scope of most architects.

The example of Prickly Mountain energized architects on hundreds of projects for almost a decade. "It suddenly occurred to students that they were going to be architects someday and that they could already build buildings," University of Pennsylvania graduate Ed d'Andrea said in 1972. So he and Gary Dwyer in the summer of 1967, the summer of the Flower Children, gathered a group of student architects up in the New Hampshire mountains at Franconia College, and designed and built a dormitory using the student labor of those who were going to live in the dorm. Students finished their own rooms as part of their college course work. The building is a five-story fortresslike castle keep built of wood, which has fifteen private apartments, or multilevel rooms, surrounding a communal space. That central well, with its balconies, stairs, bridges, and lower-level common lounge, is a central arena of dorm life, not unlike the wooden Os of Elizabethan stages, not unlike the performance spaces of environmental theatres designed by Jerry Rojo. It gives an appropriate bear-pit-like focus for communal dormitory living as well as expressing the design and construction process of the building. Anywhere from nine to twelve students made up a crew who worked from June to Christmas, learning about building as they went along, and

Ed d'Andrea and Gary Dwyer: Dormitory interior, Franconia College, Franconia, New Hampshire. 1967. *Photograph by Ed d'Andrea.*

Haus-Rucker, Inc. Inflatable mattress happening, Museum of Contemporary Crafts, New York City. 1970. *Photograph by Hy Rothman for the New York* Daily News

living a natural life outdoors in the mountains, on the land, and among the trees. It was an architectural commune that they called "The New Nude Lewd Improved Family Size Franconia Electric Summer Workshop."

Countless other young architects and students rebelled against paper architecture, picture-making expertise, and imaginary programs, and involved themselves in real buildings for real people. Both in curriculum projects and in after-school workshops, students from Yale, Washington University, Carnegie Tech, Cincinnati, the University of Pennsylvania, and elsewhere, demonstrated that the best way of learning architecture is *doing* architecture. They worked in Appalachia, in Vermont, in New Hampshire, in California, and wherever active involvement was possible.

Following the earlier lead of England's Archigram group or the Cambridge Seven, design communes similarly involved in *doing* devised names for their groups and their workshops as if they were ball teams or rock groups: Ant Farm, Southcoast, Onyx, Truth Commandos, Intangible, Elm City Electric Light Sculpture Co., The Grocery Store, Zomeworks, Kamakazi Design Group, Mind Huns, Space Cowboys, All Electric Medicine Show, Crystal Springs Celery Gardens, Crash City, Archi-Week, Globe City, Hog Farm, and Peoples Architecture. They went around the countryside designing and building wherever they could.

Haus-Rucker, a Viennese design group composed of Laurids Ortner, Claus Pinter, and Zamp, did Pop-space sculptures, drawings, and live-ins at museums and elsewhere in Europe before moving to New York in the mid-1960s. Here, they staged live-ins and happenings: At New York's Museum of Contemporary Crafts in 1970 they produced a four-foot-high, street-wide inflatable mattress on which people could bounce, roll, and jump, along with a self-destroying sculpture of the museum building made of cake, which was devoured by those who attended the opening night party. And in Central Park in 1972 they re-created Frederick Law Olmsted's plan for Central Park as a cake for his sesquicentennial celebration. Primarily they were interested in new life-styles and new options for flexibility and mobility and in plug-in solutions for urban problems, expressed in happenings, demonstrations, and graphics, as well as in some minienvironments and in new furniture concepts—and they put their interests into real action.

After Prickly Mountain, David Sellers moved on in 1970 to Goddard College in Plainfield, Vermont, where he and John Mallery directed the design and construction of two other buildings using student involvement and student labor—a design center and a sculpture studio building. And in the early 1970s, Sim Van der Ryn ran an off-campus course for the University of California at Berkeley, at Inverness, California; it was a "build-in" workshop. Later Southcoast also managed to show that they could produce a building: for Antioch College's original campus in Yellow Springs, Ohio, Southcoast designed an arts building that looks like a large machine part, with long skylighted extensions, sliding doors, and, in the original design, a chrome-yellow exterior. Southcoast, with Doug Michels, Tom Morey, and others, designed a preliminary scheme, got approval, and produced working drawings. "They worked hard," their associate architect in Ohio, Richard Cook, said, "using his drafting room as an all-day camping ground, working all night and sleeping in their sleeping bags off and on during the day. And they got the job done." It took some coordination and supervision and perseverance on the part of their associate architect, but the building got built and was well received by the college clients and students, both for its functional efficiency and for its unusual form.

Visitors to architecture schools during the second half of the 1960s were frequently impressed by the contrast between fifth-year students diligently bending over their drafting boards, and first-year students up and painting, building, subdividing their drafting studios, personalizing, "customizing" their individual areas, regardless of the resulting aesthetic images.

Student project: Fifth-year architecture drafting room, MIT, Cambridge, Massachusetts. 1967.

David Sellers and John Mallery: Design Center, Goddard College, Plainfield, Vermont. 1970.

This contrast was marked at MIT, Yale, New Mexico, Austin, and other schools, where drafting studios were restructured to define individual programs, or to dissociate envelope from furniture, or merely to express student self-determination. They were the ones, in the eyes of the new breed of designers, who were "doing architecture."

PROCESSES OF DESIGNING

The design process itself—that phase of architecture dealing with putting conceptions on paper—was also explored as a separate subsystem of architectural process, both to expedite and facilitate building design and to discover new ways of seeing things. These concentrations on the process of designing were exemplary of an age interested in non-architecture or anti-architecture, an age when the intention of the designer and his "concepts" were considered more important than his products, an age when there was "greater intellectual than visual interest," as Harold Rosenberg wrote. It was also to a high degree an age of aesthetic self-consciousness, which is another aspect of the interest—though by no means sweeping involvement—in design processes.

Among these new investigations into processes that led from inspiration to formal design, from spontaneity to product, are Walter Netsch's Field Theory, a method of using forms as a process of designing; the Visual Syntax of Peter Eisenman and Michael Graves, who see architecture as a language; and investigations into urban design, such as systems analysts' "urban games" with computer models; Lawrence Halprin's Motation, and other urbanography.

Field Theory

"We keep trying to find new ways to see things," architect Walter Netsch said of his design group at Skidmore, Owings & Merrill in Chicago. "We look at models and buildings through fish-eye lenses and other devices; we make films as other means of seeing things differently. Our Field Theory is a process of looking at things differently, and of ordering too."

Field theory as defined by Webster's Third New International Dictionary—anyone who has heard Walter Netsch talk will not be surprised by academic terminology—is "a method of analysis in behavioral science that describes actions or events as the resultant of dynamic interplay among sociocultural, biomechanical, and motivational forces."

The architectural connotation of the term *Field Theory* for Netsch and the design group is, similarly, a planning analysis based on human functions. Since the term also refers to optical fields, the planning process manifests itself as a fluid, manual manipulation of geometric forms. A "field" is the spatial unit of the "environmental module" that the architects manipulate to compose a building. It is a method of using forms as a process of designing. Netsch and his colleagues have planned buildings over the past ten years with basic square bays through which they envision an X formed by diagonals. Sometimes they add a smaller concentric square within the larger square; sometimes they superimpose on the larger square an identical square and rotate it—turn it diagonally. This manipulation provides the basic grid patterns of their structures. It is a process of building up an imagery, rather than imposing a preconceived concept. The process has produced varied and dissimilar-looking

Skidmore, Owings & Merrill/Chicago: Art and Architecture Building, University of Illinois, Chicago Circle Campus. 1968.

star-shaped fields as the overall modules of buildings. By truncating or cutting off the projections of the stars, octagonal forms are created. Repeating this procedure with a smaller inner square or with larger squares outside the bays, and by combining the star-shaped field, the architects arrive at "lattice" patterns of interlocked lines. In Netsch's view, the lattice creates "a linear expansion of the progression of different activities and communications for which the building is used," so the behavioral science basis of the theory is valid for him.

To facilitate visualizing this language of patterns, the architects devised a series of acetate overlays covered with various elements of the lattice. With two acetate patterns of separate squares, one laid over the other, they can visualize the rotation of the forms to achieve their lattice and star-shaped units. With two acetate sheets of interconnected larger and smaller squares, they can slide the patterns along to arrive at more complicated lattice systems of squares-within-squares. These simple acetate overlays are Netsch's basic tools for Field Theory. The technique of superimposition is analogous to John Cage's "unstructured" music, some of which is written on pieces of cellophane and shuffled like cards.

But Netsch's process produces a strict organizing design discipline along whose lines all partitions, and, ultimately, furnishings, are laid out. The lattice system indicates all the available options for complicated design layouts, which may not be immediately perceivable with simple squares or single rectangles.

Field Theory developed in practice, not as pure theory. The architects had been working toward such a design system for some time before the tools and the procedure were formulated and before the name Field Theory was adopted. The first of Skidmore, Owings & Merrill's (Chicago) buildings to break away from the simple rectangular grid was the U.S. Air Force Academy chapel in Colorado Springs, Colorado (1956–1960), with its composite structure, the upper part of which utilized diagonals and tetrahedrons. Next came a design for graduate housing at Northwestern University in Evanston, Illinois, which was never built, and subsequently the library for Northwestern University, announced early in 1964 and completed in 1970. None of the lattice is followed in the layout of the library's exterior walls, but the radial arrangement of stacks and study areas spreading outward from central information desks led to the planning considerations demonstrated in a Field Theory film that Netsch made in 1966 as a study for three Field Theory science buildings.

The first completed building to use elements of the theory was the College Forum (1965), a community social center at Iowa's Grinnell College. That simple rectangular structure shows a lattice system in its plan, layout, structural system, and to some degree in section. Then came the design for the Art and Architecture Building at the Chicago Circle Campus of the University of Illinois. Phase one of this building was opened in October 1968 to much-rumored student discontent. A & A has a spiral plan of interconnected star-form pavilions, arrived at

Skidmore, Owings & Merrill/Chicago:
Stills from Field Theory film showing radial development. 1968.

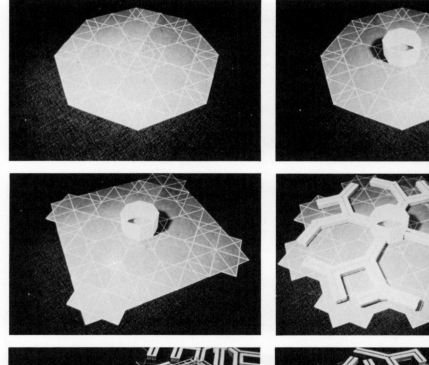

by Field Theory planning. It is a remarkable building; a glorification of the corridor, it is completely ambiguous in its windowless circulation route, even mystifying and alienating, which was, no doubt, the cause of student unrest.

In this same period, the architects designed and built the Wells College Library (1968) in Aurora, New York, which, with the A & A building, was one of the first structures designed strictly by the Field Theory process. Like a hazy cloud, the roof of the Wells College Library covers a field of nine stars—not the heavenly variety (though the analogy is not inappropriate), nor the performer species (though many a Wells College girl gets top billing). Instead the stars of Skidmore, Owings & Merrill's library are nine interlocking units that compose the floor plan. The grid pattern shows each star-shaped unit centered on a "rotated" (or diagonally placed) square column. The star-shaped units —or "fields"—that are developed by this systematic process are inter-meshed so thoroughly in the library, and the perimeter of the building is manipulated with such seeming freedom, that the existence of Field Theory as the basis of the design is not immediately apparent. The sections reveal that Field Theory has also been tentatively employed in the vertical dimension, producing a billowing, angular roof. None of this form-making looks contrary, however, either outside or inside. Even the faceted planes of the building seem to give only slight raised edges to the gentle setting, formalizing the rolling hillside terrain above Lake Cayuga, which is to the west. Further, it demonstrates the freedom that the architects achieved in working within a seemingly rigid geometric design system.

In the next five years these stars were joined by a galaxy of other Field Theory buildings—Chicago Circle Campus' Science and Engineering Center and (appropriately enough) its Behavioral Science Center; Northwestern University's Biological Science Building; and the University of Iowa's Basic Science Building, Educational Research Building, and Health Science Library, in Iowa City. These structures realize fully the three-dimensional extension of Field Theory that was tentatively stated in the Wells College Library.

For the Field Theory buildings designed since then, Netsch's design team has refined the design process, has developed more sophisticated tools, and has worked toward greater fluidity of planning. Grids of different sizes have been superimposed, arranged radially, and offset. The command of the process is impressive if sometimes incomprehensible, and the buildings produced are among the most significant—if ambiguously expressive—of our day. As Netsch notes, they "avoid the willful, cute angularities that are sometimes designed in for sculptural variety." And in fact, the very discipline of the lattice removes all suspicion of arbitrariness. Since all the forms are additive, the system also provides open-ended options versus finite planning. It provides a preestablished direction for changing the environment without disrespect for the basic unity of the original design. "In this way," Netsch says, "we are trying to tackle the infinity problem." The real benefit of Field Theory will be as a more speedy organizing tool or language with which to design a great number of buildings. And Netsch points out that his colleagues have recently been responsible for building 800,000 square feet of space per year. In a day when we must think on a mammoth scale—a scale on which entire buildings must be given the consideration details were given in the past—such design systems as Field Theory point a way.

Motation of Cities

Lawrence Halprin, landscape architect and city planner, developed an aid to the design of city spaces that accommodates the movement and speed at which we often perceive cities—from automobiles and other moving vehicles on the streets and on the freeways—and records it all. Called Motation, the system begins as a shorthand notation of what we see as we move through our urban environments. It was a continuation of the work of Kevin Lynch and Gyorgy Kepes at MIT and of Philip Thiel at the University of Washington. It posits a series of symbols—for vertical and horizontal elements, diagonal and curved elements, buildings of various heights, underpasses, valleys, water, trees, cars, trains, bicycles—all of which are notated in successive frames, like an animated film. Direction and acceleration indicators and a title block indicating motive power, duration, distance of individual frames, and total distance of movement complete the Motation system. With this device, which is analogous to the notation of music and dance, Halprin presents a process of recording the movement through exterior, or interior, spaces and environments. But further, once the system is assimilated as a mastered craft, like a shorthand language, a planner can use it to design, frame by frame, the kinds of vistas, sequence by sequence, that he envisions a city, interior, or other environment to have. The Motation system offers a quick sequential symbology. As a process it has enormous potential—as yet unrealized—for future design.

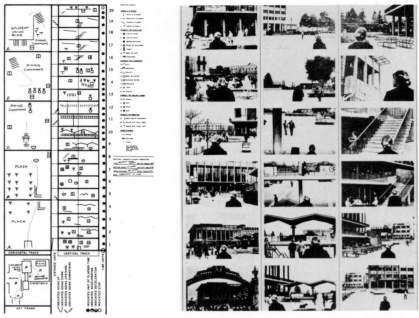

Lawrence Halprin: Motation system for urban
data collection and design. 1965.

Visual Syntax

From about 1969 on, another systematic approach to the design process
that began to interest architects was the Visual Syntax of Peter Eisenman and the Visual Semantics of Michael Graves, who have been
loosely grouped together with other neo-Corbusier architects such as
Richard Meier, John Hejduk, and (even more loosely) Charles Gwathmey as the New York School. The *New York School* is a term applied to
this group whose work was published in a book called *Five Architects*
(1972), and discussed in *Architectural Forum* (May 1973) in a series
of articles by different architects and planners called "Five on Five," or
five critics on *Five Architects*.

Although, except for Michael Graves, all of the Five live and work
in New York City (Graves lives and works mostly in Princeton, New
Jersey), the New York School is a loose designation at best. Not the
least of the reasons for this is that there are six thousand other architects

in New York City and New York State, most of whom do not share the ideals or methods of the Five. Meier and Gwathmey live and work in New York City and have produced the majority of their architecture here, on Long Island, and in upstate New York. Peter Eisenman directs the Institute for Architecture and Urban Studies in New York City, but has produced none of his few works of architecture in the city or the state. Graves has produced most of his work in New Jersey and the Midwest and none of it in New York. And John Hejduk, who heads the architecture department at Cooper Union in New York City, had built no architecture until his remodeling (1974) of the mid-nineteenth-century Cooper Union building. What does the New York School as a term refer to? The answer seems to be that the Five occasionally meet, dine, and confer together in New York City. They no longer share common attitudes, if they ever did.

Eisenman has developed theories of designing buildings as he would construct sentences with a language. Graves is interested in reading the meanings of such architectural sentences. Like other specialists, such as anthropologist E. T. Hall, Fred I. Steele, and Robert G. Hershberger, who are working on the assumption that architecture is a language, that architects express underlying cultural messages that can be read by knowledgeable experts—anthropologists, sociologists, psychologists, and certain specialized architects—Eisenman and Graves attempt to assemble columns and walls, panels and beams, volumes and columns, volumes and walls in both additive and subtractive ways to create an interrelated system of architectural language and, for Eisenman, a dialogue among the individual elements.

As specialists in the design process agree, the physical-spatial environment is undeniably important in determining how a person feels, what he can do, and how he interacts with other people, "but there is relatively little research today to guide psychologists and designers toward an understanding of the impact of the environment on man's behavior," Fred I. Steele has said. And Robert G. Hershberger has written: "We do need to concentrate on what it is that makes laymen fail to appreciate some 'potent' buildings which architects appreciate. We should also try to determine which characteristics of buildings cause them to appear organized to laymen and pre-architects but not to architects, and vice versa."

For Eisenman and Graves, as for Hall, Steele, Hershberger, and others, if architecture is a language, we must know how it is written and how it is read. Graves, educated at Cincinnati and Harvard, and now working in Princeton, aims at communicating those meanings of architecture—symbolic meanings that are built up by the culture. He investigates how architecture is read. For Eisenman, educated at Cornell, Columbia, and Cambridge, and now working in New York, the goal is to use the grammar of architecture in a meaningful, logical order of syntax. His interest is primarily how architecture is said.

Eisenman, writing in language that is as abstruse, alienating, and noncommunicative as any aesthetician's, expounds a complex and highly codified mythology. He has also produced several buildings that he uses to demonstrate his theory—although all aesthetic theory is necessarily ex post facto. Eisenman's Visual Syntax is an architectural analogy to the work in linguistics by Noam Chomsky, who revolutionized linguistic theory and research by rejecting the notion of common usage as a determinant and indicator of language functions. Instead, Chomsky posits a codex of inflexible grammatical laws, a fixed syntax existing in every language, which are there to be isolated, discovered, and revealed.

Like Chomsky, Eisenman aims to isolate and demonstrate the underlying architectural laws that are independent of external reference and communication, the syntax of architecture that he calls "deep stucture." To Eisenman, these underlying laws are the generators of rooms, of spaces, and of order; to him, this system of architectural laws generates meanings. Eisenman therefore treats the problem-solving system of architecture as a process of examination, investigation, and research by which the meaning of architecture can be understood and the language of architectural forms explained. He is content to work in the pure and independent sphere of the laws, without concern for whatever meanings are communicated. Unlike Eisenman, Graves is interested in the results of architectural syntax—its semantics—the communication of its meanings to observers along with the communication of the meaning of architectural history and heritage.

Eisenman's Visual Syntax is an inductive and reductive process rather than an inclusive and perceptual one; it is basically unconcerned with function, structure, or user involvement on a physical level. In its concentration on buildings as systems of language, as communicators like paintings, Visual Syntax is highly intellectual, uninvolved with living architecture as an applied, functioning art. It returns to an almost Minimalist concentration—on a single phase of design. Yet in its attention to the creative act as a structured and systematic theory, Visual Syntax illustrates the current expansion and explosion of the separate phases of the process of architecture that have interested architects for the past decade.

BUILDING SYSTEMS

After architects go through the process of determining what to build, they must turn next to the process of determining *how* to build. "Industrialized building," "boxes and tinkertoys," "twentieth-century bricks," and other similar phrases on the lips of architects and designers evidence an ever more committed involvement and interest in the process of actual building. Building systems are methods of constructing with standardized components that can be assembled in different ways to produce personalized designs, buildings, and environments. The systems approach to construction aims to expedite construction processes, to lower costs, and to improve the man-made environment. As long as there has been architecture, there have been systems of building—orders of masonry, balloon-frame systems, steel-frame skyscraper systems, and steel-and-glass systems that developed from Sir Joseph Paxton's Crystal Palace to the curtain walls of the 1950s and the 1960s. In the past decade, however, the scale of components in building systems vastly increased along with the need to build economically and efficiently. The urgent social need for mass housing has compelled new thinking about processes of construction.

With visions of superscale building blocks and tinkertoy systems dancing in their heads, architects are dreaming of building good low-cost mass housing at last. They acclaim the inevitable reality of industrialization, prefabrication, and construction technology—as well as the *real* in the real estate of architecture. This time, those dreams may not remain mere unfulfilled wishes. What makes low-cost, systems-built housing an imminent possibility now is the coming together at a single point in time of seemingly all the factors and forces needed to usher it along: The crying needs of destitute urban areas for even minimal accommodation are recognized by the general public and the professionals alike. The lack of insulating space against the heat and pressures of summer in these overpopulated and underaccommodated ghettos, which has caused almost annual spontaneous combustion, has forcibly brought attention to the slums and to their real and very basic architectural requirements.

The response of politicians and local governments to protests and needs has been a combination of genuine desire to alleviate the situation and genuine political expediency. That interest gives a legislative nod to those anxious to produce building systems for low-cost housing and it also provides a source of government funding. Among other favorable factors, manufacturers of mobile homes claim an existing technology and industry that can produce urban modules at a far lower figure than has been done up to now, and they are ready to offer their services for the urgent cause of urban housing. In addition, producers of raw materials and suppliers of products for housing are eager, naturally, to further this cause.

On the design side, innovations in engineering and construction—notably the lifting power of cranes and helicopters and the structural power of lightweight, thin-wall concrete—are bringing the fanciful visions of architects nearer to realization. Helicopters are used to lift, transport, and construct stacked complexes. Even the members of the architecture profession, which has struggled impatiently and ineffectually for years to alter the process of building construction, are now striking out on their own as entrepreneurs of prefabricated systems. House construction—the only major-market business, it has been said, in which an eighteenth-century workman could show up at a job site, work with his own tools, and earn today's pay—is changing, slowly but

Sikorsky Aircraft: A Sikorsky Skycrane making aerial delivery of prefabricated box house by Utility Services, Inc. 1967.

inevitably, from a crafts business to a manufacturing and retail industry. As General Electric's George T. Bogard pointed out, "What is badly needed is to accelerate an evolution in the building process comparable to that which has been under way in other major industries. [Building] is the only major industry failing to participate in the greatest economic boom the world has ever known." Architects who are really "with it" insist on bringing the construction of buildings more into phase with the construction of the rest of our contemporary environment; their goal is to build houses as Detroit builds automobiles. And some architects are succeeding.

The technological advances in building systems offer three courses: first, subsystems of prefabricated components, often called tinkertoys, which can be used to compose structural subsystems, subsystems for enclosing spaces, and mechanical subsystems; second, projects that move technology out of the structural-grid age such as plastics technology, which has developed filament-wound cocoonlike and domelike modules, spray-foam construction, and other methodologies beyond standard architectural technology; and third, much-larger-scale prefabricated components, often called boxes, which constitute complete living spaces or rooms that are moved into place all in one piece. Such technologies are now sufficiently developed to be used to expedite the construction and lower the cost, not only of housing, but also of schools, office buildings, industrial buildings, and hotels.

Many architects believe that prefabricated components—columns, beams, panels, windows, doors, stairs, and mechanical subsystems—tinkertoys—offer a better way to build because they provide more options in planning and more flexibility for meeting site, activity, and design requirements. Components range in size from thirty-foot-long concrete walls down to patented connections for joining wall panels. In between these extremes lie the beam-and-column systems that proponents claim have superior planning versatility. Another claimed advantage of tinkertoy systems of beams and columns is that individual components can be manhandled without the aid of heavy lifting equipment. Some of the new developments in components for building systems include a staggered truss system developed at MIT; a curtain wall that provides an incombustible monolithic exterior over conventional construction, a dry floor plank system that speeds construction, and a studless partition, all three developed at Pratt Institute; and Carl Koch's "Techbilt" developments. Most prominent of the decade's component systems was Ezra Ehrenkrantz's SCSD (School Construction Systems Development), which utilized a series of standard components from different manufacturers as an integrated construction system for schools in California and other buildings throughout the country.

For many other architects, the half-century-old dreams of stacking up building blocks are now joined by an entirely new vision of an urban superscale. As elements of plug-in, clip-on systems, "boxes" raise the tinkertoy construction system idea to an even larger dimension than before, up to a point where a whole living box is a tinkertoy part for a plug-in cage or structural frame. This major step is the acceptance of a new building module, based not on what a workman can comfortably pick up by hand but by what the highway authorities will allow on the road: this new dimension for building is the twelve-foot by sixty-foot trailer—with few exceptions the largest unit that can be towed on a highway—which Paul Rudolph calls the "twentieth-century brick." In the twentieth century the scale of components had to increase beyond the traditional five-inch by eight-inch brick. As Rudolph says,

> Fifty years after all the theorists made very clear the possibilities of industrialization of structure, we have—without any help from architects—a truly industrialized organization of the utmost importance—the mobile-house industry. Now, the mobile-house industry is extremely naïve: They are littering the countryside with the ugliest things imaginable; they are outlawed in most municipalities; yet they pull themselves up by their bootstraps. The mobile-house industry accounts for one out of every five new housing starts in the United States today and the graph goes up and up and up. It isn't that they are technically advanced, quite the opposite. (If you go through a mobile-house plant, you're amazed at the low level of sophistication.) But it's the buying power. They can produce a quite decent equivalent of a two-bedroom house, air conditioned for $6,000. They also produce a $3,000 house. Now where else can you buy this kind of thing?

Many architects see the box as the new scale in megalopolis, expressing on the exterior the scale of a whole family-size living unit—it is no longer the scale of a single individual, which was formerly expressed by the single window. They see the supercage of a tower of boxes as leading toward their large-scale urban image. During the 1960s exposure to Pop art principles relaxed architects into recognizing the values of the previously disdained roadside trailer, at the same time the appearance of the mobile house was markedly improved. In addition, everyone in the construction industry, except perhaps the unions, recognizes that to effect any significant savings in building construction more work must be done in plants and less work on the site. Prefabrication is the watchword, and boxes are in the fore. Architects and manufacturers alike envision "piggyback units," sectionalized units of "double wides" that are combinations of two boxes, fold-out units, and other variations on the theme.

Although panels prefabricated in a plant and assembled in the field have been used for many years, boxes as complete units with walls, floor, and roof remained on wheels as mobile homes until the Canadian government financed Moshe Safdie's Habitat for Montreal's Expo '67. Most highly touted of all box-component projects, Habitat is a $20 million assemblage of 354 prefabricated concrete boxes clustered and staggered up into an open-network hillsidelike apartment complex for 158 families. The apartments range in size from one-bedroom, 600-square-foot units, to four-bedroom, 1,700-square-foot units. The exterior of each modular box measures 17 feet 6 inches by 38 feet 6 inches, and the interior measures 16 feet 2 inches by 37 feet 4 inches. Walls vary in thickness from 5 to 12 inches of structural content plus an additional 3 inches consisting of panelboards, metal studs, insulation, and

Moshe Safdie & Associates: Habitat, Montreal, Canada. 1967.

finish. This project, beautifully executed and courageously forwarded with indomitable perseverance by Safdie and his team, showed the developers, the government officials, and the architecture professionals among the seven million people who visited it that there are realizable benefits in such construction systems. Habitat is visually exciting, varied yet strong, monumental yet personal, livable and explorable, and an image for the future. If Habitat, like the ensuing box-assembly projects Safdie has designed—and described so movingly in his book *Beyond Habitat* (1970) and elsewhere—aesthetically belonged more to an older imagery—to a tradition of fixed, static, and permanent constructions—than the new designers seemed interested in, Habitat as surely served as a catalyst to overcome many of the misapprehensions felt about stacking prefabricated boxes.

Other notable stacked-box constructions of the decade were the Palacio del Rio Hilton Hotel designed by Cerna & Garza for San Antonio's Hemisfair exhibition in 1968, Paul Rudolph's stacked-wood boxes in New Haven (Oriental Masonic Gardens, 1968–1971), and numerous other designs in that idiom by Patrick Moreau and Sim Van der Ryn; Uniment's apartment house in Richmond, California; Dalton-Dalton Associates' steel-framed boxes project (unbuilt) for Jones & Laughlin Steel Corporation; William Morgan's series of stacked proposals; and designs by Conklin & Rossant, Ziegelman & Ziegelman, Moore-Turnbull, and others.

So far, except for the few outstanding experiments noted, these units usually have been stacked three high, since housing above three stories requires additional structural strength and fireproofing, and complicates mechanical systems. But new technologies for these construction processes are constantly evolving. Although back at the real real estate, urban life continues in too many tenements, this kind of building system is getting closer to commonplace actuality.

Boxes as Plug-Ins

Stacked-box building systems are the one great hope of the "plug-in architecture" that dominates the vision of many futuristic architects. Far-out drawings of completely new cities, ideally to be built on virgin land or over water, which include plug-in towers and structural grids that can accommodate housing units, filled the pages of architecture and design publications throughout the 1960s. Such schemes envisioned industrialized housing modules, based on the "mobile" trailer idea—science labs,

educational spaces, or medical facilities that are mobile, interchangeable, and suspendible on cables so that the occupants can winch down
their environments and ship them or fly them to some other utopian
city.

The dream seemed unassailable, if not immediately realizable by
present-day technology; but there were and are objections. In 1967,
Charles Moore wrote in *Perspecta* that plug-in visions "seem to be based
on the stage of the industrial revolution when mechanization meant
repetition, a stage which even Detroit seems to have gotten through."
What is at the root of this inspiration is the idea of freedom: "People
wanted to be free to move," said Kenneth Isaacs. This freedom of
movement is actually a chimera, however, since most mobile homes
move only once—from factory finishing to site attachment. Sociologically, also, building systems using boxes are questioned with regard to
the choices our society and our construction industry will reasonably be
able to provide. Will these systems merely box people in? While many
members of the architecture profession acclaim boxes as a means of
providing a choice of housing units to satisfy every desire and to make
housing as available as automobiles, many others do not. The former
group sees the exercise of personal choice, through boxes, as an emanci-
pation—"freeing up people's minds," but not all architects and planners
who favor choice and who zealously yearn to provide low-cost environments for our increasing population agree that this will be best accomplished by energizing the industry to produce more boxes. For every
architect who feels that "it is so inevitable that housing will eventually
be done through mobile-house techniques," as Paul Rudolph does, there
is some soberly balancing disagreement. Now that a truly industrialized
prefabricated house appears to be realistically within reach, we seem to
want something more than industrialization seems geared to provide. We
no longer see as adequate or relevant the mere box—its shelter and
sustenance—now that we have elevated to prominence and have ver-
bally and officially recognized the importance of the "environment."
Today, we want to go beyond industrialization to something more
spiritual, more psychologically fulfilling; we want to get back to the
basic need for individuality. Walter Netsch says strongly,

> In the ghettos, we have discovered that the question of space is a criti-
> cal one, and to give people less space—such as a trailer—would be a
> cultural disaster. We did not succeed in taking the accepted condi-

tions of the American bungalow or the three-story apartment and make an American city. To do just another living unit as the glue of a city is a fallacy. If you do just move this in on a critical path and you substitute trailer for house, you come up with the same mess. Look at trailers in the public school areas and you will see the constraints you will have with them!

Harry Weese agrees, "The trailer is one of the most expensive kinds of housing you can have. Look how people trade them in every three or four years, like an automobile. First cost is one thing, but obsolescence and longevity are something else. What we should build is a supply of housing good enough and that can be reused for more than one decade." Joseph Passonneau summarizes, "There is a connotation of jerry-building in trailerishness—that the society is dumping this junk on an under-privileged element."

Yet, as Craig Hodgetts points out, "For many people who have been living in tenements or government housing, the possession of their own trailer—fully equipped home—is a giant step." Choice of available housing units, in the long run, will always be dependent on financial position, and in this respect the analogy of the automobile holds true. The dream of multiple choice may be a youthful, or perhaps even a greedy, one on the part of affluent segments of our society, more than it is a dream of the needy poor. For they will, no doubt, always feel fortunate to acquire even one living unit.

How can our technology satisfy the requirements of individuation? As Columbia University sociologist Daniel Bell revealingly explains, there is a conflict involved in providing a housing module that would, on the one hand, offer the best good for the most people; "a group welfare function model" in sociologists' words, and, on the other hand, would also satisfy "individual utility preference." Bell and others refer to this conflict as "the paradox of the cyclical majority." As Bell says when writing about the post-industrial society:

> When one turns from individual decision making to that of groups, when one considers the problem of how best to amalgamate the discordant preference patterns of the members of a society so as to arrive at a compromise preference pattern for society as a whole, we seem to be at a theoretical impasse . . . This problem—of seeking to produce a single social ordering of alternative social choices which would correspond to individual orderings—is academic, in the best sense of the word.

What will happen, as we realize our dreams of low-cost building systems, as we broaden perspectives on our total society, is that we will recognize that a large group of people live in what Bell calls "new and higher substandard conditions."

After distinguishing and elaborating these subprocesses within the overall process of architecture, it is still left to the profession to analyze and to put into effect the subprocess of reevaluation. After the final products of architecture have been completed and put to user testing, we must evaluate them systematically for the ultimate knowledge of the profession. This is an expansion joint for the 1970s. But in the 1960s the expansion of understanding about what constitutes the process of architecture was a new attitude of inclusiveness.

An Inclusive, Simultaneous Aesthetic, Too

For all their bewildering multiplicity, the art forms of our day have been shaped by a single, omnipresent force that assaults and batters down rigid distinctions—categories devised by the idealists of preceding decades, classifications that convince us all the more that life and individuality defy classification. It is the business of artists in every age to sortie beyond the boundaries set up by habit and convention, and to show us new insights on the meaning and reality of life. In the 1960s artists went to work with revolutionary intensity to burst out beyond all barriers, then to accept all categories, activities, and interests realistically and, if not quite equally, at least with far less prejudice and exclusion than in the past. Iconoclasts stormed the barricades of habit and convention with the goal of dissolving them and then involving, interweaving, one side with the other.

Painting became intermixed with sculpture so that we cannot tell where one begins and the other leaves off. Robert Rauschenberg, James Rosenquist, and others added actual chairs, leftover painters' tools, and found objects of all sorts to their painted canvases as sculptural appendages.

In literature, fiction merged with nonfiction as Truman Capote wrote a "nonfiction novel" and Tom Wolfe, Gay Talese, Jimmy Breslin, and others expanded their reporting into the realm of playwriting and poetry. The impersonal view of traditional news reporting merged with the highly personal to produce the New Journalism.

In music, formal and popular works alike were interwoven with

46

instrumentation, compositional methods, and motifs that were adopted from each other's traditions, materials, and crafts. Rock groups led us through a maze of altogetherness with inclusions of historical music (baroque-rock as in "The Rock Bach" and rococo-rock in "Swingle Mozart"), religious music (organs and gospel singing), country and oriental music (folk-rock and raga-rock, country, western, and the blues). The Beatles and virtually every rock group that followed played updated classical music, sang gospel, hymn, and folk tunes to a flailing tribal beat. They orchestrated this vibrating, pulsating music for organ, violins, and classical sitar as well as for electric guitar. Formal musicians attempted a similar synthesis. Among others, Gian Carlo Menotti in his opera *The Last Savage* (1963), Leonard Bernstein in his *Mass* (1970–1971), and composer-lyricist-musical-director-priest Al Carmines in his musicals as well as in his multiple professional involvements, all exemplified this crossing of traditional barriers.

John Cage reached out to incorporate silence as a part of music. He had his performers sit silent in front of their instruments for ten minutes while the audience listened to its own coughs, shuffles, rustles, whispers, giggles, and to outside noises. For Cage, such sounds are as much part of music as is silence, which is what occurs between musical notes. In the theatre this musical device became integral to Harold Pinter's plays, in which the Pinterpause is nearly as significant as the Pinter text. Elsewhere in the theatre, the attempt to transcend the traditions of the performance event produced the New, Environmental, or Experiential theatre, in which distinctions between acting area and audience area, between the audience and the performer, between the performers' roles and the performers' personal lives, and between the play and the discussion of the play were continually erased.

Art historians and sociologists have studied these forays across traditional boundaries in painting and sculpture, music and theatre, but they have largely excluded architecture and design from their overviews. I hope to show in this book how architecture, too, in our day, has made a move toward crossing barriers and toward making interdisciplinary mergers, toward bursting out beyond the boundaries of academic design, toward a homogeneous vernacular. There has been a democratization of architecture, as of the other arts and of society, a homogenizing that is colloquially described as "getting it all together." The new design has gone beyond established design, merging it with life, in two significant and influential ways: beyond the traditional technology and process of architecture, and, secondly, beyond the traditional aesthetic of architects' inspiration, content, and products.

GETTING IT ALL TOGETHER AESTHETICALLY

A generation supercharged with a new sense of involvement, participation, and activism was bound to develop a new aesthetic. Its predecessors' preoccupation with reaching tidy, conceptual, pictorial goals seemed sterile, limited. Marshall McLuhan was with it when he spoke of "total and simultaneous use of all the senses." To the new designers, that meant accepting multisensory experience as part of the reality of design, just as much as it is part of life. It meant including the unpredictable and the nonquantifiable tensions, feelings, emotions, and perceptions that make up our experience of living. "I am for an art that takes its form from the lines of life itself," Claes Oldenburg wrote in his journal, "that twists and extends and accumulates and spits and drips, and is heavy and coarse and blunt and sweet and stupid as life itself." The new designers responded with a resounding "Right On!," and opened their arms to embrace speed and motion as well as monumental stillness, disorder and confusion as well as clarity and regularity, whimsy and humor, puns and witticisms, not merely the high seriousness of a monumental order. Their design approach recognizes and admits boredom as well as the interesting; nudity, profanity, and scandalizing as well as the polite and decorous. Among its new elements are anonymity, availability and accessibility, emotional expressivity and subjectivity, and qualities such as irony, mystery, ambiguity, awkwardness, contrasting juxtapositions and conflict, perversity and paradox. It is a superscale expansion of our design vocabulary, design attitudes, and design goals.

The new design claims to be the first stylistic movement to recognize this multiplicity of our visual environment, and to accept it all as much as possible. It dares to open the architecture school doors and consort with practitioners of the building crafts. It sees that there is a world of valid design beyond academic theory entirely, beyond all prescriptions except the intuitive animal-emotional responses of the people, of the users, of the clients and inhabitants of architecture and designed environments.

The now generation feels there was too much purification of our environment in previous decades, preventing sensory involvement, extending no invitation to human activity, to the joys of hustle and bustle and interaction. It aims at putting vitality back into planning and design—not rejecting purification entirely, just adding liveliness to cleanliness. It considers feeling levels to be basic design determinants—the feelings of warm and cool, of dry and damp, of glare and gloom, of quiet and blare. It therefore discards the view *of* the designed object as the predominant criterion and adopts the view *from* and the feelings produced by use and occupation.

The new design realists reject the status quo of established rules, and the imposition onto humanity of somebody else's ideal world. They renounce authoritarian respect for the wise old parent-teacher; they refuse to submit to the imposition by master "form-givers" of an idealized view of architectural perfection. They strive for a new humanism grounded on respect for the individual and for the obvious realities of daily life. These realities include the existence of accidents in design and execution, things not fitting exactly, and what happens in between. This is a behavioristic empirical approach that Yale architecture historian Vincent Scully calls "the current architecture of realism."

If the previous design idiom held a fixed vision of pure, clean boxes, the new design attempts to look at the facts for what they are first; it rejects "pure form" and looks at the site for what it is, accepts what it sees—including mess or chaos—and works with those realities, reinforcing them, doing it harder. It accepts the sloping site and works with it, without imposing a leveling podium. Hugh Hardy's game in designing a playroom ceiling "was a question of accepting the restriction that a multigabled roof already went down around your ears and straight up over your head," he explained. "We said that if the ceiling is something that goes up and down, we'll make it go up and down as much as we conceivably can." That was the new realistic vision of accepting actualities—actualities of the site, existing structure, clients, desires, and preconceptions—and attempting to use these real conditions as determinants of design, rather than sweeping them away and creating something else (see p. 107).

"You start with what people do," said John Johansen in 1971, "not with what you think they ought to do." The new architects and designers strive to start out with no preconception. They open their eyes wide to what we have and to what we need—functionally—to our activities, to our life-styles, and then they work to provide new solutions and new forms. They take into account their own and their clients' do-it-yourself functions. They tell it like it is. They aim for a straightforward all-embracing view of human behavior, and then for direct expression of that behavior in design. Their aim is to produce something richer, more vital, ever changing, continually rewarding.

By accepting a wider range of our visual experience as candidates for our design vocabulary, the new designers include elements of our environment that we have previously considered as undesigned and as unworthy of designers' attention. Some find sources of inspiration in rural structures-simple, anonymous, traditional farm outbuildings. Some accept elements from the everyday world—kitsch, the folksy and anonymous, and the banal. Some accept and admire the influence of our commercial art environment on our academically designed environment. They look to the automobile, the commercial strip—"roadside America," as Robert Venturi calls it—with special praise for the spectacular effervescence of nighttime illuminations on such commercial strips as Times Square and Las Vegas.

Art critic Harold Rosenberg has written in *The De-Definition of Art:* "The new post-modern outlook aims at an aesthetic liberated from all traditions including the tradition of the new." Consequently, inclusive design accepts historical traditions once again. It accepts historical allusions. It acclaims the preservation and the recycling of buildings for new uses, with some startling effects—such as the basketball court for Long Island University that is located on the stage and lower orchestra of an old, gilded baroque movie palace. To sit in the balcony among the gilded putti and watch the gymnastic action on the polished wood court is to experience an architectural recycling that has few if any precedents before the past decade.

The new design also accepts decoration, applied pattern, and ornament. Decoration had become such a dirty word to the design professions during the 1940s and the 1950s that even professional interior decorators changed the name of their institute. At the same time the new breed of designers was experimenting wildly with decoration at a new scale, in new colors, in new locations, and for new architectural purposes. This breed accepted, first of all, the historical endorsement of decoration as at least integral to architecture and design. They were

Lionel K. Levy: Gymnasium built into the Brooklyn Paramount Theatre (1928) for Long Island University, Brooklyn, New York. 1962. *Photograph by Legg Bros., Ltd.*

giving expression to what Edgar Kaufmann, Jr., wrote, in apparent heresy, early in 1962: "Decoration is almost surely the older art" when compared with architecture, "if the cave men painted for reasons of magic and not for mere self-expression." At the same time critic Kaufmann wrote, with startling prescience, that architects "may find that those who design for interior use will increasingly be designing for outside construction. That is to say, designers may be influencing architects rather than the other way around."

By the mid-1960s this prediction was realized when such non-architect professionals as industrial designers came to influence architecture, and conversely, when interior schemes designed by architects began to abound with a new kind of decoration and when urban mural programs increased across the country. It was the bold, new, polyexpanded megadecoration. That new decoration manifests attitudes of perverse trickery (both optical and intellectual), devices of explosive scale (transparency, reflectiveness, and simultaneity), and the permissive acceptance of chaos in existing "tasteful" spaces. Ambiguity of surface, trompe-l'oeil, fake symmetry, and reverse perspective are other decorative devices that are newly included.

The new design also accepts superimposition—things laid one on top of the other, things spilling over from one area to the next, the layering of plane on plane, and the interplaying of pattern and reflection. It cherishes fusion and the ambiguity that this creates when the various levels of perception weave in and out, overlap and return.

Finally, the inclusive new design often aims at "getting it all together" simultaneously to incorporate all the new dimensions along with the old traditions into a single, rich, lumpy, carbuncular compound of surprises and delights. Marshall McLuhan called this simultaneity of our life-style and of our vision *allatonceness:* "Ours is a brand-new world of allatonceness. 'Time' has ceased, 'space' has vanished. We now live in a global village . . . a simultaneous happening." Hugh Hardy makes the point, with regard to theatre architecture, that, "as in life today wherever you are—things are not happening in any single direction but simultaneously in many directions—in all directions at all times."

Houston's Southcoast Group said of a trip to New Haven that they had "a nude thanksgiving brown rice ritual in Harkness Chapel with candles, incense, etc. and happiness is a warm gun-bang-bang in gregorian chant followed by a costume feast in the common room upstairs followed by a stone at Dwight Street."

The predecessor of this concept of simultaneity is in Cubism with its

multiple simultaneous time-space overlays. In the 1960s and earlier
other artists, such as M. C. Escher, used different perspectives simultaneously. Al Held constructed perspective with simultaneous and contradictory systems.

In Charles Moore's New Haven house (1966), objects considered
incongruous a decade earlier jostled each other: stained-glass panels,
Turkish carpets, Mexican pottery, and nineteenth-century family portraits mingled with industrial lighting equipment, exposed plumbing, a
Wurlitzer jukebox, neon sculpture, negative-positive design motifs,
mirror tricks, silver mylar, and a host of pop-mod-freak objects (see
p. 239).

More than any other building of the 1960s the one that got it all
together is the Faculty Club at the University of California at Santa
Barbara, where Moore and his associates pushed simultaneity of dis-
parate elements to the most attenuated limit of discordant togetherness.
There, crude pop objects are combined with the most bizarre and
incompatible objects from other more refined but unacceptable periods.
There, amid the most pristine modern lighting fixtures and neon banners

MLTW/Moore-Turnbull: Faculty Club, University of
California, Santa Barbara. 1968. *Photograph by Morley Baer.*

hangs a nineteenth-century Louis Philippe crystal chandelier; on one wall are pictures of the Beatles in ice-cream-cup-cover portraits and on the opposite wall are stuffed rams' heads from an old hunting lodge; Knoll dining room furniture nestles under a Moorish (appropriately) Alhambra-like carved-wood ceiling; Jacobean furniture and a quasi-Gothic, German renaissance fireplace are juxtaposed to a layered construction of two apparently different structural systems. The whole is a section through modern history, a simultaneous "allatonceness" that sounds arbitrary, but somehow works, with a kind of vitality that is completely new.

The new design movement is therefore called the design of "inclusion" and of "accommodation," since it accommodates a more inclusive design vocabulary and a more inclusive outlook—and attempts to make meaningful fantasy of them all. If it is the essence of art to go beyond traditional vision, beyond boundaries, to break down classifications in order to expand our perceptions of reality, the new design is art by virtue of this overall attitude of greater inclusiveness.

This cumulative theory of the new design is made up, naturally, of the individual theories, penchants and prejudices, approaches and whims of half a dozen leading, innovative practitioners and theorists. Robert Venturi, the most original, provocative, and widely published architectural theorist of our day and his wife, Denise Scott-Brown Venturi, see the new design as the architecture of "accommodation," which accommodates within our design interest an inclusive "both/and" attitude, including not only the standard vision of modern architecture but also the anonymous "undesigned" world of "popular" life (the roadway, plastics, the chaos of conglomeration), together with the disparity between the inside and the outside. He also feels that architecture must accommodate all the "complexities" and juxtaposed contradictions of our visual world, as he proposed in his book *Complexity and Contradiction in Architecture* (1966), in numerous articles, and in *Learning from Las Vegas* (1972). Even within this newly included area of Las Vegas, Venturi sees an inclusive new order:

> two types of order on the Strip: the obvious visual order of street elements and the difficult visual order of buildings and signs. The zone *of* the highway is a shared order. The zone *off* the highway is an individual order. In combination they embrace continuity *and* discontinuity, going *and* stopping, clarity *and* ambiguity, cooperation *and* competition, the community *and* rugged individualism.

Other critics and historians also, such as Yale's Vincent Scully and many of his former students, use the term *accommodation* for the movement. "To me," Scully said, "accommodation is based on a rigorous pluralism and a willingness to face the complexity that surrounds us."

Charles Moore, the most witty, human, and accessible aesthetician-architect of our time, calls the new design the architecture of "inclusion," distinguishing it from the older architecture of "exclusion," which "attempted to find order by excluding disorder and confusion" and which organized all into a simplistic system of "less is more." To him the architecture "extends our sensibilities and dares to strive for a more complex unity of diverse elements. This is an acceptance of the diversity of human experience," Moore says. "It is an inclusive, T. S. Eliot-like view of life." Robert A. M. Stern in his book *New Directions in American Architecture* (1969) contrasts predominantly "inclusive" architects with "exclusive" architects.

None of these theorists sees the architecture of inclusion or accommodation as barring the architecture of exclusion, although the formalizing and packaging of architectural programs into static, fixed, geometric forms, which was the basic approach of architects from the Bauhaus through the International Style, is the element most nearly excluded from the architecture of inclusion. The point is that the new approach is viewed not as a substitute for the old, but as *an addition to,* and expansion beyond, the old. As Hugh Hardy said, what this new movement attempts to do is to permit architects "to accept *all* the world."

Hardy is one of the new design's most articulate and challenging spokesmen, not only because of his clear explanations but also because of his staccato hip new speech, which sounds like the New Journalism drawn right from the conversation of his contemporaries. He forcefully proclaims new, young, vital, forceful, bust-out, revolution. As he said:

> The world is so full of shapes and none of them appear in architecture. Architects are still bound up in Euclid: When we plan cities, houses, we make choices between long malls, thin towers, and squares. If you look at the shiny polished surfaces on all those monumental Park Avenue buildings, you realize what a tiny book has been opened to design them. That's only a portion of the world. Architecture can benefit by accepting all of the environment—instead of just that academic stuff. Our architectural vocabulary is destitute. Have you ever seen the way an architect draws a car? It's a box. Car

is chrome, moving, flashing. If you're still in the arms of Euclid, you can't accept 60 foot stretch pants on the side of a bus. . . . It could be misinterpreted that billboards themselves were the thing—as Reston misinterprets that fuzzy textural plazas and funny niddily-diddilies are the thing and Lincoln Center presumes that travertine is the thing. It would certainly be sad if anybody really thought that the only solution to interior or exterior design. It would certainly be sad if anybody really thought that the solution to New York City subways was only to put stripes in them, or that the solution to interior or exterior design was only supergraphics, mirrors, and mylar. That's only a way of doing something. All these fix-me-cure-me's are too short a view. The new design comes from a recognition of the entire urban environment. It's exactly what you see outdoors. The kids are involved with the new stuff because it's just like the old T-bird blasting around the turnpike. And that also is only a portion of the world. We still have spheres and travertine and fuzzy plazas. The next phase is to get both together—Lincoln Center in stripes, not just stripes.

. . . What is going on is whether you should try and make the environment whole. Should a responsible architect admit to his vocabulary Williamsburg and the jet plane and what's out on Third Avenue, or should he limit himself to saying the world really ought to be my way.

So he expressed the viewpoint of the inclusive aesthetic.

Richard Oliver, who studied with Kahn at Penn and with Moore at Berkeley, said, "In this age of pluralism, the point seems to be to expand our vocabulary rather than restrict it, to make our architecture more diverse rather than less so. Supermannerism encourages us to seek complex order, ambiguous order, and allows us to include things rather than exclude things. I want the choice of Supermannerism or anything else that seems suitable to the problem at hand." Vincent Scully said, "It includes all and rejects gentility." Others rejected nothing. Mass housing is an absolute necessity but there should be no restrictions on houses as jewelry-sculpture for the rich who will always be able to afford them. Nothing is to be stopped—except restriction itself—the principal force is to release restrictions and add all new dimensions.

The new designers, therefore, accept incongruous juxtapositions, which they call the "duality" of life. Accepting duality means that we can include in our vocabulary both sides of a design coin, both polarities of a visual situation. Michael Graves elaborated this theory at the end of the decade and posited pairs of opposites as "duality" and their juxtaposition as "plurality." Throughout the decade the more common term was *simultaneity*.

So the new designers urge a free, open-minded acceptance of this additive, broader, wider, more spacious, visual, textural, functional, and emotional world. They include more effects of humanity by which they can arrest our accustomed and habitually unseeing eyes. The new design then is inclusive since it accepts the box as well as the stripe, the undesigned as well as the designed, the elegant as well as the vulgar, the loose as well as the uptight, the kinky as well as the straight, the old as well as the new, perhaps the bad as well as the good—even if this makes criticism ambiguous. "The idea is that you can have everything," Doug Michels summarized. This is the philosophy of the young in the 1960s, those who feel that they can have, get, and do anything, or everything, and that the entire world is open to them.

Genealogy of the New Design

Every generation rebelliously rejects the aims of its parents and joyously endorses those of its grandparents. That is the cyclic axiom. For all that revolutionaries have always emphasized the newness of their ideas and accomplishments, history as well as etymology insist that revolution also means return. From decade to decade, throughout the ages, the design cycles spin from classic to romantic, from rigid to liberated, from spare to exuberant. Today, to confuse the issue, the cycles are accelerating and the time between them decreasing almost to the vanishing point. It is a change in time scale that is critical for our age. Sociologist Daniel Bell writes of the post-industrial society:

> It was once exceedingly rare to be able to observe the formation of institutions *de novo*. Social change was crescive and moved slowly. Adaptations were piecemeal and contradictory, the process of diffusion halting . . . Today, not only are we aware of, and trying to identify, processes of change, even when they cannot be "dated" but there has been a speeding up of the "time-machine," so that the interval between the initial impetus to change and its realization has been radically reduced.

In architecture the time lag between Mies van der Rohe's initial probes in 1919 toward a skyscraper entirely sheathed in glass and the realization of that idea in Skidmore, Owings & Merrill's Lever House of 1953 shows how slowly techincal achievement used to follow theoretical innovation. But the time lag between acceptance of this glass curtain wall inspiration in 1953 and rejection of it as "monotonous" in 1962 shows how the time machine has speeded up. Says Bell, "The average time span between the initial discovery of a new technological innovation and the recognition of its commercial potential decreased from 30 years (for technological innovations introduced during the early part of this century, 1880–1919) to 16 years (for innovations introduced during the post World War I period) to 9 years (for the post World War II period)."

"Communication in our time is instant," architect Howard Barnstone and others observed in the mid-1960s—what happens in New York or London, Chicago or Sydney is known everywhere within two hours. Sociologist Toffler describes "the astonishing expansion of the scale and the scope of change" in our day. It has created "time skips" that are bringing millions to the verge of "future shock." He writes,

> In the past one rarely saw a fundamental change in an art style within a man's lifetime. A style or school endured, as a rule, for generations at a time. Today the pace of turnover in art is vision-blurring—the viewer scarcely has time to "see" a school develop, to learn its language, so to speak, before it vanishes. . . . The most enduring twentieth-century school, Abstract Expressionism, held sway for at most twenty years, from 1940 to 1960, then to be followed by a wild succession—"Pop" lasting perhaps five years, "Op" managing to grip the public's attention for two or three years, then the emergence, appropriately enough, of "Kinetic Art" whose very *raison d'être* is transience.

Most architects, accustomed to greater longevity and conditioned to the notion of permanence, viewed such changes as faddism.

The world of instant communications makes instant era of both design and fashion. The old and the "now" come together, and the solid-thinking designer is sometimes blamed for being a flimsy fashionist. The boundary between reality and fashion has never been as irregular or as treacherous as it is today, but the important distinction to be insisted upon is that design and fashion have *not* become one and the same.

Peter Hoppner admits that architects are more interested in fashion now than they were ten years ago. "But then," he continues, "they are more interested in the world, in art, in slums, in everything than they were ten years ago." Frederick (Derek) Romley observed, "We have a freedom now and look into anything that we think will work. So we sometimes find that we are using the same things that the fashion people are using. What we do lasts longer." "It will be increasingly difficult to make a distinction between "design and fad in the future," Hugh Hardy believes.

> It is extremely academic to say what is popular is not important. I thought we had been through all that. Why can't something that is important for the present not be important for all time? I suspect that "for all time" will be an increasingly meaningless thing. Today we are interested in the simultaneity of the two. And we recognize that the hierarchical establisher who says today that the popular is superficial is speaking from just as superficial a pose.

Despite the truisms of revolutionary cycles—"there is nothing new" and *"plus ça change"*—there *is* something new in our age: it is this headlong drive to do it faster, as well as bigger, thereby decreasing time lags to the degree that we have virtually doubled back on ourselves. "We will soon be nostalgic about the future," said Joseph Sweeney. (It is not coincidental that recycling is a major activity in our day.) In the 1960s, the forward thrust of the Minimal style met its own backlash head on, almost being swamped by its own wake.

Minimalism

Of all the directions in twentieth-century architecture—and they included several—the one the new generation of architects rejected most completely was the International Style. By the late 1950s the purgative International Style crusade had reached its peak of refinement. It became Minimal architecture—the mainstream of American architecture from the mid-1950s on—which continues to play out its course. As handed down from the Bauhaus by Walter Gropius at Harvard and by Mies van der Rohe at the Illinois Institute of Technology in Chicago, it dominated the generation of architects born around 1920 and educated in the 1940s. The generation brought up at Harvard under Gropius included Philip Johnson, Paul Rudolph, Edward Barnes, John Johansen, Ulrich Franzen, I. M. Pei, and (earlier) Gordon Bunshaft. They were "the Last of the Machine Age" generation, to use Reyner Banham's phrase. To many of that generation the ultimate distillation of Bauhaus principles was the work of Mies, their peerless model.

Mies was the purest architectural Minimalist. His towering faith in an architecture founded on logic and reason never swerved throughout his long lifetime. He died in 1969 at the age of eighty-three. Since he lived and taught in Chicago for more than thirty years (from 1938 to

1969), his exposure as an educator and his architectural productivity as an example were a monumental influence on American architecture —ultimately even stronger and more visible than Gropius's at Harvard. Mies's architecture was characterized by poetic clarity, homogeneity, and restrained yet unparalleled elegance. It was exquisite by instinct as well as through meticulous endeavor. His poetic architectural syntax was expressed in the dictum: "God is in the details." His overall diction was classical, monumental, fixed, and balanced, if not symmetrical. Yet his use of space was undeniably romantic—open and sculptural in its fluidity. And he displayed a sensual appreciation of visually enjoyable textures and of richness in the pure planes of polished natural materials—travertine, onyx, bronze, steel, and glass.

Mies's faith that form must follow structural function led him to make structural bones visible through transparent skins of pristine glass. His "Less is more" became the first commandment of design in the 1950s. Visual elimination, intended to flush away organic wastes, too soon began to drown out humanity by its abstraction. Whereas Mies aimed to make a democratic architecture for a technological society—a machine age median for everyman in those industrially fabricated loft spaces—his imitators left that architecture functionless and spiritless for no man. If with Mies "Less is more," with the late Minimalists "Nothing is all." Minimal architecture in the early 1960s aimed for a sparse, flat, understated look, stripped, clean, pure; it eliminated even the structural articulation that Bauhaus designers had devised as a decorative motif. Bauhaus designers ostensibly eliminated ornamentation. Actually, they only simplified it. They restricted ornamentation to structural articulation. Theirs was jointy decorating. The new generation saw this and was not silenced by reverence. As David Sellers accused, "Even Mies had excess extrusions." The Minimal style eliminated ornamentation even of this kind; it stripped nonessentials and minimized or miniaturized everything that might possibly be considered extraneous: joints, reveals, moldings, and the like. This neat technique looked effortless, but it was a kind of acrobatic prestidigitation that aimed to go unnoticed; it concealed extremely complicated internal systems of structural, mechanical, electrical, and joining elements.

This Minimal movement was a final working out of its ancestral aesthetics—going beyond Mies in denial and exclusion. It was, in effect, a repudiation of the basic tenet of functionalism that form follows structural function. By concealing the elements of all subsystems—

structural, mechanical, and electrical—the ideal of industrialized, systematized architecture was subverted. Employing regularity of parts, precise proportions, and general symmetry produced coldness, abstractness, and virtual anonymity.

Because of its surface simplicity, Minimal architecture goes almost unnoticed as a distinct substyle, yet the comparison with Minimal art is nearly exact, and revealing. Minimal painting and sculpture showed how far the fine arts, unfettered by the requirements of applied function as architecture is, could lead the Minimal movement. During the 1960s, painters and sculptors continued to exclude subject matter and soared away into purer and purer realms of logical fantasy, intellectual elaborations of ever more refined and precise Euclidean geometry. It was an art based almost exclusively on logic and reason, mathematics and geometry. It used numbers to organize; it excluded motion and symbolism, turning instead to arithmetical series, algebraic compounds, and modular arrangements in almost mystical proportions. The appeal was to the mind, to engage the intellect alone.

Barnett Newman's paintings, precursive of the Minimalists, showed a way to make the most of the fewest elements—massive scale and expansive color—with which he surprisingly proclaimed an ever warmer and more radiant romanticism and a stretching, continually expanding scale. Josef Albers concentrated on squares. This reductive abstractness led to similar experiments in sculpture. Donald Judd and Sol LeWitt were prominent among the later sculptors whose geometric smoothness and rhythmic repetition of square and rectangular forms in shiny metal and plastic proclaimed the ultimate supremacy of technology and intellectual discipline. Often only a knowledge of the rational system within which these sculptors operated could connect the viewer to the sculptors' work. There was no other communication, no general human understanding shared by all mankind that could make these works meaningful—only the logical premises on which they were based. In the work of Don Judd, for example, there was, as *Time* art critic Robert Hughes observed, no movement, no gesture, no direction, no metaphor, no image, and especially no relation to the human figure. There was no interaction between the forms themselves, only a transaction between the critical comment on the system that the sculptor and the observer shared—or didn't share. If that language was unknown to the viewer, the works were pure, refined, austere, ascetic, remote, and inaccessible.

Other Minimalist pieces turned out in the 1960s by artists like Robert Irwin, Larry Bell, Peter Alexander, and Robert Morris portend a kind of plastic-glossy, mystical purity.

Art critic Barbara Rose admitted of Minimal art that "its reductiveness allowed for a relatively limited art experience." Others admitted that simplification reduced the sensory input, and that overcomplication may be chaos, but oversimplification is monotony. It was "sterility through simplicity," as another critic wrote.

For the Constructivists Naum [Pevsner] Gabo, Antoine Pevsner, Kasimir Malevich, and Vladimir Tatlin to merge their abstractions of the machine age with architecture was prohibitive, but for architecture, further abstraction was a route to professional suicide.

The latest buildings in this direction show simple geometric forms of greatly increased scale, with immediate clarity and diminished interest due to flatter profiles, thinner skins, and larger areas with smoother surfaces. They have jewellike wall membranes—mirror-wrapped or black-sheathed towers, pylons, or boxes that look like monolithic packaging. In contrast to my term, *Supermannerism,* Ada Louise Huxtable, late in 1968, called this *superclassicism.* Some of these structures look so elemental that they seem like early design schemes or *projets* that were constructed as originally conceived. Most prominent among the exponents of the Minimal substyle were: Eero Saarinen in his black-velvet CBS Building (1965); Gordon Bunshaft of Skidmore, Owings & Merrill; Kevin Roche of Roche, Dinkeloo Associates; and I. M. Pei. It was an unlikely and inharmonious group that sometimes shared only the aim of large scale and smooth concealment.

A few notable interiors epitomized the Minimal movement perhaps more clearly than architectural exteriors. The work of the Knoll Planning Unit under the direction of Florence Knoll Bassett and the New York office of Skidmore, Owings & Merrill, sometimes jointly, often separately, was the pinnacle of Minimalist achievement in interior design: from the Connecticut General Building (1957), which they designed together, to the Union Carbide (1961) and Olivetti (formerly Pepsi-Cola, 1959) buildings, which were SOM's alone, and on through the CBS Building, designed not with SOM but by a team led by the Knoll Planning Unit. Benjamin Baldwin's designs with their rarefied simplicity, yet uncommon humanism; Ward Bennett's elegant sculptural interiors and furniture; offices and other interiors by Nicos Zographos, all were designed by a generation trained in purgative puritan exclusion

Skidmore, Owings & Merrill/New York: Marine Midland Bank, New York City. 1967. *Photograph by Cervin Robinson.*

and alignment—the straight and narrow way. They seemed to equate aesthetic with ascetic.

In these interiors, the Minimal style produced simple, white plaster boxes with broad expanses of plain surfaces, including bare, glossy floors. Door and window openings were flush, frameless, and trimless— sliced severely into the planes. Window coverings were spare and ascetic. Only natural-grown textures in deep wools and burl woods enriched the pure, "clean" envelopes with their crisp machine-age furnishings, which were placed in space like objects exhibited in a museum. The aim was to focus on what is most variable in our environments: that is, on portable, changeable objects such as paintings, artworks, plants, and (ostensibly) people. These Minimalist spaces depend on meticulous detailing to conceal functioning supportive systems. But this pure perfection in the alignment of grids and objects, this pictorial emphasis, produced some environments so fixed and static that they allowed no interaction with the user. They became boring. The snide comments on the dictum "Less is more" went from "Mies is more" to

Ward Bennett: Glickman offices,
New York City. 1962. *Photograph by Louis Reens.*

"More is less" to "Less is less" to "Nothing is all" to "Mess is more" to "Less is a bore."

That opulence could be created from "simplicity" and that simplicity could be achieved by complex detailing are paradoxes of the Miesian and Minimal idioms. As the boldest illustration of this effort, the invisible use of marble as the baseboard in SOM's Banque Lambert penthouse in Brussels (1965) is the most elaborately minimal detail. White plaster walls appear to come down to the travertine floor line. But since a plaster base would be impractical for cleaning, the baseboard is actually white marble—white marble painted white to match the plaster wall. If the white paint chips, the white marble underneath will still appear continuous with the plaster walls. One further point about the baseboard demonstrates the difference between Miesian and Minimalist detailing: no scored line is used between plaster and marble to denote a change of materials; no spacer or recess connects baseboard to floor. "Maybe in the past we used to have too many notches all over the place," Gordon Bunshaft mused. "But there is no need to give a name to this. It is just a plain wall." Yet Bunshaft's concern for the totality of projects, his control of meticulous detailing and quality of craftmanship, and his own designs for furniture are sure enough indications of his esteem for interior design detailing. But, this revealless refinement on Miesian design is something of a late repudiation of Mies's godly details.

One underpublicized leader of American interior designers, Benjamin Baldwin, is an architect who, after an early partnership with his brother-in-law Harry Weese, now specializes in interior design. Working virtually on his own, the soft-spoken designer is almost Oriental in his purity and connoisseur's discrimination. His combination of the Minimal approach with a sophisticated casualness that is ravishing. In a minimal apartment he designed for his own use in 1964, the interplay of rectangular voids with paintings on the walls was the strong yet subtle design force. Broad, ceiling-height doors pivoted back against storage cores like unnoticed walls; planes met without reveals; nearly invisible, narrow-slatted, undraped Venetian blinds served as the only window coverings; the sofa was a frameless, built-in nook, carpeted and filled with loose pillows. The alignment of the linear elements was meticulous and furniture was kept to a minimum. "My work in interior design expresses my opposition to the chaotic world man creates," he wrote. "It is a constant search for the calm tranquility one finds in nature. In

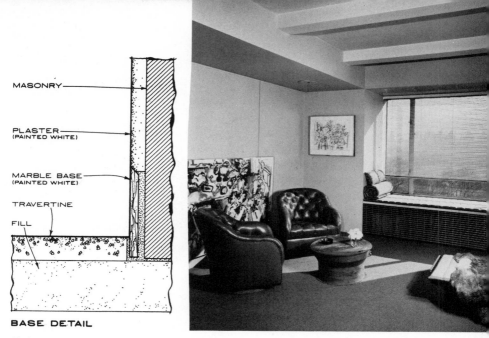

MASONRY

PLASTER
(PAINTED WHITE)

MARBLE BASE
(PAINTED WHITE)

TRAVERTINE

FILL

BASE DETAIL

(*left*) Skidmore, Owings & Merrill/New York: Baseboard detail, Banque Lambert penthouse, Brussels, Belgium. 1965. (*right*) Benjamin Baldwin: Baldwin apartment, New York City. 1964. *Photograph by Louis Reens.*

nature I find a sense of order—logical and lyrical—which I would like my work to express."

In the office designed for the New York advertising agency, Papert, Koenig, Lois, in 1967, Nicos Zographos retained some functionalist structural articulation, but he distilled and refined it to an almost surreal essence. Even the most luxurious executive spaces had no overlay of so-called elegance, no carpets, no draperies. Zographos commented that "this design is romantic in its way: It is a throwback to the early days of the Bauhaus, but brought up to date."

The aseptic puritanism of the post–Beaux Arts period produced the Minimalist idiom, whose most important word was *simplicity*. Designers were trained to see "the offensive clutter and honky-tonk" of our cities, the random growth of our animal habitations and urban environments, and to reject or strive to abolish all that busy, unclean, crotchety visual squalor (and much of it was just that). What they aimed to do was to provide purer, clearer, cleaner visual scenes for our Athenian delecta-

Nicos Zographos: Papert, Koenig, Lois, Inc.,
offices, New York City. 1966. *Photograph by Carl Fischer.*

tion. What they designed were simple geometric forms, "similar glass cages for dissimilar uses," isolated each from each, surrounded by as much space as possible, increasingly flatter, cleaner, textureless of facade, accented only by some token artwork, fountain, or smaller pavilionlike building set off from the main tower. This was the Minimalist refinement of Bauhaus goals in the 1960s—a democratic style that would produce handsome environments evenly in all building types, that would be depersonalized and therefore supposedly usable by all types of people.

The First Uprisings
Fast on the tide of action came the wave of reaction. No sooner was the Minimalist crusade successful, than design revolutionaries began to overthrow established Miesian and Minimal principles. It was at first a gentle, sometimes witty revolution—more in the realm of whimsical disobedience than of combat.

When the 1960s began, the pure, refined, sublimely proportioned towers of Mies van der Rohe had been realized in his elegant yet industrialized-looking apartment buildings in Chicago, and in his ultra-luxurious bronze Seagram Building in New York, designed with Philip Johnson, his then devoted disciple. Gordon Bunshaft of Skidmore, Owings & Merrill's New York office had also produced sterling refinements on Mies's industrial idiom in the Connecticut General Life Insurance Building, Hartford, Connecticut, Lever House, the Union Carbide

Building, and the Olivetti Building (formerly Pepsi-Cola) in New York. But even as these models of the Minimal were climbing to an airy peak of classical aesthetic refinement, a new flamboyance in structural design was assaulting the very validity of ever achieving that peak. An inquisitive romanticism and daredeviltry produced a stream of parabolic, hyperbolic paraboloids and other convoluted structural forms that critic Thomas Creighton called "the New Sensualism." It reflected the advances of the Second Generation of Modern Architects—those whom Frank Lloyd Wright, Mies, Le Corbusier, and Walter Gropius had directly influenced or taught—who strove for more warmth, new forms, and new "delight," as Minoru Yamasaki called it. These architects built craggy and fluttery roofs, fanciful shapes; they performed structural acrobatics or added cake-icing decoration—Greek, Gothic, Indian, Islamic, and countless other awkward borrowings from older or foreign architectural idioms. Yamasaki affected Gothic forms for small pavilions, where they were somewhat appropriate and justifiable, but he also used them for the twin towers of what had been planned as "the world's tallest building" ("for the world's shortest time!," said *The New York Times*)— The World Trade Center in New York. Edward Durrell Stone translated Indian grillwork into concrete block for a generally admired embassy in New Delhi, but then into ubiquitous houses, and a Belgian World's Fair pavilion. It was, as critic James T. Burns, Jr., said, "an eminently salable brand of bland gorgeousness."

Late in the 1950s and early in the 1960s, an interest in "fantastic architecture" also helped pave the way for design permissiveness. Any number of European and American architecture, magazines, as well as several books, were devoted to nonrectilinear, free-form sculptural or jagged and jarring building designs, which were considered "fantastic" from the vangage point of the then accepted rigid rectangle. What fascinated in this category ranged from the most intellectualized and intentionally bizarre images to the simplest nonrectilinear architecture in primitive villages. Among the rediscoveries of this period were the dreamworld, melting, sculptural architecture of Antonio Gaudí and the latter-day expressionism of Frederick Kiesler's egg-shaped "endless house" as well as the free-for-all architecture of Bruce Goff and Herb Greene. Simon Rodia's personal assemblage of his Watts Towers in Los Angeles also attracted architects, as did the seemingly zany buildings of Amancio Guedes in Mozambique, and the nonrectilinear work of Hans Scharoun in Germany.

In a similar vein, futuristic, slick constructions such as hotel-top revolving restaurants, flying-saucer-like houses by John Lautner, and other science-fiction imagery clearly out of the mainstream of accepted architectural theory were beginning to interest more and more respected architects. At the same time Bauhaus principles became enriched by the sensuous colors of Abstract Expressionism—the colors of Mark Rothko, Hans Hofmann, and Barnett Newman. And in fabric design the vibrant work of Dorothy Liebes, Alexander Girard, and Jack Lenor Larsen made palatable to more people the spare designs derived from Miesian principles.

In 1958, therefore, when the Museum of Contemporary Crafts mounted an exhibition of Louis Comfort Tiffany's technological delicacies of Art Nouveau glass and metalwork, the design world was prepared to accept whiplash curves and sensuous colors as a new direction, leading to what would soon become a new visual order.

Within the mainstream of American architectural theory, the first permissive breaks were made by Eero Saarinen, Philip Johnson, and other former disciples of Mies. First came some elaborately convoluted sculpturing that expressed a dissatisfaction with the established rules and proclaimed an independence from the Miesian rectangle as well as from the taboo against ornamentation. Eero Saarinen astonished his contemporaries with the world's biggest, molded free-form sculpture—the TWA Terminal at J. F. Kennedy Airport (then Idlewild) in New York. But the strongest rebellion came from Philip Johnson, who had been Mies's most voluble and energetic disciple. In contrast to his own Miesian Glass House in New Canaan, Connecticut (1949), Johnson unfurled a quasi-Chinese parasol of shingles over a shrine with an open garden considered as part of the building called The Roofless Church in New Harmony, Indiana (1960). The world of architecture was beginning to be turned upside down.

Among the rebellious design jokesters, Johnson had the wryest laugh of all. As architect of The Museum of Modern Art's expansion program in the early 1960s, he designed another handsome classic room in the Miesian idiom, but he sent it sky-high; some critics considered it a sick architectural sacrilege, and others recognized it as an irresistibly funny parody. At first glance, the Founders Room atop Johnson's annex to the museum appears to be merely a domed version of the Miesian idiom that Johnson mastered so well. An exposed I-beam structure of modular bays apparently supports plaster Gothic vaults lighted with strips of

Philip Johnson: Founders Room, The Museum of Modern Art, New York City. 1967. *Photograph by Louis Reens.*

exposed, unfrosted incandescent bulbs. The immediate effect is Mies-cum-Gothic-cum-carnival-midway of the Gay Nineties. But as the eye follows the steelwork from the ceiling downward, one sees that the structure simply stops—a foot and a half above the floor. It is, quite literally, a Miesian takeoff. It gets off the ground by inverting the Miesian idiom, bringing it indoors, painting it white (instead of black or bronze), and using it frankly as pure decoration.

In a similar foolery, Charles Moore mocked the early Modern goal of integrating the inside and the outside of a building and literally brought the outdoors indoors in his own 1962 house at Orinda, California, by opening up the corners with sliding walls made of barn doors. He laughed at Miesian propriety and placed Doric columns around the latter-day conversation pit as well as around the shower.

Moore, Lyndon, Turnbull, Whitaker:
Moore house, Orinda, California. 1962. *Photograph by Morley Baer.*

Moore's first office in New Haven, Connecticut, destroyed the lines established in Mies's office in Chicago. Moore used a screen at one end of the reception room in a strangely Adamesque way—setting it out several feet from the sink visible on the end wall, and supporting it on two Doric columns of unequal height, which the screen jogged up and down to accommodate. Another support was an Ionic column capital,

(*left*) Ludwig Mies van der Rohe: Mies van der Rohe office, Chicago. 1967. *Photograph by C. Ray Smith.*

MLTW/ Moore-Turnbull: Moore-Turnbull offices, New Haven, Connecticut. 1967. *Photograph by Steven Izenour.*

which was used as a plinth on the floor. Roadway reflectors trimmed the edge of the screen as a new kind of Greek key. No architectural office had ever before displayed this kind of wild abandon. Architect Moore proclaimed "I include irreverence and puncture whatever architectural balloons I can find lying around."

Architect Robert Venturi wrote in *Complexity and Contradiction in Architecture,* "I welcome the problems and exploit the uncertainties. I aim for vitality as well as validity." Venturi also made some sprightly design jokes early in the permissive decade. For a house in Chestnut Hill, Pennsylvania, he winked at the ordinary Cape Cod cottage and twisted a simple peaked-roof scheme around so that the front door is in the gable end; then he made the gable end into a broken pediment that, perhaps pretentiously, recalls the great English mannerist historical houses he is so fond of. Inside, the most celebrated of his design jokes is a stair that leads to nowhere; it can be used as a large whatnot and as a ladder to aid in washing a window, but otherwise there is no function. It is, nevertheless, a gantry to the sky, an infinity stair that is a clear symbol of our age.

Venturi & Rauch: House, Chestnut Hill,
Pennsylvania. 1962. *Photograph by Rollin R. La France.*

Some time in 1963, Ronald Beckman, Director of the Research and Design Institute of Providence, Rhode Island, but then an associate of George Nelson's in New York, said that architects had refused to face the industrial revolution as a challenge and to *use* mass-produced industrial products. Instead, he pointed out, architects have continued to make ever more handcrafted buildings. "Buildings have become more and more esoteric—made out of bronze, or zinc, or lodestone," he wryly stated. "This is a retreat from the problems of mass production and automation, and from that even more pressing contemporary problem— the population explosion." The first seeds of a rebellious viewpoint were sprouting in several directions.

Taking the lead from these pioneers, today's architects and designers reject the uptight, packaged formality of the past—that Minimalist purity, which created monotonous, sterilized, easy-to-copy-badly pigeon crates, and massive, impenetrable, tight-skinned box-buildings. Above all, to the designers of those Minimalist schemes, tidy "tastefulness" was the goal. Today tastefulness is a dirty word to many designers.

When graphic design took a Minimalist direction, cartographer Richard Edes Harrison trounced it in *The New York Times Book Review* in 1964: ". . . the designer . . . is apparently one of those who conceive the ideal page as a solid rectangle of gray on white, no indentations for paragraphs, no running chapter heads, no footnotes; maximum purity, minimum readability. The reader can consider himself

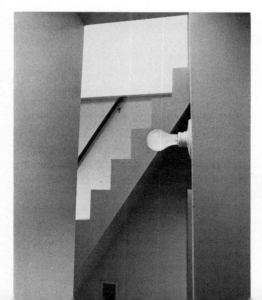

Venturi & Rauch: Nowhere stair, house, Chestnut Hill, Pennsylvania. 1962. *Photograph by Rollin R. La France.*

lucky that the pages are numbered." To that reviewer, as to many architecture critics, then and now, the people—readers and building users—were more important than the purity of the design.

"Purity is the problem of our age," T. S. Eliot had observed anent the process of literary creation. What purism did was depreciate, uproot, and abstract our lives from the soil and from our emotional responses. Purity and perfect alignment hide humanity. Lewis Mumford wrote in the *Architectural Record* in 1962 that "in so far as modern architecture has succeeded in expressing modern life, it has done better in calling attention to its lapses, its rigidities, its failures, than in bringing out, with the aid of the architect's creative imagination, its immense latent potentialities."

"One of the older generation's chief hang-ups," says North Carolina State University associate professor of product design Frederick Eichenberger,

> is our inability to evaluate design problems, decisions, and solutions in operational terms. To fill the void, we have invented a metaphysical aesthetic that says certain things are better than others because they are better—and never mind why, because anyone with sensibility knows why without being told. This may help to give form and substance to our days, and grant us a modicum of comfort, but it is not particularly useful to the young. They know it just ain't so. If God is not dead, he has at least gone into seclusion.

The governing principle of the new movement, according to Howard Barnstone, "is freedom and open-mindedness. The works of Mies, Yamasaki and I. M. Pei are new constrictors," he explains, "new sealed envelopes, new Establishments, and not-so-new vocabularies. The reign of the Knoll Planning Unit as the major factor in interiors lasted well over ten years, from 1955 to 1966 at least. Some change was bound to come to this fixed set of rules." The change was to an architectural equivalent of Laurence Sterne's *Tristram Shandy*.

Rule-making—"form-giving"—was the hallmark of 1950s architecture. Architects brought an established vision to every problem and automatically imposed that vision onto the problem before they ever started to cope with programming, site, or budgetary requirements. They used essentially preconceived systems of massing and structure, preconceived doctrines of joinery and detailing, preconceived ideas on the uses of materials. It was an architecture of the intellect—rational, conceptual, based on what a "form-giver" could conceive, could "give." Whatever did not fit into that established vision was excluded. "In about 1955," as Tim Vreeland recalls,

> a number of people, younger people who were deeply involved in architecture and thoroughly knowledgeable in architecture—traditional, historic, and modern architecture, who knew what its tenets, canons, principles were, who, being imaginative men, had already reached a limit of the possibilities of this "rational" architecture. The rules had been so clearly established, understood, and practiced by everyone that the early victories in which the early champions of the 20's and 30's prided themselves on had begun to ring hollow. Modern architecture had scored its victories so completely and was so completely teachable, that it had become a formula.

"In the late 50s, I was getting disillusioned with the way things were going," Joseph Esherick affirmed, "not just the work I was doing, but the work everybody was doing. The questions were about how you design a certain wall or a suspended ceiling or a partitioning system—questions about things that could be solved in any one of a variety of ways, but always arbitrarily. It didn't seem to me that this was leading anywhere." And Sim Van der Ryn added, "And the people doing it and the reasons it was being done seemed to be increasingly fatuous."

"Even in the creative process," Stuart Pertz continued, "you did not discover any more when you were finished than you knew when you began."

Accepting the world as it is, all of it, became an article of faith for the new breed. Instead of relying on preconceptions, instead of squeezing program requirements to fit an imposed image, architects of the 1960s began more realistically. Their buildings were developed not by applying rules of geometry, structure, and detailing but rather by allowing solutions to emerge that were inherent in the site, in the program, in the materials to be used, in the clients themselves. Instead of fitting rooms into packages—mammoth matchbox towers or eighteenth-century-inspired pavilions—architects began to design the forms of buildings according to the users' actual living patterns and to their psychological requirements.

It was a new thing to deal with the actualities of physical and psychological functions, to focus on human activities, and develop an idiom from them. It was a further development of Louis Kahn's "what the building wants to be," toward a consideration of what the owner wants the building to be. It was not coincidental that critics began to assert that great architecture requires great clients as well as great architects.

The major change in architecture from the 1950s to the 1960s was, in fact, from rationalism to concentration on feelings and emotions, from pure design to human concern. That, after all, was what was happening in society at large: everyone everywhere was striving for heightened sensitivity to every kind of physical and psychological stimulus. Architects began to concern themselves with what people see, feel, and hear, or don't see, feel, and hear, and how they react to all this. They tried viewing models with periscopes or with fish-eye and other lenses in their attempts to find new ways of seeing and presenting architecture.

Architects "went back to try to see new ways of seeing things," Walter Netsch said. "It doesn't make much difference what is out there so much as the way you can see it, how you perceive it," Joseph Esherick said. In Tim Vreeland's view, the difference between the architecture of the 1950s and the 1960s was the difference between the "Architecture of Conception and the Architecture of Perception." David Sellers said, "To me, it is existential; it all has to do with how we feel about how one has to act, and live, and be aware, and be alive, and have his senses in his fingertips in this particular age." Colin Rowe had said it was a distinction between the thing as it *is* and as it *appears.* Ulrich Franzen wrote of "new connections between eye and mind," which were being considered as a "reconciliation with an existing world." And Cesar Pelli said that architects were interested in "what it is and not an image of what it should be . . . We are concerned with what people actually feel and not with what they should feel."

If all that really matters is what you see, and if what you see is produced by no more than a millimeter of paint or something even less substantial, such as projected light, nevertheless that is what you experience and that is what you feel. From this position, then, Tim Vreeland could distinguish the "architecture of conception" from the "architecture of perception." He pointed out that Renaissance architecture also had been one of conception, "predicated on such considerations as, for example, that the Pantheon accommodates a perfect sphere within its domed space, though half the people who see it are not aware of it. Then, Dr. Rudolf Wittkower pointed out, that view gave way in the following century to Guarini's view that the only important thing is what man can see." So in the 1960s, architects were concerned with perception—with trompe-l'oeil, false perspective, and stagecraft. They were supported by countless experiments by perceptual psychologists and aestheticians—Vreeland mentions Gombrich, Ames, Gibson, and Koffka—people who experimented in Gestalt psychology, with distortion chambers. "Architects had taken for granted that they operate in the geographic environment," Vreeland said, "when in actuality their most important contributions may be to the behavioral or perceptual environment."

THE SUPERMANNERISTS' EDUCATION

It should not have been surprising to learn—but it was—that most of the Supermannerists came from three eastern schools of architecture: Princeton University, the University of Pennsylvania, and Yale University. So many came from Princeton in the late 1950s that in the University of California at Berkeley faculty they formed a "Princeton clique" around 1960. By 1971 the Princeton classes of 1955 to 1960 alone had produced at least nine deans of architecture schools and six full-time professors who spread the new design to budding architects across the country: among them were Charles Moore and Ralph Drury at Yale, Keith McPheeters at Auburn University, Delbert Highlands at Carnegie-Mellon, Donlyn Lyndon at the Massachusetts Institute of Technology, Norval White at the City University of New York, Richard Peters at the University of California at Berkeley, W. G. Gilland, R. S. Harris, and T. W. Kleinsasser at the University of Oregon, A. Von K. Anderson, Jr., at the University of Miami, Robert B. Church II (now deceased) at the University of Tennessee, and J. M. Powell, Jr., at Louisiana State University.

The Princeton influence has been largely unrecognized. Currently, critics speak of the Yale and Philadelphia axis, omitting Princeton. In the mid-1960s the spotlight was on Yale, where Venturi was a faculty member, Charles Moore was dean, and socially involved students came together to effect a widely publicized activism. By the early 1970s, the spotlight focused on Philadelphia, where Kahn and Venturi's associates held center stage. But all of them had first got it together at Princeton.

In the second half of the 1950s most architecture schools provided rigorous training in established principles, as handed down by Beaux

Arts–trained teachers. A solid indoctrination into the tenets of the Bauhaus and the International Style was the base of architectural education. During those years, there was no question that the work of the First Generation of Modern Architects—Frank Lloyd Wright, Mies van der Rohe, and Le Corbusier—was the rock on which all was founded, and there was still a great deal to learn from them. Directions that other early Modern masters may have pursued, such as Aalto's, were neglected, if not rejected as unacceptable.

However, tender new influences were springing up. At Princeton in the late 1950s Jean Labatut, director of the graduate architecture program, instilled an infectious love of the history of architecture without threatening the Modern ideals of his students. Labatut's curriculum provided his classes "an art historical base that sensitized the eyeballs," as William Turnbull describes it. "You had your eyeballs permanently pounded into very sensitive objects, with a good basic background in history and in terms of how ideas related over time, who had done what, and how well they had done it; you had all the nuances down." Labatut was "perceptive at developing nuances," Charles Moore recalls. "He pointed out the kinds of things where you see this and then you see that and then they all relate." Labatut's was a protopsychological approach to architectural vision—concerned with what a viewer actually sees from various perspectives and distances. He also showed his students the value and interest of nonmaterial or nonsolid design elements—water, light, smoke, sound—which had been a personal concern of his since he designed the sound-light-water-and-fireworks pageants at the 1939 New York World's Fair. Professor Labatut wrote in early 1972 that he had fostered "an educational system which is against the creeping architectural sameness promoted by dictatorial educators," that is, against the "mental slavery which leads to a type of man's environment good enough for a community of ants but not good enough for the comprehensive phenomena of the community of man."

To Princeton after the mid-1950s Enrico Peressutti came from Italy, where his firm, BBPR, was known for attempting "to establish a poetic style by reference to tradition and local atmosphere." Peressutti brought to his students this sense of the peculiarities of the site as well as his low-keyed sense of humor, his ability to make them aware of the possibility that architecture could be fun. "Peressutti tweaked our noses by giving us an exercise to do our modern buildings in Palladian proportions," Turnbull recalls. Perhaps most importantly, Peressutti stressed the difference between the diagram for a building, the chosen system or idea, on the one hand, and the real building, on the other. Throughout the 1960s, because of the strong Beaux Arts emphasis on drawing, architects needed continual prodding to recognize that a building is brick and mortar not pen and paper: that despite Plato, the idea of a building is not a building. So Peressutti prodded his Princeton classes.

Kahn

But the supreme teacher, the magical Pied Piper of the Supermannerist band, was, until his death in March 1974, Louis Kahn. Unknown except to some few architects in Philadelphia until 1951, when he was fifty, unknown to the profession at large until the early 1960s, unknown to the lay public until the mid-1960s, Louis Kahn was nevertheless the most mesmerizing and liberating teacher of architecture in the United States throughout the 1950s. When the architectural world first heard of him in 1960, 1961, and 1962 through the pages of *Perspecta* and *Progressive Architecture,* and through Vincent Scully's book, *Louis I. Kahn* (1962), Kahn's mystique, mythology, and vision had already imbued a whole generation of architects at the University of Pennsylvania, at Yale, and at Princeton. Yet throughout the 1950s and 1960s this fact, as well as the depth of his influence, was recognized only by his close associates and his students.

Kahn is the pivotal influence that pervades all the Supermannerists who studied under him in the 1950s at Princeton, Yale, and Pennsylvania, and those who worked with him in Philadelphia during those years. They were the ones who, as second-generation Kahnians, became the acknowledged innovators of the new design when their first works began to appear in the early 1960s. Younger students who were graduated in the mid-1960s, and who form a third generation of Kahnians, can inevitably trace their interests in the new design back to Revised Standard Kahn through these innovators: through Robert Venturi, who studied at Princeton from 1947 to 1950 and then worked in Kahn's office until 1958; or through Charles Moore, who did his doctoral work at Princeton and taught there from 1955 to 1960, taking Kahn's first master class, then carrying those teachings to Berkeley and then to Yale; or through other second-generation Kahnians who became influential designers and teachers—Tim Vreeland, James Polshek, Romaldo Giurgola. As Moore says, "it is all derived from Kahn, as everything is."

Kahn's theories and his work began to coalesce and solidify only

Louis I. Kahn: The Jonas Salk Institute for Biological Studies, La Jolla, California. 1959–1965. *Photograph courtesy The Salk Institute.*

around 1949, when he opened his own office and, at the same time, began to teach at Yale. Then the electricity of his statements, both in words and drawings, exploded in the minds of his students. All great systems of design and thought are supported by rich, complete theories, or mythologies, and Louis Kahn's resonant metaphysical justifications are no exception. As a philosopher-poet, he ultimately captured the attentive, eager souls of architects whose dreams of ideal spaces and godly designs were constantly hindered by human fallibility. Kahn fanned their dreams, leading them into ever more imaginary, visionary yet human methodologies of creation—methodologies for uncovering the truly significant factors of their clients' programs, the realities of their sites, and the rationales of their structural systems. He gave architects at mid-century an Existence Will to search for what he maintained each building "wants to be"—two phrases that were keynotes of his organizing rationale. But it is important to remember that in the mid-1950s this experience had been shared only by those who were exposed to him personally at the three eastern architecture schools where he taught and by those who actually worked in his office.

As Charles Moore recalls, "When I first went to Princeton early in 1955, Kahn and Rudolph were on a symposium together. I didn't know who Kahn was, but I thought he was kind of an interesting old duffer. However he didn't come to teach at Princeton until 1958, when Labatut was on sabbatical." And William Turnbull says "Labatut had to get someone to be the master-class critic and so he pulled in a funny old man named Kahn, who was absolutely unknown to us at the time." In fact, Kahn went to Princeton only a couple of times for that class; in the main, his students traveled with their drawings to his office in Philadelphia, where the master exploded their vision and held them spellbound till late at night. Then they all left, "dumping their drawings disgustedly in the garbage outside, leaving the old man still hard at his own work," one student recalls.

"Kahn really opened everybody's eyes to the fact that making a beautiful sensitive building was not where it was at," Turnbull states. "Kahn said, 'don't do anything unless you have some idea why you're doing it.' " He demanded conceptual clarity above all. He gave architects a strong sense of structure, reaching into levels of design that had not been tapped by the Internationalists; like them, he felt strongly that we should see how a building is made, yet his desire to express structure more clearly brought the innermost workings of buildings to sight—the activity functions and the mechanical systems. His was a latter-day functionalism, beyond the structural functions or expressionistic structuralism of Mies. Kahn imparted a new intellectual rigor to thinking about light, materials, structure, and spaces. He was the tremendous generative force of the decade.

Naturally, his thinking has foundations in architectural history. As Joseph Esherick sees it, "There is a moral injunction and an ethical character about Kahn's pronouncements. It is familiar in the writings of Julien Gaudet, whose *Éléments et Théorie de l'Architecture* in four volumes (1870–1880) posits that the elements of architecture are not the ancient orders but they are windows, walls, floors, and light. The idea that a wall wants to be a wall and the idea of master spaces and slave spaces are both in Gaudet. I remember," Esherick adds, "that the prominent thing on Kahn's desk when I first went to meet him in the late 50's was a copy of Gaudet's old testament."

What is important about Kahn's capacity as a teacher is that he showed his students how to push and prod and pry about these elements in order to find the problem within the problem. "The problem is not the two-bedroom, three-baths that the client wants; the problem is that he wants a special place or has some other unexpressed intent," Turnbull said, as an example of Kahn's vision. Kahn showed that the design answer could come from the design problem—should not be superimposed by the architect or his idiom—that it is inherent in the building.

By expressing the concept of what a building "wants to be," Kahn found a valid philosophical way through the wall of consistency that had previously held firm—that the structural form should follow the activity function, that the visual expression should reiterate the structural expression. Critics who described buildings in terms of exterior "skins" and "muscular" structure had begun to sound foolish, since they were forced to pursue the analogy and pretend that the exterior skin of a building was consistent with the building interior design, as if a human or animal skin is consistent with a human or animal interior. In Kahnian theory, Form comes from a careful consideration of the human activities that will go on in the building and of the other functional requirements also. Design, on the other hand, is a secondary consideration, not tied in with Form but almost independent of it. Design, in Kahn's new view, could be an expression of the individual shape an architect wants it to be. He insisted that architects should not merely make pretty things without good reason but that a strong idea, if related to programmatic concept, could be idiosyncratic and valid. In this regard he was the first influential architect to show a way through to a duality of architectural expression, although he himself did not permit departure from the theories of consistency and integration.

He was, as Vreeland said, "unalterably opposed to an art of that kind"—meaning duality—"because he believed so strongly in the physical body of architecture. The second-generation Kahnians, his students in the 1950s, went on to design buildings that were very different on the inside from the outside. They, the Third Generation of Modern Architects, were liberated by Kahn. He was the new American Gropius—although unsung in this regard until the students of his first mature decade had passed his doctrine on to yet another generation of students.

"He taught me how to think, how to design," is a typical memory. "It was primarily his attitude about things, because he himself is an infinitely better teacher than an architect," said a Penn graduate from the last years of the 1960s, "a really superb old man that everyone just fell in love with. It was a stance from which he saw things, even his body position."

Kahn had a totally different concept of evaluating a project: rather than saying a building is out of scale or that the proportions are not great, the structure or materials inappropriate, he talked about a building in terms of what its effect on the human being is. He asked what the building does beyond housing a family. Besides, as Ulrich Franzen lauds him, "He is a poet of materials." Kahn joined the handcraft of nineteenth-century brickwork to the Modern movement's passion for industrial and factory buildings, and that endeared him to all architects interested in the craft of building. Those were the years in Kahn's career that Moore regards as "Kahn's high period—when he hadn't found the answers yet, when he was still anguishing over whether to lay the bricks flat or turn them on their sides."

At Princeton, then, the influences were a combination of Labatut, who sensitized vision; Peressutti, who spiked architecture with wit; and the late-maturing Kahn, who liberated his students from a very classical background and brought a special view all his own. Stuart Pertz makes a distinction between these influences: "The bigger than life images that are the most recognizable in Kahn's architecture—the exaggeration, the oversimplification without sterility—that is Kahn's influence. But the subtle interplay of things that are not easily described—that don't easily generate from anything that have to do with program, but have to do more with a visual sensitivity—has to do with Labatut."

Among the Princetonians who were exposed to this combination of influences, Charles Moore completed his Ph.D. work in 1956, in the same class with Keith McPheeters, Alfred DeVido, John Woodbridge, and Hugh Hardy (whose processes have as much to do with his work in the theatre, he feels, as with Kahn and Venturi). Moore stayed on to teach, among others, Bill Turnbull and Donlyn Lyndon, who later became his partners. Also from Princeton classes around 1960 came Steve Kilment, Willis Mills, Jr., Stuart Pertz, and Hobart Betts.

Robert Venturi, not suprisingly, had the same educational exposure.

He had studied at Princeton under Labatut from 1947 to 1950, subsequently was directly exposed to Italian wit at the American Academy in Rome, and then worked with Kahn in Philadelphia from 1956 to 1958. He was on the faculty at Penn in those same years, and discussed his own work, especially the proposed house for his mother in Chestnut Hill, which captured the attention of Moore, Hardy, Turnbull, and others. The interaction between Kahn and Venturi during this period—who was the greater influence on the other—has been discussed by Vincent Scully and others. I stress another point: that the education at Princeton under Labatut and the subsequent exposure to Kahn were similar occurrences for Venturi, Moore, Hardy, and the Princeton Supermannerists who came later. It is this inspirational background that links the Supermannerists.

To the architects who studied at Penn from 1952 on, similarly, Kahn was accessible as a teacher and in his prominent Philadelphia career. With him on the faculty were Robert Venturi, Tim Vreeland, Romaldo Giurgola, Robert Geddes, George Qualls, Ian McHarg, Robert LeRicolais, and August Kommendant, under the deanship of Holmes Perkins. From the time that Kahn taught his first master class at Penn in 1957, as a three-teacher team along with LeRicolais and Norman Rice, students there could be exposed to the two leading theorists and inspirations of Supermannerism on their home soil. Among the Penn graduates of those days were Richard Saul Wurman and Louis Sauer (1959); Jordan Gruzen (1961); Charles Gwathmey (1961, and going on to Yale the next year); John Lobell (1963); Barton Myers and Todd Lee (1964); Denise Venturi and Steven Izenour (1965); and Edward D'Andrea (1967).

Some Yale-trained architects in the early 1950s, notably Peter Millard and Tim Vreeland, had an exposure similar to the Princetonians: Vreeland, an exact contemporary of Venturi's and Moore's, finished Yale in 1954, then worked in Kahn's office in 1955, and taught at Penn. Vreeland lived in Philadelphia and had known Kahn and Venturi there, so he was an exception among Yalies in coming to know Kahnian theory so early. Although Kahn had been teaching at Yale since 1949, most Yale students in the early 1950s and even in the 1960s did not get to know him because he was involved with master classes generally made up of students from outside Yale. Besides, Kahn's personal influence was not strong until the mid-1950s, when his work and theories crystallized in the Trenton Bath Houses in New Jersey.

Another architect who was influential in the development of the new design in the early 1960s was Joseph Esherick, who also lived in Philadelphia and had gone to Penn, and who met Kahn in the late 1950s. Esherick had "always known about Kahn" he says, because Kahn was an old friend of his uncle, Wharton Esherick—the wood craftsman whose artistry with wood produced some of the most poetic and elegantly expressionistic furniture. Wharton Esherick had always wanted his nephew to work for Kahn, but that never happened. Instead, Joseph Esherick carried what he had learned personally from Kahn to the West Coast, where he taught at Berkeley and where he practices in the Bay Area.

Through this early group of Philadelphians and Princetonians, the Kahnian mystique spread across the country to countless students before anything on his work was published. From Princeton, Richard Peters went to teach at Berkeley and was instrumental in Vernon DeMars's bringing Charles Moore there in 1959 and Donlyn Lyndon in 1960. In the meantime, John Woodbridge had moved to San Francisco; William Turnbull settled there in 1961; and W. G. Gilland was also teaching at Berkeley. Richard Peters, now chairman of the department, recalls that in all about a dozen Princetonians who were at Berkeley in the early 1960s formed what was known as the "Princeton clique." At this same time, Hans Hollein was there from Vienna, studying and conceiving his aircraft carrier in the middle of the desert and his Rolls-Royce grille as a Pop art New York skyscraper; so began Hollein's formally obvious but otherwise biographically unclear connection to the Supermannerists.

Hans Hollein: New York skyline collage. 1962.

In much the same way as the Princeton clique at Berkeley spread the new design ideas, Yale students came under the Kahnian influence most forcefully through Robert Venturi, who was invited there by Paul Rudolph to expound his version of the new design in 1962. Yale students from those years recall starving for something new amid the final drought of the New Canaan School—Philip Johnson, John Johansen, Victor Christ-Janer, and others, whose reverence for the classical Miesian discipline still lingered, even if on the wane. They were inspired by studying in Kahn's 1954 art gallery, but the arrival of Venturi signaled something entirely new. It brought the Princeton vision of Labatut and the liberating influence of Kahn as revealed through the special mannerist brilliance of Venturi's mind.

Another exponent of the Kahnian outlook had been exposing Yale students to that approach since 1955: Peter Millard, who was in the Yale class of 1951, continued to be a forceful though underpublicized critic from the mid-1950s until the present. When Millard began to teach at Yale, Kahn was in charge only of master classes under Paul Schweikher's chairmanship; so Millard became the direct connection between Kahnian approaches and most Yale architecture students. Millard says of Kahn: "The man himself is a force, when you are in his presence. You either love him or hate him, but you cannot ignore him." One of Millard's students, Russell Childs, recalls, "Under Millard I learned that building is not just forms, but also mud and materials put together by people's hands. Millard had the gift to throw one back to absolute beginnings and to destroy preconceptions. He urged that a building grow out of the real program." And so the development of Kahnian thought proceeded.

Among the Yale graduates of that period were Hugh Jacobsen and James Polshek (1955); Herbert Newman (1959); James Baker, T. Merrill Prentice, Jr., and Stanley Tigerman (1960); Warren Cox, Walk C. Jones, Jacquelin T. Robertson, Der Scutt, Rurik Ekstrom (1961); Charles Gwathmey and Keith R. Kroeger (1962); Jonathan Barnett and Louis Skidmore, Jr. (1963); Peter Hoppner, Charles Hosford, Etel Kramer, Robert Mittelstadt, and Robert Nerrie (1964); Michael Altschuler, Peter Gluck, John Hagmann, David Sellers, and Robert A. M. Stern (1965); Michael Hollander, Thomas Luckey, and William Rienecke (1966); and Craig Hodgetts (1967), among many others.

By that time, of course, Kahn's reputation had expanded to international scale and had begun to influence older architects who were first

(above) Venturi & Short: Grand's Restaurant renovation, West Philadelphia. 1962. *Photograph by Lawrence S. Williams.* *(below)* Venturi & Short: Isometric, Grand's Restaurant renovation, West Philadelphia. 1962.

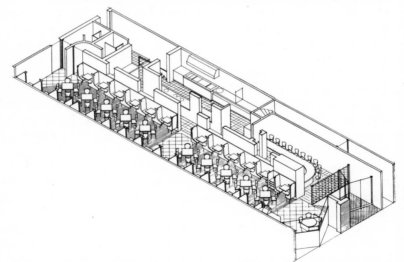

exposed to him through the publication of countless articles—especially in *Perspecta* and Jan Rowan's "The Philadelphia School" in *Progressive Architecture* in 1961. At that time also, the first work of the second-generation Kahnian architects began to be published: Robert Venturi completed Grand's Restaurant in Philadelphia (1962)—an Italianate diner with industrial parts and common materials and a then strangely incomprehensible overlay of graphics. Charles Moore with Lyndon and Turnbull won instant acclaim with a Citation in *Progressive Architecture* for Moore's house in Orinda, California (1962)—a box with a multilayered interior that I likened to Baroque stage design before I came to see it as a mannerist composition with recycled architectural elements.

In 1965, to complete the circle, Moore followed Paul Rudolph as chairman of the architecture department at Yale. And so the leadership in architectural education seemed to pass from Pennsylvania and Princeton to Yale, which more than one student of architecture at the time felt to be the great citadel of all fine artistic creations. In 1966 works of the Yale class of 1965 burst on the scene through the Prickly Mountain boys—David Sellers, Bill Rienecke, Louis Mackall, and others. Also in 1966, Robert Venturi's book *Complexity and Contradiction in Architecture* was published by The Museum of Modern Art; also in 1966 Robert A. M. Stern put together the Architectural League's "40 under 40" exhibition, which was the first broad exhibition outside the pages of architecture magazines of the group of designers that I was later that year to call the Supermannerists.

In 1967 the new design exploded into full flower. The first athletic club at The Sea Ranch in California painted by Barbara Stauffacher Solomon was widely publicized. The term *supergraphics* was coined (see p. 272), the first collection of supergraphic designs published, and the movement and some of its aspects described. Projections, discotheques, drugs, hippies, revolution, and long hair all were flourishing. In 1968 *Progressive Architecture* published a full issue on this movement. Reactions to the idea of a new movement included such accusations as "mostly an invention of *P/A*" . . . "confined to a half dozen personalities" . . . "restricted to a few Eastern schools." Yale architecture students at that time, with an air of pride, dubbed *P/A* "The Yale Alumni Magazine" because students and graduates of that university brought so much work to its attention. Now, we see that these accusations were right, although the accusers generally did not know why the movement had *started* at a few eastern schools, nor which ones besides Yale.

The new design was transported to the University of Houston in the mid-1960s by Howard Barnstone, who had studied at Yale in 1948 and came to know Kahn when teaching there subsequently. At Houston, the design group Southcoast developed at the same time as a rebellion against the school administration. Ironically, the student rebellions in the late 1960s at Houston, Yale, and elsewhere had been foreshadowed by a similar plot to overthrow the head of the school at Princeton in 1957. The new design reached the University of Texas at Austin through Richard Oliver, who had been a student of Kahn's at Pennsylvania, then of Moore's at Berkeley. And, as Chip Lord explained in 1968, it reached Tulane University in New Orleans "mostly through the periodicals," showing the acceleration of communications within one decade. By then mass outcry and outrage arose in professional circles. Cries of "shame," "ghastly chaos," and "trivial fad" were rending the heavens of the Design Establishment.

In 1968, the wave seemed to crest. Was it that beginner's luck and the first flushes of enthusiasm on the part of the class of 1965 were only then beginning to be splashed with the cold water of human fallibility? Certainly, at that time, many prodigies seemed to fade from view—or to have their views fade from them. Had their "LSDesign" become too much? Had it damaged their brains? Would they produce anything so arresting again? Were designers' interests evaporated by overexposure in the press?

Whenever any comprehensive explanation is published about an avant-garde or unknown movement, direction, person or development, in the arts at least, it seems that such publication causes the avant-garde to feel their domain has been exposed to the masses. In reaction, they often immediately begin to pursue some other course. What such publications seem to do is to wrap up the accomplished works succinctly enough for all to comprehend, so that those newly introduced can immediately pursue the published direction—through imitation. But the already knowledgeable feel bored or are pressed to move on to other things. That was the reaction to the 1968 and 1969 publications on Supermannerism. It had also been the reaction to the 1961 publication on "The Philadelphia School," which produced masses of Kahn-worshipers immediately, and which alienated Kahn from *P/A* instantly—since he did not want identification as the founder of a school but wanted to be considered an independent and pure poet. At that time, those who felt that they were doing work that was new and different from Kahn also did not like being lumped in as derivative; so they turned to the unknown Kahn about that time, that is, they turned from Kahn to Venturi, and in some cases to Moore. "By the time most people caught up with Kahn," Vreeland remembered, "he was already something to be critical of," by which he indicated the change in Kahn's work from what Moore had earlier called "Kahn's high period" to what he later called Kahn's "international acclaim period."

In 1969, Mies died; miraculously, but only coincidentally, the fight was over. At the same time, a recession began. Nixon was securely in favor with the majority; peace certainly seemed on its way; moratoriums expressed activity as much as desire. And a period of sobriety and ecological-mindedness, a period of settling into a new phase prompted people to say that all the razzle-dazzle of the 1960s was over, that it was only a silly fad.

That is a faddist's view of history. A decade of mature work by so may architects cannot be dismissed so easily. The plateau of sobriety lasted from 1969 to 1971. Then by 1972 the architects and designers who had started doing small, wood beach houses and apartment remodeling in the early 1960s were suddenly doing major housing, university buildings, and large-scale planning. Their styles and idioms were in full force. Not many of them have made major monuments in prominent urban centers as yet, but they are producing highly professional, prime-of-career work. They comprise a new design school. They have developed an idiom that I believe can well be called Supermannerism.

MANNERISM

The design that developed in the decade from 1962 to 1972 exhibits so many parallels with design in the century from 1520 to 1620—the period of Mannerism—that we can hardly escape applying that term analogously. In fact, the analogy was drawn by several prominent architects during the 1960s, including Philip Johnson, Robert Venturi, Charles Moore, Thomas Vreeland, and others. Johnson said of his underground art gallery in New Canaan, "I wanted to create an ambiguous, let us say, a *mannerist* clarity" (*Esquire,* 1969). Robert Venturi discusses Mannerism throughout his *Complexity and Contradiction in Architecture* and compares today's approach as "an attitude common in the Mannerist periods: the sixteenth century in Italy or the Hellenistic period in Classical art . . ." He also draws parallels with Mannerism in literature, art, and architecture in several other periods, showing similar elements of chaos, ambiguity, paradox, and other complexities and contradictions. Vreeland has said of Venturi, Moore, and other colleagues, "One cannot help but be aware of the historical parallel with the 16th Century in Italy, when a lot of very clever architects had reached the same limit of the possibilities of the preceding architecture, had learned their lessons so well that they knew what it was all about and had to move on to something new." Hardy has said that the parallel with the sixteenth century demonstrates the seriousness of our new direction in design, but he emphasized that the new academicism originates from a "curiosity about people, instead of systems and things."

In sixteenth-century Italy, as in America during the past decade, the swell of social change and the rapid developments in science were reflected in the change in architectural attitude—away from the ordered, disciplined, and rational Renaissance architectural systems of Alberti, Bramante, Brunelleschi, and Raphael. Sir Nikolaus Pevsner has written that the "creators of Mannerism were rebels against the purity and humanism of Raphael and Titian." It was a change brought about by such sixteenth-century architectural rebels as Michelangelo (all of whose architecture was produced after 1520), Sebastiano Serlio (1475–1554), Giulio Romano (1499–1546), Baldassare Peruzzi (1481–1536), Michelle Sammicheli (1484–1559), Giacomo da Vignola (1507–1573), Andrea Palladio (1508–1580), Giorgio Vasari (1511–1574), Domenico Fontana (1543–1607), Vicenzo Scamozzi (1552–1616), and Carlo Maderna (1556–1627), as well as the painters Fiorentino Rosso (1494–1541), Francesco Primaticcio (1504–1570), Bartolommeo Ammanati (1511–1592), and Flaminio Ponzio (1560–1633)—to name those mentioned by Dr. Pevsner and Dr. Rudolf Wittkower in various works.

The term *mannerism*, first applied to painting by art historians such as Dvorak, Pinder, and Pevsner, and others in the early 1920s (the period, incidentally, of Dada and Surrealist mannerism), was adopted in the 1930s by architecture historians who continued to clarify the term as it relates to sixteenth-century Italian architecture and its subsequent transfer to England. Dr. Pevsner, the pioneer in this area in his *Outline of European Architecture* (1943; rev. ed. 1960), delved further into the correspondences between Italian and English Mannerist architecture in an article "The Architecture of Mannerism," which was published in *The Mint* in 1946, and in the same year Anthony Blunt delivered a lecture at the Royal Institute of British Architects on "Mannerism in Architecture," which was subsequently published in the *RIBA Journal* in March 1949. Dr. Rudolf Wittkower and others continued to investigate this early period of Mannerism off and on through the 1950s.

The terminology that they apply to Mannerism makes clear the correspondences between earlier Italian and English Mannerism and American Mannerism in the 1960s and 1970s. Dr. Pevsner variously describes the effects of Michelangelo, Palladio, and other sixteenth-century Italian Mannerists as: "the reverse of balance and harmony . . . unbalanced, discordant . . . distorted . . . meagre . . . slim, elegant . . . stiff and highly self-conscious . . . sophisticated . . . overcivilized, intellectual . . . capricious . . . demonstrative . . . daring . . . having a surreptitious license . . . heretical detail . . . uncomfortable, arbitrary and illogical . . . conscious discordance . . . incongruous . . . ," and so on.

Dr. Wittkower writes in *Art and Architecture in Italy, 1600 to 1750* (1958) that between 1550 and 1590 the Mannerists

> practised a formalistic, anti-classical, and anti-naturalistic style, a style of stereotyped formulas, for which the Italians coined the word *maniera* and which we now call "Mannerism" without attaching a derogatory meaning to the term. Virtuosity of execution and highly decorative surface qualities go with compositional decentralisation and spatial and colouristic complexities; in addition, it is not uncommon that deliberate physical and psychic ambiguities puzzle the beholder. Finally, the intricacies of handling are often matched by the intricacies of content.

This could have been written to describe a piece of architecture from the 1960s as well as from the 1560s. Other qualities that Dr. Wittkower ascribes to Mannerism are: "formalism, stylisation, superimposition of motifs . . . peculiar vacillation," and he summarizes, most succinctly, "Florentine Mannerist traits are very strong in the subtle reversal of architectural motifs and in the overlapping interpenetration of elements as well as in the use of decorative features."

These words read as clearly about the strongest supergraphics as about Palladio's two scales of orders superimposed on the church of San Giorgio Maggiore in Venice, one scale slithered through the other. They read as clearly about Philip Johnson's Founders Room at The Museum of Modern Art as they do about Michelangelo's Laurenziana Library (1524–1557), which Dr. Pevsner considers "Mannerism in its most sublime architectural form." His description of that work is a paradigm of the spirit of the Mannerism of today:

Michelangelo: Laurenziana Library, Florence, Italy. 1524–1557.

The anteroom is high and narrow. This alone gives an uncomfortable feeling. Michelangelo wanted to emphasize the contrast to the long, comparatively low and more restful library itself . . . As for the chief structural members, the columns, one would expect them to project and carry the architraves, as had always been the function of columns. Michelangelo reversed the relations. He recessed his columns and projected his panels so that they painfully encase the columns. Even the architraves go forward over the panels and backward over the columns. This seems arbitrary . . . It is certainly illogical, because it makes the carrying strength of the columns appear wasted. Moreover, they have slender corbels at their feet which do not look substantial enough to support them, and in fact do not support them at all . . . The staircase tells of the same willful originality . . . there is conscious discordance all the way through . . . What Michelangelo's Laurenziana reveals is indeed Mannerism in its most sublime architectural form and not Baroque—a world of frustration much more tragic than the Baroque world of struggles between mind and matter. In Michelangelo's architecture every force seems paralyzed. The load does not weigh, the support does not carry, natural reactions play no part—a highly artificial system upheld by the severest discipline. In its spatial treatment, the Laurenziana is just as novel and characteristic. Michelangelo had exchanged the balanced proportions of Renaissance rooms for an anteroom as tall and narrow as the shaft of a pit, and a library proper, reached by a staircase, as long and narrow as a corridor. They both force us, even against our wills, to follow their pull, upward first and then forward. This tendency to enforce movement through space within rigid boundaries is the chief spatial quality of Mannerism.

Emil Kaufmann in *Architecture in the Age of Reason* (1951–1955) says, "What we see in 'mannerism' is uncertainty, dilemma, and bold effort to exhibit, in the strongest terms, contradictory trends." There, we also hear prophetic echoes of the 1960s. If, on the one side, Kaufmann continues, "we see weakness, inconsistency, affectation, and 'unnaturalness'; on the other, we find dramatic eruptions. We see changes in balance, distortions of the logical relationship between supported and supporting elements, and attempts to revise the conventional disposition."

In an article relating Elizabethan architecture to Italian Mannerism, "Double Profile" (*Architectural Review,* March 1950), Dr. Pevsner wrote of "the post-Renaissance return to medieval ideals" in that disturbed, transitional period: "Mannerism is an uncomfortable style, as the age which made it was an uncomfortable age," he began.

The Reformation had finally broken up the unity of Western thought. Science was not yet there as an equally international if secular force. There were religious wars and religious persecutions everywhere . . . Counter-Reformation and Calvinism tried to impose a bondage on the mind . . . as rigid as the conventions of Sixteenth Century poetry making. In art Mannerism appears in the cold, forced intricacies of Bronzino and Vasari, of the Schools of Fontainebleau and of Harlem, in the self-conscious sinuosities of attitude in Cellini, Goujon, and Giambologna, in the attenuated, spiritualized and yet so ballet-like figures of Pontormo, Rosso, Tintoretto, and Greco.

The transfer of Mannerism from Italy to England, as Dr. Pevsner has shown, was not felt until Inigo Jones returned with his carefully annotated copy of Palladio's *Quattro Libri* and built the Queen's House at Greenwich (1616), and subsequently the Banqueting House in Whitehall (1619–1622). The Queen's House is clearly a direct mannerist reversal of the architectural motifs in Palladio's Palazzo Chiericati —screens substituted for solids and solids for screens.

To explain further how English mannerist architecture expressed the social forces of its time, Dr. Pevsner outlines some correspondences with Elizabethan literature. He finds that the works of Sir Edmund Spenser, especially *The Faerie Queene,* and of the chroniclers Holinshed and Camden reflect an interest in a form of British historicism that was not unlike the antiquarianism of the architectural classicists of sixteenth-century Italy. But these works predate the transfer of Italian Mannerism to England. The theatre historian George Kernodle, in "The Mannerist Stage of Comic Detachment" (1970, 1973), pointed out later parallels in the literary works of early seventeenth-century English writers, including the mature Shakespeare of *Hamlet, Lear,* and *The Tempest.* He notes that these works show a spirit of restlessness and tortured complexity, of doubt and conflict, that reflects "the crisis in man's definition of reality" in the seventeenth century.

An even more forceful literary correspondent of Mannerism in English architecture is Metaphysical poetry, produced by a group of poets who wrote primarily between 1600 and 1675—a period that indicates an eighty- to one-hundred-year time lag in the transfer of styles from Italy to England. Among the English Metaphysical poets, most notably, John Donne (1572–1631) extolled the fact that in the new science and philosophy of the time he saw "All coherence gone." Other Metaphysical poets, including Robert Herrick (1591–1674), George Herbert (1593–1633), Richard Crashaw (1612–1649), Henry Vaughan (1622–1695), Abraham Cowley (1618–1667), and John Cleveland (1613–1658), used both the new blank verse and freer forms as well as intellectual gymnastics, arbitrary, and wild "conceits." Their vividly realistic interpretations of physical detail follow the style of the Neapolitan poet Giambattista Marino (1569–1625) called *Marinism.*

Of these writers, Dr. Samuel Johnson said in his *Lives of the Poets* (1779–1781):

> The metaphysical poets were men of learning, and to show their learning was their whole endeavor . . . if [wit] be that which he that never found it wonders how he missed, to wit of this kind the metaphysical poets have seldom risen. Their thoughts are often new,

but seldom natural; they are not obvious, but neither are they just; and the reader, far from wondering that he missed them, wonders more frequently by what perverseness of industry they were ever found.

So we often feel about certain 1960s designs: far from wondering why we did not think of such a scheme, we wonder how the designer ever did. Then Dr. Johnson continues, "But wit may be considered as a kind of *discordia concors;* a combination of dissimilar images, or discovery of occult resemblances in things apparently unlike. Of wit, thus defined, they have more than enough. The most heterogeneous ideas are yoked by violence together; nature and art are ransacked for illustrations, comparison, and allusions; their learning instructs, and their subtlety surprises." *Discordia concors*—discordant harmony—is, I feel, the key-note of all Mannerism.

It was Colin Rowe who first made a detailed comparison between sixteenth- and seventeenth-century Mannerism and the architecture of the early twentieth century. In his "Mannerism and Modern Architec-ture" (*Architectural Review,* May 1950), Professor Rowe compares elements of Le Corbusier's villa at La Chaux-de-Fonds of 1916 with earlier Mannerism—with Peruzzi and Palladio. A mere listing of the features he notes is a revelation: "transparent . . . dematerializing . . . overlapping . . . discord between elements of different scale placed in immediate juxtaposition . . . crushed in the harshest juxta-position . . . complexities and repercussions . . . uneasy violence . . . process of inversion . . . inverted spatial effects . . . stri-dently incompatible details . . . the diagonal . . . light screens . . . ambiguity . . . both subordinate and contradictory." This list reads like the opening chapter in Robert Venturi's *Complexity and Contradic-tion in Architecture,* which is headed "A Gentle Manifesto." Professor Rowe had remarked that the villa at La Chaux-de-Fonds is itself in the way of being "a manifesto." Other features of modern architectural Mannerism that Colin Rowe pointed out in 1950 (when Venturi was still a student at Princeton) were *inclusive* and *duality*—both key words in the 1960s. He also noted that the mind is "baffled by so elaborately conceived an ambiguity," that these effects produce "both a disturbance and a delight," and that certain motifs are "sufficiently abnormal and recondite to stimulate curiosity." The attitude here is virtually identical with the appraisal of the Metaphysical poets by Dr. Johnson, although Professor Rowe is more favorably inclined toward the Modern movement than Dr. Johnson's patience permitted him to be in the face of similar *discordia concors.*

It may not be coincidental that the villa at La Chaux-de-Fonds has as the principal motif of its main facade a flat white panel, divided into three—"the central one, elaborately framed, comprises an unrelieved blank white surface." Although the sources of Le Corbusier's panel are obviously different, the formal similarities to Venturi & Rauch's white brick billboard panels at the Guild House (1960–1965) and Fire Station No. 4 (1965) are unmistakable. Professor Rowe emphasized that "it is not imagined that a mere correspondence of forms necessitates an analogous content" and he outlined an intentional approach on the part of Mannerists in all centuries, saying: "The Mannerist architect, working within the classical system, inverts the natural logic of its implied structural function; modern architecture makes no overt reference to the classical system." But Professor Rowe was writing before the classical system of Mies was so firmly established in America, and before the Supermannerists began to invert it. He continued, "The Mannerist architect works towards the visual elimination of the idea of mass, the denial of the ideas of load, or apparent stability. He exploits contradictory elements in a facade, employs harshly rectilinear forms, and emphasizes a type of arrested movement." Then he said,

> An unavoidable state of mind, and not a mere desire to break rules, sixteenth-century Mannerism appears to consist in the deliberate inversion of the classical High Renaissance norm as established by Bramante to include the very human desire to impart perfection when once it has been achieved; and to represent, too, a collapse of confidence in the theoretical programmage of the earlier Renaissance, which it is able neither to abandon nor to affirm. As a state of inhibition, it is essentially dependent on the awareness of a preexisting order: as an attitude of dissent, it demands orthodoxy within whose frame it might be heretical.

Finally, "If, in the sixteenth century, Mannerism is the visual index of acute spiritual crisis," Professor Rowe wrote in 1950, "the recurrence of similar attitudes at the present day should not be unexpected, and corresponding conflicts should scarcely require indication."

It is no long step from the elaborate and meticulous conceits of the Metaphysical poets or from their passionate interest in God and his cosmic influence to arrive at the metaphysical architectural theory of

Louis Kahn and the meticulous conceits of his architectural construction. By the use of the term *metaphysical* alone the analogy between Kahn and Donne is enforced. And the magnificent art-historical conceits of Venturi, Moore, and the other Supermannerists elaborate the mannerist mode further.

So it was that throughout the 1950s and the 1960s Professor Labatut at Princeton could discuss with his students "direct structural expression (functionalism) versus mannerism (what is called disruptive pattern in camouflage lingo)." So it was that Robert Venturi expressed such an interest in the history of mannerist architecture in Italy and England. And finally, so it was that I wrote in 1966 and 1967, not on this evidence but quite intuitively, that our current school of American architecture might be called "Supermannerism."

In the following chapters of this book, I am going to discuss the principal attitudes of this new design: "Permissiveness and Chaos," "Ambiguity and Invisibility," "Wit and Whimsy or Campopop," "Superscale and Superimposition," and their interrelationships in "User Systems and Adaptability to Change." Most of these overlap with one another. Together they comprise the new, inclusive aesthetic.

Permissiveness and Chaos

THE DECADE OF THE DIAGONAL

The new rebellious visual order is permissive first of all. It permissively rejects the Establishment; it then permissively includes and accommodates. It is permissive in questioning the aims and methods of the older generation as the fixed and only viable way for our day, and in inventing new ways for today.

To express its permissive attitudes the new design naturally adopted new forms. If the 1950s, with its sensual structural extravagance was the decade of the parabola—with Brasilia and Saarinen's Saint Louis arch as alpha and omega—the 1960s was the decade of the diagonal. Symbolically, the diagonal was adopted as the line that cut across established traditions, breaking out of the box and exploding "the architecture of squares." This is not to say that diagonals had not appeared in Modern architecture before the 1960s. Besides the lightning patterns in Art Deco pieces that were included in early Modern architecture, in the late 1940s and the 1950s diagonal wood siding was used for wind bracing in small houses. Louis Kahn's Goldberger house project (1959) shows strong diagonals. Luis Barragán's Chapel at Tlulpan, Mexico (1952–1953), had a strong diagonal in the plan, but his work remained largely unknown in the United States until the 1970s. Le Corbusier's Carpenter Center at Harvard University (1963) has a serpentine roadway running through the building on the diagonal. But in the late 1960s the more intense use of diagonals seemed to one observer, Rita Reif of *The New York Times,* to "promote astigmatism as the vibrating lines in an op art painting do." Philip Johnson said,

(*top*) Edward Larrabee Barnes: House, Wayzata, Minnesota. 1968. *Photograph courtesy Retoria Yukio Futagawa.* (*above*) Moore, Lyndon, Turnbull, Whitaker: Condominium apartments, The Sea Ranch, California. 1965. *Photograph courtesy Retoria Yukio Futagawa.*

There is a love of the 3:1 angle. All modern buildings, with the English as the leaders, are using either 45° or 60° angles—flaring out at the top or coming together like a pyramid. The breakup of the International Style came not only with Kahn, but especially with English architects, who use angles to splay out over the top of the building—the arbitrary 45° angle.

The first signs of the ascendance of the diagonal came early with the faceted, prismatic shed-roof clusters by Edward Larrabee Barnes. Shed roofs became motifs of the day, and were elaborately manipulated in strong forms by Joseph Esherick, Charles Moore, and countless others.

Diagonals were seen in the space frames of 1960s architecture. Louis Kahn's 1961 project for a new Philadelphia City Hall tower was a kind of vertical space frame of multiple diagonals that seemed incomprehensible, although its imagery was unforgettable. From 1963 on, siting, massing, elevations, and interior planning began to be full of diagonal motifs.

In 1964, Alvar Aalto's second project in the United States—the Edgar Kaufmann, Jr., Conference Rooms at New York's Institute for

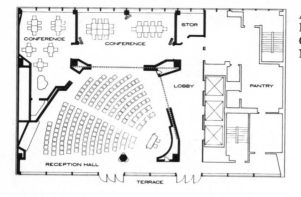

Alvar Aalto: Plan,
Edgar Kaufmann, Jr.,
Conference Rooms,
New York City. 1964.

International Education—exhibited a then seemingly arbitrary but now enduringly vital diagonal seating arrangement. In fact, Aalto, since the 1920s, in his quiet way was doing many of the formal exercises that captivated American architects of the 1960s. Shortly thereafter, the Perkins & Will Partnership sited a tower for U.S. Gypsum diagonally on a corner plot in Chicago. Robert Venturi's Chestnut Hill house (1962) had already used a diagonal entry plan "to relate to directional space." Venturi & Rauch's small medical office buiding for Drs. Varga and Brigio in Bridgeton, New Jersey (see p. 263), has chamfered corners and a zigzagging entry. And at the same time Alexander Girard was working in interior design with his patterns-on-patterns of rotated

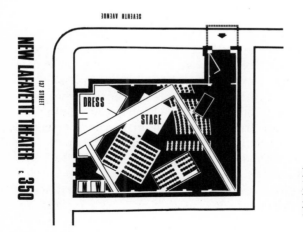

Hardy Holzman
Pfeiffer: Plan, New
Lafayette Theatre,
New York City. 1968.

squares. Detroit architects Meathe-Kessler designed a courtroom that was laid out on the bias. And Hardy Holzman Pfeiffer Associates rang a series of changes on diagonal interior plans for theatre seating layouts—at Simon's Rock College, the New Lafayette Theatre, and elsewhere—and in many house plans.

Walter A. Netsch of Skidmore, Owings & Merrill, Chicago, designed his Field Theory buildings, resulting in elaborate plans and roofs of diagonals that resemble origami. In his Art and Architecture Building (1969) for the Chicago Circle Campus of the University of Illinois, Netsch designed prismatic, crystalline space-frame windows that are jewels of diagonal architecture. Harry Weese's Christian Science Church in Chicago (1968), an otherwise clean and pure travertine temple, shows diagonal fenestration details—some of the revolutionary's blood pulses through that International Style architect's veins. Even those leaders in Miesian and Minimal interiors, Knoll International, turned in 1969 to diagonal plans for the firm's new Boston and New York show-rooms by Gae Aulenti.

In 1966, Barnstone & Aubry designed the New York offices of Schlumberger Limited with a plan of diagonal partitions that gave greater importance and space to the corridors. What most catches the eye in the Schlumberger offices is the wide wiggle of diagonal walls that partition off the clerical cubicles from the circulation corridor. The walls are more than merely "in" like the twisting, frugging, wriggling dances of the period.

Howard Barnstone and Eugene Aubry:
Schlumberger Limited offices, New York City. 1966.

Around 1965 Bill N. Lacy with Ronald Beckman laid out variable partitions around drafting tables for the University of Tennessee in Knoxville, based on diagonal plans. Young Yale graduates Doug Michels and Bob Feild sited their unbuilt project, Paddock House, diagonally. They designed an administration building renovation in 1968 for Federal City College in Washington, D.C., that showed random diagonal-plan office partitioning around a free-form hallway. Their plan utilized diagonals not for extending vistas, but seemingly to scandalize and to contradict the established tradition.

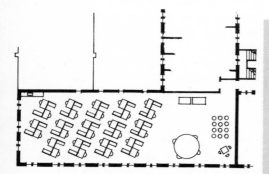

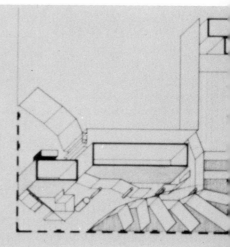

(*above*) Ronald Beckman and Bill N. Lacy: Plan, Architecture school drafting room, University of Tennessee, Knoxville. 1965. (*right*) Doug Michels and Bob Feild: Plan, Federal City College, Washington, D.C. 1968.

By the end of the decade, Skidmore, Owings & Merrill had produced the Alcoa Building in San Francisco and the John Hancock Center in Chicago with diagonal trusses for wind bracing that are exposed on the exterior like bridge design. And as the 1970s opened, the New York skyline was crowned with its monument to the shed-roof era: atop One Astor Plaza—the Times Square office tower designed by Der Scutt of Kahn & Jacobs/Hok—is a pinwheel of diagonal fins that rise from a low center to high points at the perimeter corners. Those forms, standing amid earlier skyscraper spires, epitomize the new design in their reversal of the historic center-peaked roof.

In 1972, Paul Rudolph completed his prismatic composition for the headquarters and research building of Burroughs Wellcome Company in Raleigh, North Carolina, with sloping structural columns, inward slanting windows, and sloping walls both inside and out. Like his scheme for the Central Library at Niagara, New York, the Burroughs Wellcome Building is a monument to the decade of the diagonal. Davis Brody & Associates in their Waterside Apartments and numerous other residential complexes in New York; Conklin & Rossant in their new town plan for Reston, Virginia, and in a series of apartment towers; Hardy Holz-

(*below*) Der Scutt of Kahn & Jacobs: One Astor Plaza, New York City. 1973. *Photograph by Norman McGrath.* (*right*) Paul Rudolph: Plan, Central Library, Niagara, New York. 1974. (*lower right*) Davis Brody & Associates: Waterside Apartments, New York City. 1962–1973. *Photograph by Robert Gray.*

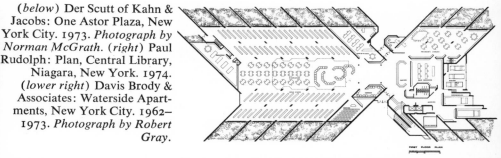

man Pfeiffer Associates in the Cincinnati condominium cluster The Cloisters; and scores of other architects—established firms as well as students—designed with diagonals in plan, in section, and in details for balconies, windows, and anywhere possible.

Berkeley art historian Spiro Kostof called it "raging diagonalism," Jaquelin Robertson called it "diagonalosis." To the supermannerist architects from Princeton, Pennsylvania, and Yale, the 45° angles that project from a building as monitors or snouts, wedges or slices, were called "zips" or "zaps"; at Penn they talked of "zoots" and "zots"—one being the male shape and the other the female; in California the 45° angle wall was often called a "zootwall." These produced explosive and joyful spatial experiences in many cases, but as often, the diagonals produced tight, pinched, squeezed spaces and shapes that were more painful than liberating. They had become a favorite motif that was early accused of being faddish but not so easily resisted by architects. It was clear, however, that the diagonals of the Supermannerists enforced movement through space, as the work of the early Mannerists had done. It could not be only accidental that the predominantly gray pietra da serena stone of Michelangelo's Laurenziana library, which is virtually without graining or veining, has, at the far end of the library in the door pediment, a white vein that shrieks startlingly across, lightninglike, on

(*left*) Michelangelo: Pediment detail, Laurenziana Library, Florence, Italy. 1524–1557. *Photograph by Guido Sansoni.*

(*below*) Hardy Holzman Pfeiffer Associates: The Cloisters, condominium cluster, Cincinnati, Ohio. 1971.

(*above*) Hardy Holzman Pfeiffer Associates: Section, children's rooms, Princeton, New Jersey. 1965. (*below*) Hardy Holzman Pfeiffer Associates, Reflected ceiling plan, children's rooms, Princeton, New Jersey. 1965.

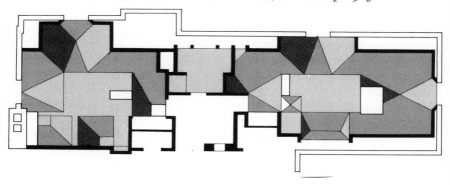

the diagonal. Or was it in fact accidental and therefore only coincidental with Mannerism in other periods?

Hip Ceiling for Two Pre-Mods

A picturesque, almost Gothic, almost Tudor house in Princeton, New Jersey, began flipping its lid in 1965, not only because of the two miniswingers aged nine and eleven who ruled the attic floor, but also because of its new ceiling, which resembled one of those folded paper swans that flaps its wings. The ceiling was a diagonal aesthetic game with facets by Hardy Holzman Pfeiffer Associates. The plaster goes up and down in pyramidal and trapezoidal shapes of various dimensions; some are steep and high to negotiate dormers, some low and wide to contain other functions; two are towerlike to accommodate monitors, which Hugh Hardy called "light grabbers." The monitor that faces north is adjacent to one that has a southern exposure; together, they present a cool-fire demonstration of the contrasts in color between light from the north and light from the south.

As Hugh Hardy explained,

> If there's one thing people are doing now who are seriously inter-
> ested in making those bizarre shapes, it's not the bizarre shapes
> themselves, it's that this generation is trying to get out of boxes.
> The generation that preceded us stripped a lot away, which was a de-
> struction of the box, but the limits within which they did it always
> included the floor and ceiling. This generation is doing it much dif-
> ferently: the world now is made entirely of diagonals. What we're
> trying to do is to bust out of the confinement of a static space—to go
> as far as we can to created spaces that are ambiguous, that don't end,
> that become something else. With the monumental—the static stuff—
> we're bored; it telegraphs to us, because when you come to the middle
> you can see the end. Here, we bent over backwards to exploit some-
> thing that is constantly shifting and moving and changing.

No diagonal drawn in the 1960s was such a clear statement of
rebellion against the past as Project Argus, a glittering, ambiguous room-
within-a-room that Charles Moore, then the chairman of the architecture department at Yale, sprawled diagonally across the jury room in
Paul Rudolph's Art and Architecture Building in 1968. Reflecting confusingly in silver from the stripes of naked fluorescent tubes, Project Argus was designed by Moore, F. R. R. Drury, and Kent Bloomer of Yale's
faculty and built by students to provide an "open-ended experimental
atmosphere," Yale officials said, presumably in contrast to Rudolph's

Charles Moore, F. R. R. Drury,
and Kent Bloomer: Project Argus, Yale School of
Architecture, New Haven, Connecticut. 1968. *Photograph by Joel Katz.*

Paul Rudolph: Plan,
Art and Architecture
Building, New Haven,
Connecticut. 1963.

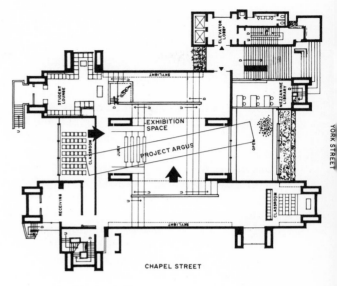

"closed" exploded-pinwheel-plan structure. Project Argus housed and reflected film clips and an all-white light show, by Pulsa, the New Haven lighting design group. The lighting was meticulously controlled, and surely the most tidily designed light show of the decade. The pulses, both aural and visual, and the flashing superimpositions inflicted a dazzling bombardment. The diagonal plan and the heavier, wider-at-the-top elevations were forcefully symbolic of the Third Generation of Modern Architects' rebellion in the 1960s.

No building was such a paradigm of the course of the 1960s as Paul Rudolph's Yale Art and Architecture Building. From 1963, when it opened, to 1972, a decade later, it had made a full orbit around the far, dark side of rejection and defacement and had returned to its originally lauded launching pad. The vicissitudes were saddening. When the A & A Building opened with a fete and distinguished international architects, critics, and historians in attendance, it was admired for all the elements of the mainstream of 1950s architecture—monumentality, texture, taste, manipulation of space, and totality of design. Though it was too early to tell, the building also exhibited most of the elements of the new design that was to burst on the scene in the next year or two. Younger critics praised the daring, the complexity, the use of uncommon materials, and historical fragments.

The plan—an orbiting pinwheel—is ambiguous, confusing, complex. The furnishings are proto-Pop: freighter cargo nets as window coverings, exposed spotlights in the lighting system. A & A also has a witty, mannerist demonstration of the strength of materials in a pair of wood capitals supported on attenuated slender metal-pipe columns; it reveals an interest in interstices in its hollow columns used as return ducts; and historical allusions and found objects are seen throughout in plaster-cast fragments of Donatello, della Robbia, and Sullivan, whose wrought-iron grilles from the Chicago Stock Exchange elevators are used as entrance gates to the art library. Applied ornament is accepted in these items and in the texture of the concrete, which was variously referred to as "collegiate shetland," "tweed," and, as Peter Andes called it, "monumental seersucker." The use of those terms at the time of the opening indicated the divided enthusiasm that the building provoked. Immediately the student painters and sculptors rebelled against the functional aspects of their studios, pelted the exterior with eggs, punctured windows with bullets, and threatened to picket the opening ceremonies. (This spirit preceded the Free Speech movement demonstration at Berkeley in 1964.) At the same time the distinguished assembly of international architects, critics, and historians praised the personal, expressionistic plasticity and complexity that could excite the imaginations of the young who were to study there. "Imaginations" and rebellion!

Two years later in 1966, when Paul Rudolph had left Yale and Charles Moore had assumed the chairmanship of the architecture department, students rejected the "too rigid" drafting carrels, and rebelled more generally against what they considered the dominating personality of the spaces. In 1968, five years after the building had opened, students and faculty collaborated in introducing Project Argus, which they considered a direct rejection, if not a repudiation, of Rudolph's design. However much Rudolph and the designers of Project Argus both considered the construction as the nadir of the Art and Architecture Building's reputation and respectability, Argus was only slightly more ambiguous than the A & A spaces had seemed in 1963 when they were new; the sensations were surprisingly similar, although Argus was clearly more jazzy and frenetic. During the next two years, this rebellion rose to heights or depths of defacement, depending on one's vantage point. Students and junior faculty members splashed the walls and floors with Magic Markers and spray cans of paint. Discussion, confrontation, and general unrest about the building as well as about the curriculum offered within it continued. Finally, in June 1969, the two upper stories were mysteriously gutted by fire. Although Yale authorities eventually dismissed charges of arson and found that there were no signs of malicious intent, the student painters and architects moved out to work elsewhere. Then came the ultimate defacement—the fire damage was repaired by an architect other than Rudolph, and in a way that can, at the kindest, be called insensitive.

Ironically, at that time, students were avidly espousing open-ended planning, ambiguity, found objects, Pop, and personalized, nonregimented environments that had what they considered greater freedom; they seemed to espouse all the things that the A & A Building had, at first, seemed such an archetype of. Then in the early 1970s, when student activism had quieted somewhat, or was directed into other areas, the A & A Building was gradually reoccupied and accepted by students and faculty alike. It was being rediscovered; early in 1972, a decade after it opened, a Yale architecture school calendar indicated that students, or at least the calendar editor, Henry Wooman, recognized "the heart of this monument of American architecture . . . the ferocious nobility and grandeur . . . concerned with an ideal . . . richer because of it. We are aware of the fact that we are in confrontation with the heart of monumental architecture, a statement of human spirit and a material manifestation of an ideal of human culture." The orbit had been completed; the wheel had come full circle. The A & A Building was accepted as it had been in 1963.

The House on Its Side

"Say, man, why did you build it on its side?," asked a guy who climbed up to the site of a house on Maple Hill outside of Plainfield, Vermont. It was designed and built in the summer of 1968 by Houston's Southcoast design group, including Kenneth Carbajal, Kelly Gloger, and John Gilbert. "Oh baby, baby, you are not going to believe this one," they crowed. The house is a three-dimensional exploitation of the diagonal—the diagonal gone cubic—it sits like a cracker box balancing precariously on one edge. Inside, too, the topsy-turvy house is turned on its ear, completely disorienting, permissive, and ambiguous. Diagonal walls and ceiling, with both horizontally and diagonally laid siding, make it hard to tell which way is up, what is wall or ceiling, or floor. When you lean back against the outward sloping wall and look up, suddenly the wall is going the other way, soaring inward to a twenty-four-foot ridge. At the

section thru studio   section thru bed/above eat live/below

Southcoast Design:
House, Plainfield, Ver-
mont. 1968. *Photo-
graph by Norman
McGrath.*

Southcoast Design:
Sections, house, Plain-
field, Vermont. 1968.

ends of the house, windows set on the diagonal are cut *enfilade,* as if a
six-foot-square solid had rammed through the full length of the house,
shaping the tops of doorways and leaving an invisible rod on which the
entire house is hung. The designers' avowed premise for this balancing

act is that the annual snowfall in Vermont made a steep pitched roof mandatory, but they removed that idea far from the hackneyed A-frame.

In the new design, the house on its side has a somewhat transitional place. On the one hand, the exterior suggests diagonal packaging, a box set on one edge, which is a paradoxical approach for a generation so opposed to packagers and so dedicated to exploding the box. On the other hand, the section was not arrived at by adopting a preconceived envelope, and the interior, with its remarkable effects of disorientation, is clearly a product of the new generation.

Nor was architecture the only field in which the diagonal made prominent appearances. In painting and sculpture, and whatever conjunctions of the two that modern artists could evolve, countless turns on the diagonal were effected. Jack Youngerman and others rotated their square canvases to search out new symmetries and to burst the limits of the canvas. Graphic artists by the dozens slipped prints and photographs on the diagonal to make readers and viewers move their heads as well as their eyes. John Hejduk and Robert Slutsky collected an exhibition for the Architectural League of New York on "The Diamond in Architecture and Painting" in 1967, and used a rotated square for the graphic imagery of their posters and fliers.

What all these "zips and zaps" of shed roofs and diagonal projections really indicated was a search for a new perspective. Architects and

John Hejduk and Robert Slutsky: Poster for "The Diamond in Architecture and Painting" exhibition, New York City. 1967.

artists gave it new dimension in the 1960s. Jiro Takamatsu built large-scale platforms that created comic-strip-like environments based on exaggerations of Renaissance perspective. (Michelangelo, after all, had planned the Campidoglio along a forced perspective.) Sven Lukin and Ron Davis created works of enormous force through precise draftsmanship with one-point and three-point perspective.

The Supermannerists' 45° angle monitors, domes, "light grabbers," and their shed roofs with high clerestory windows blasted the occupants' visions off into outer space—"rocketed the vision of the vanishing point along 12,000 times faster," as Hugh Newell Jacobsen said. The diagonals of Supermannerism stretched man's vision, not inward—as a pair of peaked shed roofs does—but outward through flopped or inverted peaks, and through clerestories. The Supermannerists looked out to a divinity in the sky—whether it was a god or a man in space was not entirely distinguishable.

Whereas Renaissance, Mannerist, and Baroque architects and painters, from Bramante to Michelangelo and Bernini, relied on perspective to convey an illusion of reality, the new painters and architects used it to place man somewhere between illusion and reality. In particular, "bird's-eye perspective," which employs three vanishing points instead of one, placed man in midair aboard some orbiting satellite, it gave him a new view of the world, and permitted him to see the dual scale that Supermannerism revealed.

Even the superclassical Minimalists were playing with diagonals by the end of the decade—I. M. Pei, the arch-Minimalist, used them in the Choate School's Fine Arts Center plan and section, in Wallingford, Connecticut, in his siting of Boston's wind-struck John Hancock Tower, and in his J. F. Kennedy Library, proposed for Boston.

SPONTANEITY

Besides sprouting out of the box with a diagonal, zigzag, ziggurat mushrooming dare, Supermannerism is permissive and perverse with regard to the process of architecture. It grants acceptance to the accidentals of design. It is a laissez-faire attitude of letting things happen in the design process as the situations spontaneously generate themselves. It permits us to include confusion and disorder, error and contingency decisions, and open-endedness. It permits architects to reject or to omit as many preconceptions as possible.

Unlike the Minimal style, Supermannerism does not attempt to hide such necessary elements as plumbing, wiring, and air conditioning, but attempts to make a design virtue of them, literally "letting it all hang out," much as the new generation aimed for in their life-styles. Attention is on process of design rather than on architectural product, as is outlined in "An Inclusive Process."

To those with more established architectural tastes, chance and indeterminacy do not seem to be real elements of art. They call it "an approval of the makeshift." To the new breed of young designers, spontaneity and self-determination are more realistic attitudes. As California artist William T. Wiley was quoted in *Time,* "chance and blind illogic play roles in art as well as in life."

Like the accidents of Action painting, of assemblage and drip in the work of Jackson Pollock and Yves Klein, like the Happenings of the New Theatre, and the apparent spontaneity that the wiggling, jiggling, jerky images of the hand-held camera and *cinéma vérité* techniques brought to the new movies, all the arts of the decade seemed to investigate chance and indeterminacy, the accidentals of production.

Accidents and randomness were part of the spirit of accepting change and mobility. From 1952, the time of John Cage's "unnamed event" at Black Mountain College in North Carolina to the Happenings of Allan Kaprow, Claes Oldenburg, and other artists throughout the 1960s, sculptors and painters programmed unstructured events, paintings, and sculpture. And the idea had precedent—Harold Rosenberg in *The De-Definition of Art* wrote that "accident is a fifty year old technique for evoking art."

Young architects adopted the device. Theirs were architectural happenings. David Sellers designed a float for a 1966 Fourth of July parade that started out as a truck full of lumber pulling an empty hay wagon on which there were eight guys with hammers, saws, and other tools. "When the parade started at 10 am, we were smack in the middle behind the band; we designed and constructed two buildings on the hay wagon from scratch. We had a generator on the truck and ran electric saws. The buildings were game booths that were used at the parade grounds after the parade." It was an architectural happening on wheels.

Doug Michels, whose proffering of chaos as a design goal prompted Catholic University administrators to reassign him from design courses to history courses, proposed to teach Mies's architectural theory by taking his students to a parking lot, placing them on a ten-foot grid, and running zigzag among them, as if he were skiing a slalom course, and whispering "Mies van der Rohe, Mies van der Rohe." It was a happening in architectural education. Among other architectural happenings were the countless architecture festivals concocted at schools throughout the 1960s. Like the rock music festivals of recent years at Woodstock and Watkins Glen, which were live-in musical happenings, architecture schools staged vigorous and imaginative seminars in a new style and with new names to match: "Arch-A-Week," "Time Slice," "The Electronic Oasis," "Sonic Mirage," "Infinity Feedback," "Enviro Lab," "Astro Daze," "ARF," "Globe City," and "Life Raft Earth."

The young designers acclaim the unfixed situation. They acclaim the building process itself as a source of design inspiration. Some of them claim that they allow things to happen as they go. Ostensibly, it is not planned and ordered like the conceptions of the preceding decade. Their aim is to get beneath the veneer of the creative process, to seize the seeds of architectural ideas and encourage germination and growth. By improvisational methods, by permitting things to happen on the site rather than designing fixed drawings, the new attitude allows architects to see what the design elements themselves are generating. Charles Moore at Yale championed visual techniques other than the rendering or the typical plan. Isometric sections are sometimes the only drawings made for a contractor by some of the young Turks. Randomness is the basic imagery behind rigidly manipulated schemes by more established architects, too, although spontaneity could not be a final effect of the more permanent concrete and steel construction.

Spontaneity goes with the work of young architects involved personally in the joy of building, the joy of creation, who are rediscovering the fun and games of architecture and building, of improvising new solutions during on-site construction, of calculating tactile surprises and imaginative detailing. What they praise is the virtue of the building process as a source of inspiration, and the virtue of allowing things to happen when they do.

Among the 1960s architects to accept spontaneity were many from Yale, Washington University at Saint Louis, and the University of Houston. As Ringo Rienecke explained, "When you have a joist that you put in that happens to be six feet too long, and you put them all in, and there are some others going the other way, they may start to develop something." "Then you can see what they are generating," Sellers added. "For instance, interior siding has to do with a visual impression entirely, so you can nail the boards up and leave spaces between them so you can see the silver insulation through; you can use boards of different thicknesses, and that's ok, too."

Charles Hosford, another Yale-trained architect, said of the numerous design changes that occurred throughout the process of constructing a ski house in Maine (1968), "My bewilderment from large and small discoveries became a habit-forming state of mind. I discovered that when the limits of a particular construction method or available material were reached, this situation produced feedback to the design process, and the information challenged me to push beyond the normal limits."

Another Yale architect who worked at Prickly Mountain, Vermont, Louis Mackall, said, "It took about two months to design my house and when I got through all I had was a cardboard model, and the only drawing I needed at the time was a foundation plan." When Hardy Holzman Pfeiffer Associates designed the Hadley house (1967) on Martha's Vineyard, Massachusetts, Malcolm Holzman said, "If we had planned some spaces consciously, they wouldn't have happened that way. Although the house is complex, the working drawings were minimal. The builder was handed two sheets: one containing floor plans, sections, and elevations; the other, electrical specifications, rough dimensions for the fireplace, and layout of the kitchen. The remainder was left to the contractor." Hardy added, "If the volumes are strong enough, virile enough, the details are less important. There are no sixteenth-century anatomical drawings for joints in this house."

The construction process of Southcoast's "House on Its Side" (1968) in Plainfield, Vermont, also illustrated a design commune's espousal of spontaneity. The house was built in two months so that Paul Nelson and his wife could have a base for his poetry teaching and writing at nearby Goddard College. In the construction process, the architects say that they "freely" followed the will of the materials available. They had no plans or sections, no working drawings, only a cardboard model to follow. "So we began to develop a feeling for what was actually happening," Kenneth Carbajal observed. Details, devised as they went along, were based on the most simple and straightforward solutions—and the most inspirational fun. "When we were deciding where to put a nail," designer Carbajal recalled, "we said, 'Well, nobody's looking, so we'll just put a whole circle of nails around.' " Client Judy Nelson elected as her own design thing to staple on the exposed black Rolex electrical wiring in a sculptural manner. As a result, the permissive design accidentals built up to enliven the Nelson's environment, and the do-it-yourself activist goal of the designers also lured the clients' involvement.

"If you have something drawn and you do all the cutting and planning," Bill Rienecke had said, "you wouldn't learn what the elements are doing themselves." "What can come out of this is another way of designing," Sellers noted.

> It might be possible to design the seed of a building; then, if you can take the simplest most important thing and call it the seed, the building may just generate itself. It is a growth process; it starts with nothing and it evolves. Improvisation is, I think, something that an architect does on a drafting board, and I think he does so with a high degree of inefficiency. When you do it on the site, all of its aspects are revealed, and any order that it sets up is automatically evident.

It was a generative style.

"What we learn from the Nelson house," Carbajal said,

> is that all the working drawings and busy work that an architectural office feels it has to go through is a waste—and the client has to pay for it. This busy work is only something to give an architect confidence and to produce a better image for his audience. Working drawings should not be necessary for small projects if an architect supervises closely and if he knows his contractor.

The spontaneous designs of 1960s architects are best described in terms of construction details. The examples, even if not all of timeless significance, demonstrate forcefully the element of permissive spontaneity. In constructing Charles Moore's New Haven house, when a tube was cut through over the kitchen, an old joist with square holes in it was uncovered. "We liked it and left it," Moore said. He also left part of the tube that covered a light switch and outlets, but simply cut a hole in it so the unit could be got at. Robert Venturi's best-known permissively

---

(*clockwise starting top left*) MLTW/Moore-Turnbull: Detail, Moore house interior, New Haven, Connecticut. 1966. *Photograph by Maud Dorr.*
MLTW/Moore-Turnbull: Detail, Moore house interior, New Haven, Connecticut. 1966. *Photograph by Maud Dorr.*   Venturi & Rauch: Stair, house, Chestnut Hill, Pennsylvania. 1962. *Photograph by Rollin R. La France.*   Venturi & Rauch: Partial plan, house, Chestnut Hill, Pennsylvania. 1962.

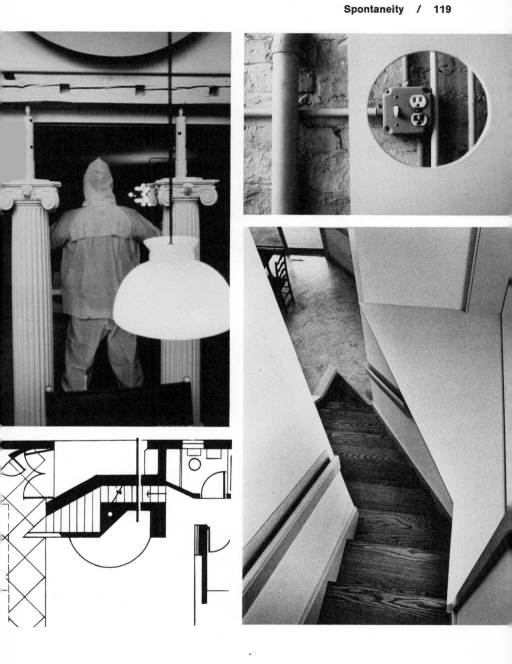

spontaneous work is the main stair of the Chestnut Hill house (1962). It runs between the fireplace and the front door and accommodates itself both to the fixed fireplace form on the one side and to the needs of the front door on the other side, for more generous width. Consequently, the stair ends up as a special "nonformalized" shape that was spontaneously induced by the conditions of its surroundings; its form is determined by the interstice between the two walls. In the same house, the rain leader that plunges haphazardly across the facade, does so, Venturi said, because "Life is like this," adding that there cannot be a single order to cover everything because there will always be something that won't fit.

The year before he finished architecture school at Yale in 1968, Louis Mackall designed and built a house for himself and his wife at Prickly Mountain, Vermont, that showed his involvement in the permissive, chance happening. Around the predetermined nucleus of a stairway with courses set at 45° angles, the house grew, accidentally its designer said, with spaces opening vertically off the stair landings. The section was multilayered and had a vertical emphasis, as might be expected from a student working in Rudolph's Art and Architecture Building at Yale, and with Charles Moore. Mackall also allowed a number of other seemingly spontaneous design solutions to occur in that house: ceiling lights that illuminate the open, balconylike spaces on several levels are controlled by a continuous rope pull that hangs down through all five levels of the stairwell; the circuit-breaker panel is prominently accessible near the entrance and serves as an allover electrical control box for the entire house. Mackall also made an innovation in plumbing—venting directly into the roof leaders through an inverted U, with the idea that warm air from the vents would keep the leaders from freezing and that the curved connection would prevent backup. And what was most expressive of the tyro-architect's desire to experiment and do it himself was his placement of the furnace, which he exposed on an open platform in the stairwell where he could work on it himself in light and air rather than in an awkward crawl space.

Other houses at the six-hundred-acre Prickly Mountain tract show Mackall, Sellers, Rienecke, and other young architects breaking out of the box into an aggressively diagonal world and putting un-common materials at the service of common functions in whimsical, sometimes witty, sometimes ambiguous, and always permissive ways. They constructed their own designs, letting them grow from isometric drawings through processes of accommodating the accidentals of design. The Tack House (1965), a sprouting pyramid designed by Sellers and Rienecke, was used as office, drafting room, and living quarters for the designers until it was destroyed by fire in 1970, and then remodeled. It started with an ordinary gable roof and grew up at one corner into a tassel of triangular windows and colored panels around a crow's-nest sleeping loft. The gable roof was a vertical extension with a cutout for a terrace and a window on the north elevation. On the east and west under the gable roof the traditional box was cut back and pierced so that it looked as if the roof were sitting on a discontinuous plinth. As a permissive, whimsical, and overtly honest expression of structure, the central column that supports the roof is brought down and exposed at its base by a square opening cut through the ceiling of the lower-level drafting room; it was supported by a steel bracket. This is another satiric jab at the proponents of functionalism. Heating pipes and plastic plumbing and soil lines also ran exposed through the ceiling opening and across the drafting room, as an expression of permissive freedom more than for decorative effect. (Fortunately they were not transparent pipes.)

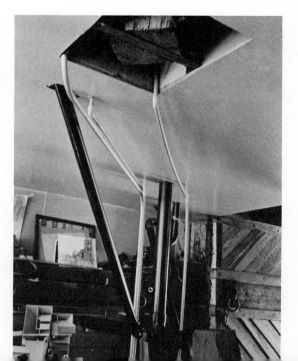

David Sellers and William Rienecke: Tack House, Prickly Mountain, Warren, Vermont. 1966. *Photograph by David Hirsch.*

In the Tack House, also, old farm-country objects were put to new uses: a rake became a tie rack; the sink was a block of wood left over after a salad bowl had been scooped out of it. The conditions of installing both plumbing and wiring also produced spontaneous design solutions at Prickly Mountain, where Sellers let his metal electrical conduit run exposed along walls and ceilings sometimes to achieve sculptural effects. In his Prickly Mountain Bridge House (1967) the conduit produces a frame of modern molding around the kitchen cooking area and, near the switch, also serves as a rack for potlids; outlet boxes sculpturally beckon to be used. In the bathroom the conduit is the shower curtain rod (I hope it will never short-circuit).

With an economy of means Hugh and Tiziana Hardy hung a kind of modern whatnot composed of shadow boxes: the smallest possible angle irons were screwed to the wall and left exposed; similarly, the electric cable for the lighted boxes was strung loosely, spontaneously, as the function required. Hardy explained, permissively, "Why not?" Not so permissively, one shelter magazine published a photograph of the wall group in full color, but retouched it to avoid showing the wires.

Hugh Hardy: Detail, apartment interior,
New York City. 1966. *Photograph by Louis Reens.*

Critics of the idea of accidentals and spontaneous improvisation point out that on-site improvisation is possible only in small-scale projects. Their strongest criticism, however, is that this permissive spontaneity can create only the kind of mess that the International Style crusaded to clean up. "Now wait a minute," Sellers objected, "I think there is a big difference between what we're doing and what they revolted against. We may pitch a roof because it is more economical and efficient, but also so that when you're at the top of your building you know you're at the top. And these are real things—how you live—rather than what somebody is going to think of the thing as a picture."

Historically, in ages of great investigation and discovery, craft is seldom refined, however. And it is true that the International Style "cleaned things up" for purely visual reasons, whereas this permissiveness lets things happen for people, for the psychological and physical requirements of the user. Ultimately, the untidy horrors of spontaneity, like the horrors of some assemblage sculpture, will be enjoyed for their acceptance of the reality of the architectural situation, for their joy in tactile surprises, and for their visual richness. Yet five years after the rush of rugged-mess, especially at Prickly Mountain, that highly touted spontaneity resembled the decrepitude and debris of any country outbuilding of a nature-oppressed mountaineer.

Some of the attempts to achieve spontaneity of design and construction in the 1960s were merely contrived pretenses of chance, and they are immediately identifiable as such. But their designers are not to be too severely blamed for their attempts. In architecture, unlike musical performance, the possibilities of freezing spontaneous accidents into permanency reach a virtual impasse. The idea of spontaneity, of chance and indeterminacy, was necessary to liberate architects from their ideas of static, "frozen music" and to let them pursue solutions to a mobile, changeable architecture.

The dewy-eyed surprise of the young 1960s designers as they learned how buildings grow was unquestionably naïve. If Americans had not been paying so much attention to the mean population age and the so-called population explosion, the "young generation" and the "under-thirties" might not have impressed us with their surprise and claims for spontaneity. It would be easy to ridicule the "eureka" that young architecture students exclaimed—as if they had suddenly recognized they had been speaking prose all their lives. But they did express it to themselves, to their clients, and to their society as they crossed the new frontiers of design in the 1960s.

CHAOS

The Design Establishment immediately decried the new approach with the satirical slogan "Mess is more." The crusading retort of the younger generation was "Down with uptight design." They continued to move from an attitude of mere permissiveness to one of accepting chaos as an aesthetic goal. In an age of aggressive ugliness in clothes, relentless cacophony in music, and squalor as an art form, chaos as an aesthetic goal reflects the intellectual and social attitudes of our time.

"There is no particular advantage to chaos," Philip Johnson said, "but that's where we are." "It is a matter of allowing dirt into the system or keeping it out," Charles Moore explained. And educator Robert Metcalf said, "This expression is not an attempt to create chaos; rather it is another way of ordering and organizing." "It is very controlled chaos," Cesar Pelli noted, "the disorder is in the right place."

Chaos as a goal has a carefully prescribed purpose. It accepts the rabbit warrens of actual life-styles, the vital mess and the messy vitality of great American cities, as Jane Jacobs described them. It accepts helter-skelter patterns based on historical traditions or habit, as Reyner Banham explained the transportation growth of Los Angeles.

If some designers accept chaos as an aesthetic goal, another group accepts chaos as a system. In two design areas for example—office planning and graphics—systematic chaos is accepted, *developed* to bring out the inclusive vitality of human endeavor. The office planning system is called "office landscape"; graphics will follow.

Office landscape, an established major current in office planning during the decade, proffers visual chaos as a means toward functional order. A method of office planning, originating in Germany, office landscape is is based, like American office planning, on studies of work flow, communication, and circulation. In contrast to the typical American rectilinear layout of furniture, however, it produces irregular arrangements. To the American eye, the results of this planning look like primitive, outrageous, free-form chaos, which architecture historian Walter C. Kidney called "office jungle, office chaos, or office finger-painting." As Edgar Kaufmann, Jr., explained the reality of office land-

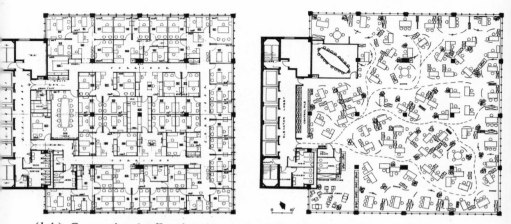

(*left*) Conventional office layout proposed for du Pont's Freon Division, Wilmington, Delaware. 1966. (*right*) Quickborner Team: Office-landscape plan, du Pont's Freon Division, Wilmington, Delaware. 1967.

scape: "Clustering is the pattern of human life; regularity is the pattern of theory." To the designers who espouse chaos, the results of office landscape are exonerated by the fact that actual uses by people are the true and proper determinants of its organized—or disorganized—design.

Office landscape was originated by the German furniture manufacturing firm, Eberhard and Wolfgang Schnelle, much as American office planning had been refined by Knoll International (formerly Knoll Associates) during the 1950s. The office-landscape system first came to America by way of several European architecture magazines—*Baumeister* and *Architectural Review*—and was introduced to architects in this country by an article I wrote for *Progressive Architecture* in 1964. Another early office-landscape designer was Sweden's Sven Kai-Larsen. From 1965 to 1967, while the organization that had originated the system in Germany continued to promote their work, by way of their American unit—the Quickborner Team—some American planning firms, mostly based in New York, were scandalized by the new chaos. They carried on a loud magazine war about the merits and/or absurdities of the system. Yet three years later, the first actual office landscape in America, designed by the Quickborner Team, was occupied by the du Pont Company's Freon Division in Wilmington, Delaware, in September 1967. In March 1968, John Hancock Mutual Life Insurance Company

Quickborner Team: Office landscape, du Pont's Freon Division, Wilmington, Delaware. 1967. *Photograph by Louis Reens.*

opened a Quickborner-designed "landscape" in Boston, and by midsummer 1968, office landscapes were springing up for Eastman Kodak in Rochester, for the New York Port Authority, and elsewhere. And American designers were adopting the idea too.

Despite the revolutionary appearance of its "messy" plans, office landscape aims primarily at an environment that will evoke greater work efficiency. It also aims at a more intensive and more economical use of space. Since the irregular furniture arrangements of office-landscape planning make rectilinear spaces impossible, the fixed metal and glass partitions that were such a pivotal part of office planning in the 1950s and the early 1960s are not used. Instead, low, movable screens—supplemented by file cabinets, wardrobes, and planters—separate work areas and provide visual privacy. These low partitions (usually around five feet high) make the floor more flexible and can utilize space more intensively, since a good deal of the circulation space required within departments can be shared by the circulation space between adjacent departments. The screens and the open plan also give more office workers a view of the windows. And lastly, office-landscape planners maintain that the visual privacy provided by glazed partitions is no greater than that provided by no partitions at all.

However, without partitions, office-landscape plans are threatened with a chaos of sound. Therefore, several new acoustical devices were proposed to keep noise levels down in offices. In addition to ceilings and screens that are acoustically treated, carpeting is used throughout the floor and ceilings are kept low to shorten sound paths. Acoustical "perfume" or white sound is added to deaden the intrusions of conversations and machines.

Office landscape, like Supermannerism, justifies itself on psychological grounds. This was something of a breakthrough at the time, although designers had been discussing the additional benefits of better environments and had been decrying the fact that inadequate research had been done in this area for some years. Office landscape also posits a chaos of movement: when faces and movement are constantly visible, there is no distraction through singular action. The idea is similar to feeling all alone in a crowd. The tenet of office landscape, then, is that when everything is distracting, nothing is distracting. Chaos is encouraged at all levels.

Among the first American designers to work with the German system, the Research and Design Institute (REDE) in Providence, Rhode Island (1966), devised an office landscape of salvaged balustrades, improvised screens and desks, and old Mission Oak furniture for the institute's headquarters. The combination of found objects and office-landscape chaos was singularly REDE's. Of the coordinated furniture and partition systems designed along office-landscape ideas, the most sophisticated and adaptable was the system developed from the theories and specifications of Robert Probst by Herman Miller, Inc. Called Action Office II, Probst's furniture system allows a worker options in the ways he can work—standing as well as seated, on high stools as well as low soft chairs, at multitables instead of single desks. But office landscape was only one kind of office chaos.

Research and Design Institute (REDE): REDE office landscape, Providence, Rhode Island. 1966. *Photo collage by Eugene Dwiggins.*

Chaos in the Drafting Room

At first in architecture schools and later in architects' offices, drafting rooms were chaotically rearranged into scramble-plan or multileveled rabbit warrens and rustic carrels. Others were painted with camouflage techniques that curiously identified and singled out work spaces. These two approaches differ in that one directly creates spaces in answer to the specific work requirements of each individual, whereas the other provides a kind of visual perfume that attempts to float an entire envelope or partitioned-off space away, and thereby isolates workers from the mass distractions.

One of the early, clear examples of this loosening-up—"free, loose, and cool" were the words of the young—occurred when the first School of Architecture at the University of Tennessee in Knoxville opened in 1965. As their initial lesson, students joined faculty in turning their hands to a do-it-yourself instant partition-and-furniture system and built their own school interior spaces to fit their own curriculum needs. What this produced was a zigzagging open plan of freestanding partitions and a spider's web of overhead wires hanging from ceiling outlets to Luxo lamps on the partition-hung drafting tables. Along with the individualized space of each occupant, the scramble slum of wires generated a scene with a totally different aesthetic from that of the previous decade. This random, flexible happening appealed to the new dean, Bill N. Lacy, whose live-wire ideas on architecture were subsequently put into national action while he was director of the National Endowment for the Arts' program on architecture and environmental design. "Architectural education at its best has been a sort of adult Montessori, changing as faculty changed," Lacy observed at the opening of the Tennessee school. So he needed a "system of space organizing elements that could be easily rearranged to accommodate the nature of the class and the individual student's working habits." He found sympathetic collaboration in Ronald Beckman, director of REDE in Providence, Rhode Island, and in Robert Probst, director of research for Herman Miller, Inc. To fulfill all the requirements of a changing curriculum and to permit students to rearrange the "space-organizing elements" themselves, they evolved a system that was half furniture and half wall. It was a hybrid system that brings the wall into the realm of movable furniture. Panels arranged in a U-plan, in an L-plan, in a Z-plan, and in pinwheel clusters could be slid around the loft space, furniture still attached, to form new arrangements in the space of an afternoon. The designers called them

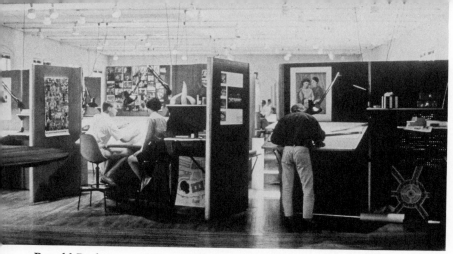

Ronald Beckman and Robert Probst, with Bill N. Lacy: Architecture school drafting room, University of Tennessee, Knoxville. 1965. *Photograph by Bill N. Lacy.*

"skiddable walls." The focus was on do-it-yourself flexibility, but the aesthetic implications of its permissive chaos were inescapable (see plan, p. 104).

In the spring of 1967, students at the Massachusetts Institute of Technology's department of architecture, overnight, turned one of their design studios into an instant *barriada* by subdividing it with salvage timber and concrete blocks. Administrators were outraged by the chaos of the design as much as by the unauthorized activism. Donlyn Lyndon, who was appointed head of the department the next fall, gained the administration's agreement for some of the students to involve themselves officially in subdividing, building, painting, and personalizing all their design studios as "space/use workshops." The resulting spaces resembled a demolition site, with more salvaged lumber and concrete blocks. New mezzanines up among the ceiling fixtures and head-menacing beams provided additional work spaces above the floor-level areas. At the entry to MIT's first-year studio, a peace movement sign appropriately proclaimed, "Destroy America to Save It." The salvation of this work by the students was to loosen up the areas and give them "use form." Students thereby became involved in construction earlier than usual in the frustrating four-year period of drawing projects without building them. (See photo, p. 27.)

Similarly, at the University of Texas at Austin, in 1968, fifth-year students partitioned their design studio and painted it with bold colors and stripes that leaped openings and overlapped into adjoining spaces. Cutouts and stripes fused the different planes into a streaked chaos. And at the University of Houston, instant mezzanines, ladders, and partitions were erected by fifth-year thesis students to fit their work patterns and life-styles.

By the end of the decade the chaos concept had found its way into open-planned schools—wall-less as well as gradeless—and into hospital planning and design.

Garblegraphics

Graphics gave designers in the 1960s their widest, mass-experience outlets for chaos. An immediate, accessible, small-scale design area, graphics epitomized the permissive rebellion and "do your own thing" involvement of the decade. That impulse to involve yourself and those you want to communicate with more completely led to chaotic and seeming amateurism in magazine layouts, advertising, posters, and most other graphic design. In opposition to the slick, machinelike conformity that had become a symbol of the Establishment, newspapers and magazines developed an apparently insatiable desire for the new graphics and the new outlook. If the new was good and improvement was better, revolution seemed the ultimate climax.

Architecture students were also exploring chaotic graphics because graphics were so much less fettered by the demands of practical requirements than architecture was. They created a messy, ugly, grab bag of graphic devices for posters, announcements, flyers, and broadsides that the older generations found virtually unreadable and undecipherable. This incommunicative communication technique was also applied to letter-and-envelope correspondence. It elaborated on the handcraft Mail Art of Ray Johnson. Most critics thought these games could be excused because they were considered disposable and obsolete on creation. And Mail Art is virtually "invisible" as an art form, but Chip Lord went further and called his own efforts in this area "trash art." Although this movement carried on investigations by Bauhaus and De Stijl graphics designers, what these newer designers produced in graphics shows the major influences of the decade: Pop art, Op art, the sexual revolution, the taste-decorum revolution, and a simultaneous use of them all.

The preceding decade had seen the rise of graphics firms as consultants to architects and the spread of comprehensive graphics and signage programs in large-scale building projects. Airports, office complexes, new towns, and city programs in the late 1950s aimed for a Minimalist purity and tastefulness in graphics and signs as exemplified by Swiss theories on graphic design. The typefaces Helvetica and Micro-Gramma prevailed. The reigning graphic style was High Helvetica.

Then, in the 1960s, the New York graphics design firm, Chermayeff & Geismar, added a new sign to The Museum of Modern Art that turned New Yorkers' heads—literally. It read from bottom to top with Helvetica letters on their sides, left to right if one turned one's head on end. It made looking at the museum like a trip to a record store to look at record jackets. That was the kind of cautious advance of the early decade, but it was also prototypical of the rebellion. The removal of that sign in 1970 and the substitution of banners epitomized the de-formalization of the decade.

Next came larger-than-traditional letters and numbers on signs, calendars, and posters. The Stendig furniture company's annual Christmas calendar, designed by Massimo Vignelli in 1967, veered toward superscale. Popular culture from childhood popped up in comic-book speech balloons—coming from the signatures of letters or from the faces on stamps. Ordinary found-in-the-office objects such as rubber stamps were repeatedly stamped, stamped, stamped across envelopes, letters, and posters—zigzagging, screeching for attention. Graphic elements of

Collage of garble-graphics and Mail Art collected by C. Ray Smith. 1967–1968.

ONYX. Broadside. 1968.

all sorts were superimposed one on the other. Lettering in script, print, and outlines was slid up and down, reversed, and staggered; words were run on, abbreviated, placed on end, run in diagonals, in circles, or squeezed into other shapes. They spelled out directions and meanings beyond mere words and created a verisimilitude of graphic and printed design. Changes from color to color to black, from print to script to typewriter type to labels and paste-on images, to pointing-finger signs and emphatic arrows moved the reader along and up and down pages. Photographs, photo negatives, Xeroxing, multiscreening—all exploited this graphic collage technique. It was a kind of kinetic reading game that involved the viewer in a treasure hunt across the page—or cloth, mylar, or banner. Letterheads on stationery became allover designs covering a page like Peruvian patchwork, creating a diaphanous scrim behind the writing or the type that was like visual static, white noise, or subliminal perfume. Walker Gee Design Group produced a mirror-image letterhead on the back of a page that could be read only when light shone through.

Lines of type were run on, filling the unit spacing from beginning to end of line and breaking words wherever those limits occurred. Kenneth Carbajal published a paper in which two typefaces of different size were *These lines of italic type are interspersed here as an illustration of* used on alternate lines to intersperse two distinct discussions. The intent *the effect of Carbajal's simultaneous and disorienting graphic effect.* was to demonstrate the interrelationships of seemingly separate gestalts. *His typefaces were a traditional elite typewriter face and a big bold one.* And the effect was confusing, alienating, and eyebrow-lifting.

The forms and the shapes of the actual paper, posters, or signs were also expanded by graphic designers in the new idiom. Tradition-breaking, iconoclastic ways of typing envelopes, letters, and so on, were matched by stationery that was folded to become its own envelope, stationery with holes for spindling or embossings for typing instructions.

There were run-on letters with solid and void interchanges like Deborah Sussman's versions of M. C. Escher's graphics. Type reading "Continuum" was run around the back and the front of an envelope; *Symmetry* was printed with the second *m* reversed to produce a typographical verisimilitude. The chaotic balloons and rubber stamps wittily

Deborah Sussman: New Year's card for 1970, Los Angeles. 1970.

defied preconceptions about the dignity of public appearance and exposure; they also aimed to involve the newly exposed "real" feeling that this defiance can bring. Op art visual techniques including phosphorescent Day-Glow colors and silver and transparent films were used. Vibrating typefaces attempted to re-create the effects of vibrating colors or of flashing, kinetic lights. Some of these were produced quite simply with superimposed, slightly offset typing. Others reiterated vibration through the use of discontinuous lettering. The sexual revolution also raised its no-longer-ugly head in graphic design, when the forms of genitalia were used as directional signs and were stretched to provide outlines for letters, digits, or storefront signs. Graphics designers crammed all these influences, inspirations, devices, techniques, forms, and colors together to produce an inclusive simultaneity of culture that cried out as planned chaos.

No one really came up with the charactonym for this kind of graphics; I attempted *garblegraphics* and *crazygraphics* to show the run-on, random superimposition of its design chaos, but they are imperfect terms. It seems worthwhile to find a descriptive term for this graphic work, since so much of architecture and the work of architecture students in the late 1960s was integrally concerned with graphics and presentation techniques. One design group in New York, called ONYX, became known because of its strongly ambiguous and splendidly confus-

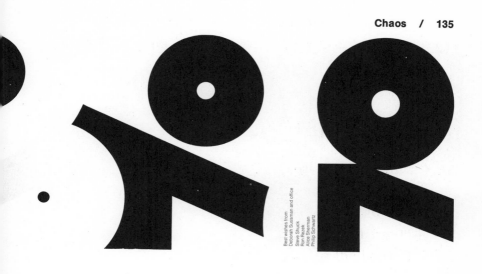

Best wishes from
Deborah Sussman and office

Steve Shuck
Ron Rezek
Alice Sherman
Philip Schwartz

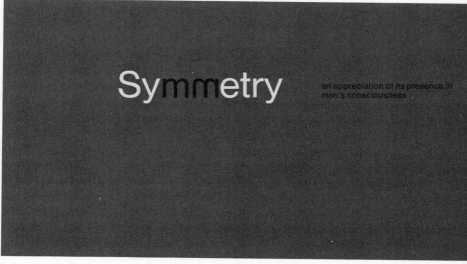

(*above*) *Symmetry* (catalogue cover). 1968. (*below*) Vibrating type-face for The New Electric Circus Discotheque, New York City. 1969.

Doug Michels, Robert Shannon, and Sal Vasi: Transparent acetate plans and model photographs for a house project. 1969.

ing broadsides that presented their work but did not explain it. ONYX's interplay of solids and voids was vital enough, it seemed, without being repeated in reverse—one image on another, letters changing to trees, to clouds, to inflatables, or to arms—as they were.

Students adapted many of these chaotic presentation techniques in architectural drawing. Plans and sections showed new arrangements of multiple levels and interrelated spaces that were labeled in a corresponding alien, unending, and inextricable graphic style. Labels used multiple colors and different typefaces that were graduated in size and positioned in seemingly random yet surprisingly directional locations like maps to point out and explain the hierarchy of levels and spaces, of functions and activities. Hardy Holzman Pfeiffer Associates, prominently among other architectural firms, produced their plans in a singularly personal idiom of overlaid tones and rubber-stamp labels that defied interpretation by some, but as often transfixed curiosity and admiration. Doug Michels, who proclaimed his rebellion from traditional drawing by labeling some of his design documents "Not-A-Plan," also labeled plans with random words that spread out to lead the reader along circulation routes or were repeated and repeated chaotically to suggest mobility. He even printed plans on sheets of transparent, invisible acetate.

Later examples of spontaneous chaos in graphics were the spray-can graffiti that were to be seen on virtually every car and wall of the New York subway system by 1973. In a move variously attributed by social psychologists to self-identity or protest at the drab environment of the subways, young spray-can artists flowered, dotted, and lettered their names and logos in vibrant, sometimes joyfully colored designs at a huge scale across train walls, windows, advertising, and maps. The movement caught on with the press almost as fast as supergraphics had done (see p. 269) and ultimately found its way onto the stage in the Joffrey Ballet's *Deuce Coup* by choreographer Twyla Tharp. It was as vital and stimulating a social phenomenon of personal, self-reliant involvement—however disrespectful of the Transit Authority's investment—as had been witnessed since the student riots of the mid-1960s. All these ambiguous and chaotic activities had camp undercurrents.

Ambiguity and Invisibility

As W. H. Auden had called the 1920s "The Age of Anxiety"; ours has been called an "age of ambiguity." In the 1960s, in politics and business, in education and the arts, people were more ambivalent, more vague and vacillating than ever before, it seemed. The new designers accepted this fact of contemporary life, and they expressed it in their theories and designs. They endorsed ambiguity—a design element, more controlled than permissiveness, more subtle than chaos, and one that was entirely excluded from early Modern and Minimal architecture.

After established traditions and theory are rejected, a void is left. What will fill it? In the new design, the first thing to fill the nebulous area was the acceptance of the ambiguous void itself. The new designers express ambiguity formally—a direct inversion of the rational clarity of the Internationalists. The new designers create spatial ambiguities that rely on dislocation, disorientation, alienation, and surprise for their effects. They confuse and distort by means of perverse trickery—through optical games and intellectual twists. Sometimes their paradoxical spaces produce painful or neurotic reactions; sometimes they elicit joy and delight; always they surprise with fundamental vagueness.

To produce these enigmatic effects, the new designers permissively include chaotic arrangements—or nonarrangements. They use a confusing plethora of inseparable forms, pattern on pattern, and the interplay of solid and void. They exploit the multiple functions of elements simultaneously. They camouflage forms with unexpected materials, confuse with unexpected textures, with color, with perspective, or with light. Among the optical tricks employed are motion parallax and multiple perspectives. This kind of ambiguity is achieved through multiple complexity; it is *discordia concors*. Another kind of ambiguity is created by a virtual immaterialization of forms, those non-objects that approach invisibility through transparency and reflectiveness. Both work with the contrast between the space as it is and the space as the architect wants it to appear.

The architectural ambiguity achieved through complexity was first clarified—if that is possible—by Robert Venturi in his *Complexity and Contradiction in Architecture*. There Venturi acclaims an "architecture based on the richness and ambiguity of modern experience." He devotes his third chapter to ambiguity, which he considers the primary element of the architecture he acclaims. He points out that "oscillating relationships, complex and contradictory, are the source of the ambiguity and tension characteristic to the medium of architecture." He sets up ambiguities by accepting "duality" as an outlook—"both/and" not "either/or." "The calculated ambiguity of expression," he continues, "is based on the confusion of experience . . . This promotes richness of meaning over clarity of meaning." In this discussion Venturi draws correspon-

Abracadabra boutique, New York City,
lighting by Marvin Gelman. 1967. *Photograph by Maud Dorr.*

dences between ambiguity in painting—in Abstract Expressionism, in Op art, and in Pop art—and he relates ambiguity in architecture to ambiguity in literature, as explained by such critics as T. S. Eliot, Cleanth Brooks, and William Empson, whose *Seven Types of Ambiguity* (1947) was so pivotal to literary criticism. Venturi was equally pivotal to modern architectural criticism, in proclaiming, "The variety inherent in the ambiguity of visual perception must once more be acknowledged and exploited." What he formulated in writing, he and his contemporaries expressed in buildings throughout the decade.

Like ambiguity in the other arts, the new design ambiguity relishes merger and fusion of inflexible opposites. It shifts from one meaning and scale to another; it thrives in situations where different levels of perception run up and down like arpeggios, or weave in and out, or slip from the past into the future and return to the starting point again. It is overlapping, intermingled, and redundant.

What is of interest to the analysis of perception and phenomenology, as to the new design, is a nebulous area between precise perception and the hallucination of infinity. In the fine arts of painting and sculpture, the precursors were Surrealism's eerie perspectives and juxtapositions of landscapes, and Abstract Expressionism's perception of emotions. Abundant ambiguity was recognized and acclaimed in the work of René Magritte, who gave seminal predictions to the new designers, and in the multiple-perspective drawings of M. C. Escher and in his almost kinetic evolution of solids as voids. Escher dramatically depicted "unlimited spaces," mirror images and inversion, and "impossible buildings." Yet only designers of space capsules could realize the kinds of ambiguous environment that he envisioned. In theatre planning, the new design ambiguity corresponds to undifferentiated and uncommitted spaces— those "little black box" experimental theatres that proliferated in performing arts centers during the decade. It is reflected in the plays of Samuel Beckett and Eugène Ionesco, of Edward Albee and Harold Pinter. It corresponds to the alienation, disorientation, and formlessness that are such prominent aspects of the New Theatre, Environmental or Experiential Theatre, and Happenings. Perhaps most tellingly, the new design ambiguity corresponds to current psychic investigations, to spaced-out highs, by aiming at expanded consciousness through expanded spaciousness. It is the architectural nirvana of the drug culture. In city planning, as the titles of Kevin Lynch's books demonstrate, he

M. C. Escher: *Another World,* 1947, wood engraving
printed from three blocks.

moved from *The Image of the City* (1960) to *What Time Is This Place?* (1972), that is, from simplex clarity to an ambiguous pun on the early Modern architecture components of time and space. Jane Jacobs had accepted the ambiguous and complex mix of vital city life and city planning in her *Death and Life of Great American Cities* (1961). And, elsewhere in architectural theory, Aldo Van Eyck, who significantly influenced many American architects during the decade, expressed an interest in "ambivalent images" and "multiphenomena."

The new ambiguous architecture varies from the literally nebulous to ambiguities in solid concrete. Perhaps the greatest number of large buildings that prominently feature ambiguity and induce reactions of ambiguity and dislocation are the work of Walter A. Netsch, Jr., of Skidmore, Owings & Merrill's Chicago office. Although he does not otherwise fit into the Supermannerist group, having had a dissimilar education at MIT, Netsch's work exhibits a commitment to many of the same goals. His Field Theory buildings, such as the Art and Architecture Building and the Behavioral Science Building at the Chicago Circle Campus of the University of Illinois, contain unsettling ambiguities in their mazes of corridors and the seemingly meandering circulation of their complex though rigidly geometric plans. Architect Netsch observes that visitors to the Art and Architecture Building in particular "try to see where they are rather than letting the building be an experience." His spatial ambiguities are a new, foreign, and, to those in tune with the new generation, an exhilarating experience (see pp. 28, 213).

Harry Weese, also an architect who is a design generation older than the Supermannerists, produced some ambiguous elevator trips that expressed the spirit of the new design in the second half of the 1960s. From an architect noted for logic and clarity, this was somewhat surprising, yet his continual rejuvenation explained it. In his explorations into the ambiguous, Weese achieved a disconcerting moment of confusion within the traditions of his own generation. The location of the elevator in his Chicago office building behind a discreet white brick wall is totally unannounced, and visitors are left to make an undirected choice of turning either right or left into the apselike space behind the brick partition. If they choose the left turn, they find an elevator door, but if they choose the right? When the elevator opens, the question is answered: an identical, double entry, one on each side of the single elevator cab. Like the lobby, the cab is a sober interior, but riders soon recognize that the light flooding in from the ceiling is not electric but

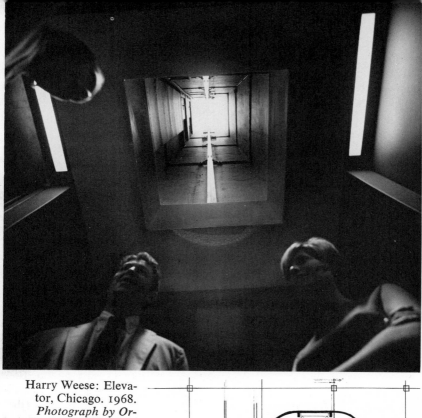

Harry Weese: Elevator, Chicago. 1968.
Photograph by Orlando R. Cabanban.

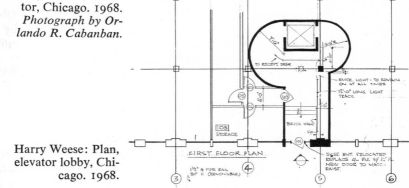

Harry Weese: Plan, elevator lobby, Chicago. 1968.

natural; that the top is open except for a clear plastic dome, that there are no cables, that the shaft is open to the sky, and that the system (hydraulic) is rapidly propelling the capsule toward the top of the gantry and . . . lift-off? It is space age ambiguity.

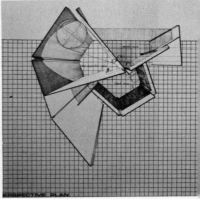

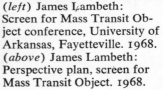

(*left*) James Lambeth:
Screen for Mass Transit Ob-
ject conference, University of
Arkansas, Fayetteville. 1968.
(*above*) James Lambeth:
Perspective plan, screen for
Mass Transit Object. 1968.

Knoll International—font of Bauhaus furniture in America, sire of
the most exquisitely orderly interiors of the past quarter century—
espoused an ambiguous, subliminal salesmanship in their Boston and
New York showrooms in 1969. There, they lure customers through
plans like webs of tangled arrows, and through ambiguous changes of
floor-level-cum-shelf-level. The effects are immediately disorienting, yet
there is method in this perverse obfuscation. Italian architect Gae
Aulenti, who designed the alienating spaces, mystifyingly forces shoppers to see the long-familiar furniture classics with the fresh eye of
rediscovery.

Architecture students of the 1960s produced some exemplary ambiguous effects. While a student at Tulane University in New Orleans,
Chip Lord painted his own staircase in glossy orange enamel and the
handrail in blue, except for the depth of the balusters, which was orange
gloss. Then, as if there were a one-point light source casting a shadow,
he painted the shadow of the balusters onto the stairs in blue (see color
plate 15). "Sometimes hard to climb," he noted. It was ambiguous Op.

Young educators also experimented with what has come to be readily identified with the new design ambiguity in their work. James Lambeth, at the University of Arkansas in Fayetteville, explained that working with "like volumes and unlike surfaces, with like areas and unlike volumes, with image on reality" creates ambiguity that can compel the involvement of viewers in puzzling out their various levels of meaning. Lambeth designed a screen-cum-poster for a conference on megastructures; the design was a series of panels overlaid with photographic murals that simulated movement, like flipping a series of cards. Eleanor Karp, a colleague on the Arkansas faculty, described the design as

a static wrap-around reality with sloped and shifted planes that imply movement. Real people standing near the envelope, entering or leaving it, merge with the people in the billboard photograph, requiring an observer constantly to readjust between what he is seeing and what he knows exists. Space and movement, light and dark, combine so that when you stand still, the envelope moves; when you move, the envelope stands still.

This is the kind of fluctuation between the thing as it is and what it appears to be that the new design ambiguity strives for.

AMBIGUITY THROUGH DE-MATERIALIZATION

Another means of achieving ambiguity in architecture that was prominent in the 1960s is through the de-materialization of forms. Through designing non-objects with transparency and reflections, materials and buildings are rendered relatively invisible. These non-object buildings or non-buildings relate to but are not to be confused with "non-architecture," as the interest in the process, practice, and "software" of architecture came to be labeled. *Non-architecture* relates to process rather than end product, although the term was also used loosely to designate buildings not designed by architects—a typically parochial professional view. Non-buildings, which express an anti-form or anti-object movement that occurred in all the arts of our decade, are invisible, by being underground; or virtually invisible by being ambiguously all white or all silver; or transparent like bubbles or inflatable structures. In the art world of the 1960s as in the world of architecture, non-object art was also investigated. Such evanescent materials as smoke, fire, gas, wind, electricity, and the non-object aspect of kinetic art were used as the subject matter of art. It harked back to Jean Labatut's enthusiasm for fountains, fireworks, smoke, and light as architectural elements. The device is an extension of the Bauhaus goal of de-materialization, which was demonstrated in countless glass membrane walls and in discontinuous, floating staircases from the 1920s to the 1950s. Yet the new design intensifies and expands this direction.

De-materialized ambiguous spaces can be created with any number of design elements. Monochromatic schemes—all white, all silver, all blue, or all red rooms—create ambiguity by making the envelope vanish. If ever there was an illustration of what University of Houston students called "LSDesign," it was Charles Coffman's ambiguous all-red room designed in 1967 when he was a fourth-year student. He converted what he called a "Grade A Acme rectangular box" into a livable bedroom by building sloping or raked walls of cardboard and by painting the space entirely in red latex gloss—floors, walls, ceiling, closets. The only exception was a blue-gloss circulation stripe that led from the entry door to a pigeonhole bed nook. The space seemed planeless, cornerless, scaleless, and disorienting—completely ambiguous (see color plate 14).

The all-white room—with its white-on-white intaglio effects, transparent glass and plastic furniture, and with its floating quality achieved by illumination—leads to ambiguity through the de-materialization of the envelope and its elements. All-white rooms have been around, popping up off and on throughout history since at least the days of

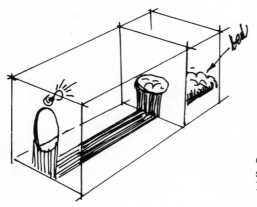

Charles Coffman: Schematic sketch, Coffman bedroom, Houston, Texas. 1968

Jacques-Ange Gabriel and Germain Boffrand in the 1700s, returning with the Mackintoshes around 1900 and again with Syrie Maugham and Lady Mendl in the 1920s. But today's all-white room—whiter than ever before and easier to maintain because of plastics and drip-dry—is with us because (though it seems maximally minimal) it involves us by means of its ambiguity. By making the envelope vanish, a dramatic emphasis is placed on growing, changing things—and on people, who take on a hypnotic air in the almost weightlessness of the all-white orbit. This architectural technique corresponds to the white-on-white intaglio artworks of Kasimir Malevich and Josef Albers, Omar Rayo, Jasper Johns, and others. Ad Reinhardt's black-on-black paintings invert the color but not the technique of noncolor ambiguity. All-white rooms sometimes start out as exercises in texture rather than in color, which is the more common interior design exercise. The goal was, purely by orchestrating the textures, to make a room that would appear warm and elegant. And the clearest demonstration of that exercise was to eliminate all color. Flat white walls, gloss-white enameled woodwork and ceiling cornices, white deck-enameled floors and wood furniture, white linen sofas (slip covered and Velcroed on for easy washing), plastic white fur rugs (washable), and chrome, silver, and mirrored furniture varied the textures in all-white schemes during the 1960s. In addition, rheostated lighting and such changing elements as fires, flowers, and people varied the color and textural effects daily. Such all-white spaces look somewhat like plaster architectural models. People become prominent focal points, haloed against the background void. All-white rooms give people a sense of weightlessness. In one of them a visitor gasped, "My God, it looks like a negative."

No one can say that the usually quiet-mannered Paul Rudolph does not dare. He dares to be primarily concerned with space and with sequences of spaces; he dares with all-white ambiguities. In his first New York office of 1965 (dismantled in 1969), he dared to build in ambiguous vertigo effects that would put off many a prospective client. When you got off the elevator, the space suddenly exploded: all-white, light, and open; floating, interconnected, striped by flying bridges; interrelated by multiple-use objects—furniture tops also serving as stairs—and multiple-use spaces that superimposed meaning on meaning and ambiguity on ambiguity. That office was canopied by precarious-looking cantilevered pods that were drafting areas; confusing and disconcerting. It seemed at first glance like a light-color version of his Art and Architec-

(*above*) Paul Rudolph: Rudolph office, New York City. 1965–1969. *Photograph by Louis Reens.* (*below*) Paul Rudolph: Section, Rudolph office, New York City. 1965–1969.

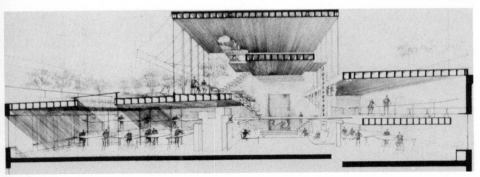

ture Building at Yale, with a similar pinwheel plan and circulation effect. To connect areas on the north front with the south rear, two narrow platforms were built at different levels on the east and west sides of the space. Because of the changes of level, the platforms produced a spiral circulation pattern. It was a dizzying feat going up and down stairs and on bridges around the space of the central well. The bridge floating out from the east wall was so narrow a strip that, as you passed, the statue of a cardinal against the wall almost thrust you off the bridge and out into space. However, Rudolph ultimately made this passage feel more secure when, as he says, "the look on a certain mayor's face said that his was one civic center I wasn't going to do." Rudolph put this tenuous, ambivalent, vertiginous effect in perspective when he explained, "This space is free-flowing vertically, like a Mies plan but turned on edge. Can one ever forget the sections of Mies—parallel horizontal lines of equal distance? What a negation of the human spirit." In contrast, Rudolph demonstrated the kind of ambiguity dared by the Second Generation of Modern Architects in their move toward the new design.

Rudolph also designed a number of all-white, ambiguous, floating or orbiting apartments from the mid-1960s onward—for himself (see color plate 13)—and houses for others. He conceived his own all-white New York apartment (1966) as a "floating platform" suspended in space above a sweeping river view. Within this space, low canti-levered seating platforms surrounding the living area are lifted off by incandescent lighting beneath their translucent white plastic planes. This platform shelf serves as a base for legless, vinyl patent leather seating units and as a step to a small outdoor terrace of white steel grating, which is like a gantry from nowhere to the floating room. Complement-ing the slick, glossy textures are hides of white kid fur on the floor, a contour map behind the sofa, and white plaster castings of Sullivan panels. At the windows hundreds of disk mirrors (suspended on invis-ible nylon wire) reflect the interior brilliance like a myriad of stars against the evening sky. In contrast to this ambiguous all-white environ-ment, Rudolph placed a grand piano across the entry; one squeezes past this black funnel into the weightless whiteness.

Weightlessness has also been a goal of the performing arts through decades of high-wire and trapeze acts and winch-hoisted flying ma-chines, but a new age of weightless performance culminated in the work of the Multigravitational Experiment Group and in Trisha Brown's dance piece *Walking on the Wall,* performed in 1971 at the Whitney

Museum of American Art in New York. Dancers ran, stood, and walked along the walls, supported by harnesses and cables hung from tracks on the ceiling. The effect was to overturn the audience into an orbiting, weightless group and the performers into a group of earthbound strollers. The new architects of the 1960s aimed for the same effects.

Like all-white spaces, monochromatic schemes with silver and mirror textures are other devices employed to demonstrate the perceptual investigations into ambiguity. Mirrors, for all their sparkling clarity, can be used to achieve disturbing or amusing spatial confusions, and in the new design they are placed to provide multiple reflections, reflections to infinity, and intimations of immensity that are clearly more ambiguous than the Galeries des Glaces of the eighteenth century. Silver interiors, like all-white ones, are no new fad either. From the time of Louis XIV's legendary silver furniture, through François Cuvilliés's silver-leafed, sea spray, rococo decoration, and down to what Alexander Girard called "the silver panic of the 20's," this white shimmering surface has shown sporadic flashes. Yet in the new design the silver wall is especially pertinent, because it is also ideally suited to the search for spatial ambiguities. As a flat wall surface, silver leaves a clean definition of the planes, yet produces a soft reflection that duplicates the statement and extends the space. Silvery reflections make the space seem to move, they confuse the image further and make it discontinuous yet interdependent. Mirror-faced buildings fascinated the Minimalist architects since Saarinen's Bell Telephone Laboratories Building in Holmdel, New Jersey (1962), but these did not aim for ambiguity. Some of the most telling of these effects in the 1960s were small-scale designs. Charles Moore's New Haven house (1966) had a fun-house mirror arrangement that made one wonder which plane the mirror was actually in. In front of the bathroom mirror was a cutout panel the same shape as the mirror frame. The reflections of the two similar frames—one with mirrors, the other a mere void—created a reflection into infinity and confused one's ability to locate the actual mirror—or oneself when reflected. Plane on plane were there, but which was forward of the other was mystifyingly ambiguous.

On a larger scale, Alexander Girard's restaurant design for L'Etoile (1967) in New York showed several mirror and silver tricks overlaid to create a series of reflections and ambiguities of planes. Glass panels etched with the great names of France were reflected in opposing mirrors; a wall of squares of mirror alternating with leather tile read sometimes as a wall surfaced with those two materials, sometimes as a leather screen open to a view beyond.

Another of Harry Weese's elevator designs, in his Time-Life Building (1968–1970) in Chicago, has technically innovative two-story or double-deck cabs with timely, ambiguous silver environments. The muted color cabs seem plain enough on entry, but as the passenger looks at the ceiling, it appears that there are windows at the top around all four sides, revealing a view of the cosmos stretching out into infinity. In fact, the panels of the cabs above head height are smoke mirrors that reflect tiny exposed bulbs in the ceiling like stars, reduplicating them by the opposing-mirror effect; it is as if the elevator were orbiting out into the celestial bodies of space. It is an architectural expression contemporary with Stanley Kubrick's film 2001: A Space Odyssey, as well as with man's first landing on the moon.

Mirrored-glass effects were relatively costly and permanent for experimentation by the student generation in the 1960s. Consequently, they searched for other materials. With silver mylar mirror, a new version of the traditional silver room came into being.

Less specific than mirror, silver mylar produced a gleaming silvery surface that briefly became a symbol of our age of ambiguity. It appeared, seemingly overnight, in restaurants, shops, apartments, houses, and even in offices and schools—at least in design offices and design schools. Yale's Project Argus, built under the direction of Charles Moore in 1968 (see "The Decade of the Diagonal"), glittered with silver mylar walls reflecting flashing fluorescent tubes all along the walls of the jury space in Paul Rudolph's Art and Architecture Building.

About the same time, former students of Rudolph's were wreaking similar new design ambiguities on houses and interiors of their own design. Peter Hoppner refurbished a hallway as a silver happening of five swinging doorways and a swiveling panel-cum-closet that closed down an archway. The reflections made a crazy-mirror fun house of the hallway (see color plate 16). Hoppner observed, "The whole spirit of today is like the spirit of the 20's. People are using silver because they are tired of all-white and colors. It's in the air." Silver also interested Derek Romley as something beyond all-white and because it provided a continuity of background with chrome and steel pieces. He demonstrated it best in a 1967 silver-mylar-walled kitchen in New York, in which the stainless steel equipment and appliances looked more consistent than in any other kitchen design; aluminum painted woodwork melded the two other metallic surfaces.

INVISIBILITY

Beyond all-white and all-silver schemes, invisibility is the only logical visual step. And the new designers took it gleefully. Architects investigated a number of non-object buildings and nearly invisible structures. These were formal analogies to the non-architectural, or the nonformal, or subsystems of design. They investigated such ambiguous buildings as those literally underground, which were virtually invisible, and such other non-object buildings and interior furnishings as reflective and transparent ones.

Vast substructures of urban towers had been underground for decades, but totally underground buildings considered as an aesthetic achievement were a new development of the 1960s. These schemes were not only underground in the sense of being radical but were actually covered wholly or partly by earth. Philip Johnson's underground art gallery (1966), adjacent to his own Glass House in New Canaan, Connecticut, was a prominent example of this non-architecture direction. As Johnson explained, "Weight is the opposition to the glass style. After all we have been through the last forty years, it leads one to earth." Yale's bermed Tandem Accelerator Building by the office of Douglas Orr, de Cossy, Winder & Associates in conjunction with landscape architects Zion and Breen, and the Campus Store at Cornell University by Earl R. Flansburgh and Associates are underground buildings on our campuses. Several university libraries also went underground at the same time: the University of Illinois library at the south mall of the Urbana campus, by associated architects Richardson, Severns, Scheeler & Associates with Clark, Atlay & Associates; and the Hendrix College Library at Conway, Arkansas, by Philip Johnson in conjunction with Wittenberg, Delony & Davidson. Other underground schemes that carried forward this non-architecture theme were the underground Student Union at the State College of Iowa in Cedar Falls, Iowa, by John Stephens Rice, and the large, amorphous, diagonal earthforms—although not actually belowground—for a performing arts center project at the University of Toledo by Hardy Holzman Pfeiffer Associates. Philip Johnson, Malcolm Wells, and others designed underground houses, Wells's more underground than most. Kevin Roche's Oakland

(*left*) Philip Johnson: Underground art gallery, New Canaan, Connecticut. 1966. (*right*) Kevin Roche, John Dinkeloo & Associates: Oakland Museum, California. 1969. *Photograph by Chalmer Alexander.*

Museum (1969) is the monument of this direction, although it is actually less underground and less invisible than the smaller buildings.

The sociological rationale behind underground buildings, and the one point agreed on by the wide diversity of the architects who designed them, is that architects cannot continue their traditional practice of dotting the landscape with single buildings—no matter how perfect those buildings. Underground buildings seemed to be a means of land conservation. As Philip Johnson stated it, "The whole idea is to get more land and to do away with the plop, plop, plop series of houses or buildings all over the countryside." The creation of nearly invisible architecture or buildings behind and under earthberms was a step in this direction. It demonstrated formally the increasing ambivalence in the profession about the validity of traditional buildings and about the historical monumentality of architecture. Underground buildings exist as architecture, but they don't exist visually. They accept the need but reject the expression of that need. This thinking was also a significant acceptance of ambiguity by the new design.

Bubbles

Those nearly invisible and often partly underground non-buildings called air structures, air-supported structures, or inflatables also captured the imaginations of the new designers. As defined by the Building Research Institute, an air structure is "an engineered building constructed of high-strength film or combination of fabric and film which achieves its structural shape, stability, and support by pretensioning with internal air pressure," or, as Ant Farm explained, by comparison to traditional building, "Technically, an inflatable is merely the outside film of paint, roof paper, and foundation vapor barrier supported by the air conditioner or heating system." That expresses the ambiguity of dematerialization.

A technology of air had been developing since 1946, when inflatable "radomes" were accepted for the government's early warning radar missile system. Engineered domes for military application included supply warehouses, field hospitals, houses, and a 210-foot-diameter bubble for the Telstar station at Andover, Maine. Victor Lundy's portable air-supported structure for the Atomic Energy Commission's "Atoms for Peace" exhibition (c. 1960) first showed the sculptural potential of these inflatable structures, and his snowball clusters of bubbles were a jolly feature of the 1963 New York World's Fair. At the end of the decade, the United States were made proud by the low-profile air-supported pavilion designed by Davis Brody & Associates, Chermayeff, Geismar and deHarak, and engineer David Geiger for that pneumatic fair Expo '70 at Osaka, Japan. That United States Pavilion was a low-air-pressure, single-membrane structure of translucent vinyl-coated fiber glass restrained by a diamond grid of steel cables in tension that were anchored to a concrete compression ring resting in earthberms. This large and light clear-span air-supported structure—274 feet by 465 feet, or the size of two football fields—was not only a technical achievement and the star of the fair, but also a triumph of the non-object building movement because of its berms and nearly invisible, low-profile, translucent bubble roof.

Throughout the 1960s, commercially designed inflatables were used to enclose large areas quickly and cheaply for scientific, educational, and cultural purposes as well as for commercial and recreational purposes—if primarily in undesigned situations. Traveling labs and warehouses, industrial clean rooms, and agricultural greenhouses (one was made for Goodyear, near Akron, as large as one acre), gymnasiums and tennis courts, swimming pools and ice rinks, communications antennae and parabolic radar reflectors were housed in countless, variously shaped inflatable structures. As the technology developed, air structures were constructed not only with cable-restrained single-membrane enclosures, but also with double-membrane or high-pressure tubular air beams, and combinations of both utilizing exhausted or negative air, like a vacuum within double-walled enclosures.

These were architectural correlatives to inflatable boats, and air-cushion vehicles or hover craft. In the art world bubble buildings had correspondences in Claes Oldenburg's "soft sculptures"—his squashed superscale light switches and typewriters, and his inflatable soft lipstick for Yale—and in Christo's "packages"—wrapping up acres of Australian coastline or buildings in plastic sheeting. The visionary beacon for designers of inflatables was Buckminster Fuller's scheme of constructing a bubble dome, albeit space-frame supported, over most of Manhattan as a new scale of climate control.

All this turned on numbers of students to inflatables in the last half of the decade. From an initial interest in non-architectural objects like parachutes and in intangible head games, nomadic design communes, like Ant Farm and Southcoast (who used the name "Intangible" as a return-mailing address), took us along a festival path of bubbles, raising a sparkling froth of inflated structures at environmental festivals, at architecture conferences, and at public events. In Cambridge, New Haven, and New York, in Florida, Arkansas, and Texas, in Berkeley and Los Angeles, students and faculty as well as public officials witnessed the construction and inflating of bubbles, in various configurations and colors, as participatory events—what Southcoast described as "twelve-hour inflato-environments and celebrations of life."

Student bubble. 1969.

Several publications detailed the methods of constructing bubbles: the *Bubble Primer* by Blair Hamilton and Bill Whitaker, and the *Inflato-book, a pneu-age tech book* by Ant Farm, made the rounds of architecture circles and design communes like best sellers. Two young designers specialized in air technology—Blair Hamilton and Charles Tilford, who called himself an "inflato-environmentalist."

With this new non-architectural technology there seemed to be a logical answer to structural flexibility and to inner-space mobility. As the *Bubble Primer* maintains, "Specifically, it is now possible—as it never was before—to build long span, open space structures, unbroken by the supporting beams or columns necessary to traditional compressive, 'stone-on-stone' buildings." This makes it "entirely feasible," the *Primer* continues, "that within the decade we will be able to enclose city-sized spaces. An enclosed city means dramatic changes in the costs and architecture of the buildings within—domestic, public and commercial . . . Finally, it will mean that previously uninhabitable areas can become attractive for settlement." Inflatables, then, have an important social potential in the minds of architects as an immediate and economical means of providing shelters, however temporary or permanent, for blighted areas—urban ghettos, underdeveloped countries, and other areas of social concern where construction of traditional buildings is less imminent.

The instant bubble is also a symbol of user involvement, capturing the childlike fascination with going into a womblike tent. As the *Inflato-book* explained:

In case you hadn't figured our reason or excuse, why to build inflatables becomes obvious as soon as you get people inside. The freedom and instability of an environment where the walls are constantly becoming the ceilings and the ceiling the floor and the door is rolling around the ceiling somewhere releases a lot of energy that is usually confined by the xyz planes of the normal box-room. The new-dimensional space becomes more or less whatever people decide it is—a temple, a fun house, a suffocation torture device, a pleasure dome. A conference, party, wedding, meeting, regular Saturday afternoon becomes a festival.

Many of these festival bubbles created silvery reflections, veiled vistas of the surrounding exterior environment, as if both were seen through the soft-focus miasma of smoky haze—and often they were.

Student bubbles were more invisible than most, being constructed of clear, transparent polyethylene sheeting. They were immaterial, mental-image analogies to solid architecture, yet as thin as architecture could seemingly be. To many design students in the late 1960s no more potent expression of involvement with fast means for furthering social concerns, with user activity, and with designer participation seemed possible than these amorphous, definitely un-square, floating, writhing, air-supported enclosures. They sparkled in the sunshine, drifted gracefully with the breezes, were inviting and entrancing, non-architectural in the old senses, and also crossed meanings, boundaries, and categories into an ambiguous new design effect. At the end of the 1960s, a bubble-topped arts facility for Antioch College's campus at Columbia, Maryland, gave promise of bringing this kind of invisibility to the educational establishment (see also p. 305).

Research and Design Institute and Rurik Ekstrom: Inflatable arts facility, Antioch College, Columbia, Maryland. 1970; demolished 1973.

Several problems remain to be solved before inflatables or underground buildings can be seen as any kind of pervasive panacea, however. Among them, the interface between the bubble or underground structure and the exterior atmosphere still requires resolution—how to deal with exhaust vents, chimneys, and stacks. Underground buildings produce a forest of stacks and vents among the trees and shrubbery above; bubbles require large outbuildings for ventilating equipment. The eight-story buildings that vent Manhattan's tunnels demonstrate the scale of the problem.

Spiros Zakas: "The
emperor's new chair,"
transparent acrylic
sheeting, New York
City. 1969.

Invisible Furniture

While invisible bubble buildings were occupying the radical architects,
invisible furniture gained a similar explosive popularity. I refer to those
visually sensational pieces made of clear acrylic plastic, both panels and
inflatables. Our most progressive designers of plastics-as-plastics have
worked with panels of acrylic plastic sheeting and inflatable bubbles to
create furniture and lighting that make use of air technology and the
aesthetic of the invisible. Their pieces are designed to eliminate the sea
of legs that obstruct and clutter the spaces we live in. Most prominently,
they have latched onto folding, bending, and cementing or pinning
sheets of transparent plastic into tables, stools, chairs, and lighting
fixtures. Designers such as Paul Mayen, Neal Small, John Mascheroni,
Kip Coburn, John A. Weick, and Spiros Zakas demonstrated abstemi-
ousness in the craft of folding sheet materials. Square tables by Neal
Small and Kip Coburn have legs bent down from single sheets of plastic
that form tabletops. Coburn duplicated plastic cylinders as a table base
to produce a multiple mirror image; John A. Weick folded and bolted a
single sheet of plastic to form a two-level book table; and John Mascheroni folded a single transparent acrylic sheet to produce a tall, self-

supporting barstool. Steve Lax of New York's plastics shop Lucidity called these pieces "transparent origami"—comparing them to the oriental art of folding paper. Many of these pieces are virtually invisible, like the emperor's new chair. Such furniture partakes of the same aesthetic as invisible bubble structures.

In coming full circle, the idea of invisible architecture leads to nonexistent architecture—another demonstration of paradoxical ambiguity that the new design creates. As Ada Louise Huxtable wrote in *The New York Times* in 1969, "Architecture as happening is leading to a maze of anbiguities in which theory is undone. But art does not get undone. Art manages to transcend paradox and theory and even the intentions of its creators, as long as it speaks accurately for its time." And our time is an age of ambiguity.

Wit and Whimsy or Campopop

The new inclusive design also accommodates whimsy and humor. In a design world long accustomed to taking itself as an endeavor of high seriousness, this addition enriches our environment with jokes and wit, the smirk and the giggle. Why not? Design, like life, can accommodate serious business, the dignified and decorous, as well as the smile and whim, the jovial and absurd.

This new whimsy manifests itself architecturally in spatial puns and visual jokes, in the humorous use of connotative items, materials, and colors, and in surprise juxtapositions. Some of these witty pow-zap-pizzaz-bang environments reach a giddy visual climax by combining, sometimes by superimposing, three recent movements—Camp, Pop, and Op—into a rich tutti-frutti for the eye that I call *Campopop*.

The strongest, most catalytic aesthetic force in our decade has been the witty recognition and (at first) ironic acceptance of the visual environment of our ordinary daily life—the popular culture that motivated Pop art. Artistic philistinism and aesthetic squalor seemed to be everywhere in America during the 1950s and at the beginning of the 1960s. A newly aware, college-trained generation made a collision comparison of this philistinism with the European sophistication that had become more and more accessible by airplane. We were training our youth for awareness, and at every glance their aesthetic toes were being trod upon: in the movies, in the new television, in the advertising that "covered the earth," in the lack of subsidy for the arts, in the lack of general appreciation for the arts.

What was awful and offensive to the sophisticated eye was the corny garishness of American "consumerama"—the commercial art, advertising, and huckstering that gave things the wrong priority, that put the bathroom, kitchen, and garage before the ideas, emotions, and sensibilities of civilization. That cornball pushiness made laundry soap and deodorants, toothpaste tubes and electric fans, toilet seats and soda bottles, radios and cigarettes, sandwiches and milk, hamburgers and, above all, automobiles the most prominent items of our visual culture. Instead of trees, we saw billboards and gasoline signs: instead of paintings, we had hokey supermarket posters and vapid cartoons like the funny papers; instead of architecture and country houses to visit, we had great tawdry old barrooms and squalid public buses. It was vulgar, garish, trashy, honky-tonk.

The situation had gotten so bad by the late 1950s that it could not get worse, it seemed; so it had to get better. But how? Artists, instead of being merely outraged and horrified by all of this, instead of rejecting it all as exclusively as possible, determined (in their hideous fascination) that the way to make those artifacts of our undesigned, uncouth, philistine, everyday culture better was to make fun of them, to make a big joking tongue in cheek put-down of them. This was Camp—at first.

Camp is a basic attitude and the singular humor of the mid-twentieth century. A detached aesthetic vision, Camp permits reversals of judgment—from bad to good, from bad to fun, from serious to humorous—and other boundary crossings. It irreverently turns things inside out for humorous ends. It can step back from its own view—of the vulgar, the kitsch object, of the coarsest unrefinement of nonacademia, of even the horrible—and be amused. It ignores content to focus on style, texture, or surface and to focus on them with a private, idiosyncratic, seemingly uninvolved vision. It is an extravagant, excessive, mannered attitude. Perverseness with a goal of humor is its core.

Perverseness and contrariness are usually manifested by children when testing authority figures. So forebears serve as whetstones to sharpen the new blades of character. Genius and invention work in similar childlike ways: all genius flips the coin. The genius children of the new design perversely use the opposite of the previous generation's methods, sneaking around authority like bad boys in prep school. They contrarily invert the expected and rebel against established authority and traditional principles to reveal or create something new—half-impish, half-better than the world that was. "Perversity basically means you challenge appearances and you look for the other side," Tim Vreeland said. "You go out and look for the other side of what is given you as natural, normal and accepted." This is a basic technique of Mannerism. In a decade of ever increasing respect and understanding for psychology, this kind of reversal became a basic tool. Psychologists advised that if we react strongly against something, we had better examine the causes of our feelings. Robert Venturi said, similarly in *Learning from Las Vegas,* "Learn from what you don't like." In the past decade this stepping back to a position of detachment so that one could reverse his views or feelings created a dichotomy somewhat equivalent to the "dissociation of sensibility" that T. S. Eliot attributed to the culture of the seventeenth century. It was a logical aesthetic extension of the conflict between culture and technology, between art and science, between business and culture. The perverseness of Camp was one of the dissociated attitudes that developed.

In 1964, William Snaith, of the industrial design firm Raymond Loewy–William Snaith, said, "Most so-called tastemakers do what they do because they wish to separate themselves from the rest of unrefined, vulgar humanity. So they say that the shiny, the golden, and the large are not good taste. But if what they now say is good taste were suddenly accepted by everybody, the next minute the tastemakers would go to gold tinsel. The most important thing for them is to be different." He described the perversity of Camp.

First widely discussed in print in the same year, 1964, by Susan Sontag, Camp had been, in fact, a growing "sensibility" of the avant-garde art world from at least the mid-1950s and perhaps from the late 1920s. It had flourished in English theatre circles; was especially polished in the work of Noel Coward and Beatrice Lillie; and was allegedly a life-style for such movie stars as Bette Davis, Tallulah Bankhead, Mae West, Marlene Dietrich, and Greta Garbo, as Susan Sontag pointed out. Most critical in a discussion of Camp is the distinction between the object and the eye of the beholder. Because she did not accept that distinction as the basic operation of Camp, Sontag got some of her examples wrong—including Tiffany glass as Camp (when the glass by Louis Comfort Tiffany was always sumptuous, gorgeously handcrafted, and among the most sophisticated and artful of creations) and Art Nouveau's best (which also didn't appeal to her taste) showed how changing appreciation can pass a camp view by. Defining objects as Camp is dangerous, therefore, because assuming the camp attitude often effects a change in our appreciation of those objects. A critic can get caught in the time lag.

A definition can be extracted from Sontag's "Notes on 'Camp'" (included in *Against Interpretation,* 1966):

> The essence of Camp is its love of the unnatural: of artifice and exaggeration . . . converts the serious into the frivolous . . . the Camp sensibility is disengaged, depoliticized—or at least apolitical . . . the triumph of the epicene style . . . the acute, the esoteric, the perverse . . . bad to the point of being enjoyable . . . The whole point of Camp is to dethrone the serious. Camp is playful, anti-serious . . . One can be serious about the frivolous, frivolous about the serious. Camp proposes a comic vision of the world . . . the democratic *esprit* of Camp . . . appreciates vulgarity . . . the connoisseur of Camp is continually amused, delighted . . . A pocket history of Camp might begin with the mannerist artists like Pontormo, Rosso, and Caravaggio.

Perverse twists akin to Camp could be found throughout the arts and society during the decade of the 1960s: in the black wit, sick and ethnic jokes of Lenny Bruce, Mort Sahl, Dick Gregory, and other comedians, in the theatre's black comedies. Wit and humor, irony and satire, paradox and travesty were used continually to shock and to inspire vitality and variety; the gaiety and humanism of high-spiritedness versus high seriousness, of high jinks and high pranks, capers and games—all interrelated with the perverseness of Camp—were fundamental attitudes of the decade. In music, John Cage's *Concert for Piano and Orchestra* (1957–1958) parodies pianistic conventions of the past century against an orchestral accompaniment scored for eggbeater, spray can, umbrella, paper bags, and hammer and saw. It is a fun-poking, nose-thumbing, humorous work—although it represents only one facet of Cage's music.

Although games for the eye are recurrent throughout the decade (some of them have been discussed in "Ambiguity and Invisibility"), the spatial playfulness of Op art was another example of the new fun, of whimsy and humor. Afterimage complements, phosphorescent effects, and vibration experiments were the staples of Op art's surprises and humor. Op created effects of apparent movement and, sometimes, responses of nausea. Bridget Riley's parallel and concentric wiggles dizzied the retina and made striped two-dimensional planes become heaving three-dimensional textures. Riley herself called it "a paradox of chaos and order in one." Jasper Johns, who had painted Pop American flags, did one in green, black, and orange to produce an Op flag with afterimage corrections. Victor Vasarely, Richard Anuszkiewicz, Larry Poons, and a host of others made art of the full complement of visual phenomena that E. H. Gombrich described in his book *Art and Illusion* (1960). In the other arts the 1960s showed the same combination of gaming reversal, escapism, and search for new areas as these games for the eye did. Exuberant comic wit is strong in the twentieth century. It culminated in Pop art in the 1960s.

ANTECEDENTS OF POP

It was not the first time that artists had crossed boundaries, opened the doors of the academy, to discover and depict popular cultures. Breughel's peasant-life scenes come immediately to mind along with the nineteenth-century Romantic composers, who wrote songs based on folk tunes and activities, and the Romantic writers from Thomas Gray to Oliver Goldsmith and George Crabbe, who extolled the virtues of village life. In the 1890s Art Nouveau had begun to blur the distinction between fine art and the applied and decorative arts. In our own century the gulf between the academy and the populace was continually narrowed from the Ashcan School to Duchamp's "urinal."

Dada and Surrealism are the direct ancestors of the 1960s irony, wit, and visual punning. Dada, the anarchistic, anti-art atmosphere that flourished after World War I, was an attempt to disrupt the stolid bourgeoisie of Europe. It was witty, ironic, sometimes erotic, and evocative. One of its most publicized products, the *Fur Covered Cup, Saucer, and Spoon* (1936) by Meret Oppenheim, exemplifies the out-of-context reversal that is the spirit, though not the content, of Camp and Pop. Subsequently, Surrealism, that more structured movement dating from André Breton's manifesto of 1924, applied Freud's theories to art and took imagery off into another world, a dreamworld. Apparently inconsistent with reality, Surrealism was above and beyond reality—as Supermannerism is above and beyond Mannerism. It espoused weightless inversions, random influences, and content, all devised to change perception, and ultimately to change the world. Like Supermannerism, Surrealism quickly confused political goals and artistic goals; like Supermannerism, Surrealism was thought of as a revolution, a system of radical change. Among the Surrealists, Arp, Klee, Picasso, Man Ray, and Miró passed through several stylistic periods, with Max Ernst staying for the longest run; Dali and Magritte mocked the merely functional from 1930s through the 1950s. The Surrealists' exodus from Europe to America during the World War II led to their direct influence on Abstract Expressionism and subsequently on Pop.

Art critic Harold Rosenberg writes of 1960s Pop in *The De-Definition of Art:* "The issue was, and is, style and creative method—mannerisms." Pop was a method of providing an embarrassed, camp excuse for the existence of American popular manners and culture. Pop artists' jokes may have been a rejection of things thought to be horrible, hideous, ugly, reprehensible, and to be avoided at all costs, yet they were also a camp acceptance of that popular culture. The Pop artists spoofed cans of soup and beer, and boxes of soap; they made travesties on candy bars, gooey wedges of plastic cake, mammoth Coke bottles, telephones, toilets, and the full vernacular of commercialism—billboards, neon signs, girlie magazines, comic books, advertising, television antennae, garages, and car washes. Their jocular preoccupation with vulgarities, with the commonplace, and with the trashy, was campily humorous. Although she was speaking primarily about clothing design, fashion arbiter Eugenia Shepherd, among others, declared at mid-decade that there was no longer anything called "vulgar"; vulgarity did not exist in our day. By analogy, the ugly, the commonplace, and the ordinary no longer exist. Her sociological theory was that when everything is vulgar, nothing seems vulgar any longer. The new vision of Pop had permeated our culture.

If "beyond" and "above" are the essential directions of art, if transforming known objects and ideas into statements and images of uncommon understanding and unsuspected reality is the task of artists, then Pop art clearly fulfilled this function of permutation. The camp joke became an art form. Through jokes at the unacceptable philistine culture of Middle America, through such camp acceptance, Pop art came about. In fact, the jokes backfired on the original camp intent and artists themselves found that this terrible, popular, ordinary culture had unsuspected merits. They began to inquire why the comic strips and the rest of popular culture were, in fact, so popular. Why did the majority of Americans prefer it to well-cultivated, university-bred, sophisticated taste? They began to capitalize on the popularity of the subject matter and its compelling, chaotic new order. Through this continuing recognition of a formerly unseeable phenomenon as a new and creative vision, the high humor of Pop shifted to more serious social awareness.

What these artists did was to take common objects and use them in uncommon ways. They gave their works a Kandy-Kolored Environment, to paraphrase Tom Wolfe. They took conventional things and used them out of context: Andy Warhol blatantly depicted banal "consumerama" and movie star idols; he took the can of soup out of the kitchen and put it on the floor of the art gallery. Jasper Johns took the American flag off the flagpole of reverent patriotism and put it on the painterly wall and into the realm of the coloring test. Roy Lichtenstein took commercially printed comic strips and turned them into single-frame, superscale easel paintings and glorifications of commercial painting. James Rosenquist took the roadside billboard and made it a luscious, superscale Madison Avenue museum collage; he monumentalized glossily gorgeous foodstuffs. But that was only the first step in altering context.

Among the other leading Pop artists were Claes Oldenburg, with his anti-art soft sculptures and non-architecture anti-monuments; Tom Wesselmann, with his nude fragments, his abstractions of nipples and toes, legs and lips; Edward Ruscha, with his vision of California gas stations and life-styles; and George Segal, with his white plaster casts of men and women on buses, in taxis, in barrooms, and so on.

Found objects—the *objets trouvés* of Marcel Duchamp—were everywhere in vogue in the pop age: in clothes, in utensils, in sculpture and painting, and in architecture. Old clothes from the 1920s and the 1930s, from grandmother's trunk and every thrift shop—funny fur coats, droopy old lace dresses and beaded bags—all contributed to a funky assemblage of found-object clothing in the mid-1960s. It was ironic that, in an age of anti-Establishment and revolution, the "bust-outs" should adopt the guise of the clergy and the armed forces: uniforms of all sorts were the fancy dress of the blue-jeans generation—army-navy store haberdashery, flags, 1930s and 1940s hats, jewelry, scarves, and other found accouterments. This was as undeniably Pop as song-freak Tiny Tim's reviving "Tiptoe Through the Tulips."

Whimsy and humor, paradox and irony were elements of the extraction from context as Pop artists subjected their materials to changes in scale—a lipstick the size of a rocket, a comic strip the size of a heroic painting. Further, the process brought about changes or reversals of weight, texture, and materials, which had stronger elements of surprise and humor—like Jasper Johns's twin ale cans of 1960, one can made of solid bronze adjacent to one of lightweight plaster, and like Oldenburg's food made of soft beanbag construction and his other soft-hard sculptures. This was Pop, but it was Camp, too. Finally the process of extraction utilized the fragment, the abstract, took it out of context, blew it up in scale, changed its color, its perspective or its weight, its texture, its materials, and its construction and put the whole Waring-blender mixture up for everyone's mental twister to unravel as he laughed.

Yet this laughter is not so frivolous as that of pure Camp; it is the laughter of irony, slightly acerbic, bitter, precarious—like the laughter caused by Harold Lloyd when he is about to slip off a skyscraper flagpole. "The important thing about humor," Claes Oldenburg was reported as saying (in *The New York Times,* 1969), "is that it opens people up. They relax their guard, and you can get your serious intentions across." It is that spirit Susan Sontag describes in *Against Interpretation* when she compares the simple fun of Camp: "Pop Art is more flat and more dry, more serious, more detached, ultimately nihilistic." Harold Rosenberg writes in *The De-Definition of Art,* "In pop, America's two cultures, highbrow and popular, meet on the neutral ground of technique," and "It is the overlay of the 'high' and 'low' aspects of contemporary art practice that characterizes Pop Art as a movement; 'real things' have nothing to do with it." "Mid Style" is what Peter Blake calls the architectural expression of all this.

In the 1960s, architects and designers, like the Pop artists, believed they had fused high or fine art with anonymous, popular low design. Helped by The Museum of Modern Art's exhibition of 1960, Art Nouveau was reintroduced to mass culture. It was adopted in that long-haired mod-art mood called "psychedelic art," which was a popular reinterpretation of Art Nouveau forms, a visual expression of the curling, smoke-inspired visions of Eastern marijuana and hashish cultures. The popular communicators—fabrics designers and display and graphic designers—gave impetus to this new current. The populace in turn adopted this high art into its advertising as the academy adopted low art into its original creations.

In architecture, the inversions or reversals that Pop art effected included the inversion of the serious (if not somber) posture of academic architecture and the substitution of an architectural image that is lighter in tone and more enjoyable—enjoyable by people, human users of architecture; it also inverted the sophisticated elegant approach for a democratic, lower-class, if not declassed, architecture. The fun and surprise with texture and mass were part of the attraction of weightless and invisible inflatable buildings. For the fun of it, also, students played textural and optical games during the 1960s. Experimental floors with bouncy surfaces of bubbles that burst when walked on (made of that bubble-plastic sheeting used as a packing material) were among examples of what University of Houston students called "funhouse architecture." Chip Lord painted the form of a pair of French doors on a wall opposite a real pair of French doors, which, in turn, were *enfilade* with another real pair across the second room. It looked as if a laser had seared through the two spaces and continued the doors as a solid element running through them—or as if it were a comic-book illustration of a door blasted through the wall.

This impetus for surprise and fun combined with ambiguity reached a height between 1967 and 1969 in the world of retail shops. Fantasy retailing environments dazzled our cities with optical and textural tricks. Merely the names of these specialized emporiums expressed their whimsical and pop orientations: Salvation, Grizzly Bear, Inter-Galactic Trading Post, Lift-Off, High Gear, Serendipity, Paraphernalia, Splendiferous, Abracadabra, Genitalia, Lucidity, Plasticity, Lady Madonna, Et Cetera, *et cetera.*

ORDINARY AS ART FORM

Two inspirations for Pop architecture run concurrently throughout the work of the new design—one is the anonymous undesigned, vernacular; the other is the garish or squalid, synthetic, and commercial. Often the two seemed to merge into a campopop compound.

At the opening of the decade there was already an architectural tradition of looking at common materials for their intrinsic design merits and of using them out of the context of their originally intended uses. The legacy of Dada, Surrealism, and Futurism in upending materials, uses, contexts, and functions was securely enough established to inspire, first, making use in interiors of industrial parts and found materials of the sleaziest manufacture, and then, futurizing the industrial inspiration and making large-scale buildings in that image. This tradition sprang from the inspiration that early Modern architects drew from industrial and factory buildings—the powerful geometric forms of chimneys, storage tanks, and vats, the acres of serrated sky-lit roofs.

Throughout the decade, an interest in vernacular architecture also bolstered a new vision of the ordinary. The intention was to search for ever more indigenous, close-to-home inspirations, to draw genealogy from existing architecture, and to create a continuity of tradition. This search was memorialized by Bernard Rudofsky in *Architecture Without Architects,* a book and an exhibition at The Museum of Modern Art in the fall of 1964, which was about anonymous, non-architect builders and their surprisingly sensitive, imaginative shelters and monuments. Rudofsky concentrated on vernacular architecture in ancient and modern provincial villages; his vision emphasized the growing rebellion against formal architecture and established architects. Similarly The Museum of Modern Art's "Twentieth Century Engineering" exhibition in the spring of 1964 was both a rebellion against traditional architecture, a movement toward non-architecture, and an expansion beyond it toward a new technology.

Literarily, the interest in vernacular architecture was continued by *Villages in the Sun* (1969), a book in which Myron Goldfinger reiterated the Rudofsky theme with a lavish and perceptive concentration on Mediterranean community architecture, and in such other more general books as *The Barn* (1972), in which Eric Arthur and Dudley Witney portray the farm buildings of North America. These were the found objects of architecture that served during our decade as the kind of strong inspiration that industrial buildings had been for early Modern architects.

People in interior design and furnishing, as usual, collected and used in their interiors all sorts of remnants and found objects from vernacular and old traditions. Carriage lamps had become a symbol of the front entrance—though how people came to want their houses to look like carriages had little to do with the desires of avant-garde architects who wanted houses to look like automobiles. Old farm weather vanes were used as wall decorations; old hip baths used as jardinieres or flowerpots became the satirical symbol of this folly. At this small scale, the acceptance of found objects meant that lighting fixtures designed for factories and warehouses—RLM shades and barn-door baffles—could be used by smart decorators as well as by young and rebellious architects; it meant that exposed mechanical systems and silver insulation batts could become more decorative than the late functionalists had ever envisioned.

David Sellers and
Charles Hosford:
Barn-door lighting in
residential use. 1968.
*Photograph by David
Hirsch.*

Next, architects took the idea into a larger scale: they brought capitals from old columns, paper boxes, and other architectural remnants into their interior designs. The device was old but the scandalizing effect of out of context was significantly new. Whereas previous transformations of objects had been made primarily for their addition of patina and texture to the new clean-lined, organic-textured buildings and interiors, the new out-of-context use of found objects was geared to shock, and to demonstrate the disposability and the ephemeral nature of all objects.

In terms of building materials, the pop vision means that anything is fair game for the construction of architecture, as of art. As Hugh Hardy said, "It meant that architects could build buildings out of anything, they did not have to use anything specifically labeled as architectural materials."

Among Pop architecture examples, earliest and easily identifiable are Philip Johnson's New York State Pavilion and Theatre for the New York World's Fair of 1963. The New York State Pavilion is clearly a reversal—the most substantial plastic tent ever built covers an outdoor room. Supported by great cylindrical concrete pylons, that mammoth indoor-outdoor tent of multicolored plastic sheeting—blue, orange, and red—makes a lively patchwork quilt of a cable-strung roof. Exposed elevators, painted signal-yellow like streetlights, ran up and down on the exterior of one of the pylons to reach the observation decks. At Johnson's New York State Theatre at Lincoln Center (1964), the audi-

Philip Johnson: New York State Pavilion for World's Fair, New York City. 1963. *Photograph by Ezra Stoller.*

torium is a line-for-line copy of the old Metropolitan Opera House interior but in new industrial materials: the chrysanthemum ceiling in industrial metal mesh, the treillage on the proscenium arch in cross-hatched wire drip, the lights on the six balconies as headlights, besides the fact that the side lobbies are hung with pop artworks. Tellingly, this pop auditorium is distinguished from the theatre's ceremonial foyer, with its tiered balconies that look like a dressed-up cellblock. Rightly so; "I saw it in a jail and I like it," Johnson said, thereby admitting a camp inversion and a black humor that clarify the distinction between the pop materials in the auditorium and the camp inspiration for the foyer.

Venturi's renovation of Mom's Restaurant in Philadelphia into Grand's (1962) was also early architectural Pop. Venturi used common things in uncommon ways. He said, "In keeping with the budget and with the character of the place, we tended to use conventional means and elements throughout in a spirited way, so that the common things took on new meaning. This was also a reaction to the overdesigned 'modern' fixtures typically available today." Their conventional means were industrial lights, bentwood chairs, old-looking high-backed booths, and exposed air-conditioning ducts.

As early Modern architects derived inspiration from industrial archi-tecture—from factories, train sheds, refineries, and large-scale "ma-chine" buildings—many new designers are inspired by barns and sheds from New England to California, and derive new images from these

Moore, Lyndon, Turnbull, Whitaker, with Lawrence Halprin: Athletic Club Number One, The Sea Ranch, California. 1966. *Photograph by C. Ray Smith.*

MLTW/Moore-Turnbull: Athletic Club Number Two, The Sea Ranch, California. 1969. *Photograph by C. Ray Smith.*

forms. Kevin Roche, not usually identified with the pop movement, used common farm-silo tiles as a facing for his Knights of Columbus Tower (1970) in New Haven. Charles Moore and Joseph Esherick took the vernacular of California outbuildings—wood structures with shed roofs, trapezoidal and triangular cutouts, and additive elements—and clustered those forms into notably sensitive massings. This is most vibrantly and richly expressed in the buildings at California's Sea Ranch (1965–1970) by Moore, Lyndon, Turnbull & Whitaker, which reflect both the spectacularly rugged terrain and ranch-country building craft. As Esherick comments, "It was interesting because we were asked to do a series of buildings to demonstrate what could be done in what really is a pretty unfriendly place as far as climate goes. It appears to be much less friendly than thirty years ago: We were given our choice of sites, and we had a plot of winds of the area: we picked where it was the strongest." The buildings of The Sea Ranch show a subtle merger of an existing vernacular and a new design imagery that produced an increasingly popular vernacular, a growing new slang—and one that Moore speaks most colorfully of all. The analogy between Moore's designs for The Sea Ranch and Palladio's deification of North Italian farm buildings is not too farfetched.

The distinction between background buildings and foreground buildings has categorized architects as well as their designs for several decades. Commonly, foreground buildings are defined as those designed to stand out from their surroundings and to make prominent monuments of themselves and, most people suspect, of their architects. Those called background buildings attempt to blend in with their surroundings, usually by employing current design motifs, and they modestly aim for contextual continuity of neighborhood. With the Lieb House (1969), Venturi & Rauch turned the self-effacing social and neighborly aim of background architecture into an offense tactic on New Jersey's Long Beach Island. Not content with merely using current vernacular beach architecture for their materials, the architects, instead, employed the boxiness of conventional beach houses along with a historical, Camp revival of 1950s two-toned coloring in asbestos-shingle sheathing. Contradictorily, the Lieb House is unprepossessing and prominent at the same time because it uniquely raises the anonymous "builder's house" into the realm of an art form. Venturi, with a typical but always unexpected inversion, singled out this direction as the "cult of the ordinary," a theory he clearly explained in an analysis of the mammoth

Co-op City apartment complex in the north Bronx, and which his firm demonstrated in the design for the Brighton Beach apartments competition and in the Yale Mathematics Building.

Venturi's theory is that in a setting of ugly and ordinary builders' houses, a setting leveled of topographical features—hills, trees, vegetation, foliage—any new design that sets out to be "pretty" or "good design" only points up the ugliness of the landscape. So Venturi & Rauch made the Lieb House (see color plate 2) a building "which was, in its way, ugly like the landscape of telephone poles and wires and the constant rhythm of these little houses plopped on their sides," Venturi said.

> We were building this in terms of what the urban planning at the beach is. We're not building it for what we think it should be . . . Most people design in terms of not what is but what should be . . . it's not like spraying a spray of perfume when you're in a pigsty. I look at this building and I see it next to the poles; the poles and the building look okay together. This building purposely is a kind of bold little ugly banal box,

he could say proudly of the Lieb House, leaving some architects amused by this intellectual twist, leaving others incredulous at his candor and pride. As familiarity with the house grew, the bold-scale boxiness stood out against the surrounding pitched roofs; its two-toned superstripes were a proclamation amid the vernacular; the form of its fragmented semicircular window on the west side and the scale of the address number 9 at the front entry was, even Venturi admitted, "high-fashion architecture." "The Lieb House," Denise Scott-Brown Venturi explained,

> is ordinary and extraordinary at the same time. It is like the landscape and not like the landscape—ugly and beautiful. It is the tension between these opposites. We are saying it is like everything else; yet it isn't like everything else; we admit that. It is like everything else in the way that the Pop artists make something like a Campbell's Soup can. It is like, but isn't like. See what I mean?

However constantly interesting the mental agility of the Venturis' doublethink aesthetic theory—and that may be the most valuable contribution they make to architecture—the Lieb House is a perfectly workable, no-nonsense house, with a straightforward acceptance of the sequential functions of beach-house living. The washer-drier is downstairs between the front entrance and the sand-shower room; the upstairs living area is entered through the kitchen. Those are the relationships to daily realities that make the house a functional as well as an artistic expression of the ordinary. Critics who ask if that is a good thing ask a superfluous question. The quest of art is no longer to show us the beauties of nature but to show us the realities and richness of life—to show us new visions of existence. In that respect, the Lieb House helps us to discover the truth of our daily "ordinary" existence.

SUPERSCALE POP

Several architects brought the world of Pop to architecture in a larger scale by using found objects to construct whole buildings. They developed systems of designing with standard industrial parts, such as industrialized architectural elements used by package builders—metal roof structures, wall systems, stairs, windows, and door units normally used only for storage buildings and behind-the-scenes architecture. Previously, most architects had considered these elements outside the realm of design. To them, each element of their pure and original sculptures should be custom-designed, and the result was that they virtually reinvented the wheel for each successive house or office building. Perhaps more than any other factor, that approach to architecture as jewelry-sculpture was responsible for the meager architectural market, since it pushed the costs of building as high as a client would permit. The new use of available materials and building systems exploited proven functions and economic efficiency. And the architects who pursued this path, did not abrogate their own design contributions.

It was not the first time in our century that architects had explored the uses of found or ordinary pop building materials. In 1910, Bernard Maybeck had designed the First Church of Christ Scientist in Berkeley with standard factory sash, adding leaded joints between panes to give them a more delicate scale. Charles Eames's house in Venice, California (1949), made the first notable use in the Modern idiom of standard building components from manufacturers catalogues. Designed and built as a "case study" house for the magazine *Arts & Architecture* edited by John Entenza, who subsequently directed the Graham Foundation, Eames's house is a virtuosic demonstration of the use of catalogue components: standard steel windows are assembled with wall panels of steel, plywood, and asbestos cement into a highly sensitive International Style, Mondrian-like composition; open bar joints supporting the roof also serve as decorative exterior fascias. In the 1950s Bruce Goff used structural ribs from the Quonset hut, interior partitions of fly screening, and columns of spun concrete sewer pipe; Herb Greene used ordinary steel reinforcing rods as stair balusters; Rafael Soriano constructed balcony fronts and fences of corrugated plastic sheeting, and Pierre Koenig used readily available steel decking as an exterior wall system, which he made elegant. Most of the uses of commercially available materials in the 1940s and the 1950s were in the mainstream of the machine age idiom.

Yet, Eames had made a penetrating statement: rejecting the custom-designed jewel architecture of the master builders, he assumed the role of selector and assembler—much as decorators assembled interiors rather than designing them, much as the fine artists made collages and assemblages. Eames took the machine age to its promised conclusion, making use of only such well-designed building materials as already existed—right off the warehouse shelves, so to speak—and devoted his energies to joinery and composition. It was the first real sally into the democratization of Modern architecture.

In the 1960s, John Johansen developed the functionalism that he had been brought up with into a new scale; he used exposed plumbing and standard corrugated siding for the exterior of several buildings. His Mummers Theatre in Oklahoma City (1970) is seemingly a pop, road-side statement—a giant-scale tinkertoy with pop plumbing imagery that Johansen compared to "electronic circuitry." His L. Frances Smith Elementary School in Columbus, Indiana (1970), is also in this mecha-nistic vein—a late monument to functionalist goals of apotheosizing the mechanical systems.

Hardy Holzman Pfeiffer Associates designed diagonal collisions of their buildings to provide a new look for rigid, foursquare, and rather pat-looking industrialized systems. They did a research study of this special range of building components from package builders—formerly the rejected competitors of architects—and began to incorporate into their buildings items they found—prefab stairs, Butler roof systems, industrial siding, greenhouse systems, and so on. Their designs consis-tently use popular, conventional building elements, virtually as they are, to produce a new, jagged Pop architecture. In the Mt. Healthy School (1972) and the Columbus Occupational Health Center (1974) in (*right*) John M. Johansen: The Mummers Theatre, Oklahoma City, Oklahoma. 1970. *Photograph by Balthazar Korab.* (*below*) Hardy Holzman Pfeiffer Associates: Columbus Occupational Health Center, Columbus, Indiana. 1972. *Photograph by Norman McGrath.* (*below, right*) Casino signs, Las Vegas, Nevada. 1969. *Photograph by C.Ray Smith.*

Columbus, Indiana, this direction has produced truly distinctive major buildings.

The Kinetic Electric Environment

The Pop art vision that accepts commercial lighting as valid good design, as in the signs at Las Vegas and Times Square, this same pop vision has made ours the "age of the nude bulb"—including fluorescent, incandescent, and bare neon. Interest in a changing, evolving environment and in nonstatic forms and growth accounts for much of the manipulation of this synthetic medium. Since the 1880s when mansions were first wired for electric lighting and all lamps went exposed, we have come full circle. From the 1920s to the 1970s the object of lighting design was to conceal the source of light and to eliminate glare. Today there is a general desire to see the light source again. At the Bauhaus, designers were interested in exposed light as a creative medium. Gerrit Rietveld designed a chandelier in the 1920s with exposed fluorescent tubes. But it has been only in the last ten years that artists have tackled light itself as a legitimate medium.

Among the painters and sculptors, David Smith and others depended more and more on light (from the sun or artificial sources) and "the animation of reflective surfaces to achieve effect of weightlessness." Light sculptor Dan Flavin uses fluorescent tubes to define and explode space—sometimes confusingly at the same time. Many artists working with light were given a home during the 1960s by Howard Wise's gallery on New York City's Fifty-seventh Street: Richard Hogle worked with flashing colored lights projected onto shaped translucent forms; Preston McClanahan used the technique of fiber optics in large-scale, transparent plexiglass rods and sheets that carried colored light to the terminal edges; John Van Saun worked with colored lights that flashed in random sequence and struck a musical note at the same time. "Lights in Orbit," an exhibition of works composed of light in motion, ran in the heyday of 1967 at the Howard Wise Gallery; as stated in the catalogue, it featured "High-intensity quartz-iodide lights; electronic circuitry; laser beams; magnetic distortion of electron beams; polarized light; plastics irradiated by gamma rays; polyester films coated with a mono-molecular layer of aluminum; new phosphors having varying controlled rates of decay." Thirty-six artist-scientists were represented in a literally dazzling display of light works: Marta Boto, Howard Branston, Jackie Cassen, Rudi Stern, John Goodyear, Richard Hogle, Julio Le Parc, Frank Malina, Preston McClanahan, Edward Meneeley, Gerald Oster, Nam June Paik, Otto Piene, Leo Rabkin, Earl Reiback, Takis, John Van Saun, Paul Williams, and Donald Zurlo. And no one can forget the pioneering Lumia works of Thomas Wilfred, who died at the end of the decade. Flashing, floating neon was used by Billy Apple, Chryssa, and others during the 1960s, and by 1972 Rudi Stern and Mel Romanoff in New York opened a SoHo gallery especially for neon signs and sculptures.

These artists' and architects' work with light realized in a new electric way the Bauhaus goal of de-materialized architecture and design. Light creates environments of non-form even *less* materially than inflatables and other invisible designs. It was part also of the interest in kinetic design and in adaptability to change.

Architectural lighting designers now feel that people are more comfortable when they are aware of the sources of light, sound, and air. The light source, and such prosaic paraphernalia as wiring, switches, and sockets, have become decorative and design elements. Ordinary plugs and sockets have become visible parts of the lighting fixture—all part of the pop attitude. And Nathan Silver wrote in 1971, "Las Vegas is the world's first twenty-four-hour city, as the Chamber of Commerce knows. Day is as night in the glittering, windowless casinos; night is bright as day along Fremont Street, ablaze with rocking and erupting lights." (At least until late 1973.)

In 1968, the Elm City Electric Light Sculpture Company, a group of New Haven designers including William Grover and Jerry and Martha Wagner, brought neon sculptures out of the art gallery and into a more permanent, practical, and everyday environment. The neon tube assumed remarkable grace in a neon chandelier designed by Jerry Wagner for Yale professor F. R. R. Drury. Long, gold and pink neon tubes on a dimmer drew attention to the dining table in the center of the all-white room. The technical mastery that hid all electrical connections was especially worthy of note; connections were concealed behind a circular, polished-chrome plate that reflected the tubes, making them appear to flow from the ceiling in a liquid motion. Since neon tubes will not support their own weight beyond a certain length, the design called for careful calculation (see color plate 8).

For Charles Moore's Faculty Club at the University of California's Santa Barbara campus, the same designers created six suspended neon banners that are the most flashy updated medieval heraldry of our turned-on age (see color plate 6).

Grover also used standard parts, readily available from the local hardware store, to make a chandelier for Charles Moore's New Haven house (1966). Inspiration came from an article in a German lighting journal, which showed a similar fixture assembled from specially manufactured parts. While Grover was installing his fixture for Moore, designer John Kyrk saw it, and later came upon the same magazine article Grover had seen. A fixture Kyrk subsequently designed, similar to

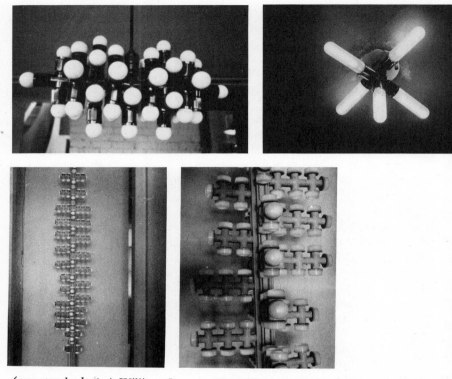

(*counterclockwise*) William Grover: Chandelier composed of double sockets, New Haven, Connecticut. 1965. *Photograph by Maud Dorr.*   Paul Rudolph: Light sculpture composed of double sockets and night-lights, New York City. 1966. *Photograph by Louis Reens.*   Peter Gluck: Lights for dressing rooms, Contessina Boutique, New York City. 1967. *Photograph by Louis Reens.*

Grover's, was widely marketed by Design Research. Kyrk feels that even if he had not seen Grover's work, he would eventually have developed his own version of the idea, simply because of his interest in bare bulbs and kit construction.

To make a hanging light sculpture in the vestibule of Paul Rudolph's Manhattan apartment (1966), orange-glow night-light lamps plugged into white, rubber, three-way sockets were ganged and strung on tap-a-line fixtures. In the orange bedroom of the same apartment, the warm glow of incandescent lighting was concentrated close to the carpet in two lines along the room's long walls. "Plug-mold" wiring channels were on the ceiling and lamps were suspended on long exposed cables.

David Sellers and Charles Hosford added coiled cable as a pop lighting element, which was functional in addition by permitting the extension of the lights to other locations. "Barn-door" fixtures with baffles on sides, top, and bottom, normally used in industrial corridors, were clustered by the same designers to create a chandelier with exposed spotlights. Industrial fixtures known as RLM's were used by the same designers with different kinds of lamp bulbs in various residences. A wall fixture by Hosford centers a single silver bowl lamp in a block of

Charles Hosford: Dining table
sconce with silver bowl lamp. 1966. *Photograph by David Hirsch.*

(*left*) Peter Hoppner: Standard lamp with shaving-mirror reflectors, New York City. 1967. *Photograph by Louis Reens.* (*right*) Alan Liddel: Lights from juice cans with beer-can-opener perforations as decoration, Mt. Rainier, Washington. 1960. *Photograph by Hugh N. Stratford.*

solid wood, whose shape is determined by the salad bowl that has been carved out of it. For a standing fixture in 1967, Peter Hoppner used two shaving mirrors attached to the top and bottom ends of a steel tube to reflect light from an exposed incandescent lamp.

Another prominent inversion in the use of architectural materials was in carpeting, which was extended beyond its traditional limits. From the confines of luxurious salons, carpeting spread into schools and hospitals; then it spread outside to stadiums and terraces and, in a double paradox, outdoor carpeting spread back inside into bathrooms and kitchens. Even in traditional locations, carpeting expanded beyond the limits of the living room rug, climbed the walls, spread across ceilings, and wrapped up the furniture as well. New outdoor carpeting known as synthetic turf, recreational surface, or more bluntly, artificial grass was originally a camp idea for playgrounds and sports fields. Next it invaded the garden in resort and hotel installations. (A resort hotel in the Catskills reportedly put down two acres of lawn in plastic grass.) It offered "low maintenance—no weeds, no mowing, no watering, and no hay fever," one observer noted. Then, as a texture-attracting advertising device, stores and hotels carpeted their sidewalks.

One double reversal in building matrials stood in Krumsville, Pennsylvania: an old fieldstone farm building was stuccoed over for insulation, then painted gray with a grid of white lines that made it look like a concrete-block building. Modern concrete block had been superimposed on fieldstone. In architectural and building materials, it seemed, anything goes.

AUTOS

A simple and clear demonstration of Pop in architecture is the use of the automobile as image and as object. If the trailer industry made an aesthetic crash when it set the house on wheels and took it out onto the road, today's designers are winning a visual drag race by putting the trailer into reverse and bringing the automobile—and the whole freeway, in fact—indoors. As they said in neo-1940s jargon, "It's super!" The "Yield" signs over college dormitory beds, the bumpers as fireplace fenders, the headlight bulbs in table lamps, the billboards in countless forms are constant reminders that the mystique of the auto has captivated man. From fiery phaeton to tin lizzie, from Model T to souped-up dragster, the young in spirit have been revved up about speed. Today, they cherish the chrome wheels and the shine-and-polish routine that accompany it. The automobile is in the forefront: it is the pop imagery of our decade.

No wonder Pop artists and architects were captivated by the commercial strip: nearly half our time is spent in the environment of the road. This is partly a romantic revival of the 1940s spirit of hot rodders, beatniks, and Jack Kerouac, in which personalized, customized, decked-out autos were treated as pets, if not as wives. The outlook appeared so fundamental to youthful designers and to middle-class America that it was examined by Marshall McLuhan in a book called *The Mechanical Bride* (1951).

With roadways going through buildings as in Le Corbusier's Carpenter Art Center at Harvard and, around 1960, more and more cars and parking being integrated into buildings as in William Tabler's hotel

George Segal: *The Truck,* 1966, plaster, metal, glass, plastic, wood, and moving picture. The Art Institute of Chicago. *Photograph courtesy The Art Institute of Chicago.*

schemes, Skidmore, Owings & Merrill's store for Macy's in Queens, New York, and the Helicoid in Caracas, the visual aspects and accouterments of the freeway were bound to be incorporated into the new design.

How did the freeway get indoors? The deification of the machine and of the industrialized process started it all, then Pop art "laxed" us further into accepting the commercial-fold aspects of our two-sided, gaudy-*versus*-designed culture. As the fine arts have shown, freeway elements can be transformed in varying degrees. In assemblages by John Chamberlain and by Cesar Pelli roadway items remain realistic, but rumpled. In Gerald Laing's work the imagery has been abstracted— chrome and rainbow-flaked metal pieces evoking mufflers, smoke, and speed. Van Ringelheim's "directionals" give a new boost to road signs. Most telling for the motion and light of our automobile society is George Segal's piece *The Truck* (1966) at the Chicago Art Institute in which the viewer, like Segal's seated white-plaster driver, watches through a windshield as the multicolored nighttime environment seemingly speeds past him in rear projections on the windshield.

In interior uses—a logical reversal of indoor-outdoor interpenetration—hot-rod "candy-apple" finishes, "California Baby Moon" hubcaps, car jacks, reflectors, horns, and the like were used as both functional and fun objects and as finishes and structural systems. Charles Moore and William Turnbull used roadside mailboxes as athletic-club lockers. David Sellers put a rubber bulb "a-OOOgah" horn from an old tin lizzie through the front door of one of his houses at Prickly Mountain, Vermont, to serve as a doorbell; it could have served as doorbell and doorknob combined. A car bumper seemed like the largest and least expensive hunk of chrome already available to offset

Moore, Lyndon, Turnbull, Whitaker, with Lawrence Halprin and Barbara Stauffacher Solomon: Mailboxes as lockers, Athletic Club Number One, The Sea Ranch, California. 1967. *Photograph by Morley Baer.*

David Sellers: Automobile horn as doorbell, Prickly Mountain, Warren, Vermont. 1967. *Photograph by David Sellers/Hirsch.*

my own traditional all-white living room; and since, in England and the South, at least, a bumper is called a "fender," a nice international design pun was made by using it as a fire fender (see p. 298).

Ulrich Franzen is credited with first using tractor seats—another automotive item—as indoor furniture when he had them chrome-plated for the shop Paraphernalia. Later, they were sold by Design Research and used as *objets trouvés* by any number of designers. David Sellers, among them, also used black leather seats from a Mustang as the sofa of prominence in his Bridge House at Prickly Mountain. Volkswagen or Fiat doors were used by Fabio De Sanctis and Ugo Sterpini in a cabinet exhibited at the Museum of Contemporary Crafts' "Fantasy Furniture" show in 1966. And by 1970, two chairs using VW parts or facsimiles were in commercial production—one by William Lansing Plumb, one by Peter Goldring; the latter used VW fenders as arms.

By extension, chrome-yellow, rubberized, all-weather road construction tarpaulins also bring the automobile indoors. Standard tarps made for the Bell Telephone System were hung on their grommets as the wall covering of my own apartment kitchen; they were tied together with Day-

(*left*) Peter Goldring: VW chair composed of
fenders and hood painted yellow. 1970. *Photograph courtesy
Lighting Associates Inc.* (*right*) William Lansing Plumb: *Volks Chair*. 1970.

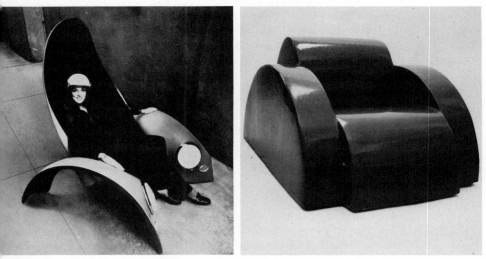

Mediterranean Car
Wash, California.
1969. *Photograph by
Arthur Golding and
Doug Meyer.*

Glow orange barricade warning tape. The all-weather materials were easily maintained and sprightly for kitchen use. A hubcap served as a reflector for the exposed spotlight in the ceiling.

Hardy Holzman Pfeiffer Associates (then Hugh Hardy & Associates) first planned the lobby of their theatre for Cincinnati's Playhouse in the Park (1968) entirely with automobile parts. Seating was to be from Ford Mustangs and Cougars; front bumpers from Ford Fairlanes were to be used as stair railings; headlight units from the same make of cars would serve as wall sconces. "The freeway is the modern jewel," Hardy said, "and the items used in its environment are the jewels of today." In the theatre, he continued, "we decided that the obvious way to call the audience back after intermission was to put the parking lights on." In the concert hall of their proposed Performing Arts Center for the University of Toledo, Hugh Hardy & Associates planned to hang automobile windshields as acoustical clouds. The windshields were to be hung on wire, complete with weather stripping and chrome trim, but upside down.

Countless other automobile- and freeway-related objects fascinated young designers, such as the car-wash facilities that Arthur Golding wrote about. But one roadside object stood out above all the others— the billboard.

BILLBOARDS

Of all the commercial roadside objects that inspired the pop imagination, billboards were the most accessible and most accommodating to architects' manipulation. The notion of using billboards as subject matter was a camp inversion, first of all, in that they began to appeal to designers just when the federal government outlawed them. When Washington finally got involved in cleaning up our highways, ridding them of 500,000 billboards by means of the Highway Beautification Act of 1965, Robert Venturi was off lecturing around the country on behalf of *bigger* billboards. As he said in Oklahoma, "Billboards, if anything, should be larger. Out here with your vast spaces, the great scale of your signs and billboards is a virtue and it should be used for public purposes as well as commercial."

Numerous other architects used billboard ads as a new kind of wallpaper. Charles Moore put up a fragment of a Volkswagen billboard in his New Haven house. Hugh Hardy papered Harlem's New Lafayette Theatre and several other projects with billboards. Yale-trained Doug Michels used a photomural of the ubiquitous VW bug purring down the street of dreams and bouncing over Ionic capitals in an apartment in New Haven. It put the image of the mechanical bride above the image of the nonmechanical bride. Paul Rudolph started out to wrap his kitchen in Gulf Oil billboards and ended up with a collage of them on walls, ceiling, and floor, on window, refrigerator, and cabinets as a cubistic fragmentation of the roadside strip. Venturi & Rauch used all this pop imagery in the Guild House in Philadelphia, in Fire Station No. 4 in Columbus, Indiana, and in the Football Hall of Fame project, which Venturi called "a Bill-Ding-Board." Yet Venturi's billboards, as he built them, are controlled and uptight in relation to the exuberant abandon of their intellectual predecessors.

In the Guild House apartments for the elderly, built in Philadelphia (1960–1965), Venturi & Rauch first combined all the elements that later became the hallmarks of their design: The building adopts the idiom of the everyday, ordinary red brick apartment house—an acceptance of our pop reality and the neighboring buildings—and combines it with historical allusions. In plan and massing the structure resembles the entrance porticoes of mannerist architecture. In the street-front facade, which is no higher than the rest of the roof line but which has two vertical slits like crenelations, the center portion has the effect of a

Doug Michels: Michels apartment with Volkswagen billboard, New Haven, Connecticut. 1966. *Photograph by John Hill.*

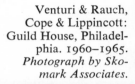

Venturi & Rauch, Cope & Lippincott: Guild House, Philadelphia. 1960–1965. *Photograph by Skomark Associates.*

parapeted screen of red brick atop a white brick base. This base, the main entry, is Venturi's first architectural billboard with oversized, purposely clumsy lettering on a white field. As another historical allusion, the entry reiterates becolumned porticoes: whimsically, a single polished-granite column is placed in the middle, as if blocking a large entry, although the entry is actually composed of two small doors flanking the false, nonstructural cylinder; above, a series of balconies, topped by an arched window to a recreation room, suggests a monumental gateway to palatial residences of old. All the facades are sensitively composed by fenestration of different square and horizontal shapes, many of them oversize double-hung windows that recall the ordinary apartment house idiom. This attention to fenestration is a design activity of Venturi & Rauch's that reaches a culmination in the skillfully varied windows punched, like a key-punch card, in the firm's Mathematics Building for Yale (1970). As a final Pop art symbol of our age, "and of the aged who spend so much time watching TV at the Guild House," as Venturi said, the first designed a nonfunctioning gold-anodized television antenna that is placed as the crowning heraldic emblem atop the arched ceremonial portal.

The effect of Guild House is unsettlingly ambivalent. It clearly presents a realistic acceptance of the everyday fact and occurrence of ordinary contemporary building, and this seems a straightforward, direct, and honest approach to our urban environment. Yet it also includes motifs of earlier, more monumental and pretentious architecture in an attempt to symbolize the residential pride of its elderly occupants; this is an intellectual overlay. What this blend of ordinary mediocrity and monumental pomp creates, therefore, is a singular and tensioned response.

As Venturi described his firm's Football Hall of Fame project of 1967–1968, it is really a building-board.

> The front is made out of one of those flashing light board systems. And you enter in a really sexy way—up ramps and through an entry door that is the shape of a football. Behind that is a long nave with chapels in ranks like a great Italian villa. There is a hierarchy of the football saints: great projections and movies on the vaulting of the nave show the great football plays, and in the chapels are relics like those of saints. Here they would have the sweatshirt of Knute Rockne —the actual object that is reflected in the movies on the vaulting and on the front, electric billboard.

At sixty miles per hour, Venturi & Rauch's Fire Station 4 in Columbus, Indiana (1965), is immediately recognizable. At the top of its hose-drying tower is a large numeral 4. A white pattern of brick, seemingly overlaid on the red brick building, is like a pasted-on advertising poster. This literary analogy may not be visually immediate, since the white poster shape is incomplete because of cutouts for doors and windows, which it permissively cuts across without alignment; but once understood, the billboard is unforgettable. The white brick is set in from

(*top*) Venturi & Rauch: Fire Station No. 4, Columbus, Indiana. 1965–1969. *Photograph by David Hirsch.* (*below*) Venturi & Rauch: Fire Station No. 4, Columbus, Indiana. 1965–1969. *Photograph by David Hirsch.*

the corners of surrounding red brick and the front elevation has a parapet or false front that is higher on the left side than on the rest of the building to give the elevation proportions different from the actual volume of the building. Indefinably, vaguely, this cutout shape of the overlaid white brick billboard suggests an inverted upside-down *4*. Like Al Held's superscale, fragmented triangle paintings of the mid-1960s, it is additional and subliminal signage.

Another minor decorative device illustrates Venturi & Rauch's pop Mannerism. Above the doors to the hose-drying tower and beneath the exposed quartz light fixture that illuminates the *4* two black bricks are set in the white coursework. They literally underline the light fixture, making another literary analogy. "We think it looks more pert this way," Venturi said, using a novel adjective for architecture, but one typical of his criticism. Similarly, the project designer of the fire station, Gerod Clark, said, "This is the first of our dumb buildings," by which he meant to indicate—as in "she's a dumb blonde"—that the building has rather basic materials but is flashily and sophisticatedly put together. Venturi used the phrase "dumb-sophisticated" for the fire station to show the contrasting and contradictory dualities that he wanted to express—the ordinary brick building in contrast to the mannerist billboard facade—again demonstrating a perverse twist of mind crackling with imaginative contradictions. Fire Station 4 is one of Venturi & Rauch's most tasteful, polished, and intricate works.

Architects and critics not in sympathy with Venturi's theories found his allusions and devices a wicked acceptance of their own rejected taboos. And his sense of wry yet scandalizing humor in using the terms *boring, ordinary, dumb, banal,* and *ugly* about his own designs continued to confuse and provoke public and professionals alike as well as to further the obscurity and inaccessibility of his design intentions.

Banking Boutique

By 1969 such supermannerist devices as billboards had been accepted widely enough for the most "serious" and traditionally conservative institutions to assume the finery of their peacock plumage. Businessmen had already begun to wear their hair, sideburns, and moustaches longer. The backbone of 1950s conformity seemed broken. This thrust of the new design deep into citadels of the Establishment caused a new excitement. Bolstered by a strong and inflationary economy, a few bankers put this all together and sponsored several supermannerist banks.

Not since 1954, when Gordon Bunshaft and Skidmore, Owings & Merrill took Manufacturers Hanover Trust Company out of its stone fortress tradition and put it into a "defenseless" glass box, had any major change occurred in the image of banks. Now, the new architects produced for the 1970s what Skidmore, Owings & Merrill had done for banking in the 1960s. For its new headquarters building in Philadelphia, the Industrial Valley Bank (IVB) did not play safe but vaulted its image into the space age, as well as responsibly providing a lively indoor-outdoor wall onto a new urban plaza and thereby enriching the city-scape. The new image and the belief in the bank's social responsibility to the urban scene took Richard Saul Wurman, of the Philadelphia firm Murphy Levy Wurman—along with an exceptional client, John C. T. Alexander, then senior vice-president of the IVB—into getting it all together with lights and synthetics, reflections and superscale, rooms-within-rooms, diagonals, and billboards.

In the 10,300-square-foot branch, which opened in January 1969, tellers face the main entrance from the street-level plaza. Circulation from the building lobby at the right of the tellers' counters to that main entrance is a diagonal line that influences the flat side of the otherwise circular officers' platform, which is a low-walled room-within-a-room to the right of the main entry. "The plan is dumb," said Wurman, revealing his Philadelphia associations, and meaning direct, straightforward, and nongimmicky. The lighting design is prominent, due to exposed fluorescent tubes; diagonally striped against a reflective glossy white ceiling, they reiterate the circulation pattern from entrance to entrance. Repetition of the tubes camouflages what purists considered the "inelegancies" of the exposed electrical connections. In addition, pendant square tubes of wood, which house incandescent spotlights, spread pools of light onto the tellers' counters. These square pendant fixtures are striped with fluorescent tubes that run down the center of each side. The effect is that

Murphy Levy Wurman: Industrial Valley Bank, Philadelphia. 1969. *Photograph by Jon Naar.*

the lights read as exploded corners and make the tubes appear like diagonally rotated squares.

In an open-ended program of changing murals, architect Wurman painted a cartoon for a new mural every six weeks and sign painters executed his designs on an eighteen-foot by thirty-seven-foot indoor billboard behind the officers' platform. The initial murals of the series presented a superscale slice of Mrs. Smith's cherry pie and a mammoth Mack truck bulldog—both of them bank customers—as well as a super-flag for Philadelphia's 1976 exhibition. Purple, blue, silver, white, and black are the colors of this banking space, and there are new materials in it too: the deep blue flooring is troweled, poured, and polished neoprene; low partitions and the tellers' counter are sheathed in panels of purple plexiglass covered in glass to prevent scratching. In deference to tradition, however, where money touches a surface, that surface is the customary marble. Check-writing desks also are of plastic—large black plastic-laminate cubes with one-inch-thick glass tops composed of four one-quarter-inch sheets. This relatively thin glass is laminated together for economy but also to produce a reduplicated optical effect. Slots for deposit and withdrawal slips are cut diagonally into the tops of the cubes

(left) Murphy Levy Wurman: Billboard in Industrial Valley Bank, Philadelphia. 1969. *Photograph by Richard Saul Wurman. (right)* Murphy Levy Wurman: Billboard in Industrial Valley Bank, Philadelphia. 1969. *Photograph by Richard Saul Wurman.*

1. Hardy Holzman Pfeiffer: MUSE, Brooklyn, New York. 1968.
Photograph by Norman McGrath. (See page 252.)

2. Venturi & Rauch: Lieb House, Long Beach Island, New Jersey. 1969.
Photograph by Steven R. Hill. (See page 173.)

3. Cesar Pelli for Daniel, Mann, Johnson & Mendenhall:
California Jewelry Mart, Los Angeles. 1968.
Photograph by Arthur Golding. (See page 280.)

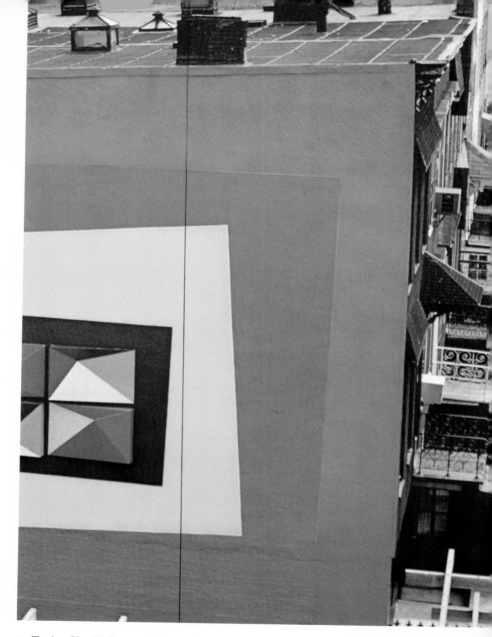

5. Tania: City Walls mural, Brooklyn, New York. 1970. *Photograph by Joel Peter Witkin.* (See page 200.)

. David Sellers and Charles Hosford: Gatehouse, Sugarbush ski area, ᐧarren, Vermont. 1967. *Photograph by David Sellers.* (See page 297.)

6. MLTW/Moore-Turnbull: Faculty Club, University of California, Santa Barbara; neon banners by Elm City Electric Light Sculpture Company. 1968. *Photograph by Martha Wagner.* (See page 179.)

7. Venturi & Rauch: Church of Saint Francis de Sales, Philadelph 1968. *Photograph by Steven R. Hill.* (See page 25

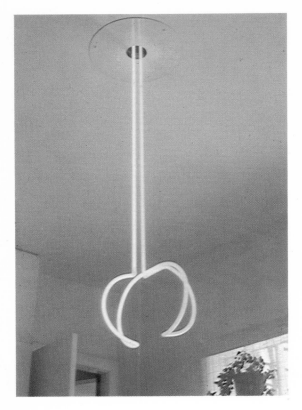

8. Jerome Wagner: Neon chandelier for F. R. R. Drury:
New Haven, Connecticut. 1968.
Photograph by Robert Perron. (See page 179.)

9. Doug Michels and Howie Knox: Storefront for Marathon Shoe Repair, New Haven, Connecticut. 1967. *Photograph by Doug Michels.* (See page 278.)

11. Student project for an exhibition, University of Texas, Austin. 1968.
Photograph by Richard Oliver. (See page 292.)

o. Robert Miles Runyan & Associates:
unburst supergraphic for
S. *Independence*. 1968.
hotograph by Martha Holmes.
See page 279.)

12. Doug Michels: Supergraphic on a window, Washington, D.C. 1968. *Photograph by Doug Michels.* (See page 278.)

13. Paul Rudolph: Rudolph apartment, New York City. 1967 *Photograph by Louis Reens.* (See page 149.)

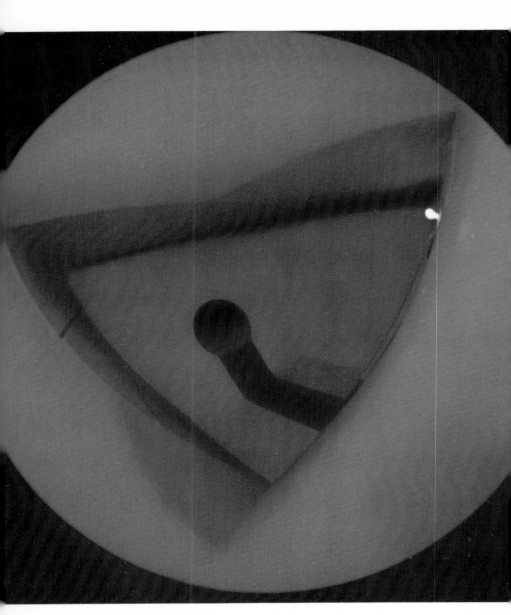

14. Charles Coffman: Coffman apartment, Houston, Texas. 1968.
Photograph by Charles Coffman. (See page 146.)

15. Chip Lord: Stair enameled orange with shadow of handrail in blue, New Orleans, Louisiana. 1968. *Photograph by Chip Lord.* (See page 144.)

17. Lester Walker: Supercube, New York City. 1967. *Photograph by Robert L. Beckhard.* (See page 241.)

Peter Hoppner: Foyer finished in reflective silver mylar,
v York City. 1967. *Photograph by Louis Reens.* (See page 151.)

18. William Grover: Hallway with reverse perspective stripe, New Haven, Connecticut. 1967. *Photograph by William Grover.* (See page 280.)

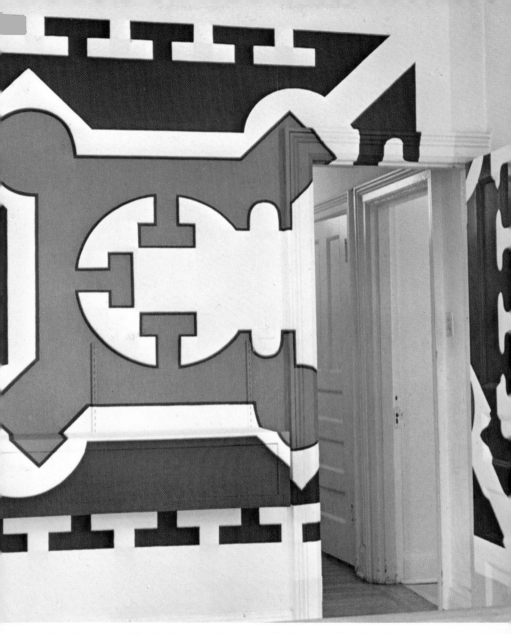

19. Barrie Briscoe: Mural, Toronto, Canada. 1968. *Photograph by Barrie Briscoe*. (See page 281.)

20. Doug Michels: Supergraphic for the offices of Moore-Turnbull, New Haven, Connecticut. 1965. *Photograph by Doug Michels.* (See page 282.)

21. Barry Briscoe: Liturgical supergraphic for Hillcrest Chur Toronto, Canada. 1969. *Photograph by Roger Jowett.* (See page 28

22. Barbara Stauffacher Solomon: Elevator design problem given to Yale architecture students, New Haven, Connecticut. 1968. *Photographs by James Righter.* (See page 290.)

23. C. Ray Smith: Smith New York City apartment with projection of Niagara Falls; executed by D. Gersztoff, J. Nuckolls, and W. Warfel; equipment courtesy of Kliegl Bros., Inc. 1968. *Photograph by Louis Reens.* (See page 297.)

24. C. Ray Smith: Smith New York City apartment with projection of The Sistine Chapel; executed by D. Gersztoff, J. Nuckolls, and W. Warfel; equipment courtesy of Kliegl Bros., Inc. 1967. *Photograph by Louis Reens.* (See page 297.)

Daniel Solomon, David Reichel, and Barbara Stauffacher Solomon: Thrift Federal Savings & Loan Association, Concord, California. 1970. *Photograph by Joshua Freiwald.*

beneath the glass. Since diagonals were already fairly modish at the time, Wurman considerd them the only *designed* elements in the bank. His word is significant, since it shows the Supermannerists' continuing negative reaction to pure form.

Wurman was more interested in what he calls "the public environment." Since, as he feels, the citizenry owns fifty percent of a city, corporations have a responsibility to the way their products—including buildings—adjoin that public environment. The branch put a brightly lighted youthful public face onto the esplanade around the building and took the world of banking another step along the road of public responsibility.

Sign as Space

Another bank—the Concord, California, branch of Thrift Federal Savings & Loan Association (1970)—was a bank-in electric billboard. The design brought the roadside imagery of lights to the old-order harmony and consistency of banking design. All the "corporate image" and "logo" design of the 1950s and the early 1960s seemingly are apotheo-

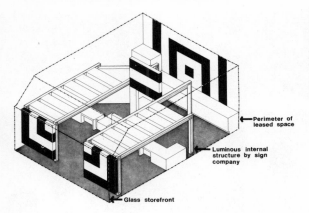

Daniel Solomon, David Reichel, and Barbara Stauffacher Solomon: Isometric, Thrift Federal Savings & Loan Association, Concord, California. 1970.

sized in this little bank; the bank's front window sign is the lighting system and the partitioning system. Literally, light creates and defines the space in a youthful and allusive interpretation of the old dictum.

Designer Daniel Solomon with architect David Reichel and graphics designer Barbara Stauffacher Solomon called in a roadside sign company to fabricate this electric bank interior. "Most of the small branch," says Daniel Solomon, "was built in the shops of Tom Wolfe's favorite neon maker—Federal Sign and Signal Company. We had the area sheet-rocked and then the neon people brought in what is really a three-dimensional space-enclosing sign, which houses the main banking activities." This is a direct and rare use of roadside Las Vegas's popular art to create the spatial essence of architecture.

The luminous sign is composed of fluorescent tubes behind fabricated acrylic panels, which are supported on a white-painted steel I-beam structure. This unit forms a red-and-white-striped background for the bank's logo display in its front show window; it continues overhead to provide a luminous ceiling for the principal work areas; further, it partitions off the rear work area with diagonal panels. The remainder of the interior design is composed of bold black-and-white stripes and several ranks of minimal white desks and counters. Daniel Solomon has been interested in the use of temporary furnishings and display materials in rented commercial work spaces, and he taught a course on the subject at Berkeley. But he admits that the bank, as a prototype, is "more permanent and more precious" than the theory of disposability purposes.

URBAN RENEWAL WITH PAINT

The painted billboards on city walls that developed in the 1960s were giant leaps in urban contribution and community involvment, as well as a prominent espousal of billboard Pop. Paint and other applied decorations were used for ghetto improvement in an admittedly superficial and temporary manner, but also for quick, economical, and revitalizing ends. In areas of New York, Detroit, Chicago, Boston, and other cities outdoor mural-painting programs assisted by municipal governments produced superscale urban billboards on both abstract and social themes. This is one of the most stimulating social and artistic phenomena in our country. As a means of revitalizing too often drab and dreary inner-city environments, blighted areas, and industrial areas, paint can make an immediate and often witty contribution. That today's cities can be made bright, cheerful, and sprightly without new construction was an idea that was virtually revolutionary to developers, who had learned their success from older urban renewal handbooks. To a number of architects and designers of the decade, this kind of applied decoration was clearly an expedient tool to get a large-scale remedial operation accomplished. And to improve our environment is the goal of all architects and designers. (See color plate 5.)

"The beauty of it is that it is a very low-cost answer," says California architect Cesar Pelli. "Architects who used to be concerned only with so-called important projects are concerned today with low-cost problems as well—problems where there is little money. And paint is a terribly important answer." Besides paint, of course, he could have included billboard appliqués of plastic, metal, and other materials. Hugh Hardy interjected a note of caution. "Talking about the device as being cheap for the ghetto sounds second best—like cleaning up the natives. It sounds condescending. Why should ghetto solutions be low cost? This sounds less appealing than that the technique is good because it is a good idea." Cesar Pelli replies, "Sometimes you have to do things with little money because the money has to go far and there is just so much to go around. And maybe you should stretch it and do more with that money. Besides, the technique is not only good for ghettos; it can also enliven commercial and other problems."

Another reason for fostering exterior decoration is that overworked word *involvement*. "With paint, the community itself can get into the act," Lee Harris Pomeroy explains. "They can't build buildings and lay bricks, but they can paint. That has real social value."

Owners of industrial areas experimented with renewal by means of this superscale decoration. As a result, some lucky fringe areas of our cities, and some even luckier inner-city areas, have been brightened up beyond their customary dreariness. For the tanks of the Slay Bulk Terminal on the west bank of the Mississippi River at Saint Louis (1968–1969), architects Hohmann & Meyer designed a paint-stripe scheme as a "low-cost beautification and aesthetic improvement." Part of their master plan for the Terminal design consisted of dark bands that frame round-cornered panels on the lighter-colored oil storage tanks.

Amusing, perhaps because it is both pretentious and deceptive, in the way that romantic novels are illusionary and dishonest, was an industrial fence that alluded to a firm's activities. At the Farmer John meat packing plant in Vernon, California, from 1965 to 1969, the roadside fence was painted with a gentle pastoral panorama: amid green fields shaded by old trees, the farmer's boy fishes in the pasture pond while the piggies gambol and frolic in a blissful springtime of unworried life. David Gebhard, director of the art galleries at the University of California, Santa Barbara, first wrote about this roadside artistry: "The uniqueness of the approach to design (and public relations) is so way out and flamboyant that there are many lessons we can learn from it. Here is a combination of a 19th century view of the farm with the billboard with illusionism tempered by an understanding of community relations. Here behind these nostalgic reminiscences of the farm, slaughter takes place and stench permeates the air."

It is hard to see an allusion to something larger than life in this romantic deception, unless it is the heavenly rest beyond the slaughterhouse. What the Farmer John fence contributed was a commercial billboard as a camp urban improvement, a perverse and witty deception for one of the most unattractive, if necessary, of our commercial environments. It was similar to the work of Art Tribe in Venice, California, and elsewhere.

A more literary billboard in industrial-area improvement was the Ron Llave rum-bottling plant (1968–1969) in Arecibo, Puerto Rico, which is housed in a refurbished lumber warehouse. New York architect

(*top*) Painted fence, Farmer John meat packing plant, Vernon, California. 1965–1969. *Photograph by David Gebhard.* (*bottom*) Painted fence, Farmer John meat packing plant, Vernon, California. 1965–1969. *Photograph by David Gebhard.*

Barrie Fez-Barringten (then Barry Feiss), with the architectural firm of Schimmelpfennig, Ruiz & Gonsales, designed a paint-renovation scheme at the first site visit. "Draw circles the height of the building," he instructed the painting contractors, "then repeat them around the building until you get back to the start." The circles express the repetitive barrels and bottles of the bottling plant, so the design has a supergraphic dimension (see "Supergraphics") in its suggestion of the barrels or tanks continuing through the building. Architect Fez-Barringten, who calls the device "metagraphics," sees a Pop art literary allusion in the circles. To him they are the projections of spotlight beams like Batman's in the comic strips. The powerful beams blot out the red building and make lighter, beige circles; in the process, the beam catches hanging lamp fixtures in its shadow. We need a mind-set to see all this, but once established, it is hard to forget the comic-strip analogy. And it creates a new scale with a simple geometric form.

Also in Puerto Rico during 1968, church members painted their own multicolored billboardlike exterior. Fez-Barringten numbered the building design in chalk and gave each church member-painter a number and paint pail, explaining, "You are color number one; you are color number four"; and so on. The action melded the congregation's involvement as well as producing a lively image for an old wood-frame tropical church.

This same spirit spurred the painting of murals in black ghettos in Detroit, Chicago, and Boston. New York City's Department of Cultural Affairs sponsored nearly two dozen murals throughout its boroughs. Most of those city murals are the work of a single artist, though the community involvement that they enlist as completed symbols is immeasurable. City Walls, a New York organization started by Allan d'Arcangelo and Jason Crum to paint urban exterior murals, was presided over by Joan Davidson, then by Doris Freedman, formerly the director of New York's Department of Cultural Affairs. City Walls' mural decorations were more abstract and pretty than the social protest billboards and peace movement murals that were painted by such artists as Dan McIlvaine in Chicago, and artists Charles Milles, Roy Cato, Jr., Dana Chandler, and Gary Rickson in Boston, where the program was sponsored by the Institute of Contemporary Art.

In the spring of 1970 a group of black teen-age youths, residents of the Al Smith Housing Project on the Lower East Side of Manhattan,

Community Arts Workshop: Mural at Al Smith Housing Project, New York City. 1970. *Photograph by Nester Cortijo.*

painted the saga of a black drug addict turning his back on drugs. With the direction of the New York City Community Arts Workshop headed by Susan Shapiro, the teen-agers staged and photographed various scenes in drug life as the young artists saw it: getting a fix, shooting up, and finally rejecting drugs. On the far right of the billboard a teen-ager turns his back on his former drug use and gives the black power salute while looking toward the future. The artists projected their slides of the scenes on panels, painted blue and red silhouettes of them, and hung the panels on the blank outside wall of the community center building in the project. Doris Freedman said that this direction "of helping the artist to move into society and also of responding to the needs of the community" is the direction in which city and government art programs should be going. "If government is going to get into the arts," she continued, "it has a dual responsibility: one to the artist, the other to all the people." With this background of ideas, art and exterior billboard decoration were forwarded for the involvement of urban populations.

Many student groups painted exterior billboards during the decade. Students of urban design at Saint Louis' Washington University executed a billboard in University City, Missouri, as a means of renewing a dreary inner-city playground in 1967. William Albinson and Robert Kearney, Jr., projected slides of their design model on the walls at night and made freehand outlines in crayon. The two nights of cartooning led the designers to incorporate their own projected shadows permissively into the painted designs.

Another billboard project in an economically depressed area, the I-II-II Club at 122 Franklin Street in Albany, New York, revitalized several abandoned buildings into a neighborhood youth center (1968). The exterior became a vertical painting of the address number. Designed by Steven L. Einhorn, Merrill H. Diamond, and Eric C. Yaffee of the

Einhorn-Sanders Associates: I-II-II Club, Albany, New York. 1968. *Photograph by E. M. Weil.*

firm Einhorn-Sanders Associates, the buildings were refurbished with no effort to repair broken shingles or cracked blocks. Instead, circles and segments were laid out on the old surfaces by using varying lengths of wood poles with one end drilled to hold a marker and the other end nailed to the wall. Sign painters then finished the design freehand.

Project Hope, a youth recreation center in Houston's black Pearl Harbor area, is a proud witness to the vigorous involvement of student designers in social causes. The center and its adjacent playground were redesigned and rebuilt by fourth-year architecture students at the University of Houston in 1968; it was a class project initiated by the students themselves. They devoted themselves to a problem that is relevant to today's society and also produced a real architectural product—an accomplishment beyond the lip-service protest that so many students exercised without further results. The students contacted Hope —Human Organization for Political and Economic Development— which had selected a site for a youth center in Houston's most depressed ghetto. The site contained a dilapidated, one-story, wedge-shaped building that Hope had painted black and named the Black Building; it had an adjoining open area that was asphalted. The students wanted to add design vitality to the area that would attract and excite the neighborhood children.

According to the course director, Houston architect John Zemanek, "The meeting with Hope brought out how times have changed: Hope was not impressed with advice and promises with strings attached, with problem solutions that created new problems. Unless Hope could help us," Professor Zemanek continued, "they were not interested in our intentions to help them. We needed help; we knew we had come to the right place. Clearly Hope was interested in community self-determination as much as the students were in the involvement of designers in relevant design." Materials for construction were donated by business establishments. Found objects, industrial rejects (such as spools for heavy cable), and other commercial design and recycled elements were assembled. Ornamental painting included an exterior billboard and signs (a lightning pattern on the front was drawn freehand from a comic book by Charles Coffman) as well as color-field patterning of the playground equipment; inside were stripes and zigzags as well as silhouettes of neighborhood kids painted from projections on the walls.

In the process the architecture students gained on-the-job training about client relations, about persuasiveness in obtaining contributions from local suppliers, and about actual construction. Even more than the demonstration of how billboards, paint, Pop, and recycling can contribute to our urban environments, it was this involvement of architecture students with a neighborhood community that was the source of such hope.

This same kind of urban revitalization was also accomplished with illuminated billboards at night. Billboards were projected onto several building exteriors as well as onto interiors. While the self-appointed "beautifiers" at the District of Columbia's Kennedy Center for the Performing Arts were lobbying for a "cleanup" of their view toward the industrial buildings on the distant Georgetown waterfront in 1969, Doug Michels and Bob Feild crashingly put down the Establishment by working out a series of startling projections on the soffit of the elevated Whitehurst Freeway and on the nearby silos of the Potomac Sand and Gravel Company, which was one of the objects of the "tasteful" Washington cleanup. Executed with the unlikely yet complete cooperation of Lloyd Green, owner of that Georgetown industrial firm, and with a grant from Washington's Gallery of Modern Art to investigate ways of revitalizing the waterfront buildings, these electric environments included Op art patterns, drawings of nudes, and slides of pop singers Bob Dylan, Paul McCartney, and Joan Baez. Kinetic artist Eric Sepler, who had worked with such rock groups as the Fugs and the Doors, was the projection technician. He was fascinated by the potential of his medium as "urban lighting." Drivers and passersby may have been stopped in their tracks, but they were also as certainly cheered by the sights.

The implications for instant horror are as great as those for instant beauty with instant billboards for nighttime advertising; they might have flashed up everywhere. Actually, exterior projection as an advertising medium had also been used to some degree. At New York's Waldorf-Astoria Hotel, a notice for a Benny Goodman engagement (in 1966) was projected onto the sidewalk on Park Avenue outside the hotel, somewhat mystifying passersby (or passers-through). And fabrics designer Jack Lenor Larsen, who pioneered the use of electric environments in the design world, projected his firm's logo onto his branch storefront in Zurich on its opening night (1963). Rumor had it that the New York Telephone Company was considering projections on the exteriors of its mammoth, windowless equipment building. Wags suggested that they

(*both photos*) Doug Michels and Bob Feild: Projected billboards, Washington, D.C. 1969. *Photograph by Steve Northrup for the* Washington Post.

might project windows—perhaps even movies of uncurtained windows with people doing interesting things inside.

Ulrich Franzen's fifth shop for Paraphernalia (1969) in New York had a billboard of flashing projections that was the principal display, sales, and design element, visible outside as well as inside. Inside, all attention was focused on the rear wall: a projection screen on which splashily colored slides of Paraphernalia merchandise were flashed from three carousel units mounted over the entry. Flip-click: a pants suit, a bejeweled skirt, a girl with the firm's "target" logo on her bosom. Flip-click: a striped miniskirt, a tasseled belt, a bosom of beads. The rest of the shop was near to being a non-object: everything but the projections and the customers was designed to vanish, to be as unobtrusive as possible. The front window was set back from the building line so that the side interior walls, sheathed in panels of shiny black acrylic plastic, seem to continue through the nearly invisible glass. A structural column was sheathed in black aluminum; the ceiling was black; tan carpeting continued the color of the sidewalk into the interior. Six four-foot, six-inch-high stainless steel arcs reiterated the color tone of the "silver screen" rear wall. From the street, the elevation through the window was silvery white from floor to ceiling, with black side walls. There were, seemingly, no display cases, no counters, no lights, no merchandise—nothing except the projected photographs of merchandise flashing on the rear wall. These views of the merchandise and the customers and the salesgirls trying things on (plus the music, music—"Freedom, FREEDOM!") were a brand-new effect for retailing—a dresscotheque! Architect Franzen explained that the shop was designed "so that from the outside, customers feel left out until they come in and join the show." Quantities of merchandise, in fact, hung on low racks within the stainless steel arcs that screen these surprises until customers come in to explore, lured by the flashing billboard. Unfortunately the franchiser did not use the billboard or keep up the rest of the shop for long.

Of exterior billboards, Doris Freedman observed, "Artists are now working in a scale that cannot be contained in an institution and so art has to come outdoors." Hardy added,

> Most of these murals are still frame oriented and there is no reason they could not take that at a bigger scale and spread the idea across lots of buildings. In a sense Times Square is that because it all goes around corners in neon. If you can take a three-dimensional solid and dematerialize its corner, that is a pretty potent vocabulary. The fact

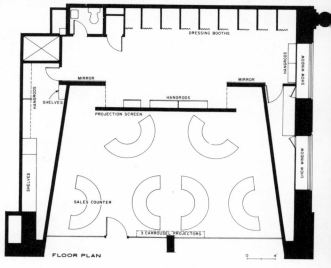

Ulrich Franzen: Shop for Paraphernalia, New York City. 1969. *Photograph by Louis Reens.*

Ulrich Franzen: Plan, shop for Paraphernalia, New York City. 1969.

DRESSING BOOTHS
HANGRODS
SHOW WINDOW
MIRROR
HANGRODS
SHELVES
MIRROR
HANGRODS
PROJECTION SCREEN
SHOW WINDOW
SHELVES
SALES COUNTER
3 CARROUSEL PROJECTORS
FLOOR PLAN
0   4'

that it costs very little is only one part. You could do it all with chrome and lapis lazuli and it would be vastly expensive. But it would still do the same job and be the same powerful core thought.

And billboards remained a powerful core thought into the 1970s.

THE SYNTHETIC ENVIRONMENT

In its inclusion of pop elements, the new design accommodates synthetic as well as natural materials. Plastics and electric light are the most prominent pop materials that are as joyfully accepted by the new designers as they were disdainfully rejected by the previous generation. This inclusive acceptance is "another step away from the vestiges of our rural heritage," as Bill Lacy observed. He questions whether this influence will grow into "a new aesthetic based on the acceptance of man-made, artificial surroundings—smooth bright plastic, shiny metal, synthetic fabrics, and imaginative lighting." Other designers declare that they are interested in "the totally synthetic and totally abstract environment." Doug Michels said, "We have to learn to design and to live in those supercontrolled environments that will be necessary when we go to the moon or to the underwater frontier." This imagery of pop materials is as fundamental to the new design generation as the inspirations from other aspects of our popular culture.

If the perspective distortion and optical games of the art world are, as has been suggested, aimed at destroying the balance between the real and the imaginary, the corresponding activity in the applied arts of architecture and interior design has, as its benefit, the creation of a connecting link between the known world and the unknown world of outer space. It is the aesthetic visual correspondent of the change from our traditional world of natural materials to the new man-made world of synthetic materials.

In interiors, the plastic world of the future seems to have arrived. Every visible interior surface has been made of test-tube, man-made synthetics—with the exception of metal elements that are self-supporting or heat-carrying. And space exploration has realized those few remaining items. All kinds of plastics are used in the furniture industry today, both thermoplastics and thermosetting plastics. ABS, SAN, polyethylene, polystyrene, polyurethane (both rigid and flexible foam), vinyl, and lesser amounts of acrylic, nylon, acetal, polycarbonate, and butyrate. They include thermosetting plastics such as melamine, phenolic, polyesters, epoxy, urea, casein, and silicone. Vinyl and polyurethane flexible foam account for the largest amounts of plastics used in furniture.

Plastics provide floor coverings, wall coverings, and the backings and adhesives for both; they go on the ceiling as well as in lighting diffusers, and in skylights. Woodwork and cabinetry are made of plastic.

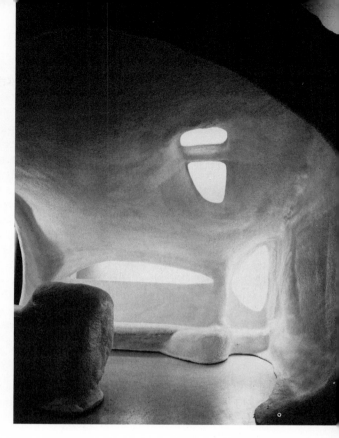

Textiles for window coverings and upholstery are both woven and sheet plastics. Door and drawer hardware, enclosures for air conditioners, television sets, and radios, every utensil needed for our common diurnal functions is produced today in tomorrow's futuristic material.

The move toward the synthetic environment could go in two directions—and did. One was the futuristic space trip of invisible furniture and spray-foamed rooms, such as plastics designer Douglas Deeds's entry for the "Plastic as Plastic" exhibition (1968) at the Museum of Contemporary Crafts, which seemed a partial realization of Frederick Kiesler's Endless House. The other was the symbolic re-creation of historical styles and kitsch in plastic, such as fake Tudor rooms with plastic "oak beams," plastic "wood-carved" linenfold panels, and plastic "antique" chests. "It is ironic" says designer Paul Mayen of Habitat, Inc., "that all our supertechnology should be used to reproduce the forms, graining, and finish of an 18th-century chair right out of the plastics oven."

There is, however, a group of furniture designers and manufacturers other than the see-through designers who use plastics as plastics. They are those leaders of the architectural furniture field—Knoll International, Herman Miller, Architectural Fiberglass, Habitat, and a few others. The designs of these firms are all elegant and interesting enough to be used in interior applications other than offices, in houses and housing, for example. Yet it is painful to see that the process for reinforced fiberglass chair shells, invented for mass production and mass use by Charles Eames and Eero Saarinen in the late 1940s, should still be witnessing a time lag in acceptance that makes such exposed chair shells desirable only as furniture for commercial uses, or for utilitarian application.

Douglas Deeds says,

> There is no limit to what shape these plastic things can be, because they are just a bunch of chemicals jumping around in a barrel until you inject them into a mold or apply them. Now the materials are more advanced than the machines. As soon as technology is up to doing things in relatively large volumes, then you could expect to mold entire rooms. And it is not beyond the realm of possibility that you could just formulate the chemicals and just throw them into a room and they would form themselves.

For a house in Stowe, Vermont (1967), David Sellers and Charles Hosford designed a plastic bathroom that had a shower made of a five-foot-diameter, eight-foot-high plexiglass cylinder; the cylinder rested on a base wall that was cut away on the diagonal, so that when the translucent shower was lighted from the inside it served as a mammoth lighting fixture for the adjacent living room. Of course, if someone had the light on while she or he was in the shower, it provided a nicely ambiguous ballet for those in the living room beyond. In the cylinder was a ring of copper tubing that ran on the inside circumference and had holes punched in it every six inches for the spray. As a bathroom finish, they used a seamless epoxy with vinyl chips that is commonly used in public toilets and a two-part epoxy paint in warning reds and yellows of the sort used by the highway department. Fine sand was added and a coating of the urethane varnish used in bowling alleys and on large truck-weighing scales was used as a protective coating.

Tom Luckey designed another unorthodox plastic bathroom in that 1967 house for Fritz Steele. Because there was not enough room to design a horizontal bathroom plan, he designed a standard plumbing tree, and then built a spiral stair around the stacked-up fixtures as access. A fiberglass textured finish was poured over this vertical bathroom to make it totally waterproof and to form an internal plastic shell. The glass fibers were laid down in reverse of the normal system: the gel coat was put on the wall, causing it to "drool a bit"; so heat lamps were

(*right*) Tom Luckey: Sketch, bathroom in fiberglass spiral stair, Steele House, Warren, Vermont. 1967.

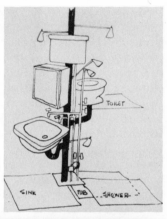

(*photos below*) Tom Luckey: Bathroom in fiberglass spiral stair, Steele House, Warren, Vermont. 1967. *Photograph by David Hirsch.*

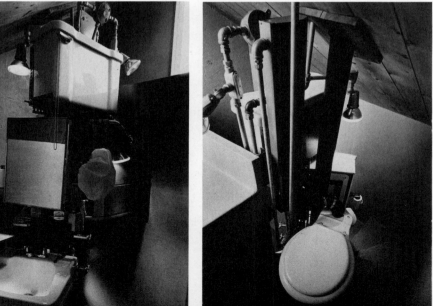

applied for curing. The system was unusually compact and efficient; and if you dropped or spilled something (or missed), all was saved or salvaged by the shower drain at the bottom of the stair. That pop plastic bath showed a camp twist, then.

CAMP *VERSUS* POP

Much of Robert Venturi's theory seemed as perverse and Camp in the 1960s as it seemed startling and new. Venturi acclaimed the decorated shed, yet that is what the neohistorical architects of the 1950s were blamed for creating—decorative screens around Bauhaus buildings. Ironically, Nikolaus Pevsner's first sentence in his *Outline of European Architecture* (1943) is "A bicycle shed is a building; Lincoln Cathedral is a piece of architecture." He continued, "Nearly everything that encloses space on a scale sufficient for a human being to move in is a building; the term architecture applies only to buildings designed with a view to aesthetic appeal." So when, twenty years later, Venturi called Rheims Cathedral "a decorated shed," it was a potently perverse twist. He said it at a time when we used to decry the false front—as in a typical western-frontier nineteenth century—as "facade architecture."

Venturi demonstrated his witty sense of paradox in an exhibition of his firm's work at Philadelphia's Art Alliance in 1968. There, besides wall-mounted drawings and photographs of the firm's work, projected slides were juxtaposed on adjacent walls, and other signs and images were superimposed on the projections. Among contradictory pairs of slides were: a commercial strip of gas stations with a forest of attenuated columns supporting vacuum-formed logo signs and, in contrast, the multicolumned court of lions in the Alhambra; Rome's populated Spanish Steps contrasted with a full American parking lot; Perpendicular Gothic fan vaulting as against the multiple parallel lines of a neon sign; archaeological ruins next to the parking lots and signs of Las Vegas; the arcade of the Doge's Palace in Venice seen adjacent to the piers of a freeway; and finally, a spaghetti tangle of roadways contrasted with the repetitive arches of the Baptistry at Pisa. These historical-contemporary, European-American juxtapositions—possible only since "the museum without walls" of photography—showed Venturi accepting a wider range of our visual environment as being comparable and evidently occupied by the same animal—man. It was an open-minded, inclusive, realistic view of the actualities of the status quo; it was novel and iconoclastic.

Skidmore, Owings & Merrill/Chicago: Stair, Art and Architecture Building, University of Illinois, Chicago Circle Campus. 1968. *Photograph by Orlando R. Cabanban.*

But although it had strong meaning, it was essentially a comic approach.

A no less remarkable example of wit in 1960s architecture is Walter Netsch's 1968 Art and Architecture Building at the Chicago Circle Campus of the University of Illinois. The building is challenging as a fun-house maze is challenging. The main stair, with its central course dividing to the right and to the left, is arrow-shaped in plan and therefore composes a directional signal that leads, in the first flight, into a dead-end corner and then forces one to turn back in the direction opposite to the pointing arrow in order to mount the next flight. This stair of Netsch's is as comic in its effect as it is a serious expression of existentialist angst; it is as mannered as Palladio's split entry stairs at the Villa Malcontenta in Venice.

By 1970, Camp had dwindled but not died. It was supercamp of the Architectural League of New York to present the exhibition by John Margolies, Billy Adler, and Robert Jensen of the hotel designs by Morris Lapidus. Lapidus is the architect of many Miami Beach hotels—with relentless decoration, with stairs that sweep majestically to nowhere, with richly encrusted columns holding up paper-thin ceiling panels. It was parody and Camp to have an interest in this work—the work of an architect whom Ada Louise Huxtable called "the High Priest of High Kitsch," work that she found "uninspired super-schlock." And since no valuable lessons were forthcoming, the exhibition can only be considered an exercise in pure Camp and humor.

About that time the editors of the underground sex sheet *Screw* appeared at a meeting of the Drama Desk, a New York organization of writers on theatre, to give their view of how to "make the Broadway area a safer and more attractive place to visit." The editors presented a plan to incorporate a legalized red light district—like those "Eros areas" in Hamburg, Amsterdam, and elsewhere—right in the heart of Broadway. It would concentrate the merchandise, they explained, provide revenue for a private police force through turnstile entrance fees, as well as additional revenue from telescope viewers across the street. Ultimately they said, customers and merchants alike would get more for their money. Traditionalists at the meeting were scandalized. The editors, however, had presented a plan that did not set out to change people's habits, to clean them up; rather they accepted the fact of human behavior and attempted to accommodate the actualities of the Broadway area.

Commenting on the proposal, Jaquelin Robertson, then with the Office of the Midtown Plan, agreed that planners should find a way to make the Times Square area a "vital, virile, and slightly vulgar forum of public entertainment—a legitimate, very democratic public forum—a high variety environment for all types of people." It was a wittily camp town-planning idea but it was also a realistic one.

It was as whimsical, humorous, and perversely imaginative to think that the architecture of Las Vegas and of Levittown were valid areas for investigation, as Denise and Robert Venturi did. They were right, but it was still a campy idea. In January 1969, "LLV," written in red neon, hung just inside the exhibition space of Yale's Art and Architecture Building. It signaled the Venturis' student research and urban planning problem called "Learning from Las Vegas," which was subsequently published in book form in 1972. Charts, maps, diagrams, and photographs hung on every wall; from the ceiling, hung boomerang-shaped, guillotinelike maps in the configuration of Las Vegas' Route 91—"the archetype of the commercial strip." All was reflected in the silver vinyl of Project Argus, which sprawled diagonally across the space (see p. 108). In attendance, with students and faculty, was a star-studded list of guests chosen from those interested in Pop architecture, with or without Pop architects. What was presented Robert Venturi called "a new kind of urban environment that simply sprawls from the social and commercial needs of contemporary life." One study, "Activity Patterns," used color-coded maps to spot the locations of gambling casinos, wedding chapels, and food stores; another research project, "User Behavior," dealt with the iconography of parking lots, with "vehicular behavior," and with the inadequacy of directional signs in herding motorists into the desired driving patterns. Others, such as "Communication System and Anatomy of Signs," dealt with the scale, visibility, and construction of Las Vegas' flashing bubbling neon super-signs. There were also some spectacular slide shows and films, including one three-screen film of the Las Vegas strip seen while driving up and down it by day and then by night; and another film taken while flying over the casinos with their outrageously joyous signs.

One observer called it a Beaux Arts presentation of the most meticulous character, and it did seem, in fact, like presenting measured drawings of outhouses. In that respect, the choice of subject matter and the high seriousness of presentation were campily witty. Yet one substantive benefit was immediately apparent: the investigation opened our eyes to a strong, vital environment in our society that had largely been ignored. The investigation was also, according to Venturi, a step forward, "getting some imagery and inspiration from commercial architecture as early modern architects looked to industrial architecture for inspiration." In this subject matter, it was unquestionably Pop.

Venturi has been called the Andy Warhol of architecture theory, and for this reason the work of Venturi & Rauch is often called Pop—a designation that is not always accurate. I think the camp aspects of Warhol's work are overlooked here. When Venturi & Rauch's work has architectural allusions to our popular "undesigned," commercial, or ordinary world—to gadgets, to roadways, to Las Vegas, or to Levittown—it is clearly Pop. At other times, however, their allusions to art history or to oriental elements—such as the moongate—have nothing to do with Pop. Surely, the allusions themselves should be distinguished from that artistic turn of mind that flips the coin as a means of revealing a subject. This mentality verges more on Camp than on Pop, although the two are similar. When Venturi urges acceptance of bigger billboards, while most others are trying to get rid of them (or at least to cluster them), he is flipping the coin so that we will not overlook whatever values there may be in them and in pop roadway imagery and communication. The content is Pop, but the attitude is Camp.

Venturi showed another kind of perversity in his books *Complexity and Contradiction in Architecture* and *Learning from Las Vegas* by printing numerous illustrations no larger than postage stamps. There is logic in this miniature recall, but it was certainly perverse, in view of the glorious four-color bleed photographs that were the backbone of most picture books, for the Venturis to include many photographs of Las Vegas less than five-sixteenths of an inch square.

When Venturi uses *dumb* to mean sophisticatedly direct, he is demonstrating a perverse, camp twist of mind that is crackling with imaginative and witty contradictions. Venturi's own theory of accepting dualities—"both/and" rather than "and/or"—was wittily one-upped by California artist William Wiley who claimed to be "both for and against."

In the same way, it was witty of Charles Moore to praise The Madonna Inn in San Luis Obispo, California, in print and lectures. That Southern California honeymoon oasis was started in 1961 by Alex and Phyllis Madonna, who began building with boulders moved by his highway contracting firm's earthmoving equipment. They produced massive masonry structures—not quite of Incan scale, perhaps highway scale—with Carpenter Gothic filigree balusters, balconies, and eaves crowned by chimneys flourishing Tudor twists. Then Phyllis Madonna styled each interior space either as Swiss grotto with Tyrolean kitsch or as Hollywood-western-frontier Victorian. The hammered brass heart-shaped appliqués and hobnail glass lamps in one dining room make it a kind of live-in gift shop; the main restaurant has a grotto base bedecked with fake pink flowers and a girl in a swing amid permanent Christmas decorations. This dining bower is the apotheosis of the card shop.

In one bedroom suite, glitterdust on a blue ceiling, pink gloss-enameled woodwork, and orange-and-pink striped, flocked wallpaper with floral paisley or madders, and a pink-red-lipstick-colored carpet makes what can be called, with certainty, a personal combination. When the sun reflects off the pink-red-lipstick-colored carpet, and blue ceiling turns purple. It may be unnecessary to point out that the designer's intention was not in the realm of baroque lighting effects.

Alex and Phyllis Madonna: The Madonna Inn, San Luis Obispo, California. 1961–1970. *Photograph by C. Ray Smith.*

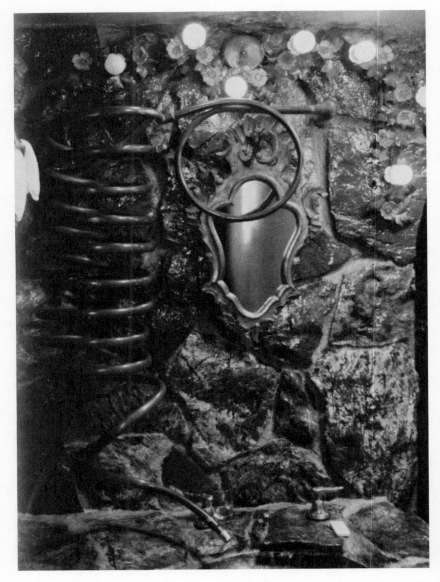

Alex and Phyllis Madonna: Bathroom with spiral copper water spigot, The
Madonna Inn, San Luis Obispo, California. 1961–1970.
Photograph by C. Ray Smith.

It is the public "rest rooms," however, that take the prize for craftsmanly invention. They are grottoes with inclusions of farm-country nostalgia and high technology. In one, beaten-copper washbasins have old-fashioned hand pumps for water spigots. In another, the urinal is a wing-armed bench made out of copper, with the trough where the bench would ordinarily be; as one approaches, an electric eye automatically turns on a waterfall that cascades down the back of the bench, turning a miniature mill wheel on its way to the trough. It takes one's mind off business.

The Madonna Inn is so sentimental and tinselly, in spite of its boulder construction and Swiss Chalet exterior, that it is the architectural apogee of Camp. It is so bad that, perversely, it has to be funny. And it is Camp of Moore, who seems to have discovered it, to appraise it. He has written in *Perspecta* of the inclusiveness of The Madonna Inn, ". . . It is rather exhilarating to note that here there is everything instead of nothing. A kind of immediate involvement with the site, with the user and his movements, indeed with everything all at once, with the vitality and the vulgarity of real commerce, quivers at a pitch of excitement which presages, more clearly than any tidy sparse geometry, an architecture for the electric present." Here Moore clearly sees simultaneity as well as humor. The Madonna Inn seems to be California's equivalent of Las Vegas' ditsy stage settings, except that its handcraft construction is real. And the Madonnas have built it for the love of craft; they have a team of Italian masons and wood-carvers to stuff every nook of the hotel. And that invention is often spontaneously just right: in one bathroom, water travels down a spiral copper pipe, reminiscent of an early refrigerator or ice-making plant, and spews directly into the sink from that exposed spiral spigot. We need only to compare this inn with that ultimate refinement of the machine-age and systems approach to hostelry—Howard Johnson's—to see how far from depersonalization and categorizing hotel design can be.

The Madonna Inn represents the whole decade of Camp, humor, wit, and fun in architecture, as the Supermannerists recognized. It is the epitome of the ethnic joke that begins "What do pink flamingos put in their front yards? . . . ," but it also presages the decade of personal involvement in customized crafts—quilting, housebuilding, and the other ecology-movement activities of the 1970s.

So, too, it was witty of Peter Blake to write in *Architectural Form* that "Disneyland, in Anaheim, California, and Disney World, in

Orlando, Florida, are the only new towns of any significance built in this country since World War II"; and for *The New York Times Magazine* to publish an article on Disney World headed "Mickey Mouse Teaches the Architects." But in their camp reversals they were also right: we have not yet mastered the valuable lessons of Disney World.

What is mannerist about Pop and camp architecture, besides the very inversion of its inspiration and material content, is that it is enlarged and self-conscious; it is remote and detached; it is glazed and impersonal. Like Mannerism in other art forms and in other ages, then, Pop architecture appeals to the manners, to the intellect not to the emotions. It is, after all, a product of the intellectual, rational 1950s training.

Superscale and Superimposition

SUPER

If the architecture of our decade is mannerist because of its inventive manipulation of scale and because of its witty conceits in juxtaposing forms, content, materials, objects, and textures, it is also Super because of its gigantic, double space scale and because of its pop-revival aspects. *Super,* a word of popular praise and exclamation since the 1920s and the 1930s, was revived during the 1960s as a resounding, ubiquitous superlative, like *great* and *terrific* in the 1950s. The historicism, revivalism, or preservation aspects of the term along with its nostalgic and pop aspects reflected the interests of 1960s designers. In *Contemporary American Usage* (1957), Bergen and Cornelia Evans wrote of the word *super:*

> It is an interesting reflection on our democratic and mass-produced times that the prefix *super,* especially in America, should be so unreservedly a term of commendation. Anything which is above the ordinary or is excessive is, apparently, admirable. We have supermarkets, and superhighways and super service stations, and, colloquially and among college humorists, the prefix itself, unprefixed to anything, is the height of praise. It was not always so. Time was that men disliked the excessive. In many older words (supercilious, supererogate, superannuated) the prefix suggests something unpleasant and undesirable.

Since we can add "superficial" to that list, the word *super* can be used as easily to condemn as to commend Supermannerism. This is the inherent ambiguity in both Mannerism and Pop. The use of the word *dumb* by critics of the Minimal sculptors, as in "the dumb box boys," and by supermannerist architects creates similar conflicts—meaning good to some and bad to others. However, the strongest claim for the use of super as a prefix to our current form of Mannerism—the choices could be neo, para, meta, and so on—is that the pop aspects of the movement are self-contained in the term, in the possible hyphenation *Superman-nerism,* which reflects the epitome of popular culture in the super-hero of all comic books.

To generations brought up on comic books, the notions of space flight, science fiction, supermen, and shazam were givens of contemporary mythology. Their apocalyptic fantasies had been the daydreams of children who grew up to see those fantasies realized—in an anarchic, uncertain, turbulent, and perverse world. Any number of comic-book allusions were made by the new designers. The designers of the S.S. *Independence* made a choice one in the ship's blue-green swimming pool by painting an action balloon on the bottom of the pool, joyously tempting people to "Splash." Ironically, while the Pop artists' systematic reversals were making jokes parodying the comics, the comic books during the 1960s were going heroic—monumentalizing all the protean heroes, actions, events, and ideals that almost all avant-garde artists were trying to knock down. The time-lagging cycles were spinning. If the old romantic comics could become today's scientific reality, it was entirely within the realm of logic and expectation that the new comics would be turned inside out to discuss turbulence and doubt in matters of sex, politics, education, and other seriousnesses in mad and zapped-out ways. The new comics of the 1960s tackled sober social problems with wit, humor, and giggles in Aesop-like parodies and fables. Those versed in these supercomics felt that only by such sickly humorous representations of despair could our age manage a giggle out of its own agony.

SUPERSCALE

The change of scale—in speed, time, space, and size—is a keynote of our singular new vision. Architecture, the art of shaping the man-made environment, violently changed its scale in the past decade. From the civilizations of Egypt and Greece, through the Renaissance, buildings were conceived primarily as single sculptural entities. Basically, man's control, power, and ability to shape his physical environment were limited to single buildings, and to earthworks—albeit of gigantic propor-

Peter Harrison of Robert
Miles Runyan Associates:
Pool decoration, S.S.
Independence. 1968.
*Photograph by Peter
Harrison.*

Student project: Waste
barrel from 55-gallon
drum, University of Hous-
ton, Texas. 1968. *Photo-
graph by Larry Brown-
back.*

tions. By the eighteenth century, man's conception of his environment had grown from single buildings to urban scale. Karlsruhe was laid out in a great star pattern; L'Enfant considered Washington, D.C., as his province; Haussman later cut great swaths through Paris. In boulevards and canals man's power to shape his environment had grown to considerably vaster scales. Beyond single buildings, man could function only in reaction to nature—the landscape, the site, and the winds and the stars. He could not change those constant, if not actually fixed, entities, but he could adapt to their patterns in the siting and puncturing of his building.

In the twentieth century all that changed. The power of man increased by leaps and bounds; first through electricity and later through atomic power, man was able to see his environment as encompassing not only all the landscape—chewing it up, moving it around, damming waters, altering it to meet whatever configurations he wanted to impose on it—but also as encompassing, by the mid-twentieth century, the possibility of affecting, however minutely at first, the stars themselves. What changed most in twentieth-century architecture was this view of the power of man to shape his environment and his subsequent view of the extent of that environment. Buildings increased in height because of steel and electricity—the structural frame and the elevator; they became comfortable the year round because of new heating and cooling systems. If architects had been master builders of single, mammoth buildings before, they could, in the twentieth century, be master builders of vast cities and regions with many buildings and complex multipurpose structures. They could impose their images of architectural perfection over whole regions. And they did. Superscale building projects included: whole new towns, omni-megastructures, air-rights buildings over streets, New York's World Trade Center and its twenty-three-and-a-half-acre landfill site, Chicago's John Hancock Building and Sears Tower.

Not since the Renaissance has man's vision shifted so completely as in the first decade of the space age. Even the advent of the machine age did not affect the outlook of man as much as the scale of speed and the distances that suddenly catapulted man into space. No longer is the vision of man conditioned by relation to the single room and to the single building, or to the single backyard or street block. The new scale opens our vistas to a vision of megalopolis, a daily awareness of outer space, and a design view stretching from whole cities and regions to whole states and continents, from a vision of spaceships to a vision of

Spaceship Earth, as Buckminster Fuller was often to call it. This is achieved primarily by the expansion of our sense from the human scale we have recognized in the past to a new superscale.

In the 1960s anthropologist Claude Lévi-Strauss said, "Most of the phenomena we encounter in mankind today and can expect in the coming decade are phenomena of a change of scale . . . The question of the size and scope of all social units is the most crucial sociological problem that arises out of the influence of number, density, and inter-action, and the consequences of diffusion and change of scale." Changes in scale throughout our society pervaded the 1960s. It was a decade when hijacking a plane became what stealing a car had been to the two previous generations; when the 1950s feat of flying around the world was trumped by a loop around the moon; when television reached an adulthood more powerful and penetrating than its parent radio, filling our eyes as well as our ears with the news as it happened; when the new superhighways of the 1960s were dotted with speed limit signs reading, appropriately enough, "60." Driving from Los Angeles streets up onto one of the freeways gives an immediate demonstration of the new change of scale in the 1960s and the 1970s. And as the 1970s dawned, the signposts of our pace, as if by necessity, read "70." No wonder it was intolerable to reduce our speeds to 50 during the gas shortage of 1973.

What is that elusive thing called scale? Historians and aestheticians from Aristotle and Vitruvius to Viollet-le-Duc and Bruno Zevi had written of the concept, but none had made clear for the twentieth century what scale was. In all meanings, scale refers to physical size; but, although many architects, artists, and designers take the words as synonymous, they are not. Size is only one of the factors of scale. As Philip Johnson said, "Size isn't important; it's what you do with the size. The human mind measures things by recognizable divisions . . . Those things which create scale, which make scale real, lie in dividing up space into meaningful units, units that make it exciting." In functionalist theory, those elements that must be dimensioned for the use of the human being—the height of windowsills, balustrades, door widths and heights—give a building "human scale." They acquire a physical size determined by human dimension, and our knowledge of human size permits us to relate those architectural elements to the overall structure. Bruno Zevi most nearly strikes the heart of the matter in his definition in *Architecture as Space* (1957): "Scale means dimension with respect to man's visual apprehension, dimension with respect to man's physical size."

As a more precise definition, scale is the aesthetic impression that is conveyed about the physical size of a mass or a space. A scale is what we measure size by. So, two relative forces are involved in scale: first, a physical aspect—size; and second, a philosophical and psychological aspect—man's image of his own stature. This perception of the size of a space or a building is the product of a gestalt—a ratio between a physical object and the mental impression conveyed to an observer about the size of that object in relation to himself. The affect on the observer, his perception of the object, and his reaction to it are the significant factors. Scale, then, is not a definitive, ontological concept, but rather an affective concept, a subjective reaction. Thus those windows and balustrades that are said "to give human scale" are only *the means* of creating the desired impression about the size of the building.

These considerations about perception became a special field of investigation in the 1960s. E. H. Gombrich's *Art and Illusion, A Study in the Psychology of Pictorial Representation* (first published in 1960) became the proto-bible of the movement. Professor Gombrich does not offer a definition of scale, nor is he guiltless of confusing scale with size, in at least two instances. And he disclaims any affinity with the tenets of Gestalt psychology; his theory differs in that illusion, perception, or impressions can be learned, whereas the Gestalt psychologists posit a constant global memory—whether we learn it or whether it is part of tribal intuition.

As in every period throughout history, scale is a keynote of our age. It always reveals man's philosophical relationship to objects and buildings—as is equally apparent in Gothic cathedrals and steel skyscrapers. In the Middle Ages, the cathedrals soared forcefully to heaven to express medieval man's aspirations toward the God on high. In the Mannerist and Baroque periods, when religious monuments of even greater dimensions were built, such as Saint Peter's in Rome, they were often designed to appear much smaller than their actual physical dimensions. The aspirations of society had changed; man's image of his own position in the universe had changed. Gothic cathedrals focused axially on the altar at the distant end and used scale to deflate the individual to his "proper" insignificance before God; in Renaissance and Mannerist churches, the focus was to put man at the center of the universe—scale was manipulated to increase man's own stature.

Contemporary painters and sculptors, architects and designers have been manipulating scale in this mannerist manner for a decade. As painters challenge the limits of the canvas and reanalyze the supporting bases of sculptures, they have questioned the shapes of canvases—not only the two-dimensional form but stretching literally into three-dimensional canvases, toward the realm of sculpture. Many of René Magritte's paintings and those of the Surrealists show a fascination with a paradox of scale—a dual scale, which confuses the beholder, asks whether—as in Magritte's *Personal Values* (1952)—a hair comb is huge or the bed it is resting on is tiny, whether the wall is sky or sky-painted wallpaper. Yet we know by the title that the comb, the shaving brush, the bar of

René Magritte: *Personal Values,* 1952.
Collection of Harry Torczyner. *Photograph by Otto E. Nelson.*

Claes Oldenburg: *Light Switch*, 1966. *Photograph by Robert R. McElroy.*

Philip Johnson: Gazebo, New Canaan, Connecticut. 1963. *Photograph by Stan Ries.*

soap, the drinking glass, and the watch loom larger in the scale of personal values than the room and its furniture. The vast geometric sculptures of Tony Smith create a landscape of nonearthly dimensions, a new scale for sculpture. The huge paintings of Al Held burst out of their frames, some of which are in themselves of an unprecedented vastness; other Held paintings reinforce the contrast of small surfaces and huge painted subjects. Both artists and architects have created playful trick effects with scale that illustrate how man can be made to look smaller or larger at will, as in the trick diagonal entryway by Haus-Rucker for an exhibition at the Museum of Contemporary Crafts in 1968/69. Claes Oldenburg's Pop art light switches, each four feet square, put us in Gulliver's giant land, Brobdingnag. Philip Johnson's half-scale Gazebo (1963) at his Glass House in New Canaan, Connecticut, makes man feel larger in Lilliput.

We frequently see photographs of large buildings today that appear to be a single story high. Hangars and single-span factories that we know to be huge often appear to be scaleless. They do not always impress us as being exceptionally long; we often cannot tell how big a space actually is. The vast Vehicle Assembly Building at Cape Kennedy, said to be the biggest building in the world, is stunningly deceptive. Buckminster Fuller was accused of lacking scale in the repetition of his single units without variation that make up his spheres and domes.

What are those recognizable divisions that could create a more measurable scale for today? "In classical architecture," Kevin Roche points out, "a building began, had a middle, ended. It had spaces beyond; it had a volume. It had a composed entity, in which all of the parts were related to each other, and they filled specific roles; they composed a total whole."

"Today," says Paul Rudolph, "the Renaissance notion that a building must have a beginning, a middle, and an end is not applicable. If you're dealing with a parking garage that is three miles long, or with a sixty-story-high office building, that notion doesn't have any meaning. These are structures which have no beginning and no end." And, as Philip Johnson said, "The new architecture will appear out of scale because our problems are out of scale." The scale of today is often said to have a kind of scalelessness, one that many architects resisted and deplored at first, one that was not immediately understood. In the 1960s, man's view of his own size in relation to the size of his most aspirational buildings is clearly not one that shows the individual either

Trick-perspective room from ABC-TV's "Voyage to
the Bottom of the Sea." 1966.

at the center of the universe, or insignificant before a distant yet omnipresent God. What is man's relationship today?

If mannerist man saw himself at the center of his universe, today's
man has a vision of scale that puts him above the earth—in orbit, as it
were—looking down on it from the viewpoint of some extraterrestrial
architect studying an earthbound model. Architects have always looked
down onto plans and into models, but the layman seldom shared this
lofty professional view. Today's scale, manipulated as in mannerist
times, makes a superarchitect of even the layman. It is a superscale for
the age of man's first landing on another planet. The superscale of the
1960s makes the viewer feel part of the bigger outer space beyond,
giving him a giant's superscale vista, and makes an orbiting superman of
him. It provides every man the position of looking back on the whole
earth from spaceflight. It makes Superman of us all. That is the mannerist approach to scale that is the origin of Supermannerism.

In addition to this vision of an astronaut, we retain, simultaneously, the earthbound view of interior spaces and exterior volumes. It is a dual, coexisting vision that our designers developed as a scale for the 1960s— a double, almost polarized vision, a hybrid, ambiguous, redundant, inclusive vision both earthbound and from orbit that we have gained from the superscale of the 1960s. The juxtaposition of two scales, discordant and seemingly out of context yet simultaneous, is the operative force of the new technique of superscale.

Paul Rudolph, in his superscale parking garage (1963) in New Haven, Connecticut, considered not only the scale of the individual automobile but simultaneously the scale of the parking facility as seen from a speeding car. Kevin Roche said,

> Many of today's buildings do not have a larger module—no group or crowd module. The total volume is simply made up of a very fine grid of modules, expressing only formless heaps of individuals. We have that which is the human scale, and then we have nothing else until we end the building. Actually, it is characteristic of these buildings that they don't end; you could add or subtract a floor without making any appreciable difference in the scale.

Roche knew what he was talking about. His Ford Foundation Head-

Paul Rudolph: Parking garage,
New Haven, Connecticut. 1963. *Photograph by George Cserna.*

Gunnar Birkerts: Federal Reserve Bank of Minneapolis, Minnesota. 1973. *Photograph by Balthazar Korab.*

quarters (1967) in New York and the Knights of Columbus Building (1970) in New Haven, especially, from project-drawing stage through completed building, looked as though they were inflated sketches of original, incipient conceptions. Of the scale in his Ford Foundation building, he explains, "We try to express two modules. One is just the individual in his office—the little cubicles; the other is the larger space, the living room garden, which really fulfills the function of being the center or heart." In Gunnar Birkerts Federal Reserve Bank of Minneapolis (1973), also, the scale of the individual is seemingly overlaid with a catenary that makes the building look like a giant stylized letter *m;* so Birkerts manipulates double scale.

Roche envisioned a kinetic changing scale as well. Of his mid-1960s Air Force Museum project (unbuilt), he said, "There is a progression of scale from the individual to the aircraft which increases in size as one progresses historically through the exhibit, to the overall building. And the building itself as a whole also expands, as one passes through it, to illustrate this progression of scale throughout the history of aviation."

This concept of kinetic scale had a direct kinship with kinetic art during the decade.

Robert Venturi, discussing his firm's Chestnut Hill residence in *Complexity and Contradiction,* explained, "The main reason for the large scale is to counterbalance the complexity. Complexity in combination with small scale in small buildings means busyness. Like other organized complexities here, the big scale in the small building achieves tension rather than nervousness—one appropriate to such architecture." Scale was a continuing discussion and investigation of Venturi & Rauch; notably in the Copley Square Competition Design (1966) and later in their ability to detach or dis-unify the symbolism of buildings from the structure. As Chip Lord wrote to me:

> I'd like to say
> A few words about scale
> In architecture and other places.
> Look at a postage stamp
> Like a branch bank
> And you begin to grasp
> The infinite vastness of the universe.

What we could see clearly was the hierarchy of design at a new dimension. The new hierarchy could be read from the individual man to his single house, thence from the street block to a half-mile-square neighborhood and from there to a city area of 100,000 people, and on to a total city. What the new vision added was the range from metropolitan area to region, to nation, to continent, to the world, and perhaps to the entire solar system. The new superscale is visible proof of the impact of space exploration on the new design.

SUPERIMPOSITION AND LAYERING

The new design uses superimposition to express in form the simultaneous perception of visual experiences common to our age. It offers spaces-within-spaces, the overlay of one use on another (see "Preservation, Historicism, and Recycling"), applied decoration, pattern-on-pattern (see "Decoration and Historical Allusion"), and pattern-on-spaces (see "Supergraphics"). Superimposition works with the space, building, or object as it is, with the thing as it appears to be, with the additive overlay, and with the interaction that they produce in combination. Like

T. Merrill Prentice, Jr.: Room-within-a-room, house, Cornwall, Connecticut.
1969. *Photograph by Norman McGrath.*

superscale devices, these superimposed phenomena can be perceived
both separately and simultaneously.

The most "architectural" kind of superimposition, using solids and
masses, came to be known by 1970 as "layering." Venturi wrote about
"things-within-things." Moore wrote of "rooms-within-rooms." Donlyn
Lyndon, "being good at clarifying fuzzy intuitive things," as Turnbull
says, called it "layering" in the early 1960s and this term was generally
adopted by the end of the decade.

Layering was not a new idea in architecture. From the peristyles of
the ancients, the screens of columns by Palladio (notably in the Palazzo
Chiericati), the multiple walls of Wies and other Baroque and Rococo
churches, to the porches of Carpenter Gothic and Shingle Style architects and to Le Corbusier's screens, the mechanism of layering was
adopted, cast aside, and readapted. Layering, in the classical concept,
was related to emphasizing perspective. What the modern movement
refers to as the open-plan and as articulation has been developed by the
Supermannerists into an interest in the spaces between the joints and the
separation of the layers. Instead of being concerned with the joint as a

continuous detail, the new designers explode the junctures of things; they separate each element from the other to produce, in effect, a discontinuous joint. This is articulation at a greatly expanded scale.

The new approach to layering was an extension of Louis Kahn's continual search for "the problem within the problem." Jean Labatut had emphasized to his Princeton students that the image of a building is different at each dimension and scale: first only a dot on the landscape, then a building, then sublayers of increasing detail—"interweaving planes" as he called them. Kahn's theory of the architectural hierarchy, of served versus servant spaces—another view of layering—captured the attention of architects when it was put to work in his Richards Medical Research Building laboratories (1957–1960) at the University of Pennsylvania, where massive vertical towers of brick powerfully express air-intake and venting systems as well as other mechanical systems that support the laboratory spaces. These were vertical interstices showing clarity of separation. His double-walled embassy project for Angola (1959–1962) explored a similar kind of layering.

Interest in the spaces between things is a corollary to layering that is also seen in the development of interstitial floors in hospitals and laboratories—those floors reserved for mechanical systems to make the floors for people more adaptable to future change. Kahn's Salk Institute laboratories (1959–1965) in Torrey Pines, California, contain the most lavish and renowned intermediate mechanical floors, and hospital after hospital in the 1960s adopted this horizontal layering as insurance against rebuilding for future requirements and to accommodate adaptability to change. Among those hospitals and laboratories are: Davis Brody & Associates' Science Building No. 2 (1966–1968) for the State University of New York at New Paltz, New York, and Ulrich Franzen's Agronomy Building (1968) at Cornell University in Ithaca, New York. Both have mechanical systems in service spaces between the laboratory floors. Franzen combines these with vertical venting towers on the perimeter, which leads to a strong vertical sculpturing of the brick exterior.

These larger interfaces, bigger interstices, distinguish the superimposition of the Supermannerists. Interstices began to interest some of them more than the layers did; to them architecture was primarily a consideration of the spaces between, of the "things that happen in the cracks," as Charles Moore said. Moore wrote that "our own places, like our lives, are not bound up in one continuous space. Our order is not made in one discrete inside neatly separated from a hostile outside. We lead lives, more importantly, in disconnected, discontinuous spaces." The discontinuity of our life-styles is confirmed by the telephone and by television, by computer relay banks and by long-distance travel, by countless other tenuous ties and remote-control electronic devices that connect our separate and mobile activities. Like the discontinuous sculptures of Kenneth Snelson, like the discontinuous prose of the Theatre of the Absurd, the new design shows superimposed systems of separate but interrelated, overlaid, and sometimes nontouching elements. This is the architectural expression of today's discontinuity.

An early, flamboyant, yet almost unrecognized example of layering was Ralph Rapson's screen for the Tyrone Guthrie Theatre (1963) in Minneapolis, Minnesota. It was an abstract frame of asymmetrically placed polygons and penantlike fins that stood outside and separate from the glass-walled theatre. At the time of the opening I wrote, "Curiously enough, the structure also makes a statement about the spirit of theatre: it is multi-layered, with several walls that may be comparable to the different levels of illusion and reality of theatre . . ." Many critics thought it "indefensible" and "extraneous," especially since it was a plywood screen stuccoed—a materials mix that was not in the

MLTW/Moore-Turnbull: Faculty Club, University of California, Santa Barbara. 1968. *Photograph by C. Ray Smith.*

MLTW/Moore-Turnbull: Layered screen of cutout numbers, Moore house, New Haven, Connecticut. 1966. *Photograph by Maud Dorr.*

established nature-of-materials usage. The screen was removed by the end of the decade, ironically, when the New York Five were coming into prominence with similar building techniques and when Moore and Turnbull were completing their multilayered college buildings at Santa Cruz California (see p. 244).

In 1966 Moore included movable panels of cutout numbers in his New Haven House; they slid and stacked at the corner, showing the kinetic multilayering of our number-conscious society. He is concerned with this discontinuity, which was held together only by airplanes, automobiles, and telephones—"electronic glue," he calls it—and he expressed it architecturally. By emphasizing interstices, such permissiveness accepts things not fitting exactly; it accepts unjointed joints—coexistence. It permits new solutions to stand adjacent to other unresolved and seemingly incompatible solutions.

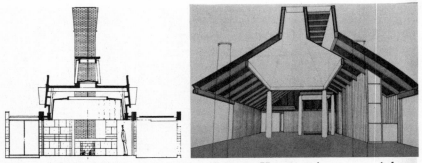

(*above, left*) Robert Venturi: Section, Pearson House project. 1957. (*above, right*) Moore, Lyndon, Turnbull, Whitaker: Section, Moore house, Orinda, California.1962. (*below*) Moore, Lyndon, Turnbull, Whitaker: Interior domed bathing area, Moore house, Orinda, California.1962. *Photograph by Morley Baer.*

Rooms-Within-Rooms

Robert Venturi's early Pearson House project (1957) had a layered inner structure of "domes." So also did Charles Moore's first house for himself. The exterior of Moore's 1962 house in Orinda, California, is simple, unassuming, and straightforward enough: a regular square wood envelope with wall-height doors and windows that slide on barn-door tracks; they open up half of each side so that the outside is closer and even more inside than with all glass walls. The house has a pyramidal roof topped by a rectangular attic skylight. In this square structure no two facades are identical, yet it is so foursquare that found-object molds for waterworks equipment, used as exterior sculptures, seem almost free-form by contrast. There is little to suggest the surprises on the interior. Inside, the house is a single space, but there is remarkable variety as well as unity of form. Two pyramidal domes, each resting on four ten-foot-high Tuscan columns that were salvaged from a San Francisco demolition, define two square areas—a living area or "conversation pit" under the larger dome and a sunken tub and shower under the smaller. Because these two areas are off-center, the smaller dome leans in toward the middle to reach into the rectangular skylight; the larger dome leans toward one end of the skylight. The domes are asymmetrical statements of the roof form. Like inverted funnels, they pull light down onto the areas they define. They and their supporting columns also compose rooms-within-rooms.

Around and between the domes, the space is open. During the day sunlight moves across the space, picking up the ceiling, the mauve and magenta paint on the capitals, the vibrant blue fascia, the soft putty-green walls, and the dark floor. In 1961 one critic of Moore's design observed that the "plan has more to do with painting and graphic design than with architecture"; he thereby presaged the emphasis that occurred during the ensuing years on graphic design and the relationship between architecture and painting. When the house was finished, I thought the interior was more akin to stage setting than to the mainstream of "solid," "permanent" architecture in America at the time, and I first compared it to the spatial and lighting effects of Baroque architecture. That was in 1963. As the decade and the new design developed, I moved my analogy back chronologically to the period of Mannerism.

In Moore's later house in New Haven, three tubular light wells were designed as rooms-within-rooms. They floated loosely within the old house and produced ambiguous interplay between the original elements

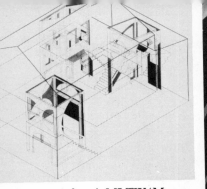

(*above*) MLTW/Moore-Turnbull: Axonometric, Moore house, New Haven, Connecticut. 1966. (*right*) Charles Moore: "Tube," looking upward, Moore house, New Haven, Connecticut. 1966. *Photograph by Norman McGrath.* (*below*) Charles Moore: Interstices and unjointed joints, Moore house, New Haven, Connecticut. 1966. *Photograph by Maud Dorr.*

and the new; three rectangular openings in one of the tubes reiterated but did not line up with the three windows behind it—that is, they were not made to fit each other. This kind of overlay or superimposition works with the elements of fusion and contrast.

Supercube

Something of a shake on the old Murphy unit that folds out of the wall to make a bed, Lester Walker's Supercube is a bed that folds out to make a room—actually five rooms (see color plate 17). Designed in 1968 by architect Walker, who studied at Penn State and at Yale, worked with Conklin & Rossant, and then formed a partnership with Craig Hodgetts, Supercube is a room-within-a-room. Located in the center of a space, this compact "living machine" is enclosed by doors that swing out on all sides to make separate areas for conversation (seating five), for dining (seating four), for dressing (with closet space), and an office (seating two) for toy store entrepreneur Stephen Miller, who was the client. Owner Miller's idea of making "a huge supertoy that could be lived in" is another manipulation of scale—both of furniture and of toys—and a superimposition technique. A double bed is the core of Walker's cozy, Pullman-berth design; a fold-down divider backrest converts the bed into two back-to-back sofas. Fold-down desks, dining and end tables, easy chairs, and benches are hinged to the enclosing winglike doors. It is a roomette, like Jefferson's bed at Monticello, but with appendages. When the wings with their circular and semicircular Kahnesque voids are folded in and out for their various functions, the strong patterns of bright red, yellow, white, and blue constantly vary the appearance of the rigid-looking red box. They also produce an effect of transparency that minimizes the volume of the cube as the psychological whims of the user may urge. Supercube almost transforms furniture moving into kinetic art.

The superficial resemblance of the design to the plywood tubes in Charles Moore's New Haven house extends only to this geometric cutout motif, which Walker rationalizes as providing diagonal bracing and preventing torque. Whereas Moore's tubes are architectural furniture to be passed through and looked at from the major living areas, Walker's Supercube is a piece of architectural furniture to be lived in as a major space in itself. Supercube systematizes ideas on prefab rooms, rooms-within-rooms, and flexible but compact systems into a playful supertoy capsule with functional and aesthetic variety to involve the user.

(*above*) Kenneth Isaacs: Living Structure, New York City. 1963. *Photograph by George Cserna.*

(*left and top of facing page*) Tom Luckey: Cylindrical rotating bedroom, Warren, Vermont. 1967. *Photograph by David Hirsch.*

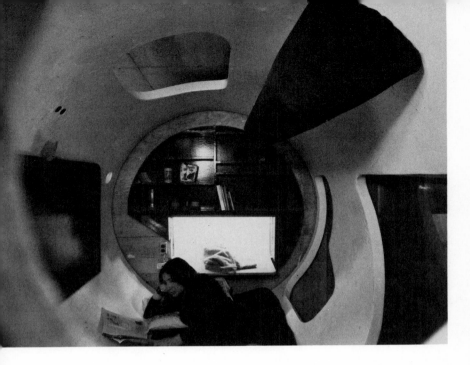

Craig Hodgetts and Michael Hollander separately developed other systems of furniture that were essentially open, wall-less rooms-within-rooms (see "User Systems and Adaptability to Change"). They were developments in idea, if not in detail, of Kenneth Isaac's Living Structure (1963)—a cage or frame structure with movable, rearrangeable pallets that accommodated desk and table space, seating, and a bed on top, and his later (1971), cube roomettes made at the Chicago Circle Campus of the University of Illinois.

The bedroom system that Tom Luckey designed and built in a house for Fritz Steele (1967) at Prickly Mountain, Vermont, explosively, ingeniously reanalyzed functions for a room-within-a-room scheme. Within a nine-foot by nine-foot room, a six-foot diameter, eight-foot-long horizontal cylinder contains a bed, a chair-sofa, a desk, and a table. The user must rotate the cylindrical room-within-a-room to lower into position the furniture that he wants to involve himself with at a specific time. Ports in the cylinder wall give access to its interior, provide a traditional sitting position, and admit lighting from the surrounding space. A black canvas upholstered bed and sofa-back was zippered to the rotating unit. Made by a cooper, the cylinder has one-and-one-quarter-inch oak hoops framing it and a double wall of one-foot, four-inch plywood painted glossy white. It rolls on four, heavy rubber, floor-mounted casters against four inch-wide, one-sixteenth-inch-thick metal strips that are overlaid on the drum. The unit is heavy enough so that it brakes itself when occupied, but it can act as a swing for sitters, and can even spin an occupant around full circle, upside down, as in the weightless sequences in Stanley Kubrick's 1968 film *2001: A Space Odyssey*. No other known system so completely reinterpreted functions, expressed them in new, inverted, exciting ways, and involved the user in the imagery of space exploration as this bedroom-within-a-bedroom by Tom Luckey.

Other giant furniture systems and systems furniture from 1965 to 1970 that created microenvironments in the midst of larger spaces included huge boxlike constructions such as Peter Hoppner's bunk bed on top of a storage room, Richard Wurman's circular officers' platform at the Industrial Valley Bank in Philadelphia, Moore's Project Argus (see p. 108), and the partitioned micro-offices-within-office landscapes, and some furniture design later in the 1960s. Moore-Turnbull's College for the University of California at Santa Cruz (1972) makes a distinc-

MLTW/Turnbull Associates: Kresge College, University of California, Santa Cruz. 1972. *Photograph by Morley Baer.*

Richard Meier: Smith House, Darien, Connecticut. 1967. *Photograph courtesy Retoria Yukio Futagawa and Associated Photographers.*

tive use of layering. In those buildings, semienclosed perimeter corridors outside the student dormitory rooms are formed by white stucco double-scale screens with openings different in size from those of the doors and windows to the rooms. As sunlight filters through the redwoods onto the sparkling white stucco screens—with their faintly Barnesian quality—the layering of crisp forms, suddenly, simultaneously, and surprisingly produces rich ambiguities. In 1973 Moore likened them to "two-dimensional stage flats or billboards."

At the end of the 1960s a similar formal effect, although derived from a different aesthetic background, is created by the thin screens of the "cardboard corbu" school—Richard Meier, Peter Eisenman, and Michael Graves. They achieve an almost porcelain brittleness by overlaying white screens of wood or stucco over metal and glass skins. In Graves's work, layering is derived from the Cubist concept of space as an interplay between plane and depth. Eisenman's use of layering is intended to be the generator of his entire architectural system, establishing the relationship of all his elements. In his method, layering refers not only to the actual layered elements but also to the relationships between layered elements.

The additive quality of layering was also explored in the clustering and stacking of pavilion-on-pavilion or shed-on-shed in the buildings at The Sea Ranch by Moore and Turnbull and by Esherick, in houses by Hardy and T. Merrill Prentice, Jr., and in many works by other architects. So the interplay between layers and interstices, between things-within-things and rooms-within-rooms developed through the decade as a technique of superimposition.

PRESERVATION, HISTORICISM, AND RECYCLING

The preservation and recycling of distinguished old buildings—found space—and of whole neighborhoods grew with a new view of our environment and ecology; it superimposed new uses and forms on our architectural heritage. That view looked at the overall environment realistically, inclusively, and accepted its totality as valid and valuable—the old as well as the new, the overall history of art and architecture as well as their present. This was a distinct change from the ideas of the early Moderns.

One of the major mistakes of the Modern movement, in its compulsion to sweep away the clutter of Victorian substyles and Art Nouveau, was to sweep away the good with the bad. In their espousal of the automated machine as the ideal of the contemporary artisan, early Modernists rejected handcraft and ornamentation—not only for themselves but also retroactively for other periods of architecture and design. The Internationalists denied, it appeared, that any design of merit could have been produced before the age of Modern architecture, or at least between the Renaissance and the Modern movement. (The authority of the Renaissance and earlier masters could not be questioned after the monumental accreditation of nineteenth-century art historians.)

So it was that for three decades, from the 1920s through the 1940s, the history of architecture was either given little emphasis in our architecture schools or not taught at all. Architects and planners, like the majority of society, were trained not to respect and protect old buildings. The result was that in the town planning and the urban renewal that followed World War II in this country our architectural heritage went undesignated, unprotected, and ignored. Countless masterpieces as well as lesser but still distinguished buildings were swept away to achieve that "pure, clean," open-space plaza effect that was a goal of the anticlutterists.

Usually, when development capital is invested in a decaying urban area, as Philadelphia-trained, Toronto-based architect Barton Myers pointed out, "The bulldozer is brought in immediately to level and destroy whatever made the area attractive in the first place. The reasoning behind this 'urban renewal' methodology is that renovation is more expensive than new construction and that, in any case, maximum coverage of a site must be accomplished in order to amortize the current high cost of new construction." "The consequence is," said Toronto architect A. J. Diamond, "that maximum capital outlay is required for competitive rental returns." This is the urban renewal method that critic Jane Jacobs so vehemently and outspokenly opposed in New York and other great American cities.

The alternative renewal method, that of preserving the continuum of urban growth, minimizes fiendish leaps of scale in both size and financing. It is a method that developers—the smaller ones, at least, if not the financial giants—can operate by since it provides high returns for small capital outlay.

In the 1960s, as population and urban areas expanded, more and more old and allegedly uneconomical or unprofitable buildings were threatened. Whether government-sponsored or speculator-inspired, urban renewal more often than not destroyed good old buildings before it built its new grid conceptions.

Civic masterpieces were toppled and superseded by replacements of stunning sleaziness. In 1963, the razing of New York's Pennsylvania Station, a civic masterpiece of 1909 by McKim Mead & White, lost for the heritage of architecture a complete city block of transitional eclectic Beaux Arts design, a reproduction of the Baths of Caracalla and the most impressive glass-and-steel train shed then left in America. In Chicago, masterpiece after masterpiece of the Chicago School—the pioneering skyscrapers of Burnham and Root, of Adler & Sullivan, and of Holabird & Root—fell by the guillotine of the real estate people's tribunal.

Mill structures in dozens of New England towns fared poorly too. Like others, most of the Amoskeag Mills (1838–1915), whose 139 brick buildings lined the Merrimack River for more than a mile in Manchester, New Hampshire, fell to the wreckers—despite the protests and efforts of local citizens, the Smithsonian Institution, and such dedicated Pratt Institute designers as K. A. Larson. Their proposals for rescue of the buildings fell on the closed ears of parking lot operators.

The industrial architecture that was the inspiration of early Modern architects slowly and irrevocably was dashed away. Nor were speculative developers and beleaguered city planning commissions much more guilty than the universities, whose avowed aims are to preserve, to promulgate, and to expound on our cultural and professional heritage. The record of the universities with regard to destruction of architectural monuments in the middle of the twentieth century is appalling. Even Frank Lloyd Wright's masterly Robie House of 1909 barely escaped the wrecker's ball before it was rescued and given its present revitalized splendor by Skidmore, Owings & Merrill's Chicago office.

Architecture as a profession could not claim a much nobler record in this destruction and disrespect. The record of architects could be explained, if not excused, by the facts of their historical disinterest or ignorance and their contractual clumsiness, which made architects' fees dependent on how much was built and how expensive the new materials were, rather than on the significance and value of architectural advice. It could also be explained by the axiom that rejects the taste of immediate predecessors, that explosively rebels to produce a new order, that blindly flails at everything to create the new.

Many architects in respected, established firms purposely did not get involved in preservation because they didn't want to provide opposition to the developers who were their major sources of income. It was more important to architects that they themselves build than that they consider the continuity of their profession's achievement through the ages. Yet, clearly, if architects themselves are not interested in preserving our architectural heritage as part of the fabric of culture, we cannot reasonably expect the public at large to work up an effective lobby in times of crisis demolition.

The interest of architects in their professional heritage began to change in the 1960s. There were always people interested in preserving older architecture, but within the profession an awareness of architectural history grew among young architects during the decade. Perhaps it was because the situation got to be more acute as renewal and rebuilding increasingly threatened more and more of that heritage. Perhaps it was because the number of preservation organizations, landmarks commissions, and historic trusts increased and multiplied their efforts. Perhaps it was because recycling old buildings was a means of getting larger-scale commissions on the smaller budget levels that young architects usually have to start with. Perhaps it was the influence of art historians Jean Labatut at Princeton and Vincent Scully at Yale on a new generation of architects. Perhaps all of the above.

The new preservation was surely caused by three general trends. First, a genuine respect grew on the part of sophisticated laymen and architects for notable and representative old buildings. Second, a wave of popular "nostalgia" helped to give support to architectural historicism. Third, all this clearly corresponded to the recycling and nonwaste of the ecological movement.

Besides acknowledged architectural masterpieces and buildings with historical associations for the city, state, or nation, it became clear that buildings of lesser importance should also be saved if they have some significance in the history of architecture—the first steel-frame skyscraper, the first space-frame structure, the earliest curtain-wall tower, and so on. (Now is the time, for instance, to put plaques or landmark designations on Lever House and the Seagram Building to protect them from new generations that may see them only as rigid, static, monotonous packages. This could help meet the challenge of accelerating cycles of taste and rediscovery.) And at a larger scale, architects and town planners recognize how important it is to the texture and fabric of a city to save streets and squares that are consistent in design, that date from a single era. It is this thinking that has fostered the designation of whole quarters and urban villages as urban landmarks. In our appreciation of preservation and restoration, there has been a heartwarming improvement in understanding and quality. Increasingly in the 1960s architects reviewed the treasure trove of found buildings, preserved them, and worked with what they offered. Using what is there—found spaces—is the new realism of availability.

It was a combination of respect for industrial buildings, for old textures and solid construction methods, along with the found-buildings tendency that led San Franciscans throughout the 1960s to remodel warehouses and brick industrial buildings—along Fisherman's Wharf, in Jackson Square, and elsewhere—into some of the most charming and pleasurable shopping-dining-recreation facilities anywhere in the country. At Ghirardelli Square (1965), which became the popular model for such recycling, the firms of Wurster, Bernardi & Emmons along with Lawrence Halprin and Joseph Esherick, under the enlightened patronage of developer William Roth, remodeled rustic red-brick and wood-structured buildings into urban shopping centers that were filled with elegant and discriminating shop designs and merchandise by sophisticated merchants and designers. The Cannery and Warehouse Number One in San Francisco followed this model. Much of this conservation was related to capitalizing on simple historical texture and patina, but the sprightly and imaginative designs of the new shops and the overriding directness that fostered these renovation schemes pointed to a new direction in preservation.

Nineteenth-century architecture gained a prominent place in the recycling movement. In Chicago, Adler & Sullivan's Auditorium (1889)—with its splendid stage machinery, balconies that can be closed off, and sumptuous decoration illuminated by the golden glitter of exposed filament bulbs—was restored (1966) by architect Harry Weese and a team of distinguished colleagues. It was a great achievement, a notable exception to that city's deplorable record of destroying its treasury of Chicago School masterpieces. In New York, the Jefferson Market Courthouse in Greenwich Village was preserved and renovated (1967) by architect Giorgio Cavaglieri into a new local library of splendid High Victorian texture. The same architect with theatre designer Ming Cho Lee renovated the "Victorian Renaissance" Astor Library (1968) for use as a varied complex of spaces for the performing arts of the New York Shakespeare Festival. In both instances the city of New York was instrumental in the preservation of the old landmarks. Also in the mid-1960s Columbus, Indiana, commissioned Alexander Girard to restore its main street of nineteenth-century buildings and thereby combat the tide of "renewals."

In Oakland, Pittsburgh, and elsewhere, old movie theatres were recycled into new performing arts centers. In Saint Louis a 1925 movie theatre, with its French Baroque ornamentation, was cleaned up and adapted for use as the home of the Saint Louis Symphony—Powell Hall—a $2.5 million feat that flashed like a beacon of financial and ecological sanity in early 1968, a time when extravagant and monumental centers for the performing arts were being completed across the nation. Wedemeyer, Cerrick, Corubia were the architects, Ben Schlanger the theatre consultant, and Cyril Harris the acoustical consultant.

And in Springfield, Illinois, the state itself sponsored the complete rebuilding and restoration (1969) of the Old State Capitol where Lincoln delivered his historic speech "A house divided against itself cannot stand . . ." Not only have those responsible preserved a national

(*both photos*) Ferry & Henderson: Reconstruction of, and reconstructed, Old State Capitol, Springfield, Illinois. 1969. *Photograph by Orlando R. Cabanban.*

monument that was once threatened with almost certain demolition and replacement, not only have they accomplished a singularly faithful restoration and preserved the historical fabric of the city, but, more importantly, they have, by that work and the municipal garage built beneath it, sparked a movement toward urban revitalization of the central business district, that surrounds the old Capitol. In addition, the $7.3 million project included, in the assembly chambers, two halls that the city can use as auditoriums, potentially enabling the building to serve as a performing arts center—for chamber music, for lectures, or for small thrust-stage productions. This preservation and restoration, a model of architectural practicality and perseverance, was sensitively led by the architectural team of Ferry & Henderson. These were some of the most promising examples of urban preservation since Jane Jacobs put into words the supremely logical and historically evident idea of urban mix and urban growth.

Although not a distinguished old building, a former pool hall and auto showroom in the depressed Bedford-Stuyvesant section of Brooklyn was recycled in 1968 by Hardy Holzman Pfeiffer Associates to create a see-touch-and-feel participatory museum for neighborhood children. MUSE, as it was named, refers to the Muses as well as being a short, childlike miniform for *museum*. As a branch of the Brooklyn Children's Museum, of which it is a prototypical storefront cultural center for needy communities, MUSE aims to involve children who might otherwise not go to such an educational and cultural facility, to involve them in a creative program of arts, poetry, theatre, music, live animals, and planetarium (see color plate 1). A curving tunnel diagonally suctions the curious from the entry door at the chamfered exterior corner into an explosion of intermeshed continuous spaces on three levels at the center of the building; drama, dance, music, art, and science studios are on the third level with the administrative offices. Angles, interpenetration, layering, ambiguity, and colors are everywhere inside. Outside, across the old front of the auto showroom, the architects emblazoned the name of the building in painted chrome-yellow letters on the diagonal. This sign becomes more than large lettering; it becomes a supergraphic when understood in terms of its analogy to stenciling on a packing crate. Like crates, which can be picked up and shipped to other places, MUSE is a pilot project for the temporary or mobile museums that the Brooklyn Children's Museum is considering for other neighbor-

Hardy Holzman Pfeiffer
Associates: Plan, MUSE,
The Brooklyn Children's
Museum, Brooklyn, New
York. 1968.

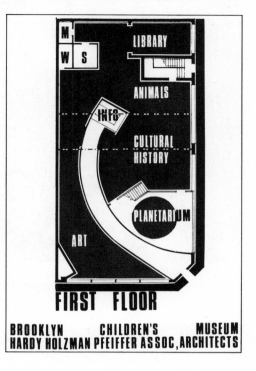

FIRST FLOOR

BROOKLYN   CHILDREN'S   MUSEUM
HARDY HOLZMAN PFEIFFER ASSOC, ARCHITECTS

hood communities. This stenciled-crate image also symbolizes the current quest of museums for mobility, and is prophetic of the days when traveling exhibitions may have entire shelters as their mobile containers, when whole museums will be shipped from community to community. The effect is to inflate the ordinary human viewer—to the size of a moving man who could lift such a crate, to a superhuman size.

Hardy Holzman Pfeiffer Associates also recycled at least half a dozen other old buildings into new spaces for the performing arts. They transformed an old park structure into a small theatre for Cincinnati's Playhouse in the Park, a movie theatre into Harlem's New Lafayette Theatre, a garage into the Harlem Dance Theatre, another garage into Newark's Community Center of the Arts, a nineteenth-century carriage house into the Taylor Theatre in Lockport, New York, and Phillips Exeter Academy's assembly hall in Exeter, New Hampshire, into a recital hall.

Hardy Holzman Pfeiffer Associates: Community Center of the Arts, Newark, New Jersey. 1969. *Photograph by Norman McGrath.*

Among the many other architectural projects based on preservation of found structures were John Cotton Moore's conversion of old industrial buildings along the Chesapeake & Ohio Canal in Georgetown, D.C., into Canal Square, another popular shopping, eating, and gathering place. Similarly in San Antonio, Atlanta, Savannah, and elsewhere whole districts of buildings and spaces from early periods in those city's histories are being preserved, recycled for new uses, and have blossomed as revitalized historical areas—San Antonio's Riverfront, Underground Atlanta, and the Old Town of Savannah.

An exemplar of reweaving a hole rent in an old and loved fabric is Hugh Hardy's proposed design for a new town house in the Greenwich Village Landmark area. He did not posit a shining forgery of Colonial Williamsburg or of his 1844 neighbors. He did not leave that tradition in a test-tube vacuum (as Gordon Bunshaft "preserved" the context for P. J. Clarke's pub). Rather, he preserved the lines of the street facade in the top and bottom stories of his design; he preserved the texture of the street in its materials, scale, and circulation patterns. Furthermore, he recalled the nineteenth-century tradition of bay and bow windows in a clear and polite, if oblique, expression of the decade of the diagonal.

New York's Landmarks Preservation Commission finally approved the design, but alas, too late. The wheels of bureaucratic buck-passing rolled too slowly. Costs had risen, and Hardy and his partners could no longer afford to build. And instead of a respectful solution to preserving a landmark street, therefore, the recalcitrant neighbors got for their visual delight a $142,000 hole-in-the-ground compost pit.

From 1968 to 1970, the deteriorating nineteenth-century building of Manhattan's Seventh District Police Court was recycled by James Stewart Polshek and Walfredo Toscanini into the lively Clinton Youth and Family Center. Located in the area long known as Hell's Kitchen and now translated sociologically as "a multiproblem area," the center once served the rough requirements of law enforcement and criminal justice —police activities, a cellblock, and a morgue—but now has been transformed into a student center. It is operated by the YMCA of Greater New York and the Rotary Club of New York. The old police court now has new spaces, brightly lighted lounges, clubrooms, crafts studios, gymnasiums, a library–meeting hall, and a senior citizens' area with kitchen. Movable furniture, nearly indestructible but more than "adequate" materials, and bright and imaginative supergraphics by David Bliss executed by Environmental Design Associates are the principal means of this recycling work. In their use of the new facility, the rowdy, dynamic occupants have permissively adapted to change by adding irreverent graffiti, by pasting posters everywhere, and by furniture rearranging.

In recycling the Clinton Center, supergraphics (see p. 269) are put to dramatic and effective use. The former main courtroom, now a basketball court and gymnasium with a preserved Victorian Renaissance coffered ceiling and classical portico, has, in addition, a kinetic-looking supergraphic of basketballs and the arcs of bounce, indicating the use of the room like a sign on the walls. Meeting rooms have bold three-dimensional-looking shadows painted around the windows to give them the appearance of greater depth—an unmistakably mannerist device. Initials on the main entry, big overlapping circles, diagonal stripes, giant numbers indicating floors, and even the shadows of nonexistent trees in the courtyard are colorfully painted on the walls to give identification, to direct circulation, and to dress up imperfections economically. The Clinton Youth and Family Center is exemplary of the decade's recycling of static old buildings for new social uses, of preserving our architectural heritage with economical and imaginative means.

James Stewart Polshek and Walfredo Toscanini: Gymnasium recycled from
former courtroom, Clinton Youth and Family Center,
New York City. 1968–1970.

Electric Demolition

By 1970, the youth movement and its symbols of vitality had such
appeal and such force, even to conservative institutions, that the new
design style was accepted by several churches as a regeneration symbol,
if not a resurrection symbol. As a kind of desperate fireworks, before the
back-to-nature movement of the Jesus Revolution, several churches
recycled their sanctuaries in the supermannerist idiom, which had always been associated with young rebels. The "new liturgy" of the
Roman Catholic Church included saying Mass in the language of each
country and also required a freestanding altar rather than the traditional
against-the-wall arrangement. Although for a number of years denomi-
nations had been making this return to the early Christian altar arrangement, the decree from Rome caused a sudden sweep of redesign
and rebuilding in older churches. In designing new sanctuaries to accommodate the new liturgy, decisions first had to be made about demol-
ishing or preserving old sanctuaries.

For the Philadelphia church of Saint Francis de Sales, Venturi &
Rauch changed the focus from the orginal neo-Byzantine sanctuary to a

new-liturgy arrangement by means of a kind of electric demolition (1968). As if they were making an editor's deletion on the statement of the original sanctuary, they literally drew a line through the old altar and its reredos, editing it out. That line is a cold cathode tube of light suspended on piano wire, ten feet above the church floor, following the gentle curve of the apse. The tube cancels out the old altar with the intensity of its electric light; yet the original statement can still be seen behind, as if in the distance (see color plate 7).

This demolition is doubly literary in that, first, it is analogous to a deletion rather than being an actual one, and second, it alludes to literary or editorial procedures. In the "electric age" this is a pivotal example of the architecture of allusion. In addition, the result is a milestone of church art and a new church image. The decision to preserve the old altar was made by the architects because they felt that its jewel-encrusted craftsmanship should be retained as an expression of the church's historical continuity. That was a decision unlike the wiping away of historical ornamentation that was indulged in by the purgative "clean" designers of the 1950s. The architects also used the line of electric demolition to focus on the new furnishings of the new sanctuary. "The shape of the magic line of cathode," as Venturi called it, is not the only element that defines the new sanctuary, of course, but it is the most supermannerist of the church's innovations. As other furnishings, the congregation required a lectern and a priest's chair in addition to the freestanding altar table. To match the new liturgy, the architects provided a completely new image for these furnishings. Three shiny objects of white plexiglass and white vinyl, with accents of yellow vinyl and

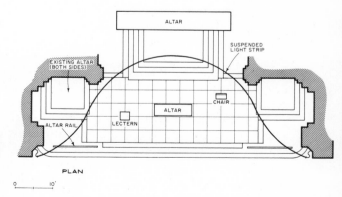

Venturi & Rauch: Sanctuary plan, Saint Francis de Sales Church, Philadelphia. 1968.

plexiglass, are set amid the neo-Byzantine surroundings. The translucent soft-curved hard plastic panels and the soft hard-edged, wet-looking vinyl in a church look like Claes Oldenburg gone pious. The architects knew, as Venturi said, that they "could not get harmony through similitude" in these new furnishings because they could not afford, much less surpass, the richness of materials—marbles, jewels, and mosaics—that had been possible when the church was built in 1907. As a consequence, they sought "harmony through contrast." The plexiglass is similar to, yet contrasts with, the marble; the soft furniture contrasts with the usual church furniture yet has harmonious forms.

Unfortunately, that design image was too totally new for a large segment of the congregation of Saint Francis de Sales. Seven months after installation, "electric demolition" took on a double and sadder meaning when the congregation removed the cathode-tube light to a storage room. They thereby blindly demolished the architects' imaginatively allusive scheme, leaving only the acrylic and vinyl furniture intact. That kind of event was not new to Venturi & Rauch, however. Once before, in a similar Kafkaesque occurrence, the architects unknowingly suffered the destruction of a scheme by client—at Grand's Restaurant (1962), also in west Philadelphia. It showed unmistakably the vehemence of the reactions that the works of the Supermannerists—or the works of Venturi & Rauch—evoked.

Urban Supertoy Subdues Renewal Bulldozer

York Square, a center of commercial buildings in Toronto, is a paradigm of the inclusive supermannerist approach of the 1960s. It combines old and new, preservation and construction, pedestrians and cars, bustle and peace, facade and mass, structure and paint. York Square (1969) was among the first large-scale exterior urban recyclings designed in the new idiom, and it went a long way toward proving that "supergames" (as the English magazine *Architectural Review* sardonically dubbed them) could be valid and meaningful when put to urban uses.

Located on the main strip of Yorkville, Toronto's Greenwich Village or Waterfront, York Square was originally a one-half-block site of decayed and mutilated structures when Toronto developer I. R. Wookey commissioned A. J. Diamond and Barton Myers to plan and design a scheme to renovate the site and to make it an economically viable commercial center. The general condition and the scale of the single

Diamond & Myers:
Plan, York Square,
Toronto, Canada. 1969.

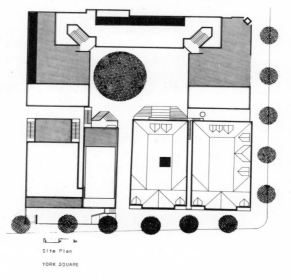

Site Plan

YORK SQUARE

buildings were intentionally maintained so that the established influx of already interested people was not disturbed.

To refurbish the old ticky-tacky row of undistinguished brick buildings on the Yorkville Avenue side, Diamond & Myers built a one-story-high, perforated red brick screen in front of them and linked it to them with skylighted roofs. The screen has huge circular openings for shop windows alternating with rectangular openings for doorways. The circles are designed to say "look through"; the rectangles to say "walk through." This is simple childlike sign making—what graphics designers call *signage*—at giant scale. It is a supertoy billboard.

"The language of the openings is really dumb," says Barton Myers, using a word that reveals his previous study at the University of Pennsylvania with Kahn and Venturi. That "dumb" geometry, unlike glass storefronts of most commercial strips, adds differentiated focus to individual establishments.

In collaboration with Barrie Briscoe, the architects superimposed supergraphics on the two street facades to serve both as signage and as circulation indicators. On the Avenue Road facade, "York Square" is telegraphically billboarded in green letters and superimposed on green and white circulation stripes. The stripes lead the eye around the corner to become an arrowhead indicator toward the passageway to the center of the York Square site. At the corner, a huge ocher-colored site plan of the complex is painted on the diagonal inside green circles. The circles relate to the *o* in *York,* Briscoe says. This overlaid diagrammatic site plan is about one-eighth the actual size of the site itself, but it is mammoth compared to the usual orientation diagram on a signboard. As a result, it makes a new scale transition between the physical actuality and the in-orbit view of the site, as well as providing a logo and identifying signage. This double-scale interaction is basic to all supergraphics, but Barrie Briscoe brings to the technique the superimposition of representational material.

All this paint is superimposed over the walls, windows, and doors of the York Square facades indiscriminately, or "permissively," as the Supermannerists view it. In the architects' minds, the graphics enhance the larger scale of the new complex and bind it all together, "much as the Victorian stringcourses of the original brick structures did," they explain. "But where diverse building elements were once combined into a whole by such devices, now whole groups of buildings are united together for the superscale of the street."

If the storefront screen and the supergraphics are included for identity, focus, and circulation, York Square's "square" is an urban

Diamond & Myers: York Square, Toronto, Canada. 1969.

amenity provided purely for the physcial and psychological well-being of the population and for their involvement and environmental improvement. That square is a central courtyard between the irregular backs of the old Yorkville Avenue buildings and a new U-plan structure that encloses the rear of the site. This brick-paved courtyard, presided over by a grand old maple tree that spreads a leafy shade overhead, is a more pastoral respite than the busy street traffic permits. It is "a place for pedestrians away from the automobile," as the architects say.

Such preservation and recycling encourage urban evolution over urban revolution. They preserve the architectural continuum while adding a measure of renewal and revitalization. As the 1970s opened, then, there was promise that a new method—the rediscovered polychromed exteriors of the past—might change the trend of bulldozer developing.

DECORATION AND HISTORICAL ALLUSION

At a smaller scale than the preservation and the recycling of complete old buildings, architects during the 1960s accepted other "givens" of our architectural heritage. They incorporated found objects from older buildings and their interiors. Sometimes they suggested or alluded to those elements with newly designed updated versions. Generally, this was a decorative device. It is in the tradition of sixteenth- and seventeenth-century Mannerism.

Decoration is another element of architecture that was reaccepted, included, in the new architecture. It is a bold new polyexpanded megadecoration. Even though the Bauhaus had a department of wall paintings chaired by Wassily Kandinsky, architects had pooh-poohed decoration for several decades. Posy-flocked wallpaper is bad, they said. And this resistance broke down only when it was recognized that Mies's I-beam mullions were structurally unnecessary and, therefore, applied decoration like structure-patterned wallpaper.

In the 1960s, the distinction between design and decoration became almost academic. What counts is imagination and invention—even if of a perverse kind. Now, to use roadside billboards or street construction tarpaulins as walls or wall coverings is entirely acceptable.

Paint—applied, unnatural, cosmetic decoration, as it had been considered—returned as a mainstay of design in the 1960s. Color was back in favor as a respectable element in architecture. It was no longer typical of architects in general, as Edgar Kaufmann, Jr., said of Eero Saarinen in 1962, his most radical color scheme was gray, black, and red. This new color freedom was encouraged by the hard-edge painters and the color-stripe and color-field painters such as Alexander Lieberman, Kenneth Noland, and Ralph Humphrey. Morris Louis, Jules Olitski, and Ellsworth Kelly had shown the potency and vitality of color. And Alexander Girard, Dorothy Liebes, and Jack Lenor Larsen had verged on Op art in their rich, vibrating color combinations for fabrics.

Some of the decorative efforts are ordering techniques, some are leveling techniques. Other goals are pure sensory envelopment, circulation clarity signage, and patterns superimposed without aiming at spatial extension. Tim Vreeland points out that the new interest in painting evidences itself in the style of presentation. "We find students using colossal size letters and numerals, juxtapositions of clashing oranges and purples, blacks and silvers, bold overscaled patterns. They also use electronic sound reinforcement, and all kinds of new projection techniques of slides and motion pictures involving distortions, reversals, and multiple images."

Such work looks insubstantial to Establishment eyes because it actively accepts, within the vocabulary of design, the thin, slick, and cheap appearances that were formerly rejected by "exclusive" designers. Yet it expanded architecture to include its full range of traditional elements again.

In recycling found objects from old architecture, Charles Moore decoratively incorporated old Ionic wood columns in several projects early in the 1960s. Hardy Holzman Pfeiffer Associates incorporated part of the old metal classical column and frieze details from the Jersey City ferry slips in an exhibition. In the vein of historical allusions, Robert Venturi's aesthetic theory is full of references to historical precedent from the beginning. His Pearson House project (1957) is said to have "domes"; the Duke House renovation (1959) is said to have "a Louis XIV scale in a Louis XVI building." His firm reiterated sixteenth- and seventeenth-century screens in the design of the facades of the Guild House, Fire Station Number 4 in Columbus, Indiana, as has been mentioned, and they alluded to oriental moongates in the Varga-Brigio Medical Building. An ancient oriental moongate in a modern occidental back fence signals the main entry to Venturi & Rauch's small medical office building of 1969 for Dr. George Varga and Dr. Frank Brigio in Bridgeton, New Jersey. The rest of the red brick building is plain, simple, unpretentious, and functionally direct. Urban planner Denise

Venturi & Rauch: Varga-Brigio medical office building, Bridgeton, New Jersey. 1965–1969. *Photograph by Norman McGrath.*

Scott-Brown Venturi says it looks "as if a Chinese restaurant rented space in a factory." Her comment is not intended as negative criticism. What the firm tries to achieve in its buildings, partner John Rauch says, is "to sex them up, just as restaurants do—but in the most inexpensive ways. In this case, we used scale to make it impressive." Instead of having a plain three-foot-by-seven-foot front door, the architects super-imposed a symbolic, plum-red, thin wood screen with a large circular opening as a means of gaining attention for the entry. A second arc, larger than the circular cutout, is overlaid on the screen "to imply a larger totality," the architects explain. Together, the two segments pro-duce a linear tension, like a mammoth curled finger beckoning toward the door.

Besides this decorative symbolism, at the entry Venturi & Rauch applied some of their other motifs to the ordinary-looking building. Diagonally sited on a suburban lot, the medical building also has its entry corner chamfered, as the other end was originally designed. Within the chamfered diagonal corner porch, the main entry behind the screen is in a zigzagging wall of white brick. The elevations show a calculated juxtaposition of voids of varying sizes: a giant fixed pane is tautly squeezed up high against the skinny roof line and crashes against the entry porch. Venturi's composition with fenestration, here as in his other

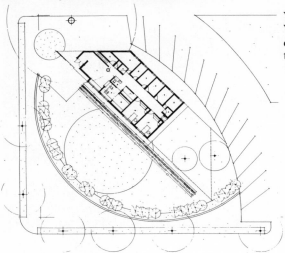

Venturi & Rauch: Plan:
Varga-Brigio medical
office building, Bridge-
ton, New Jersey. 1965–
1969.

buildings, creates a tension between contrasting sizes, between two scales, and gives the building an appearance of unusual depth for so thin a structure. Yet the historical oriental allusion is Venturi & Rauch's most kinkily whimsical and the most potently novel detail in the building.

Few houses support so much discussion and analysis in their first decades as Robert Venturi's house (1962) in Chestnut Hill, outside Philadelphia. The house is a simple-looking building on a suburban lot. Its overall form is that of a gabled and chimneyed cottage, but Venturi has twisted it around in plan as we have seen (see p. 73) and put the entrance on the gable side. That north elevation is reminiscent of a

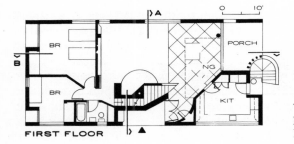

Venturi & Rauch: Plan,
house, Chestnut Hill,
Pennsylvania. 1962.

Sir John Vanbrugh: Pediment detail, Blenheim Palace, Oxfordshire, England. Designed 1705. *Photograph by Popperfoto.*

detail of Blenheim Palace—the attic of the principal courtyard portico—one of the mannerist works of Sir John Vanbrugh that Venturi is so fond of. Like a new broken pediment, the two side pavilions are extended toward the center in plan, like a detail of historical architecture blown up to make an entire building for our domestic decade. The exterior is otherwise austerely sited, stripped of podium and landscaping, like Palladian villas in Italy and England. Then, whimsically, the Palladian hallmark, the arched window, is alluded to by a tacked-on broken arch in wood trim, which presages the half-vault ceiling of the dining room. These means are used both to make historical allusions and also to use them perversely, campily, ironically, sardonically.

The front door, clearly situated at the center of the broken pediment, is nevertheless concealed, placed on the side with a diagonal "inflection" toward it, as Venturi says. Inside, the rectangular plan is spiked with diagonals, from the entry into other rooms and to the fireplace plan. Some of these angles are seemingly arbitrary, but lively and whimsical. The entry funnels one into the dining area, past the kitchen and past the adjacent stair to the second floor. The stair and kitchen walls are inflected like directional signals to lead occupants and to accommodate their movement. The house also rings variations on other supermannerist devices besides historical allusions and diagonals. The screen of walls, multilayered like a three-dimensional facade architecture, can be seen in the front elevation, where they appear as superimposed on other screens that make up the elevation. And the painterly composition of the ordinary if irregular windows began a direction that Venturi & Rauch developed more intricately in the Nantucket cottages (1971) and in the Mathematics Building for Yale (1970).

Few observers would have discovered the secret historical code to Venturi's work if he had not provided detailed written explications. Did the Chestnut Hill house really appear monumental, or was that imagery fostered by the monumental explanations on historical analogy that the

(*left*) Venturi & Rauch: Entry and living room, house, Chestnut Hill, Pennsylvania. 1962. *Photograph by Rollin R. La France.*

(*opposite page*) Philip Johnson and Richard Foster: Elmer Holmes Bobst Library, New York University, New York City. 1973. *Photograph by Casey Allen.*

architect provided? Nevertheless, the historical analogy superimposes another scale of the mannerist age's ritualism onto the personalized twentieth-century dollhouse. It is the superimposition of supermannerist superscale in one of its most intellectualized forms. Venturi as theorist traversed a complex argument of contradictory justification for the house that reflects more the wily inventiveness of his mind than the elaborateness of the house. And this can be said safely, since aestheticians recognize all design theory as ex post facto musing and rationalizing. Venturi explained the contradictions he expected everyone to find in the house. Its starkness elicited a cry that it was willful, ugly, and offensive. Its allusions and manipulations were greeted by others as cheerful, sprightly, fresh, and vital. Architecture critic Ellen Perry Berkeley said the house had "a serious whimsy, a rational ambiguity, a consistent distortion." We can add that it also has a studied chaos, a stark elaborateness, and a forced lightness.

Philip Johnson was the pioneer in historical allusion late in the 1940s. The domes within his New Canan, Connecticut, guest house (1953) and Kneses Tifereth Israel Synagogue, Port Chester, New York (1956), recall the dome in Sir John Soane's breakfast room. He later alluded directly to Palladio by including a Palladian design of black, gray, and white checkered marble floor in the atrium of his Elmer Holmes Bobst Library and Study Center for New York University (1973). The trompe-l'oeil, three-dimensional-looking floor pattern is adopted from Palladio's flooring in the sanctuary of the Church of San

Giorgio Maggiore in Venice. And the allusion does not stop there. As Palladio had superimposed one scale of order on another in the church —large columns supporting the bays rest on head-height plinths while smaller pilasters rest on approximately eighteen-inch bases—so Johnson has juxtaposed the vast interior twelve-story-high atrium, which feels like an exterior space, adjacent to glass-walled library and study spaces on the perimeter. Looking across the atrium from the south side and through the glass-walled interior spaces out to the open-air atrium of Washington Square to the north of the building is as mannered a view as Palladio strove for. This is a witty, grand allusion by a witty architect imbued with the force of architectural history.

Venturi had compared the Guild House facade with the Château at Anêt.

In 1971, Charles Moore was playing with the ordering motif of Borromini's Collegio di Propaganda Fide, where seven bays of the facade are united by a single overall entablature, and where, as Moore viewed it, the five inner bays and the three center bays are each joined by separate and overlapping elements. Adapting this motif to his first row-house block in the Church Street South Housing at New Haven, Moore painted the seven entry stoops with striped pediments—both pointed and rounded—that have inversions of the colored stripes, so that the three central stoops form a distinct group and the five middle stoops form another group. It was, for Moore as well, a bit of questionable art-historical gamesmanship, but it was fun to puzzle out.

Later, the New York Five incorporated formal elements of 1920s and 1930s designs into their work, although they often considered them to be in the direct tradition of Le Corbusier rather than as allusions to him. Michael Graves, however, did recognize the allusive process.

The firm of Stern & Hagmann seemed to make such historical allusions an ordering technique for their houses from the late 1960s through the 1970s. Most notably, the Paul Henry Lang house (1974) in Washington, Connecticut, is a flamboyant concoction of Mannerist, Edwardian, and even Gothic devices. And by 1976 Mitchell/Giurgola Associates had included a reconstructed nineteenth-century facade—a complete house front—in the exterior skin of the high-rise office tower for Penn Mutual Tower in Philadelphia.

Early in the 1960s Venturi called these inclusions "historical allusions"; and Vincent Scully called it the "architecture of allusion"; early in the 1970s Graves called this technique "quotations" from the archi-

Charles W. Moore & Associates: Church Street South Housing, New Haven, Connecticut. 1971.

tectural "repository." To them and to the many others who made historical allusions throughout the decade, these metaphors were acts of superimposition, historicism, and recycling that were comparable to the manipulation of Renaissance architecture and its motifs by earlier mannerist architects.

SUPERGRAPHICS

Not a decorative device, repeat, not a decorative device, supergraphics were the most immediately popular technique of superimposition developed by the Supermannerists. Supergraphics are gigantic, superscale, and double-scale designs painted or otherwise applied to architectural surfaces, either exterior or interior, in order to produce an optical effect of expanding a space or volume. Supergraphics start with two-dimensional forms that become three-dimensional explosions. Supergraphic designs can be abstracts of two-dimensional typefaces, flat outlines of solid geometric forms—spheres, cones, or cylinders—or fragments of representational photomurals from billboard advertising. Generally they create optical effects; always they destroy architectural planes, distort corners, explode the rectangular boxes that we construct as rooms, and consequently change architectural scale. In the purest supergraphics the fragments of forms cannot be contained within the interior volume or the exterior volume. As a consequence, the viewer completes the fragment as a gestalt in his mind's eye. His vision expands beyond the size of the room, envisioning that the fragment continues beyond the volume into the outer space of a bigger world. However, many of these allusive designs are so literary in their approaches that they are not immediately understandable. Once the designer's intention is known, though, as is usual with most optical tricks, the design can be seen in no other than in the intended way.

Although they are often highly decorative and employ decorative techniques, supergraphics are not primarily decorative devices. The Supermannerists' use of bold stripes, geometric forms, and three-dimensional images at superscale is emphatically *spatial* experimentation. Space expansion is the principal aim of this graphic technique, and discordant scale is its fundamental force; images are juxtaposed at a scale that is out of context to the room in which they appear. Diagonals indicating section cuts through a room suggest that the room is the size of an architectural model, and that a bigger architect somewhere beyond the section cut is studying it.

Supergraphics have precedents in the history of indigenous Western architecture: painted barns in Ireland, French Canada, and the Pennsylvania Dutch country; trompe l'oeil; and the picking up of architectural elements such as painted moldings around doors and windows, which is still done in Mediterranean countries. In the 1920s and the 1930s, Herbert Bayer's graphics and especially his Dadaist cigarette shop design—a shop with a projecting cigarette for the chimney—was a direct precursor of supergraphics.

At mid-decade, the thrust of Al Held's paintings was not that they

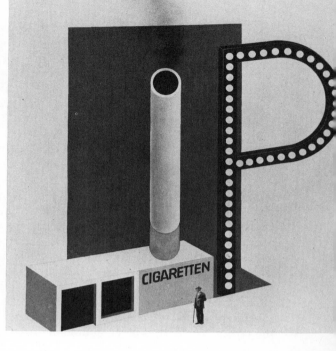

Herbert Bayer: Cigarette shop design for selling and advertising "P" Cigarettes, tempera. 1924. *Photograph courtesy Herbert Bayer.*

were outsized—his *Greek Garden* (1966) was twelve feet high by fifty-six feet long—but rather that they bulldozed their way into our vision with fragments of a circle, a square (or rectangle), and a triangle—each a solid band of outline at least a foot wide. There was no space, no distance, no concern for staying within the limits of the frame; instead the gigantic geometric forms seemed to force our attentions outward beyond the paintings to complete the three-sided square and the chamfered triangle. Another of the inspirations for supergraphics was teen-agers' interest in customizing old cars with stripes, reminiscent of the two-toned cars in the 1940s and the 1950s. The inspiration for these stripes can still be seen in mobile-home trailers, in airplanes, and in the joyous, almost anthropomorphic way the cabs of some long-distance trailer trucks are painted. But none of these inspirations and precedents was like true supergraphics. Some of the teen-agers who painted such cars in the 1950s transformed their ideas, when they got into design school in the 1960s, into supergraphics.

Houston's Southcoast group called supergraphics "hard-edge interiors." A flamboyant manifestation of supergraphics is highway billboards used as supermurals. Not only do they bring the freeway indoors, but they are an extension of the supergraphic technique with three-dimensional elements from our popular daily experience. Billboard photomurals can make a man feel he is as big as the fragmented human images he sees—almost as large as Gulliver in Lilliput.

An early superimposition of color and graphic lettering in 1960s architecture occurred in Grand's Restaurant in Philadelphia, a university campus eatery designed by Venturi & Short in 1962, opened in 1963, and redecorated by the owners almost immediately, in 1964. On the long interior side walls of the restaurant, which were painted gray with white squares, pale, dull-yellow letters spelled out the name of the proprietor and his establishment—Grand's Restaurant. The painted design looked like four-foot-high stenciled letterings tied by a thin pink line at the top; it was repeated in mirror image on the opposite wall. No one used the term *supergraphics* at the time. Robert Venturi saw the lettering as having "the character of conventional stencils" consistent with the motif of conventional objects and materials used throughout the design. Yet the graphics, which superimposed double scale on the small dining space, were brought into the purest realm of three-dimensional supergraphics by being mirrored on the opposite wall, suggesting that the type was one solid block continuing from wall to wall (see p. 88).

Charles Moore had been superimposing designs at California's Sea Ranch, after Barbara Stauffacher's work at the first athletic club (1966), but it was not until his own house in New Haven, Connecticut, was completed that he demonstrated his most imaginative manipulation of the technique. In 1965 when he moved from Berkeley to Yale to assume the chairmanship of the department of architecture, Moore designed a flamboyant and joyful house for himself. Ambiguous duality it had in abundance. The house itself was recycled, preserved from the early nineteenth century and left virtually unaltered on the exterior; but the urban calm that the exterior preserved was riotously shattered inside. The interior was an exercise in manipulating space vertically, in ambiguity, permissiveness, superscale, and superimposition, as has already been mentioned—a total inclusion of the supermannerist aesthetic. Standing independent of both the original structure and its interior were three light wells, like small interior courtyards, which Moore called "tubes." These were inserted to link and manipulate the open-plan spaces in the vertical dimension. The tubes were tall rooms-within-rooms that Moore envisioned as "giant furniture inside the dinky house—the biggest pieces of furniture you could get in a house this size." Like whatnots from Jupiter, the double-skin plywood tubes had enormous cutouts that made them resemble eyeletwork embroidery on a cosmic scale. There were nominal extensions or literary allusions in the tubes too: one was named Howard after a dog in New Orleans; the center tube was Berengaria (wife of Richard I); and Ethel was the tube over the kitchen. Several cutout arcs were a story and a half to two stories high. Onto the domestic scale of the house they superimposed the suggestion of enormous circles, "like pieces of great wheels, rolling around and grinding over you," Moore said. "I wanted these graphics to seem like part of an even bigger world. It is a latter-day manifestation of my Piranesi complex. The 18th Century got its kicks by drawing the people too small, and I thought I could get mine by making the graphics twice too big." Moore's arcs, then, superimposed a double scale, a superscale that the viewer completed as extraworldly wheels.

Besides, the tubes partition the small house more than ever, acting as screens to confuse the open-plan space, making it more ambiguous, less claustrophobic. In this way they were space extenders. Yet they achieved that goal by paradoxical means, jostling up too tightly against the chimney breast to make an impassable squeeze-through view, crashing up against the front door of the house to make a backstair space of the main entry. It was clear that Moore was fascinated by the idea of things-within-things, with what happened between the joints. And a great deal did happen between the joints: The outside of the tubes, like the rest of the house interior, was painted a bland eye-ease green; inside the tubes were white; but between the double walls, the interstices were painted in splashy, vibrant colors and filled with objects. Almost every other surface reworked some aspect of ambiguity, discontinuity, or superscale. The stair rail to the kitchen had a gap in it, making it discontinuous; yet a beam of light was an electrical connection that made the rail continuous. It was another example of Moore's "electric glue." Where one of the tubes continued over an electric switch, a miniature cutout was permissively made as a reach-through passage. Pop-component systems of electrical elements made some of the first pop chandeliers with exposed bulbs. A full-size photo of Shirley Temple as a child star was mounted on a plywood easel and stood in the study area like another person, and as an exercise in scale as well as in Camp,

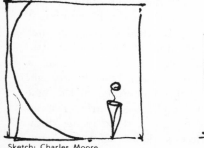

Sketch: Charles Moore

MLTW/Moore-Turn-bull: Supergraphic wheels, Moore house, New Haven, Connecticut. 1966. *Photograph by Maud Dorr.*

Charles Moore: Sketch of supergraphic wheels by the architect, Moore house, New Haven, Connecticut. 1966.

MLTW/Moore-Turnbull: Billboard mural, Moore house, New Haven, Connecticut. 1966. *Photograph by Maud Dorr.*

nostalgia, and Pop. On the wall of the staircase leading down to the kitchen Moore superimposed a fragment of a billboard advertisement showing a superscale man. (The complete billboard showed a man squatting down to inspect a Volkswagen.) It was placed to make the man appear to be looking out the back door or over the newel-post. The photomural was the left side of a billboard advertisement—another pop inclusion.

All in all, Moore's New Haven house was a laboratory demonstration of supermannerist ideas and invention, a flamboyant essay in sprightliness and wit, a forceful statement of the juxtapositions and layering between exterior and interior architecture that are commonly accepted in restaurants, shops, and hotels throughout the country. So riotous was the interior in relation to the calm exterior that Robert

Hugh and Tiziana Hardy:
Supergraphic cone, Hardy
apartment, New York City.
1966. *Photograph by Louis
Reens.*

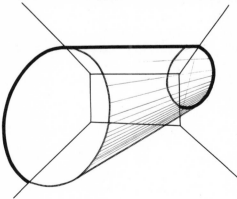

Hugh and Tiziana Hardy:
Sketch of supergraphic cone,
New York City. 1966.

Venturi claimed to love the house because, as his paradoxical mind expressed it, it was so boring.

Hardy Holzman Pfeiffer Associates started on supergraphics, Hugh Hardy says, by "passing imaginary geometric planes and solids through a room so that each plane is cut irregularly." Hardy and his wife, Tiziana, both architects, started by painting such outline forms in their apartment in 1966. Stripes in the kitchen and living room became the lines of cuts through the rooms, like sections taken on the diagonal. A stripe in the bedroom outlined a huge three-dimensional cone extending beyond the room and outside the building. The cone was not entirely accurate, the Hardys admitted, but it worked. The most self-evident and powerful example of passing these planes and solids through spaces was the segment of a circle painted in the upper corner of that same bedroom, where dime-store mirrors extended the segment on the ceiling and adjacent wall. The mirrors forced observers to complete the circle in their minds' eyes, extending the circle beyond the room, outside the building and into the street. From there it was no great leap to read the segment as part of another cylinder that cut, like a giant cookie cutter, through the upper corner. No supergraphic more clearly demonstrated the implication of gigantic solid forms from another larger world collid-

Hugh and Tiziana Hardy: Supergraphic segment of a circle continued by mirrors, Hardy apartment, New York City. 1966. *Photograph by Louis Reens.*

ing with our own earthly scale. Hardy was interested that "what is on the surface is the result of something that is left over when the solid form goes through." He was concerned with this as spatial manipulation, not as decoration. This was the purest architectural direction of supergraphics.

A variation on this fragmented circle was rung by Doug Michels in 1968 in his own Washington, D.C., apartment where a pair of concentric white segments was painted on the glass window wall. Since the building was I. M. Pei's modular, concrete-framed Southwest Village Apartments, the viewer's imagination completed the circle on the adjacent panes (see color plate 12). What made this two-dimensional form seem three-dimensional were the constantly moving, changing shadows that the design cast on the walls and floor as the sun moved along during the day and the shadows and reflections that the headlights of passing cars made on the ceiling at night. Earlier, when he was a student at Yale, Michels had installed a billboard of a Volkswagen on the wall behind his bed (see p. 188), roaring down the street of dreams. The billboard, though, had a further supergraphic dimension. The car in Michels's apartment was the one that the man in Moore's house was squatting to inspect. This was a space extender of over three miles.

Exterior Supergraphics

Marathon Shoe Repair "While U Wait" in New Haven, Connecticut, showed what could be done in preserving the urban sphere simply with paint. The shop was fairly drab when Doug Michels, then a student at the Yale Architecture School across the street, was having his shoes shined, and he told the owner so. When fellow student Howie Knox in the next chair strongly concurred, the owner commissioned the two to design and execute a painted sign for $30.00. Marathon Shoe Repair got a whole new supergraphic storefront out of that sign commission, and New Haven's parade of urban improvements gained a glossy slipper cover from the upbeat generation. Knox's and Michels's design, which they painted themselves, depicted a bright red shoe on a blue background: the front elevation of the shoe was seen on the side of the shop and the side elevation of the shoe on the broader entrance front. The sole and heel were at ground level; then the shoe jumped the window, which was untouched by the design, and was completed, shoe buttons and all, up above. The image was mammoth even though the sign kept within the New Haven regulation of three square feet of sign per lineal foot of building. What made the design a supergraphic was not this large size, however; rather, it qualified because it had two scales of vision, two levels on which it read. At one scale, the design read as an overall sign on a shoe store; at another scale as a red shoe. Visualize a man standing in that shoe—a man bigger than the Art and Architecture Building across the street—and the mental picture will demonstrate what supergraphics are all about (see color plate 9).

This double-scale graphic technique was applied to buildings in rural settings as well as to those in urban surroundings. In the skiing season of 1967, David Sellers and Charles Hosford designed a supergraphic front for the gatehouse of the Sugarbush, Vermont, ski area. The redesigned building could be read as a sign from three different distances: From afar, the basic red tones stood out against the snowy terrain, providing a directional signal to drivers en route to the parking field. As they drove closer, previously ambiguous lettering—gigantic, superimposed, and multicolored—began to read as *gate* on the left side and *house* on the right. Also, a huge arrow cutout was revealed as the doorway entry to the lifts, simultaneously directing skiers to tickets, food, telephones, and other services. Close up, at a third scale, the large whitish circle on the left became legible as a map of the ski trails (see color plate 4). The jet set and those "under thirty" thought the three-scale sign was great; the rest hated it, and since they were the majority, the gatehouse front was restored, really touchingly, shortly thereafter as an indigenous little Swiss chalet in Vermont. And that imagery is the doublethink of the pure and unadapted commercial idiom.

As early as 1963, shortly after he had been impressed by the mirror-image graphics inside Robert Venturi's Grand's Restaurant in Philadelphia, Donlyn Lyndon designed a 105-foot-long sign, like a billboard, for the Fashion Fabrics shop in the Fremont Professional Center at Seaside, California. Similar to the lettering on Sellers and Hosford's gatehouse, the motif was a series of signs with variable-scale lettering, with close juxtaposition of the letters, and with superimposition of colors—pink, red, blue, brown, and white. What was actually built was a fragment of that mammoth early concept.

Perhaps the largest of all billboards was a commercial live-in logo— a gigantic 500-foot-long yellow sunburst with leering Jean Harlow eyes surrounded by a corona of tangerine-and-strawberry-colored rays, which was painted along the hull and the upper decks of the cruise ship S.S. *Independence* to give her a "swinging" new image. The aim was to use supergraphics as a means to capture the imaginations of the under-thirties and to lure them to winter cruises in the Caribbean. The painted sunrays bounced up over the rails, bulkheads, lifeboats, and funnels and seemed to envelope passengers on the upper decks in a riot of color stripes (see color plate 10). The message was unmistakable, but it might have given a submarine's periscope viewer an Icarus-attack.

Window Washer in Wonderland

One abstract supergraphic design outdoors also demonstrated the liter-ary, if not metaphysical, manipulation of the device. Cesar Pelli, then Daniel, Mann, Johnson & Mendenhall's director of design, refurbished the old Consolidated Building in Los Angeles as a California Jewelry Mart (1967–1968). The architects turned the formerly dreary central light well into a flashy, bejeweled fantascape: The walls of the Jewelry Mart court were painted with big geometric shapes in blues and white with smaller areas of red and yellow. At the bottom of the court, the pyramidal skylights were faced with mirrors. The wall designs were open-ended so that they would not be interrupted by sunlight but would be added to by sun and shadows. "The moving diagonals of reflection and shadow," as Cesar Pelli says, "shift in and out of phase with the fixed diagonals of paint. A bright blue in shadow approximates a darker blue in sun; a reflection of sky and a highlight on a wall are the same color; a reflected ray of sun makes a deep blue brighter than a light blue above it." From inside the building, glimpses of these flashing faceted views offered an extension of the diamond appraisers' and jewelry designers' work. "The mirrored skylights inevitably suggest gigantic diamonds," Pelli says, "and when the window man washes them with a big squeegee the whole landscape takes on an Alice in Wonderland quality." (See color plate 3).

Perspective distortion is the energizing principle of a hallway by Yale-trained Bill Grover. His hallway to a basement playroom for the Vlock family (1967) in New Haven is thirty feet long with seven doors on one side. By broadening a red glossy stripe from eighteen inches at the near end to four feet at the far end as it goes along the hall, the perspective is inverted: the railroad tracks no longer merge, and the hallway is shortened. Grover, who later worked with Charles Moore and was a founder of the Elm City Electric Light Sculpture Company, says

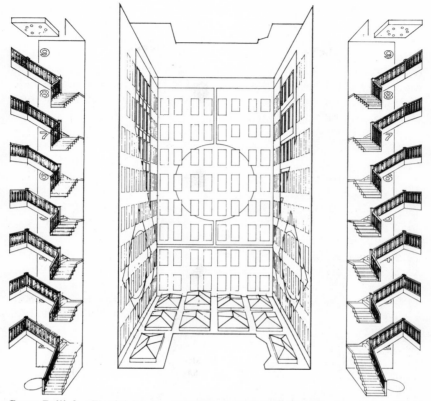

Cesar Pelli for Daniel Mann, Johnson & Mendenhall: Sketch, courtyard of the California Jewelry Mart, Los Angeles. 1967–1968.

that perspective distortion with paint "is a way to change architectural space without punching holes in walls." (See color plate 18.)

In any number of houses and apartments, Toronto-based, English-born Barrie Briscoe wrapped superscale murals around partitions and from one open-plan space into another from 1967 to 1971. Briscoe, trained in fine arts, engineering, and architecture at Washington State, Penn, and Yale, worked with Skidmore, Owings & Merrill and theatre engineer George Izenour, then in 1969 founded Supergrafitti—a Toronto firm specializing in the new graphics. For one dining-room mural (1967) he accommodated a door in the same oblivious way that eighteenth-century architects blithely cut closet doors through their boiserie. Briscoe's Op-like dining-room mural opens out on the pivoting door: when the door is opened, the lower right-hand corner of the mural appears on the other side of the door—not in reverse, but in mirror image. Therefore the mural appears to slide out against the adjacent wall as the door swings in (see color plate 19).

For Barton Myers's Toronto apartment (1968), Briscoe superimposed a painted silver-poché plan of the Château of Coucy across the

Barrie Briscoe: Mural, Toronto, Canada. 1967.

walls and ceiling. The allusions to changes in time, distance, construction, and romantic space are hard to ignore, as are the allusions in another of his designs discussed later. Toward the end of the 1960s Briscoe gained ever larger commissions, including a supergraphics scheme for the New York offices of Max Urbahn, and other types of buildings.

For the New Haven drafting room of Moore-Turnbull in 1965 Doug Michels designed an intricate interwoven fabric of painted planes. The red, blue, and green stripes passed over floor, walls, and ceiling and also over, under, and through the radiator and bookcase. Glossy red paint and glossy gray paint offset the mat blue; they also set up reflections that produced other levels and dimensions. Michels was amused because people were hesitant about stepping on the painted floor pattern. He noted mockingly that they thought it was "art" in contrast to his own looser view of them as "space trips" (see color plate 20).

Hardy Holzmann Pfeiffer Associates also chose supergraphics for their New York office image in the winter of 1967. Down the hallway between the drafting room and the partners' offices, a cylinder or cylindrical paint stripe cut through the entire length and, in Hardy's view, implied that it went on forever. Another cylinder segment cut through the reception area perpendicular to the hallway; a bold green one blasted open the reception desk, and a red cylinder at the entry had fluorescent tubes fixed onto the cut line, exploding its intersection with the wall/ceiling. Diagonal lines bisected the entry, implying sections through the room. In addition, there was an assortment of objects isolated out of context and looking singularly new: a chrome-yellow traffic light sitting on a bed of pebbles like a Japanese lantern, a pair of detached theatre seats, a moose head. When the office needed repainting in 1969, the architects merely painted the white background around the still-intact stripes. But by 1971 they longed for some new experiment, and the supergraphics were painted out.

Industrial oil tank supergraphics slyly amused motorists near New York and Chicago during the decade's last three or more years. A three-dimensional, sculptural, fifty-foot-long tiger tail constructed of painted steel wagged out of a storage tank at the Humble Oil Terminal in Chicago. A painted, two-dimensional version curled over the top of a tank at Humble's Bayway Refinery, visible from the New Jersey Turnpike between exits 12 and 13 going north. The two tails were fragmentary allusions to the company's advertising campaign slogan that their products "put a tiger in your tank." Although in commercial art it was not unusual in the 1960s to admit fairly sophisticated amusement, this feline fragment was a rare and witty example in advertising of supergraphic allusion.

One of the most successful and boldest of the supergraphic shop interiors was San Francisco's Hear-Hear. While sitting in Ghirardelli Square to discuss the design of a new record shop with Barbara Stauffacher Solomon, James T. Burns, Jr., spun out the name "Hear-Hear." Barbara Solomon spun it around even further in her logo design as

Humble Oil: "Tiger in your tank," Bayway, New Jersey. 1967.
Photograph by Frutchey Associates.

ЯAƎHEAR—after all it was 1969. She then added more of her meaningful stripes to Daniel Solomon's series of diagonal archway partitions
that define the space. Facing the prospective record buyer at Ghirardelli
Square are megasymbols of recordings—huge, representational circles
of black with red center labels. Diagonal supergrooves spread their
concentric sound waves—first in purple and black bands, then in red
and white bands and in arcs. The banded scheme resounds on all
partitions facing the street. But when the customer gets to the back of
the shop and turns toward the street, Barbara Solomon slows him down
on his way out with the danger symbol—black and yellow diagonal
stripes. These are not-so-hidden, persuasive superstripes: perhaps the
longer the customer lingers or is detained, the more likely he will be to
buy—or at least to Hear-Hear here.

Painted, striped supergraphic shops designed in late 1968 by New
York architect Alan Buchsbaum used the bold-stripe motif to band the

shops together into an overall image more powerful than the individual bits of merchandise. For a shop that sells all-plastic items—perfectly named Lucidity—Buchsbaum designed a superscale environment of black and white stripes with Art Deco overtones. Against these glossy black stripes and mat-white walls, shop owners Steve Lax and Lloyd Jordan displayed multicolored and transparent plastic merchandise on glass shelves among the ferns and other greenery. Mirrors reduplicated the stripes and gave depth to the shop. Ambiguously, then, the interior scheme both made the merchandise disappear as a constant glitter and melded it all into an even stronger, all-pervasive graphic presentation of the translucent imagery that the merchandise conveys.

Superscale Frescoes

Supergraphics, or superscale graphic symbols, also came to be accepted by churches—at least by Toronto's ecumenical Hillcrest Church (1969), designed by architects Dunlop, Wardell, Natusi & Aitken.

Alan Buchsbaum: In-
terior, hair salon,
Great Neck, New
York. 1968. *Photo-
graph by Norman
McGrath.*

When three different religious sects band together to build an ecumenical church, what clearer contemporary expression of their united venture could a designer make than continuous bands of wall color that tie all their interior spaces together? That is what the architects' graphics designer, Barrie Briscoe, used at the Hillcrest Church. Briscoe visually banded together the three congregations—Anglican, Presbyterian, and United Church of Canada—with unifying ties of wall stripery, then he superimposed religious symbols in multiples of three onto them. It was as though the spaces were immersed in a mammoth, all-encompassing illuminated Celtic manuscript. The architectural antecedents are the allover Gothic decoration of stained-glass walls or "as if veils of . . . painted narration swathed the structures," as critic Edgar Kaufmann, Jr., has described the decoration of the temples of ancient Egypt and Mesopotamia. Yet Briscoe's symbols are at an entirely new scale. The congregations were open-minded, says Barrie Briscoe, "because the design is all symbols and has a very religious feeling." The lobby sets the mood: on the wall facing the entry there is a pink circle inside which are three pale blue arrows tied together. The device is a pre-Christian symbol for unity, and it aptly connotes three congregations as well as the Christian Trinity (see color plate 21).

Behind that lobby symbol, the stripes on which it is superimposed

Barrie Briscoe: Elevations for
supergraphic murals, Hillcrest Church, Toronto, Canada. 1969.

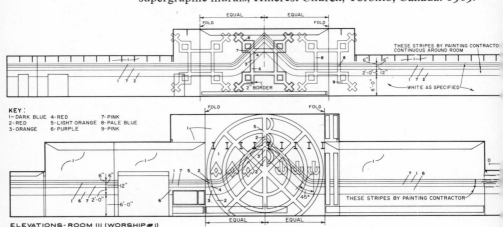

meet in a symbolic gesture—one side pointing to the earth, the other to heaven. This gesture is also a device of joinery for the series of colors that rises from a white-painted base to a dark-blue ceiling: the bottom band on one side of the building is purple and on the other side it is orange. Beyond the lobby, the stripes run continuously around two "worship rooms" and a "fellowship room," and rise to pointed arches—heavenward—on the accent walls of the worship rooms. At these points other threefold symbols are superimposed. One of the worship rooms has a symbol of multiple squares and crosses that was devised from the orb—a circle with a cross on top of it—that, according to designer Briscoe, "signifies all-encompassing, all-powerful, all-being, and also the earth itself. So I used three of them in a row, again to signify the Trinity and the three churches that built the building." As these crossed-square symbols rise from the floor to ceiling, they change color at the intersections with the stripes on which they are superimposed—the center one changing from purple through orange and red and back to purple at the top, and the two side ones changing from pale pink at the base to pale blue at the ceiling. In the taller of the two worship rooms, Briscoe devised a symbol of three circle-bounded, superimposed chi-rho's, the first two letters of the Greek word for Christ, into each of which are inserted an alpha and an omega. The liveliness of the Hillcrest Church congregations and their interior design strongly suggested that the "Death of God" so widely reported in the mid-1960s was, indeed, grossly exaggerated.

The environmental rooms painted by New York-based, Texas-born artist William Tapley from 1968 to 1972 were more painterly and intricately colored than most of the hard-edge interiors designed by architects and graphic artists. And there were supergraphic spatial effects among them. The first architectural space that Tapley painted was a lower-level stairwell and salesroom for the New York boutique, On First, in 1968, where horizontal bands of increasingly warmer colors in the spiral stairwell and horizontal bands of increasingly deeper underwater colors in the sales space created a live-in color-field painting. For the foyer and hallway of an apartment in Philadelphia (1969), a commission he received through Robert Venturi, Tapley painted a fragment of a magnificent spread-winged eagle—like the totems of Egypt, the Aztecs, and North American Indians—but in personal colors. The blue and green imbricated breast of the bird—actually an Andean

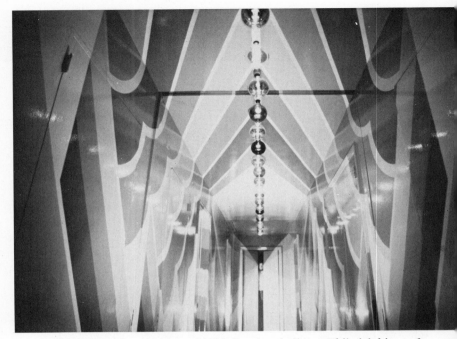

William Tapley: Supergraphic bird's wing, hallway, Philadelphia. 1969.

lapwing—is in the foyer and stretching down the hallway are the yellow and orange wing feathers, which fold down on both side walls. The wing feathers have a perspective vanishing point on the door at the end of the hallway, just at the height of a person's head. The scale of the bird seems colossal. Tapley's work is more in the vein of color theory by his own intent, but he, like Briscoe, understands the spatial manipulation of the supergraphic technique and manipulates it in a fine painterly way—and sometimes in a representational idiom—that is some of the finest work in the technique.

In June 1971, the "California Living Magazine" section of the San Francisco *Sunday Examiner* collected twenty-one examples in the San Francisco area of supergraphic storefronts. The front doors of Building Systems Development designed by Ivan Plansil depicted a multicolored isometric of a mechanical system as installed. A bagel shop by Marget Larsen has storefront-high letters spelling BAGEL; Shandy Gaff ran building-high letters around its storefront as both design and sign; The Camels by Arthur Skinner reproduced a storefront-scale version of the old Camel cigarette package. This last was a version of Herbert Bayer's cigarette kiosk project from Bauhaus days. Other San Francisco shops showed waves—water or sound—comic-strip-like images, peaceable kingdom scenes, rainbows, and M. C. Escher-like ribbons. A bank displayed a mammoth dollar sign.

By 1972, real estate developers were introducing freer, new design lobbies, plazas, elevators, hallways, and rooftops into their developments. The William Kaufman Organization in New York showed this approach at 77 Water Street, 127 John Street, and 747 Third Avenue. And prison inmates were investigating decoration and supergraphics to enliven their drab environments. One of the most amusing supergraphic designs was painted on the exterior of the black architecture firm James Donan & Associates at 202 East Twenty-fifth Street in New York. There, associate Glean Chase superimposed giant blueprints on the outside walls to describe, like working drawings, the proposed renovation of the building. It is an immediately telling sign of the work of these architects and of their aims to improve the environments of their community.

Cesar Pelli sums up the aesthetic potential of this device.

Supergraphics is a minor thing, but it is a new possibility that has been incorporated into architecture. It is a widening of the range of what architecture is. Paint used to be something outside the pale. And this is a breaking away from that—that colors in themselves can become architecture. It is one more tool. It is not the answer to everything but in many cases it is the best answer.

CIRCULATION GRAPHICS

This visual madness, ostensibly, is an expression of functional sanity. The stripes and arrows of supergraphics are not always outrageous aesthetic fortune. Some of them also provide new insights to function, circulation, materials, and objects. They are used practically: to extend the efficiency of traffic patterns, to point the way for a population unfamiliar with the circulation pattern in a public environment.

San Francisco graphics designer Barbara Stauffacher Solomon developed large-scale and colorful signage, circulation, and decorative programs into a new dimension. Strongly disciplined by Swiss graphic techniques, she designs signs and walls that are strong, vital, and immediately accessible. Her work shows none of the intellectualizing about optical tricks for which people need a key or a clue in order to understand; neither does it concern itself with graphic designs that imply the third dimension. At The Sea Ranch Athletic Club Number One (1966), she painted red and black stripes jagging across the men's locker room; and blue stripes on the women's locker room, which slide down the stairs, spin around the corner, and climb back up again. An arrow at a corner window vertically shoves us toward the view; other arrows direct us to turn corners, hop up the stairs, and swing around the landing to the second floor (see p. 185). The designs reemphasize the doubling back traffic movement throughout the building. The allover design of stripes and arrows, Barbara Stauffacher Solomon said, was "like a three-dimensional internal sculpture house that you can walk into . . . a kinesthetic world of shapes and color." It is one of the great riots of movement and color painted in an interior during the decade, and it was the first such scheme to receive widespread attention. Architects Moore and Turnbull, who designed the Athletic Club in joint venture with Lawrence Halprin & Associates, and Sea Ranch developer Al Boeke pioneered in commissioning designer Solomon to provide so total a painted decoration throughout a modern building.

Elevator Design

Literally a capsule demonstration of Supermannerism was the elevator design problem given to second-year architecture students at Yale during the 1968 spring semester, under the direction of Barbara Stauffacher Solomon, with the assistance of Gilbert E. B. Hoffman. It revealed all the inclusive aspects of superimposition, ambiguity, Pop, Op, lighting, reflectiveness, scale, diagonals, and intensified involvement and activism. Students were given the assignment of redesigning, modifying, and enlivening the two elevators in their Art and Architecture Building, using only paint as a medium (see color plate 22). A jury chose fourteen schemes that met the criteria of using a hard-edge technique to modify and enliven the boxlike enclosures with impact, of appropriate development of a theme, of originality, or of effective application of color and line for their own sake. The designers then executed their own schemes, two each week until the end of the school term. The constant, restricted scale and the single limited medium set up a comparison with the student's other work, and the chance to see their designs realized at full scale almost immediately was an experience that schools seldom provide in their regular curricula. The range of new design elements demonstrated was impressive: Diagonal line themes by John Badman, Terry Wagner, and John Christiansen successfully destroyed the confines of the box. Pop brought automobiles into the elevators in the diagonal forms of Dan Scully's multicolored mechanical drawing of a Ferrari engine and also in Glen Hodges's aerial view of a Ferrari on the highway. When Hodges's exaggerated perspective of the vanishing highway on the elevator doors opened, either the car brakes slammed you to the back of the elevator or you were catapulted out of the cab into sudden visual collision with the obstacles ahead. Other pop elevators dealt literally with the symbols of love spelled out in mammoth graphics. Peter Rose's scheme was ambiguously all white; John Jacobson's was an Op art red-on-red. The elevator by James Righter and James Caldwell demonstrated the ambiguous infinity reflections of silver mylar (the only nonpaint design). These experiments in scale were wittily contrasted by Thomas Dryer's inclusion of Le Corbusier's Modulor, which split down the middle at the elevator doors; fortunately for architects—the Modulor happened to be the right height. In Peter Woerner's and Thomas Platt's superscale American flag design, which was called "Peace," the ambiguous black-on-white forms on the doors became more clear as the doors closed and the amorphous forms became part of the protest against the Vietnam war. Wagner's vibrating "Red and Green" diagonally striped scheme included flashing red and green lights; when only the red lights were on, the scheme was all red, and when only the green lights were on, it was all green, and when the white lights were on, it was, as called, "Red and Green." The design problem was a valuable lesson for the Yale students and was adopted by other design schools in succeeding years.

Barbara Solomon continued to explore this area—"architectural graphics," as she called them—elsewhere at The Sea Ranch and in banks (p. 195), shops (p. 283), and schools, on office buildings and car service centers. Her scheme for enlivening subway systems with bold broad stripes of paint and glowing stripes of neon was exhibited at the Architectural League of New York in June 1968. Circulation graphics included follow-the-stripes flooring and ceiling patterns, door-height "exit" signs, and ten-foot-high street numbering for stations. Ironically, at the time Barbara Solomon and other designers in Boston, San Francisco, Chicago, and elsewhere were proposing the brightening of subway environments with the simple superimposition of paint, porcelain enamel panels, and new lighting, Robert Venturi was proclaiming that subways, being black holes, should in fact have their inherent real characteristics reinforced and be made even blacker. Barbara Solomon asserted that designs such as hers were for use in the real world and "not just in 'refined' environments." She said, "I don't do them to create cute chaos." By the beginning of the 1970s she and her architect husband Daniel Solomon were working toward animated architectural graphics on building exteriors.

Any number of critics felt that designer Solomon's work was stronger, more effective, and more communicative than the supergraphic designs aimed at spatial manipulation by means of gestalt. And in a decade when decoration suddenly became creditable, acceptable, again, they leaned to the potency and immediacy of Barbara Solomon's work rather than to the ambitious three-dimensional designs of some of her colleagues. As much as her work is espoused by the leading Superman-nerists, Barbara Solomon indulges in few of their convolutions of the mind. She suggests few literary analogies, plays less complicated spatial tricks. So she has a special place as one of the straightest, least mannered Supermannerists.

Among other circulation graphics, Doug Michels, in his New Haven apartment in 1966, painted a big black arrow pointing to the wall-hung telephone, below which the phone number was lettered large so that both would be easy to find. Conscious of the prominence of the telephone in our society, and also of the functional problem of available notepaper for messages, Michels painted the arrow sign with "blackboard paint" to serve as an always-ready memo pad for chalked-on numbers.

A twenty-foot-high yellow arrow signaled a 1968 exhibition in the Architecture Building of the University of Texas at Austin. Richard Oliver, then on the faculty, reported that the arrow became "a powerful sculptural artifact on the main mall and was moved on two occasions to announce functions at the Union." Spatially, the arrow elicited the kind of ambiguous responses that Tony Smith's superscale sculptures do. A shape normally recognized as two-dimensional and small, at its magni-fied scale it was both forceful and something of a humorous travesty on customary directional signs. But there was no ambiguity about this superscale graphic symbol pointing the way (see color plate 11).

Similarly for the eighth annual New Haven Festival of the Arts,

Doug Michels: Telephone locator and pad, Michels apartment, New Haven, Connecticut. 1966. *Photograph by John Hill.*

Student project: Direction indicator, University of Houston, Texas. 1968.
Photograph by Larry Brownback.

Garry D. Harley, of Carlin, Pozzi & Associates, painted arrows pointing downward onto the door to indicate the entry to the festival's exhibition space.

A red stripe oozed from under a sidewalk manhole cover, crossed the sidewalk and snaked up over the entry door becoming an arrow directing shoppers to the door handle of Fraction, a shop in Birmingham, Alabama. Designed by Gray Plosser, Jr., who studied architecture at Tulane, the graphics and entry door became the eye-catching commercial signage of the building as well as a bright spot in the urban shopping environment.

Similarly at shops across the country, flowers, peace symbols, and directional signs were painted on sidewalks, doors, and glass fronts; from Greenwich Village, to Georgetown, to Haight-Ashbury, the devices blossomed as directional signals.

On the ninth-floor executive offices of the Industrial Valley Bank in Philadelphia, designed by Murphy Levy Wurman, the chaos of office landscape was installed as one of the first such installations of the system to be designed with an up-to-date American eye. It incorporated circulation graphics, and as such was one of the first real tests of the acceptability of the system to this country's design taste. A red-and-cinnamon stripe zigzags from floor to ceiling around the core, creating diagonal, arrow-form circulation indicators to each doorway. Supergraphics and circulation graphics are an appropriate American addition to the European office-planning method, and could be developed into work-area demarcations. What was still overlooked in this kind of installation was the ceiling as a design element. Since ceilings are the single largest completely visible element throughout office-landscape spaces, they seem the logical, if neglected, areas for overall supergraphic or circulation graphic treatment.

Large Graphics But Non-Super

Supergraphics is such a seemingly self-explanatory term that it seems as if it had always been in our language. So it is easy for me to doubt the fact that I coined the word in the spring of 1967. The phenomenon had begun, so far as we can distinguish it from its precursors, around 1962 with the mirror-image lettering designed by Robert Venturi for Grand's Restaurant and on the West Coast in the work of Charles Moore and Donlyn Lyndon. It reached more splashy proportions from 1965 to 1967 in the work of Hugh Hardy, Doug Michels, and David Sellers. Barbara Stauffacher Solomon's large-scale graphics at The Sea Ranch did much to encourage interest. By mid-1967, there were enough new examples to make up an article on the subject, and I did so for *Progressive Architecture* that November. It was then that the word *supergraphics* was first published—as the title of that article. Within two months, it seemed, the word was on the lips of every design student and professional designer who was even vaguely interested in the idiom of Supermannerism.

In 1969 Yale student Martha Wagner wrote a masters thesis on the subject of supergraphics. And so it was that by 1970 and 1971, when the nearly ten-year-old examples of the pioneers were just being re-painted or replaced, the technique had attracted mass interest and predictions on its future could not yet be made conclusively with any safety.

The word *supergraphics* became synonymous with *large graphics,* and as such was adopted by professionals and laymen across the country to mean, simply, large graphics. Whatever spatial definition a critic might maintain, the population could see only the directional and the decorative meanings. As a consequence, by the end of the 1960s, the word *supergraphics* had become identified in the minds of retail consumers primarily with indoor wall decorations. Many other large graphics were produced by architects and interior and graphic designers that were stylistically similar in appearance but either did not make functional contributions to circulation or produce space-expanding effects. These large graphics were merely splashy, eye-catching, large graphics. Many of them used the same symbols from pop culture, from the roadside; many were ambiguous superimpositions, permissively flowing from plane to plane. What they did not do was to force the viewer to complete a fragment in his own mind; they did not create the double image of both fragment and completed object—cylinder, wheel, eagle, or man; they did not produce a superscale space-viewing platform for the viewer. So they were not supergraphics—although, in our drab cityscapes and in many of our pristine interior spaces, large graphics are undeniable brighteners, enliveners, contributors.

In 1969, a New York architect began to market packaged stripes that could be applied around corners; he called them supergraphics. In that same year Pittsburgh Paints brought out a brochure on how to paint stripes and straight lines and circles and arcs on your walls. It stated on one project, "would you believe the hallway at right is eight feet long. We foreshortened it by painting stripes across the door and its wall, then tapering them along the hall walls. The drawing shows you how it is done. Now don't think painted effects like this call for an artist," the brochure went on, "you can do them. They're really quite easy." Bill Grover made no comment.

At the end of 1971, Congoleum Industries introduced "The Now Floor" in daring patterns of the 1970s—a stripe of mod tile, inset and running diagonally across a blazing solid. About that time architect Joseph Grimaldi with Raymond Waites designed and packaged kits of adhesive-backed vinyl graphics for a firm called Supergraphic Originals; they became available in a number of stores. The eight-foot-long designs included a hand, an arrow, four circles, and stripes and sphere combinations. Another collection of kits, called Instant Supergraphics, offered a variety of press-on parts consisting of elbows, arcs, and straight pieces designed by Corinne McGrady. In 1972, *New York* magazine ran an article with favorite supergraphic designs by well-known graphic designers. It was called "Free Do-It-Yourself Supergraphics by Milton Glaser, Massimo Vignelli, and Thomas H. Geismar." At the beginning of 1972, the New York mural group City Walls authorized an exhibition of the outdoor murals their artists had executed. The exhibition announced a sales program offering the City Walls designs at reduced size in lithograph reproductions. In the exhibition space I was told that the artists did not like having their work referred to as supergraphics (not many of their designs could actually be considered space-expanding supergraphics, in fact). The designs were, however, being promoted as supergraphics, and it was admitted that at the time the word had been taken over by the interior wall coverings market, and was by no means an architectural term any longer.

Some pioneers considered this mass availability the death knell for their idiom. Doug Michels wrote to me that "the frontier spirit is gone; supergraphicscraysmithsandarchitecture are in the past now." Ten years after the first architectural supergraphics, the full architectural circle of the design technique had run its course—from interior to exterior and back to interior, debased as pure bigness, the object of this Pop art joke on the American dream.

SUPERSUPERIMPOSITION

Supergraphic superimposition has also been achieved with projected light. After instant food, instant sleep, and instant dreams, turned-on environments are a product of our instant age. Instant interiors: Why not? We can change a room simply by flicking a button and projecting a new slide. At night, we can change outdoor environments by the same means. Instant exteriors can be an inexpensive brightener of our nighttime urban environments. Projections provide decoration in a permissive, disposable, portable, mobile, changing kit of systematic chaos that can synthesize all the elements of the new design and its attempts to involve us. It is an architecture of multimedia.

One day the Sistine Chapel, the next day a sunset seen from beneath fall foliage; when guests come, the lambent light of a lingering meteor. It is instant planetarium—but on home or office ceilings and walls. Or, projections can be on floors: a priceless and otherwise unavailable Sarouk carpet, an elegant Baroque parquet, a fresh spring carpet of bluebells and daffodils—can be projected from the ceiling onto the floor (see color plates 23 and 24).

C. Ray Smith: Projection of Guggenheim Museum dome in Smith apartment, New York City; executed by D. Gersztoff, J. Nuckolls, and W. Warfel; equipment courtesy Kliegl Bros. Inc. 1967. *Photograph by Louis Reens.*

Instant interiors or "electric wallpaper" can include scenes of known geographic vistas—vacation photographs can change the weather during work seasons—and can change memories and responses to one's surroundings. I enjoyed a visual escape from urban New York by having Niagara Falls spilling down over my fireplace wall (without putting out the fire). Portraits and crowd scenes on the walls can make an instant party, can make one lonely or jolly. Even closer to the heart of Supermannerism, historical allusions can be superimposed—domes of Baroque or Rococo churches, or the dome of The Guggenheim Museum, with its spiral ramps and circular skylight, as I demonstrated in my own apartment to a considerably overpublicized degree, can produce space-expanding effects. This is decorating with found objects of a new, discontinuous nature.

Architects' renderings, projected inside all-white rooms, could give clients an immediate idea of a planned building. I projected the walls of the Paul Rudolph–designed Christian Science Reading Room in Urbana, Illinois, into Rudolph's own apartment. It produced instant monumental-seersucker walls and brought a Rudolph interior in Illinois into a Rudolph interior in New York. The full potential of projected environments has not yet been realized.

This superimposition of projections goes hand-in-hand with our electric-synthetic age. Yet the technique has antecedents: the theatre has been seriously working with projected scenes for at least thirty years. Usually those scenic projections have been frontally or axially oriented and framed on a single screen or plane, like a movie. Nontheatre projections, similarly, were first confined to easel-type artworks that were recessed rear-projection installations, as in the "Lumia" works of Thomas Wilfred and Earl Reiback. Most of these were based on a preconception about avoiding light in people's eyes, which was as much responsible for the slow acceptance of projected environments as any other factor. This forced designers to consider only expensive rear-projection installations—and then usually to reject them.

Yet early in 1962, Ken Isaacs designed his Knowledge Box—a learning device that was a twelve-foot cube that had twenty-four projectors flooding the interior with images. Cramming as much pictorial knowledge and information as possible onto the walls, the Knowledge Box was intended to provide an ultraquick, rapid progression of thoughts and ideas. Projected onto walls, ceiling, and floor, the pictures, words, texts, light patterns and paintings covered with a wealth of civilizations' cultures in minutes and literally projected information onto the students inside the Knowledge Box.

With the new design, those problem areas began to disappear. Elaborate, multiple, and freer effects bring the technique to new heights in discotheques, light-show environments, and for religio-aesthetic "psychedelic experiences." The new permissiveness accepts things that spill over from one area to another, from one object to the next. Under this new sense of liberation projections in the theatre have become loose, frameless, allover superimpositions. They are combined with live action by live actors, as in Josef Svoboda's *Laterna Magicka* productions throughout the 1960s. They are overlaid on performers as well as on walls and screens, as in Alwin Nikolais's multimedia dance productions. Ultimately they are overlaid on the audience—although more kindly than Merce Cunningham's follow spots that shine directly into the audience's eyes. In projected environments this means that we can accept a projection spilling onto the people in the room. This permits enormously simplified installations; no longer are recessed rear projections necessary or even desirable. Now the exposed light source is an accepted aesthetic object. Projectors and wires can be overhead or table-mounted. Now we accept, even admire, the effect of people moving through a projected image and of shadows on the projections as part of the projected environments.

Although not many apartments or houses seemed to take up this idea of instant decoration, designers still think about its potentials. The development of holography—that mysterious, three-dimensional photography—will permit us to project three-dimensional environments to give us an even more complete spatial surrounding. A peak in the development of holography and holograms came in 1967. It had been five years since Dr. Emmett Leith and Juris Upatnieks at the University of Michigan had combined the newly invented laser with Dr. Dennis Gabor's "hologram" discovery. Holograms produced by this method seemed to fill out a three-dimensional space and made viewers feel that they could put their hands into the picture. Other optics researchers at Michigan and at IBM made the process less cumbersome and more accessible. Then, in 1967, projected holograms came to public attention. General Motors put small holograms on display in Detroit and in New York; McDonnell Douglas Electronics Company mass-produced holograms for the first time; Edmund Scientific Company offered holograms for sale; and avant-garde architects took off for Michigan to see the experiments firsthand. About that time I speculated whether one would feel, on seeing a projected holograph of a room with freestanding columns, that he had to walk around the columns or through them. In 1970 International Holographics Corporation introduced the first holographic products for the consumer market. By 1972, Salvador Dali had teamed with Dr. Dennis Gabor to create what were called the first "art holograms."

In such discotheques as the participatory, sight-and-sound show environment of the refurbished Electric Circus II, on New York's St. Mark's Place, the completely electric environment envisioned by clients Jerry Brandt and Stan Freeman was brought one step closer by Gwathmey & Henderson. The two elements of the discotheque environment were interrelated: the space itself and the light-and-sound production. In the first Electric Circus these elements were kept distinct by treating its major space as a negative black volume hung with a white sculptured tent by Charles Forberg that was a separate projection

Gwathmey & Henderson: The Electric Circus II,
New York City. 1969. *Photograph by John Veltri.*

screen. In Gwathmey & Henderson's Electric Circus design of 1969, the entire space was the projection screen; the light show was the space. Gone was the black void; pristine white were the walls. It was a move out of the darkened movie-theatre atmosphere into an environment that more cohesively integrated the light-and-sound show throughout the space. The funkies had come clean. The circle had spun round in one decade. Revolutions come fast in our day.

In another projected interior of the decade, what you do at home while grazing—privately and quietly—was provided briefly in New York's night spot Cerebrum as a public, commercially available entertainment. Cerebrum offered tour guides and organized games for those who did not know how to amuse themselves while on a trip. No smoking of any kind was the rule of the place, and, of course, no alcohol was served, but no one said that you could not come prepared. Cerebrum provided taste sensations; light, sound, and tactile sensations; and group games for grown-ups (such as jump ropes, stretch-line tugs-of-war, super-balloons, projections as individual play toys). The aim was to elicit fun in the total involvement of all five senses. It looked like a cross between *A Night at the Opera* and A Night at the Turkish Baths. The "pot architecture" of this Nirvana, which was designed by Princeton-trained John Storyk, was appropriately spaced out. It presented a progression from small, black, disorienting voids to white, weightless infinity. The space exploded into a long all-white rectangular volume, sixty-six feet by thirteen feet and thirteen feet high, that was superimposed with projections and with overlays of sound. At each end of this space was a black cutout for a doorway and for a projection gallery above; the cutouts were identical but flopped. The floor, the major architectural elaboration, was a floating, carpeted platform in a Greek-key design. It had a center walkway, off which branched a series of square platforms—all elevated a foot and a half above a black-painted dry moat. The light-and-sound show was intended to help send participants into an outer space of emotional freedom. Paradoxically, it was an ordered and preset "information theory" of slide tracks, film reels, and film loops, except for some "semiclassified" encore sets. The multimedia imagery aimed to free the space from its physical solidness as well as free the mind and the body. If Cerebrum's owner, Ruffin Cooper, and John Storyk and his crew broke any new ground, it was in the nebulous area between personal involvement and the condition of the public

John Storyk: Cere-
brum, New York City.
1969. *Photograph by
John Veltri.*

spectator. Cerebrum was on the way to turning spectator passivity into participatory activity.

Don Snyder, who devised projections for Dr. Timothy Leary's "psychedelic celebrations," pointed the way for residential-scale projections by his overlaying of pattern on people in several demonstrations in New York City. One of these, initiated in 1966 by Jack Lenor Larsen, Allied Chemical Corporation, and the New York Home Fashions League, used multiple abstract projections moving constantly over futuristically clad dancer-models in motion. Snyder calls his kinetic projections "multimedia," aiming at "the architecture of the mind and of the senses." Larsen, who was responsible for showing the New York Institute of Design how projections could be used in residential and fabric design, believed that "interior design, using an ever changing array of projected color and pattern, can be as universally and inexpensively available as recorded music."

This kinetic, flexible, changeable new method of creating environments has meaningful messages for the space age. Its all-inclusiveness —all allusions to all periods to all aspects of our visual life, our physical and even our psychological life—which is the potential of the nearly infinite variety of projected materials available to us, produced the all-at-onceness that Marshall McLuhan described.

User Systems and Adaptability to Change

By all these means the new design in its concern for perception, for the affective response of the observer, involves itself in numerous options for variety and change. Promising new environments for alternative lifestyles, the new design attempts to satisfy, ever more broadly, deeply, and precisely, the actual needs, psychological as well as physical, of clients and users, as well as of architects, planners, and designers themselves.

When today's architects investigate such building systems as boxes and mobile trailerlike modules or the structure of inflatables, they are concerned with adaptability to change as well as with the technology of mobility. Mobile architectural environments express only one physical aspect of the concept, which Bill Lacy has called "the realization of growth and change as a building determinant, implying dynamic rather than static forms." Architects are concerned with the qualities of transience, impermanence, and disposability, and they turn to open-ended design systems as a means of expressing and accommodating these qualities. As Cesar Pelli says,"We understand change as being the natural condition of things and permanence as the exception." Adaptability to change realizes the changing needs of an ever changing society. The recognition of growth and decay, of fixed and lasting versus short-lived components or environments, of long-range and short-range elements, of mobile and interchangeable items for the changing requirements of our changing lives is a fundamental new reality in today's architecture and in the new design.

It is seen in mobility of the environment, in kinetic artworks and in interior designs, and in systems and in kits of parts, some of which are described in the following pages. It is seen in architects' interest in distance, speed, and outer space, which reflects their dissatisfaction with earthbound buildings. As Hugh Hardy observed:

> The pip-pop-squeal-bang-zoom-flash-look-at-me-go-90-miles-an-hour that's all around creates a desire to make buildings that can fly. Buildings seem so dumb, inert; they just sit on the ground. So there are all kinds of tricks and devices to make them float and fool around, and become balloons, become evanescent, to make them disappear, to become nothings that whoosh and they're gone.

The young design communes expressed this interest in mobility by their own nomadic life-styles—traveling around the country on call, from festival to festival, inflating bubbles, from one client's house site to another, living in trailers or buses as they built. They demonstrated mobility of practice, the ability to pick up from Houston and go to Vermont to build as well as the ability to build their own designs in a free, loose, unprogrammed, fluid manner that is correspondingly mobile. This was not new in America's automobile culture, which was founded on the tradition of frontiersmen in their Conestoga wagons and reiterated by modern nomads in their Model Ts, trailers, and campers. This portability or mobility is an essential part of the attraction that "invisible" inflated structures hold for the new designers.

The "Nomadic/Pneumatic Campus"

Within one bubble for education at the end of the 1960s the strength of this new design activity gave promise of expanded possibilities for the next decades. It was a bermed low-profile bubble-topped arts facility for Antioch College's new campus in Columbia, Maryland. The students' and design communes' involvement in the design and planning, and the mobility of the somewhat chaotic, office-landscape-like or open-plans of the interior arrangement captured the imagination (see p. 157).

Students and faculty—with the aid of architect Rurik Ekstrom, the Research and Design Institute (REDE) of Providence, and with Charles Tilford, Blair Hamilton, and with early impetus from the Southcoast nomad-designers, plus financial and technical assistance from the

Research Division of Goodyear Tire and Rubber Company and Educational Facilities Laboratories—planned a one-acre campus, two hundred and ten feet on a side, enclosed by a forty-foot-high structure composed of six- to eight-foot earthberms and a cable-restrained air-supported vinyl membrane. Inside, the campus could accommodate three hundred students and included separate "microspaces" for classrooms, for art and drama studios, for administrative functions, and for an updated version of a college quadrangle. The interior space-planning concept, by REDE's Ronald Beckman, Howard Yarme, and Jeff Blydenburgh, is an expansion of previous explorations with office landscape. They aimed to "maximize flexibility" on the grounds that "An unchanging and/or unchangeable environment encourages, and frequently enforces, stagnation in the realm of educational change." By accepting the inflatable roof's capacity to dispense with interior walls as supporting members, REDE divorces rooms entirely from the weather envelope and lets them stand, independent of the main structure, as smaller spaces within the major space. These subspaces can be varied to meet various needs: they can be either enclosed or roofless rooms under the translucent bubble; they can be freely placed furniture clusters within freestanding partitions. REDE's scheme for Antioch College showed that planning and furniture arrangements could be at a new larger scale in interiors than the portable furniture of the previous generation. Like large-scale furni-

Research and Design Institute and Rurik Ekstrom:
Inflatable arts facility, Antioch College, Columbia, Maryland. 1970–1973.

ture, these subspaces can be reanalyzed, replanned, and moved about as the needs of the campus change. The separate subsystems of rooms therefore permit maximum flexibility in terms of subsystem choice to accommodate changing needs—as we move toward individual education and toward the open classroom and the open curriculum—and in terms of aesthetic manipulation of space for psychological effect. Using stock manufactured items—portable domes, boxes, booths, trailers, tents, huts, stairs, scaffolding and decking, and other prefabricated small enclosures and building possibilities—REDE creates a subsystem that they call "micro-environments" within the larger-scale environment of the bubble roof. These too are rooms-within-rooms. The interfaces of this grab bag of elements are also considered a design area by REDE, and their concern for these interstitial spaces reiterates that special interest of the new design.

Yet of the two premises underlying bubble structures—that we need flexibility and disposability—only the former remains visible for the overall structures themselves. The idea of disposability was briefly explored in the art world in the impermanence of Jean Tinguely's self-destroying sculptures and such conceptual pieces as Claes Oldenburg's buried trench and other Earthworks. The short-lived nature of these pieces is similar to the works of the nomadic design communes. Yet disposability has been largely discredited by the ecology movement: it debunked the possibilities of the "throw-away society," which was a logical if unexamined extension of the "mobile society." "The 'disposable environment' is a fraud," said one slogan, for if it was fraudulent to think we could endlessly discard paper, it was even more fraudulent for the plastics of which bubbles were made, since they are not decomposable or recyclable. Paul Mayen warned in 1970:

> The new highly scientific technology of producing plastic furniture in ever increasing numbers is based on the philosophy of "expendable furniture." Strangely, furniture pollution is keeping pace with molecular technology but not with molecular biology. New plastic furniture is actually more durable than ourselves, our governments, and our society. The right disposal should be thought of in terms of a world that must metabolize all its activities and products.

The flexibility of mobile architecture also had a correspondent in the art world's kinetic sculptures. Hans Haacke's work with magnetic fragmented fibers and moving powders; Paul Matisse's work with ice and condensation, with fluids and viscosities, motivated by motion, heat, or static electricity; and the use of objects in motion by other designers was mobile or kinetic design at a smaller scale. And architects yearned to achieve it in their work.

The concepts of change and mobility were slow in coming to architects and other design professionals during the 1960s. The dream of the ideal theatre, the perfect hospital, and the faultless school lingered through all kinds of systems intended to achieve flexibility for all options —manual systems, motorized automatic systems, open-ended non-mechanical systems—until the recognition came that the client who helped to prescribe the building would probably no longer be there to operate it as it was envisioned when the building was completed. The theatre director and technician would have moved on; the hospital administrator would have a new assignment; the laboratory administrator would be consulting on another, even larger project. Architects had to recognize that if a building was out-of-date when completed, it was because of the nomadic nature of our administrative population, as well as because of changing requirements and technology. Mobile buildings were one of the answers, but not necessarily a successful one, as operable roof stadiums and mechanized multiform theatres proved through years of not being moved. The completed bubbles for education made clear that they were by no means so mobile as the diaphanous sculptures inflated for college festival programs. Their evanescent membranes might be mobile, might even blow away as the Antioch College bubble did, but earthberms and concrete compression rings are nonportable physicalities. Still, they did demonstrate that greater mobility, flexibility, and disposability were possible inside bubbles than inside most traditional buildings.

Besides, architects have seen mobility at a greater scale than they may ever achieve for ordinary housing, schools, and other environments. The rocket-conveyor platforms at Cape Kennedy can transport twenty- and forty-story skyscraper rockets and gantries with self-contained elevator systems and mechanical and electrical systems from one launching pad to another miles away. This is a scale of mobility and of change that inspires but still eludes architecture. For most architects, although the dream of a mobile, plug-in world persisted, their achievements in the areas of mobility and adaptability to change were at a comparatively smaller scale.

Investigation of adaptability to change led inevitably to systems furniture design—the design of interchangeable, rearrangeable, and easily assembled components that adapt to the changing needs of clients and situations with a new kind of mobility.

Today's designers, aware that refinement of forms is no longer sufficient to maintain a rapid change of response, suggest that the scope of our furniture vocabulary be expanded to include versatility and functional change—a chair is a table is a bed—within a single design system. This is also part of the current manipulation of scale that expands furniture design to include monumentality. "Systems furniture," "space kits," and "component interiors" are phrases on the lips of young designers. What makes the designs that those phrases designate so noteworthy is not their visual effect, which is so often claimed as the sole concern of these designers, but rather their greater flexibility and greater sophistication in function, in orientation, and in designing for use. Now, designers claim a fresh goal of making the actual uses by people serve as the true determinants of organized design. This extension is based on a careful, if sometimes intuitive, reanalysis of uses, and on a more refined and open awareness of the physical and psychological needs of users. They are larger-scale toys with which to educate nonprofessional designers about their environments and, I hope, to enrich their lives.

Systems building and kit furniture focus on actual do-it-yourself designer and owner manipulation, on rearrangement of one's surroundings, on instant flexibility for functional variety, on multiple functions of designed environments, on a practicable mobility of the environment, on adaptability to spatial requirements, on a participatory democracy. This new humanism is one of the most praiseworthy aspects of the new design.

As Houston's Lee Maxwell said, "Since laymen have little or no basis for understanding the furniture forms that surround them, they may be more aware of and have more identity with their designed environment if they have a hand in its actual manipulation."

If the idea sounds suspiciously like designing for modular flexibility, it also has a new improved ingredient, for modular flexibility, like much "movable furniture," did not, in fact, always make for true flexibility. Its elements were often too heavy or too permanently fixed. The do-it-yourself emphasis of systems and kits aims for a flexibility that works.

Although some of the interest in this concern for awareness of "life-styles" is motivated by a desire to cut costs, it is also based on a youthful optimism that wants everything for everybody all at the same time and thinks that everything is possible and right for everybody.

Among the notable examples of systems/kits in the 1960s were the following:

Walter Netsch's design team at Skidmore, Owings & Merrill in Chicago produced for the central atrium space of the Illinois State Bar Association headquarters in Springfield, Illinois (1968), a system of furnishings planned for do-it-yourself flexibility to accommodate three formal arrangements: for informal receptions, for quiet conversation (without disturbing the staff on the surrounding upper level), and for formal occasions. One of the truly distinguished interiors of the 1960s, the half-level central courts, which Netsch calls an "interspace," is approached from the lower level by axial stairs on the long sides; the second level is approached diagonally by stairs at the corners. These latter steps are continued down along the sides of the axial stairs in what project interior designer Don Powell calls "a topological definition of the

Skidmore, Owings & Merrill/Chicago: Illinois State Bar Association head-quarters, Springfield. 1968. *Photograph by Orlando R. Cabanban.*

sides." The skylighted space is "a variation," as Netsch says, "on the Mayan temple step form. It's diagonal geometry further dramatized by red carpeting." Black silk cubelike chairs and rosewood cube tables by project designer Robert W. Peters are used around bronze planters to negotiate the variations in function requirements without "the lethal razor sharp weapons of Mies tables slicing through quiet conversation

Skidmore, Owings & Merrill/Chicago: Second-floor plan, Illinois State Bar Association headquarters, Springfield. 1968.

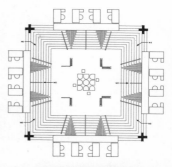

Derek Romley: Movable closets as partitions, Romley apartment, New York City. 1966. *Photograph by Louis Reens.*

Lee Maxwell: Partitioning with cardboard cubes, Houston, Texas. 1968.

groups." Movable furniture does not always constitute systems furniture as this controlled scheme does.

Lee Maxwell designed a system of partitioning, room-dividing, wall cubes that accommodated expanding or diminishing functional and aesthetic needs. He called it "space kit with plug-on surface." Like a large-scale tinkertoy, his system could be made of other materials; Maxwell chose sixteen-inch corrugated paperboard cubes, which he joined staple-fashion with industrial plastic straps. Any occupant could rearrange the interior spaces easily with such a system, could find storage space aplenty within the cubes; only the lack of refinement might be a deterrent.

Tom Luckey is a Yale-Architecture-trained designer whose gold-rush-mountaineer-cabin style of woodworking is a worthy successor in the tradition of Wharton Esherick. His designs in Vermont houses showed an iconoclastic reanalysis of function (see "Superimposition and Layering") as well as caressing woodcraft. His lively innovative approach to systems was expressed in fixed and static, if diagonal and discontinuous looking, forms in a kitchen for Louis Mackall (1967) at Prickly Mountain, Vermont, and in "the space landscape" that he designed in 1967 for the living room of Yale Professor Fritz Steele's house, also at Prickly Mountain. There, the floor is contoured up and down to form anonymous furniture for universal uses. The system of undulating plywood steps padded with two inches of urethane foam and upholstered in moss-green carpeting replaces chairs, sofas, and tables; it also provides recessed lighting with red gelatin lenses. This landscape accommodates the changing activities of the occupants, but in fact the occupants have to accommodate themselves to the universal-use landscape. In this system Luckey's only physical step toward mobility of the environment is in the walking surface, which is bouncy but does not affect general coordination.

In 1969, for an apartment in Brooklyn, Dennis Holloway designed a similar furniture system of stepped platforms that are rectangular, regular, but movable on casters. With three identical units of three steps each, a user could devise at least thirty-six different configurations for sitting, for reclining, and for extra sleeping space for guests. The yellow-painted three-quarter-inch plywood units were twenty-five inches wide, ninety inches long, thirty inches high, and hollow to accommodate storage.

Rather more inclusive as movable furniture, Craig Hodgetts's prototypal Rapid Assembly Total Floor, made for his New York living room in 1968, was composed of six movable rectangular units with triangular backrests. The system allowed a variety of "locking" combinations—rectangular, star, and pinwheel plans—to make more accessi-

Craig Hodgetts: Rapid Assembly
Total Floor, New York City. 1968. *Photograph by Louis Reens.*

ble and more functional the equipment they contain. To alter the character of what Hodgetts calls the "raft," all seating, foldout tables, and storage for books, records, phonograph, and projector were built-in and ready for family use. An umbilical made of vacuum-cleaner tubing fed electricity, audio, and telephone wires into the system, so that various combinations of the units were not impeded by a web of wires. Surreal in appearance, the non-object topography was, in Hodgetts's mind, "less pop and more machine funk." An open room-within-a-room, the raft changed from non-object to personal as the user changed activities, functions, and moods.

Multiform Bedroom

The system that Yale-trained architect Michael Hollander designed in 1967 for a bedroom-study blasted out of gravity-bound tradition. Hollander's design for the room in a New York brownstone—an eight-foot-by-twelve-foot room with one window and a door opposite—is based on interleafing the activities of a study-office with those of an overflow space for entertaining and with those of a bedroom. For this multiple-activity space, flexibility is the determinant, and Hollander produced a multiform bedroom to organize it. The system forced the involvement of the occupant in restructuring his environment for each different activity. The systems furniture for these multiple functions is a layered series of three floating, room-width platforms that slide on wall-hung horizontal rails from one end of the room to the other. Conventional half-inch ball-bearing casters mobilize the plywood platforms, which Hollander calls "trays." For sleeping, the bed on the uppermost tray is moved to the window end and the two lower platforms are arranged as steps up to it; file cabinets serve as intermediate steps. For work and study, the bed is moved out of the way toward the other end of the room and the middle platform, which holds the desk and table space, is moved near the window and the sunlight. The bottom platform keeps all furniture off the floor and allows unimpeded mobility of the trays. For overflow entertaining from the adjacent living room, all three platforms are moved to the window end, clearing the room as much as possible and making the bottom platform available as a bench.

The system has secondary advantages: first, since the bed is elevated, it is easier to make up (in a standing position) and it is easier to

Michael Hollander: Convertible office/bedroom, New York City. 1967.
Photograph by David Hirsch.

get to the other side by ducking under the mobile platform; second, the layered arrangement permits the occupant to put all work out of sight merely by climbing up to the lofty perch and hiding the cluttered desk-tray beneath it. Hollander points out that the lower platform is needed "both compositionally and ritualistically" to show the independence of the system from the room in which it is housed. "This re-creating to the actual space in contrapuntal restatement," he elaborates, "puts a new world inside the larger world." The system is a mobile room-within-a-room.

John Hanna: Air-float furniture, Urbana, Illinois. 1968.

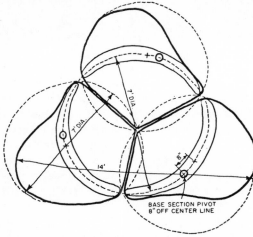

PLAN VIEW OF BASE SECTIONS SHOWS RELATIONSHIP OF PARTS FORMING 5'-9" DIA. INTERIOR SPACE.

John Hanna: Plan, air-float furniture, Urbana, Illinois. 1968.

Air-Float Furniture

As air-cushion or air-float vehicles became more and more visible on land and on water during the 1960s, and as blocks of audience seating were moved by the same technique, designer John Hanna developed a mobile, prototypic room-within-a-room system in 1968 that pioneered the use of air-float mobility in furniture design. It gave the user push-button mobility and variety in his environment. Hanna, who moved on from student work at the University of Illinois to teaching at Cornell, powered his movable furniture, Environmental Design Concept, on industrial vacuum-cleaner motors with one-gallon paint cans as air manifolds. Each of the three separate eight-foot-high sections of the system could be airlifted sufficiently to move four adults into different relationships with the other units. The mobile system offered enclosed or open seating, lighting, storage, stereo, and television in an original sculptural form that looked like stratified amoebas. The four tiers of each vertical section could pivot three hundred and sixty degrees to alter the six-and-a-half-foot cylindrical interior space into an irregular interior space and into an irregular exterior form that was fourteen feet wide in its tightest configuration. The unlikely materials were tiers of corrugated board used in honeycomb fashion, like hollow-core doors, and paper tubes that served as pivots for the tiers; only the air-float system required a wood base for support. In this system, space-vehicle lift-off imagery was combined with the pop world of found objects.

Kinetic Kit Environment

Almost completely abstract, like a painting by Adolph Gottlieb, a weightless, all-white environment designed in 1969 by Romauld Witwicki housed a system of floating, flexible, multidirectional furniture units, which pull out, lift up, spin around, and interlock, to produce a myriad of complexities from minimal components. This is an appropriate combination "for our industrial context," said designer Witwicki, a young French architect who worked here for I. M. Pei and Skidmore, Owings & Merrill before returning to France in 1970. Besides conceiving his systems interior, he also was involved in building it. Like all such systems, Witwicki's catered to owner involvement with nonstatic objects—almost with nonstatic non-objects. The design provides instant flexibility—a really practicable (if heavy) mobile environment—for the multiple functions of its owner's life-style.

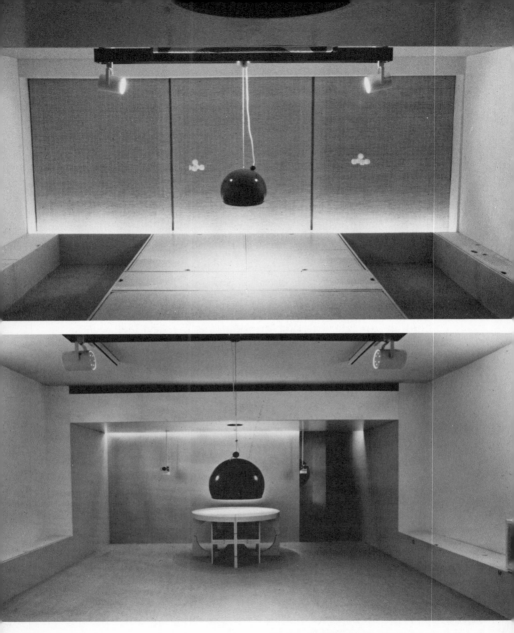

Romauld Witwicki: Flexible apartment,
New York City. 1969.

The space was a one-room apartment designed in that haven of the New York design world, I. M. Pei's Kips Bay Plaza, for architect Ivanka Mihailovich. Designer Witwicki envisioned the sixteen-foot by twenty-foot by eight-foot, two-inch space as composed of two interlocked and interacting volumes—the larger, higher, and brighter one next to the windows; the smaller, lower, and "shadow-of-white" volume next to the inner wall (which is silver-papered to reiterate the windows opposite). The change in ceiling height is effected by a fifteen-inch-deep, built-in, overhead cabinet that spans the width of the room against the inside wall. It contains equipment and objects for the multiple uses of the space—cushions, backrests, projectors, and so on.

The flexible furnishings system is composed of several subsystems. First, the units of a white platform of furniture that, when compacted against the window wall, form a mass corresponding to the overhead cabinet at the opposite end of the room. As these units break out of their long, boxlike cocoon, sliding around on casters, a bed pulls out from

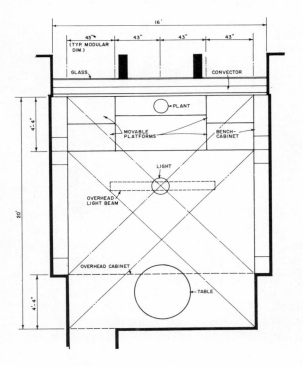

Romauld Witwicki: Plan, flexible apartment, New York City. 1969.

beneath the platform, cushions from storage space in the unit make a low sofa of the bed; lift-up tops of the side platforms can be propped and furnished with other cushions to form neo-Récamiers; and all can be moved about the room to arrange various conversation and use groups. Second, opposite the windows, a yellow supertoy of a dining unit is another subsystem of separable components that breaks down like a Chinese puzzle into table and stool units. These can also be rearranged into numerous configurations, and to interact with the white lacquer platform units and to provide further elaborations of backrests, chairs, sofas, and occasional tables, which designer Witwicki negotiated with virtuosic variety. Third, a ceiling-mounted, track-sliding beam slashes a red streak across the ceiling, moving from the windows to support flexible partitioning for the space. This red-painted beam supports lighting fixtures and pulldown roller-shade fabric panels that define and give focus to the furniture microenvironments, creating countless room-within-room configurations. Besides this colorful and decorative element, exposed pole-suspended projectors hanging from the red beam can overlay instant decoration.

Witwicki's prototype system within his double-volume white apartment stands squarely astride the contradictory design forces of our complex transitional period in that it combines a generous system of flexibility for various life-styles within a rigid, almost-too-pretty packagelike minimal visual order. Yet it is a model that industry could use for versatile, flexible, interlocking, mass-produced furniture systems.

Playgrounds for Retailing

Several children's shops during the decade were also designed with systems that successfully involved the participation of their customers. They broke away from trying to sell to the adults who actually pay the bills and aimed at encouraging the participation of the children for whom the merchandise is intended. In these educational and aesthetic playgrounds, distinctions between don't-touch merchandise and active-use playthings were made ambiguous and the functional aspects of children—their sizes, strengths, and interest levels—became the actual determinants of the designs. Creative Playthings' New York shop, designed in 1969 by the design combine of Godard/Hodgetts/Mangurian/Walker, presented a single system that formed the space as well as housing the toy display, the lighting, a push-button sound system, and clip-on graphics. In an orange-painted shop one hundred feet by fifteen feet, the designers assembled a kit of large-scale aluminum parts that are interlocking and interchangeable for display flexibility as well as being pop-oriented common building materials—they are riveted air-conditioning ducts. Where the shop provides involvement is in a built-in system of levers and buttons that children push to activate blinking lights and to create their own electronic music combinations, as well as in the touch-me merchandise. A rear room provided a carpeted, multi-level indoor playground with demonstration models of the merchandise. On the walls, a continuous slide show presented other products in action. These user-system shops achieved the decade's goals of involvement and participation with undeniable success.

Conclusion: Critical Evaluation and Predictions

Much of the work in the new design idiom that developed in the 1960s has been exciting, youthful, and brilliant. It is highly oriented to actualities and to physical sensations. It claims to be new and much of it is. Certainly it is new enough to have provoked vehement opposition within the profession. What Ada Louise Huxtable wrote about the acceptance of Robert Venturi by the profession in 1971 could almost be applied to all the Supermannerists: "The profession is split down the middle—90 per cent against." In the first five or so years those opposed insisted that "it will not last" and is "only a passing fad." Although in our age of acceleration of instant communications, instant understanding, and nearly as instant boredom and instant rejection, it is hard to know what is a substantial period of endurance; five- and ten-year increments in stylistic and technical developments may be our maximum expectancy.

Of the negative comments I collected in a poll of architecture educators in 1968, the most amusing (especially since it came from an area near San Francisco hippiedom) stated: "I am pleased to report that we observe only the normal superficial interest in mirrors, silver, stripes, permissiveness, and chaos, etc. To the foregoing you might add fluorescent colors, posters, old boards, bare feet, long hair, moustaches, loud music and girls." Appropriately, that whiplash ending makes the statement ambiguous. Those who spoke out against the new design maintained that it was "precocious experiment," "undesirable," and "irresponsible." In Chicago, the recognized stronghold of the Miesians even today, University of Illinois historian H. F. Koeper said that architects

Sprayed-on comment outside Venturi & Rauch office, Philadelphia. 1968.
Photograph by C. Ray Smith.

there reject "this kind of triviality because it is a kind of architecture of
incident and anecdote, which people look to for entertainment, like
clothes. Most Miesians are against what Frank Lloyd Wright called
'architectural millinery,' " he added. In Houston, Eugene George said,
"The participation fools one into thinking that one has accomplished
something of great merit. It seems to solve problems in a superficial way
that does not really approach the main problem at all. Instant success
seems to be a substitute for work."

Other statements that poured in to *Progressive Architecture* in 1967
and 1968 included such accusations as: "It substitutes wit for intelli-
gence, queerness for charm, and adroitness for skill. Who needs it?"
And ". . . they must be kidding. Snap, Crackle, Pop! . . . Zip, Zap,
zonk!," and ". . . in general, whimsical, shallow, commercial and insignificant," and "flamboyant, meretricious, and ingenious . . . novelty
for novelty's sake." One objector (a 1949 Yale architect) said of a
superscale exposed ductwork ceiling design, "That stupid hood over that

ridiculous . . . accenting plumbing, indeed!" Yet he expressed this while admiring Louis Kahn's Richards Medical Center with its separation and exposure of services. This diversity of opinion on the merits of the new design was expressed within the same faculty groups, and by contemporaries with different educations. Washington State University's Donald R. Heil said, superconservatively, "Such irrational experimentation may well persist until there is a cyclic reacceptance of the validity of reason as the most productive method of surviving in an alien environment."

The strongest criticism against the new design is that its aesthetic investigations "glorify subjectiveness and purely personal expression," as Robert P. Burns put it, "at the expense of the more serious architectural needs of society." Those dedicated to the "serious" involvement of architects in social issues criticized the aesthetic investigation as only "a minor part" of the total picture of architectural practice, which, they feel, must be increased in scope, not intensified by additional visual games. "The solution offered is one of style and not substance," wrote Tician Papachristos and James Stewart Polshek in *The New York Times* in 1971. It sounds like a replay. In the 1950s we had been through all that, when science and technical education were winning out over liberal arts education. By 1960, I thought, everyone recognized that life, like education, consisted of both—both together throughout the totality of society, if not balanced in every individual. All serious work and no games make architecture a dull boy. Besides, the history of art is founded on subjectivity and purely personal expression, and unless our entire understanding and definition of art changes, rather than expands, we cannot rule out those contributions. Do we say that Michelangelo and Palladio offered style not substance? Obviously an architectural philosophy cannot be based entirely on humor, and although most admit that the surface techniques add valuable wit to our architecture, they would probably agree with Gunnar Birkerts that this particular humor "reveals the creators laughing at themselves, clowning, but at the same time hiding truth behind their masks. This superficiality indicates an inability to formulate any appropriate new architectural principles."

The critical consideration in the balance is whether the new social concern of architects and the wit and the aesthetic investigations are (or can be) part of the same new movement, or whether they are opposing activities. I believe they are part and parcel of the new spirit that both fosters and is expressed by the new design. Any number of designers and architects whose work is discussed in these pages have been and are involved both with social considerations and with the new aesthetic investigations; their view is inclusive. Combinations in architecture are the promise for the future.

On the other side, there has been no lack of strong and cogent criticism in favor of the new design. Bill Lacy maintained that "A new direction is always healthy, since it forces evaluation of the old and the new." Frederick Eichenberger of North Carolina State University said, "The benefits are 'purgative,' and the only dangers are to custom, which should be threatened continually. The use of such pejoratives as ambiguity, permissiveness, and chaos are indicative of the Calvinistic concern for truth and noble thought that was and is the dark side of the modern movement."

As most of those in favor of the new design agree, the movement contributes "vitality and excitement," adds to "our vocabulary of vision," and releases "liveliness and imaginativeness and a heightened sense of design." What looked superficial and supercilious to one generation looked playful, witty, elegant, and sprightly to the next. As in all revolutions, moral liberty and physical freedom are the banners of the new design. "It is no surprise," Eichenberger added,

> that the kids who cut their eyeteeth on computers and who are fed systems and systematic thought with their pablum have embraced the joyous, spontaneous sensuality of all the aforementioned responses. They know that not every design decision is an equally big moral deal. Having at their disposal, as we never did, the tools and techniques for rational, objective, rigorous design, they are not afraid to wing it where winging it is appropriate.

This very activity of winging it should be a cause for rejoicing. "The kids are alive and kicking," commented Michigan's Robert Metcalf. "They don't believe the old ways have worked. We should all be glad for that belief."

Those who closed their eyes to the possible benefits of the new approach were resisting their own professional rejuvenation. "To fear the movement," said the University of Texas at Austin's Alan Y. Taniguchi, "would be like fearing the new generation." Yet there was and is some diversity of opinion on the merits of the movement even among those who are fundamentally in favor of the new.

Aesthetics alone seems recognized as the greatest danger for the Supermannerists. That is, if architecture students devote all their attention, interest, and energy to room decoration, how are they going to keep buildings from falling down? "They should learn to be architects and study engineering," said graphic artist Barbara Stauffacher Solomon, "and not rely on graphics as a crutch." In reply, Howard Barnstone said,

> Students don't spend all their time painting stripes and photographing things or discussing the value of straight talking. They go to structure classes, building techniques classes, cost and estimating classes, and office practice classes. If, in design, they spend time discussing the value of straight talk, it is better than coughing back a warmed-over Yamasaki.

Yet Tim Vreeland, then at the University of New Mexico, and Yale's F. R. Drury agreed that the surface and presentation techniques sometimes become so engrossing and exciting that designers forget to include any content, such as development of program or structure. However, these would be extreme compensations for regimentation and monotony, as the educators pointed out.

The experience of the first years in new design taught architects and practitioners a new range. As they matured they could look back on a decade of contributions and some excesses. By 1972, Tim Vreeland could say, "In the hands of skilled architects, it was very exciting. It had many benefits. It introduced a kind of permissiveness that was difficult to control. In the field of education, at first I had high hopes and thought it would be a new force in teaching. I worked on a series of courses in perception because it seemed to me that this would be a new way of teaching design." It did not seem to work for Vreeland, however, and he appears to have retrenched or to be developing a new approach both in his educational methods and in his design work.

The decade had been the professional adolescence of the new designers, an adolescence that every designer must go through. And that was not surprising since the largest segment of our population in the 1960s was between sixteen and twenty-five years old. That majority is what gave the decade its dominant influence on youth, and it was equally dominant in the architecture and design professions.

But wasn't it all fourth-generation Bauhaus, with emphasis on some new areas? All these experimentations with speed and scale, ambiguity and disorientation, projection and inversion had also been the enthusiasms of youthful experimenters at the Bauhaus. There, a similar Dadaist playfulness accompanied the purgative classicizing of architectural expression, at least in the beginning. The Bauhaus had espoused the industrial world as a democratizing step toward popular culture and the freer open-plan. Herbert Bayer used decoration almost like supergraphics in his shop designs. And the Bauhaus theatre experimented with abstract wit.

Perhaps these extra-architectural elements and attitudes are what the young in every idiom reach out for in order to expand the boundaries of their art forms. Yet by 1969, this experimentation was revealed to be playful and youthful games, good enough in themselves, but not a panacea. Astronaut Edwin Aldrin said in 1973 that it seemed as if we had achieved our goals, and there was no challenge left to meet. It was good to have had the experience, but clearly many of the directions of the 1960s would not lead to any solution of world architectural problems. To paraphrase Alexander Pope's "The proper study of mankind is man," the proper study of architects is architecture. What happened after 1969 was the maturation of the early Supermannerists. Their dual or double perception of the space age showed them afresh that everything in our world is finite, that everything we do affects the closed system of our fragile Earth. This awareness of our total environment and of its ecological balance led many of them further away from aesthetic considerations, away from the practice of architecture and into recycling and dropout, into government and land development. They questioned, even more, the basic assumptions of architecture. The energy crisis finally brought about the demise of the glass-walled, climate-controlled building with its excessive use of energy to compensate for identical exposure on all sides of a building.

Yet in 1973, the young design generation still insisted that their expansion of the scope of architecture, of architectural vocabulary and outlook, was a contribution to the already solid architectural view. They believe it is bringing blood and life, vitality and humanity, to the rigid exclusivity of previous decades. If the overall social change in our decade has been antielitist and antiacademic supremacy, anti-intellectual and theoretical supremacy, the academic centers themselves were, by the 1970s, no longer the elitist focal points they had been in 1957. The ivory towers and walls had been split wide open and the rest of life had been admitted in the form of a new architectural humanism. This has its dangers. Will clients really like what the new design proposes? There remains, after all, a vast lack of fundamental psychological research on emotional requirements, on the psychology of space and designed space. Will architects be able to complete their work on time and within a prescribed budget? Will they be able to muster the power—not electrical but political—to provide shelter and housing for those masses of society that could not individually afford to be the sponsors of architecture?

And we have to question the quality of the work of the Supermannerists. We see the value in the new mobility and adaptability to change that many are striving for. We see the contribution of new evanescent materials—mylar, paper, and paint. Although less than the durable monuments of architecture, they add new vitality and visual stimulation.

Where the new design first succeeded was in the areas of houses, drafting rooms, shops, wall paintings, and graphics—playful, delightful, continually surprising, and fascinating. This greater humanism also produced a new line of small parks and playgrounds, fountains and sculpture settings for the physical enjoyment, relaxation, and rejuvenation of people, as well as for their aesthetic vision. The work of landscape architects Lawrence Halprin and M. Paul Friedberg is notable in this regard.

The new designers aim at housing first; they aim to do their work where the greatest needs of the people they aim to serve are. Yet there will always be the need for the huge hospital in which sick people can be taken care of, industrial plants where people work, university laboratories where people can do research, and performing arts labs where people can perform other art forms for people. Are there any signs that the new designers will build up skills and vocabularies and professional managerial crafts strong enough to carry through these larger projects? ·

As many critics and architects observed, "the large-scale projects of architects had more appropriate solutions than the smaller, where the overexuberance of the architect took over"; as Romaldo Giurgola said, "You cannot approach a large design project as a field for personal expression. Schools, campus planning, and urban design represent the best contemporary architecture because they represent the real motivations of our time. It is not so much a matter of their being large scale, but rather that they meet the real needs of today."

Working toward those larger projects in the 1970s, Charles Moore and his partners are producing work that is ever more elaborate and complicated, if richer through manipulation of scale, devious or tricky planning, and historical allusion. Moore's firm has already built a good number of university buildings and some high-rise housing for the elderly as well as the Church Street South Housing in New Haven. Hugh Hardy and his partners appear set in their dedication to found-object architecture, with wit and decoration and the permissive perverseness of the decade's taunting lessons. Hardy's firm has built a major school and a health center in Columbus, Indiana; the Brooklyn Children's Museum in New York is in progress along with the Cooper-Hewitt Museum in New York.

Venturi's firm has designed, though not yet built, major apartment and civil complexes, the Mathematics Building at Yale, and has plans for other large projects. Venturi and his partners continue to reinforce their interest in signs and logos and communication, and in the non-architectural aspects of popular roadway aesthetics. They continue to raise questions about the line between the art form they aim to create and the vernacular from which they draw inspiration. That line is so fine that the crossing of the boundary sometimes appears to achieve no major change. "The real difference between Pop art and Pop architecture," Peter Blake has said, "is that the former is detached from its context and becomes a form of social criticism; whereas the latter—Pop architecture—merges with or melts into a deplorable social situation and implies acceptance." Some people feel that Venturi is saying we should be satisfied with what we have because we cannot do any better. Venturi claims to be showing a new view.

And the "cardboard corbu" school is heading toward greater stylization and revivalism of Le Corbusier's principles, except in the case of larger-scale work such as Richard Meier's Twin Parks Northeast housing (1973) in the Bronx, which appears to have adopted the stripped status quo or undesigned vernacular of ordinary speculative apartment buildings. Here, Meier and Venturi meet on the common ground of Venturi's Brighton Beach competition entry and the Yale Mathematics Building, although the New York Five seem loath to admit it.

Cesar Pelli and his design team at Gruen Associates are raising the standards of shopping center design and other commercial structures, refining them as vast superscale billboards for better salesmanship, as at Queens Center, the Pacific Design Center, and elsewhere. Davis Brody &

Associates veer closer to the supermannerist idiom in their exuberant, sprouting apartment complexes, Waterside and East Midtown Plaza in Manhattan, and in their Boston Road Apartments and Harlem River Park Houses in the Bronx. Conklin & Rossant, who brought a new humanism to the new town of Reston, have got it *all* together in their multilevel shopping-cultural-institutional park project, Myriad Gardens in Oklahoma City. The new design is showing maturity—and new acceptance.

If the design rebellion was aimed at breaking down rigid rules and forms, the substitution, it seems, was other forms, different forms. It is a ruptured, fractured, fragmented set of forms to express the breakaway from the old, but it is still forms, although a number of architects did investigate the nonformal, anti-object, and non-architectural. For architecture this can never be entirely a censure. Forms are the essential elements of architecture, and without form of some kind, no architecture can exist. Supermannerism is a formal style appropriately striving for a new humanism.

Concerning forms, Supermannerism found itself in the midst of an unresolved paradox. It claimed the broader social goal of answering the needs of a greater number of people and accepted in its democratization of style the commonly available undesigned or ordinary elements of our visual environment. Both directions acclaimed the fact that we can no longer fiddle with jewelry detailing, with "handcrafted, form-frenzied, nail-laden monuments," as Charles Hosford said. Architecture now requires broader strokes and sweeps to accommodate the increasing population and the increasing demands for building in our time. Although jewelry will always be commissioned by the rich, our society demands more socially conscious architect-builders to meet the accelerating needs of today. Supermannerism espoused this thinking, but it is still, very strongly, a formal style. It recognizes the goals, but paradoxically, holds onto a traditional expression of them in forms. To many critics, impatient with the apparent need of architecture to transcend its traditional scope, the recognition of the need and the diagnosis of the problem that the new design of the 1960s had been able to isolate did not seem a sufficiently substantial step forward toward a solution. They look for the great leap, and continue to denigrate the small step forward that the Supermannerists have been able to make. To them the revolution of the 1960s seems empty, rhetorical, and symbolic. It looks like the presumption and optimism of youth, a youth not yet aware of the interaction of people, forces, and fundamental human motivations. This was less true for architecture than for politics. But in design as well, at times, in their enthusiasm, in their lack of maturity, in their being somewhat too facile in philosophizing, the young went too far. The supermannerist architects eagerly accepted the spirit of the times yet often failed to recognize that art also reflects the enduring values of man. The young showed a typical youthful idealism, in which the clear goals of the head and the intellect had got separated from the heart. Like the new social activism they often acted with heartfelt enthusiasm in behalf of purely intellectual goals. Both had some similarity in their "dissociation of sensibility," which T. S. Eliot had attributed to the earlier part of our century and to the seventeenth-century mannerist period. This accounted for the literariness and in-joking of super-graphics, of Pop architecture, and of historical allusions in today's architecture. All shared in a dissociation of emotions from the intellect, a concentration on mental games and tricks. Yet the addition of wit and laughter to architecture is more emotional, has more heart and greater freedom than the purity of the Internationalists and the Minimalists. And other additives or inclusions of the new design also moved us toward a new humanism.

Again, the work of the New York Five also reveals an interest in a number of the same forms and elements that the Supermannerists espouse: diagonals in elevation and plan, wood as a basic material, silolike forms and barnlike cantilevers, and even pure decoration. Not surprisingly, the use of layering by both groups produces qualities of ambiguity and disorientation concerning the relationship of the planes. This screen effect is the single most telling element in the work of the New York School, although similar form doesn't denote similar content, intent, or inspiration. Their layering reveals their common attitude of admiration for and their indebtedness to the work of Le Corbusier—his screens on houses in India, the monastery at La Tourette, and buildings in France, Brazil, and Cambridge, Massachusetts. Le Corbusier is the fundamental inspiration for the New York Five. Where did they first gain an admiration of his work? It was through the English historian Colin Rowe, who has written incisively on Le Corbusier's contribution; as a professor at Cornell University and as a participant in the Institute for Architecture and Urban Studies, Rowe has had the opportunity to convey his admiration for Le Corbusier to the New York Five. Their interest shows sufficiently in their work to have gained them the appellation "neo-Corbu architects" and 1920s revival architects. And because of their forms and because their materials are generally thin wood screens, rather than the heavy textured concrete that Le Corbusier made so rich and monumental, their architecture has also been called "cardboard corbu."

The elements that the Supermannerists and the New York Five share—although it must be clearly stated that they do not use *all* of the same elements, attitudes, or devices—are essentially mannerist devices. They all manipulate scale, perspective, ambiguity, duality, wit, superimposition, and in many cases, Pop, which relies on the mannerist principle of inversion—inversion of established principles of traditional materials, of architectural clarity, of context, and so on. In sharing this mannerist tendency, the Supermannerists and the New York Five have another common denominator, which has not been emphasized by other critics. Regardless of their locations, educations, and ages, they owe to Colin Rowe the influence of being the first to discuss the relationship of sixteenth- and seventeenth-century Mannerism to Modern architecture. Professor Rowe did not invent modern Mannerism; he did not even forward it in his teaching directly, his students relate. But it was his insight that first gave to modern vision an awareness of the historical precedent by which we can measure the Mannerists of our day—long before his New York lecture series at the Institute for Architecture and Urban Studies in 1974. Meier's architecture has been called "elegant to the point of being mannered," and it is safe to say that the New York Five are concerned with the most mannered aspects of Le Corbusier's principles and forms. Their analytical techniques are undeniably mannered. And this Mannerism makes the New York School and the Supermannerists closer than most critics have explained.

It hardly seems fair to use the authority of previous criticism regarding sixteenth- and seventeenth-century Mannerism as a measure of the Supermannerists, but the comparisons are inevitable. The Mannerists of our day, like their predecessors, are intellectual, willful, and consciously arbitrary in their work. In their manner, dress, and life-styles more than a few of them, personally, show the overcivilized bankers'-gray-flannel-suit imagery of their 1950s backgrounds in paradoxical and even discordant juxtaposition to their freer, looser, capricious statements, actions, and designs. In their daring to forge beyond the previous system and by their inversions of it, they are in their work often distorted, affected, sometimes tortured and unnatural. Their work was, in the beginning, and still continues to be, sometimes, self-conscious and sometimes uncomfortable. All these are terms from the historical criticism of the early Mannerists, and they are equally applicable today. Yet the work of the Supermannerists is also often elegant, sophisticated, and virtuosic through its very intellectual nature. It is highly stylized, intricate. It surely shows *discordia concors* in virtually every area of architectural aesthetics and practice. And it has, more often than not, the quality of "enforcing movement through space," as Nikolaus Pevsner said of early Mannerism—but augmented by the new dimension of spaceflight.

What, then, is the ultimate significance of Supermannerism? Visual illiteracy and apathy have been shaken up, jostled by the introduction of a fuller kind of earthy humanism. Certainly this is an expression of our revolutionary age, our age of activism. Surely the statement that the supermannerist view of scale has made about our time is significant. Future historians may say that the twentieth century visibly expressed the depressing inconsequentiality of the individual—vis-à-vis the collective activity of society—the scalelessness of man himself within vast megalopolitan complexes and even vaster outer space. On the other hand, future historians may agree with me that the 1960s began to change all that, began to show a new humanism in the midst of this scalelessness, began to show it by contrasting the two in a dual scale, simultaneously.

For, Supermannerism (or whatever they choose to call the movement) is a valid expansion of optical, textural, and formal games to amuse us and move us during a wrenching shift of scale. It is a transitional, decorative, new formalist means to the spatial goal of expanding our vision—from the single room and the single building toward the superscale of megalopolis and toward the daily awareness of outer space. And it aims to do so while acclaiming the continuing importance of the individual and his personal scale. It raises our vision to another measure—from a concern for our walls and backyards to whole streets and cities, from states and regions to whole continents,

Doug Michels: Exhibition room, The Corcoran Gallery of Art, Washington, D.C. 1968. *Photograph by Steve Szabo.*

and from a vision of spaceships to a vision of Spaceship Earth. Yet it insists that the vision of individual men never be neglected. It opposes the deluge of individualism by technology as a kind of humanistic fin de siècle. It inspires the functional analysis of life systems and life-styles in fresh and original, if intuitive, ways. These directions of our art are the social concerns and the life-forces of the 1970s.

It will be seen in the 1970s whether the Supermannerists can get beyond their initial work—its microcosms of private houses, offices, small shops, decorative interiors, exterior walls, and neighborhood environments. The question is whether their ambitions to involve their inclusive aesthetic and inclusive process in a macrocosmic way can be realized in major buildings and in town planning, at a new scale of work, of materials, and of humanism.

For all their rhetoric about overthrowing all forms and all functions, for all their inability to perceive what they were doing, they were in fact working in the oldest tradition of all—to relate to the involvement and humanity of man. The question is whether we can preserve their valuable youthful attitudes and devices in architecture. Will all the new aspects, attitudes, and areas investigated and enjoyed by these young designers be incorporated in their mature work? Will they be transmitted to others in ways that can be adapted? Or will they be forgotten, put away as childish things to be replaced by an even sterner, more rigid classicism than the Supermannerists opposed? Will architects learn the lessons of the past decade or will they merely discard them and begin the cycle anew?

If they do not ignore the lessons of the Supermannerists, architects in the 1970s can bring the heart closer to the architecture for our lives. Although not a prophet, I am confident that a substantial body of good architecture will be produced by the new designers so that history will look back on a joyous turbulent age with pleasure. The Supermannerists will have matured into responsible masters in the 1970s.

Bibliography

American Institute of Architects. *Comprehensive Architectural Services.* Washington, D.C., 1962–1965.

Arthur, Eric, and Witney, Dudley. *The Barn: A Vanishing Landmark in North America.* Greenwich, Conn.: New York Graphic Society, 1972.

Bell, Daniel. *The Coming of Post-Industrial Society: A Venture in Social Forecasting.* New York: Basic Books, 1973.

Blake, Peter. *The New Forces.* Melbourne: The Royal Australian Institute of Architects, Victorian Chapter, 1971.

Blunt, Anthony. "Mannerism in Architecture." *RIBA Journal* (March 1949).

"California Living Magazine." *San Francisco Sunday Examiner* (June 1971).

Chomsky, Noam. *Aspects of the Theory of Syntax.* Cambridge, Mass.: Massachusetts Institute of Technology Press, 1965.

Eisenman, Peter; Graves, Michael; Gwathmey, Charles; Hejduk, John; and Meier, Richard. *Five Architects.* New York: George Wittenborn, Inc., 1972.

"Free Do-It-Yourself Supergraphics by Milton Glaser, Massimo Vignelli, and Thomas H. Geismar." *New York* (1972).

Futagawa, Yukio. *Houses in U.S.A. #2* ("Global Interior" series). vol. 6. Tokyo: A.D.A. Edita Company Limited, 1974.

Gaudet, Julien. *Éléments et Théorie de l'Architecture.* 4 vols. Paris, 1870–1880.

Goldfinger, Myron. *Villages in the Sun: Mediterranean Vernacular Architecture.* New York: Praeger Publishers, 1969.

Gombrich, E. H. *Art and Illusion, A Study in the Psychology of Pictorial Representation.* London: Phaidon Press, 1960.

Halprin, Lawrence. "Motation." *Progressive Architecture* (July 1965).

Huxtable, Ada Louise. "Kicked a Building Lately?" *The New York Times,* January 12, 1967. Reprinted in *Will They Ever Finish Bruckner Boulevard?* New York: The Macmillan Company, 1972.

Jacobs, Jane. *The Death and Life of Great American Cities.* New York: Random House, Inc., 1961.

Kaufmann, Emil. *Architecture in the Age of Reason: Baroque and Post-Baroque in England, Italy, and France.* Cambridge, Mass.: Harvard University Press, 1955.

Kernodle, George. "The Mannerist Stage of Comic Detachment." In *The Elizabethan Theatre 3,* edited by David Galloway. Hamden, Conn.: Shoe String Press, 1973.

Lynch, Kevin. *The Image of the City.* Cambridge, Mass.: Massachusetts Institute of Technology Press, 1960.

————. *What Time Is This Place?* Cambridge, Mass.: Massachusetts Institute of Technology Press, 1972.

McLuhan, Marshall. *The Mechanical Bride: Folklore of Industrial Man.* New York: Vanguard Press, 1951.

————. *Understanding Media: The Extensions of Man.* New York: McGraw-Hill Book Company, 1964.

Moore, Charles. "Plug It In, Rameses, and See If It Lights Up." *Perspecta* (Yale University, 1967). Reprinted as "Inclusive and Exclusive" in *Dimensions: Space, Shape, and Scale in Architecture,* Gerald Allen, joint author. New York: Architectural Record Books, 1976.

————; Allen, Gerald; and Lyndon, Donlyn. *The Place of Houses.* New York: Holt, Rinehart & Winston, Inc., 1974.

Passonneau, Joseph R., and Wurman, R. S. *Urban Atlas: Twenty American Cities, a Communication Study Notating Selected Urban Data.* Cambridge, Mass.: Massachusetts Institute of Technology Press, 1966.

Pevsner, Nikolaus. "The Architecture of Mannerism." *The Mint* (1946).

————. "Double Profile." *Architectural Review* (March 1950).

————. *Outline of European Architecture.* rev. ed. Baltimore, Md.: Penguin Books, 1960.

Rosenberg, Harold. *The De-Definition of Art: Action Art to Pop to Earthworks.* New York: Horizon Press, 1971.

Rowan, Jan. "The Philadelphia School." *Progressive Architecture* (February 1961).

Rowe, Colin. "Mannerism and Modern Architecture." *Architectural Review* (May 1950).

Rudofsky, Bernard. *Architecture Without Architects.* New York: Doubleday & Company (for The Museum of Modern Art), 1964.

Safdie, Moshe. *Beyond Habitat.* Cambridge, Mass.: Massachusetts Institute of Technology Press, 1970.

Scully, Vincent. *Louis I. Kahn* ("Makers of Contemporary Architecture" series). New York: George Braziller, Inc., 1962.

Silver, Nathan. "The Playboy Contagion in American Building." *Columbia Forum* (Winter 1971). Reprinted in *Empire State Architect* (September 1974).

Smith, C. Ray. "Aalto in New York." *Progressive Architecture* (February 1965). Kaufmann conference rooms.

————. "Airline Designs for Passengers." *P/A* (March 1966). Girard: Braniff.

————. "Alienation Reveals the Familiar." *P/A* (February 1970). Aulenti: Knoll Showroom, Boston.

————. "Architectural Products by Industrial Designers." *P/A* (June 1964). Nelson, Snaith, Muller-Munk, Dreyfuss, Teague, Beckman, etc.

————. "The Architecture of Interiors." Special issue of *P/A* edited by the author (February 1962).

————. "Architecture Swings Like a Pendulum Do." *P/A* (May 1966). Prickly Mountain, Vermont.

————. "Banking Boutique." *P/A* (August 1969). Murphy Levy Wurman: Industrial Valley Bank, Philadelphia.

————. "Boutiques, a New World of Color." *P/A* (December 1967). Work by Brill, Hollein, Michels, etc.

————. "Burolandschaft U.S.A." *P/A* (May 1968). Du Pont's Freon Division, Wilmington, Delaware.

————. "Camp Mies." *P/A* (December 1967). P. C. Johnson: Founders' Room, The Museum of Modern Art, New York.

————. "The Changing Practice." Special issue of *P/A* on theatres edited by the author (October 1965).

————. "Citation, Residential Design." *P/A* (January 1962). Moore: House, Orinda, California.

————. "The Designers." *P/A* (May 1967). Moore, Rudolph, Hardy, Hoppner, Romley: Their own residences.

————. "Down for Decoration—Upping the Nature of Materials." *P/A* (March 1966).

————. "Electric Demolition." *P/A* (September 1970). Venturi & Rauch: Saint Francis de Sales Church, Philadelphia.

————. "Exterior Supergraphics." *P/A* (December 1968).

————. "Five Decades of Interior Design." *P/A* (June 1970).

————. "Forms as Process." *P/A* (March 1969). Netsch: Field Theory.

————. "The Freeway Comes Indoors." *P/A* (October 1967).

————. "Grinnell's Social Geometry." *P/A* (December 1965). Skidmore, Owings & Merrill/Netsch: Student Union, Grinnell, Iowa.

————. "Guest Apartment." *P/A* (February 1963). Girard: Hallmark apartment, Kansas City, Missouri.

————. "High Style for a Campus Eatery." *P/A* (December 1963). Venturi & Short: Grand's Restaurant, Philadelphia.

————. "Hip Ceiling for Two Mods." *P/A* (February 1966). Hardy Holzman Pfeiffer: Children's rooms, Princeton, New Jersey.

————. "The House on Its Side." *P/A* (June 1969). Southcoast: Vermont house.

————. "Hybrid Walls." *P/A* (August 1966). Beckman & Probst: University of Tennessee Architecture School, Knoxville.

————. "Instant Exteriors." *P/A* (March 1968). Projections.

————. "Instant Interiors." *P/A* (June 1967). Projected interiors.

————. "Interior Volume." *P/A* (June 1965). Scale.

————. "Inward-Looking Ski Lodge." *P/A* (May 1968). Charles Hosford: Kingfield, Maine.

————. "Johnson's Interior Details." *P/A* (March 1965).

————. "Kinetic Boutiques and Campopop Shops." *P/A* (April 1969). Franzen, Stauffacher, Buchsbaum, American Thought Combine, etc.

————. "Kinetic Kit Environment." *P/A* (September 1969). Witwicki: Apartment, New York.

————. "The Library-Museum at Lincoln Center." *P/A* (April 1966). Skidmore, Owings & Merrill, New York.

————. "Lowering the Cost of Housing." Special issue, with Peter Green, of *P/A* (June 1968). Boxes and tinkertoys.

————. "Minimal Interiors." *P/A* (March 1967).

————. "Minirooms as Superfurniture." *P/A* (February 1968). Les Walker: Supercube.

————. "Multiform Bedroom." *P/A* (July 1969). Michael Hollander: Apartment, New York.

————. "Office Landscape." *P/A* (September 1964).

————. "Ordinary as Art Form." *P/A* (April 1970). Venturi & Rauch: Lieb House, Long Beach Island, New Jersey.

————. "The Permissiveness of Supermannerism." *P/A* (October 1967).

————. "The Phoenix: An Additive Assemblage." *P/A* (May 1966). T. M. Prentice, Jr., and Hugh Hardy: The Phoenix House.

————. "Plastics: The Future Has Arrived." *P/A* (October 1970).

————. "Redwood Walls in a Redwood Canyon." *P/A* (June 1963). Moore: Jobson House, Palo Colorado Canyon, California.

————. "Restored National Monument Sparks Renewal." *P/A* (February 1970). Ferry & Henderson: Springfield State House, Illinois.

————. "Revolution in Interior Design: The Bold New Polyexpanded Megadecoration." Special issue of *P/A* (October 1968).

————. "Rudolph's Dare-Devil Office Destroyed." *P/A* (April 1969).

————. "Sign as Space." *P/A* (May 1970). Solomon: Thrift Federal Savings & Loan Association, Concord, California.

————. "SOM Details for the Minimal Age." *P/A* (September 1967). Banque Lambert apartment, Brussels, Belgium.

————. "Supergraphics." *P/A* (November 1967).

————. "Superscale Frescoes." *P/A* (September 1970). Briscoe: Hillcrest Church, Toronto, Ontario.

————. "Two New Buildings by Venturi & Rauch." *P/A* (November 1968). Fire Station No. 4, Columbus, Indiana, and Varga-Brigio medical office building, Bridgeton, New Jersey.

————. "The Tyrone Guthrie Theater." *P/A* (December 1963). Work of Ralph Rapson.

————. "Uncommon Uses of Common Components." *P/A* (June 1964). Written with John Morris Dixon.

————. "Urban Renewal with Paint." *P/A* (November 1970). Billboards and city walls.

————. "Urban Supertoy Subdues Renewal Bulldozer." *P/A* (September 1969). Diamond & Myers: York Square, Toronto, Ontario.

————. "Wiggle Walls." *P/A* (August 1966). Barnstone & Aubry: Offices for Schlumberger Ltd., New York.

————. "Yale's School of Art and Architecture." *P/A* (February 1964). Work of Paul Rudolph, New Haven, Connecticut.

Sontag, Susan. *Against Interpretation.* New York: Dell Publishing Company, Inc., 1966.

Stern, Robert A. M. *New Directions in American Architecture.* New York: George Braziller, Inc., 1969.

Toffler, Alvin. *Future Shock.* New York, Random House, Inc., 1970.

Venturi, Robert. *Complexity and Contradiction in Architecture.* New York: Doubleday & Company (for The Museum of Modern Art), 1966.

————; Venturi, Denise Scott-Brown; and Izenour, Steven. *Learning from Las Vegas.* Cambridge, Mass.: Massachusetts Institute of Technology Press, 1972.

Wittkower, Rudolf. *Art and Architecture in Italy, 1600 to 1750.* Baltimore, Md.: Penguin Books, 1958.

Wolfe, Tom. *Kandy-Kolored Tangerine-Flake Streamline Baby.* New York: Farrar, Straus & Giroux, Inc., 1965.

Zevi, Bruno. *Architecture as Space.* Edited by Joseph A. Barry. Translated by Milton Gendel. New York: Horizon Press, 1957.

Index

Page numbers in **boldface** type indicate illustrations.